"The London
and
"Castle of Doom"

TWO CLASSIC ADVENTURES OF

THE *Shadow* ™

by Walter B. Gibson
writing as Maxwell Grant

with New Historical Essays by
Will Murray and Anthony Tollin

Published by Sanctum Productions for
NOSTALGIA VENTURES, INC.
P.O. Box 231183; Encinitas, CA 92023-1183

"Introduction" copyright © 2007 by Will Murray.
"Shadows Over England" copyright © 2007 by Anthony Tollin.

This Nostalgia Ventures edition is an unabridged republication of the text and illustrations of two stories from *The Shadow Magazine,* as originally published by Street & Smith Publications, Inc., N.Y.: *The London Crimes* from the September 15, 1935 issue, and *Castle of Doom* from the January 15, 1936 issue. Typographical errors have been tacitly corrected in this edition.

International Standard Book Numbers:
ISBN 1-932806-61-X   13 digit 978-1-932806-61-8

First printing: June 2007

Series editor: Anthony Tollin
P.O. Box 761474
San Antonio, TX 78245-1474
sanctumotr@earthlink.net

Consulting editor: Will Murray

Copy editor: Joseph Wrzos

Cover restoration: Michael Piper

Nostalgia Ventures, Inc.
P.O. Box 231183; Encinitas, CA 92023-1183

Visit The Shadow at www.shadowsanctum.com & www.nostalgiatown.com

Volume 8

CONTENTS

Two Complete Novels From The Shadow's Private Annals As told to Maxwell Grant

Thrilling Tales and Features

Cover art by George Rozen
Interior illustrations by Tom Lovell

INTRODUCTION by Will Murray

From the beginning, Walter B. Gibson hinted that The Shadow operated outside of the continental United States. His long reach extended far beyond our shores, and the Dark Avenger's shuddery laugh had petrified criminals in Paris, Rome, Madrid, Moscow, and other world capitals. Maxwell Grant only hinted at these exotic adventures, perhaps thinking American readers preferred to see him concentrate on crushing stateside crime.

In the early years of *The Shadow Magazine,* these hints might focus on a few chapters set in Paris, or a globe-spanning adventure climaxing in Berlin. But these off-trail mysteries were always rooted in American interests. While the millionaire sportsman whose identity The Shadow usurped was often said to be off exploring the Amazon, or on safari in Africa, the human enigma behind the mask of Lamont Cranston was no bored globe-trotter. The Shadow hunted men. And the most exciting game seemed to be in the States.

But after four relentless years, with almost a hundred riveting Shadow novels behind him, Gibson decided it was time to expand the Knight of Darkness' sphere of operations. He sat down in conference with editor John L. Nanovic and Street & Smith's Henry W. Ralston to hash out the next few Shadow plots. The magazine was being published every two weeks, and to keep up they plotted three or four issues at a time.

Gibson felt that London would make a good setting for The Shadow's next case. Perhaps the idea had been germinating in his mind since penning *The Man from Scotland Yard* the previous year. That novel introduced C.I.D. Inspector Eric Delka, whom The Shadow encountered in Washington, DC. Now Gibson was proposing that the Master of Darkness meet the Scotland Yard official on his home turf. Further, that The Shadow would remain in England for another adventure centering around a mysterious British castle.

Gibson later recalled that Nanovic and Ralston were cool to the second premise, feeling that Shadow readers wouldn't relate to dark doings in a weird faraway keep. But Gibson pressed his point. And won them over. But to stay on the safe side of the readers, Nanovic decided to space the stories months apart. Gibson could write his English excursions contiguously, provided he kept that in mind.

Once he had his approvals, Gibson left New York to turn them into reality.

"By March of 1935," he recounted, "I was going south in the winter and north in the summer, picking up plot material both ways and stopping in New York between times, while planning stories with a foreign setting. That summer I did much of my work in a Maine cabin that was literally built around me, as it was not finished until after I had moved in. The carpenter fashioned some of the leftover pinewood into furniture, including a desk specially suited for writing the Shadow stories. By then I was carrying two portable typewriters in case one needed repair, and I had a third available as a spare."

All did not go smoothly at first.

"I had just gotten back from Florida and I got a start on those and I got an attack of lumbago—oh boy, that was miserable—and I just sat around, and could hardly move. So I got all the data that I had on England and London and Paris and just worked on that and made notes galore. Then I wrote the stories one after the other."

In the first tale, The Shadow encounters one of his most notable adversaries, the master of disguise who calls himself The Harvester, after a species of British spider. One wonders if "Maxwell Grant" wasn't taking a sly jab at his American rival—The Spider, Master of Men.

In the second British yarn, Gibson switches locales to a moody 300-year-old haunted castle where, abandoning his usual chameleon ways, the Master of Darkness stalks mystery and murder attired only in the ebony robes of The Shadow.

If it were possible to top *The London Crimes,* Gibson may very well have done so in *Castle of Doom.* You decide.

While researching the second story, another idea germinated.

"I was doing research into castles in England," he related, "and came across a description of the Golden Arrow train. I began to think of some murders taking place on this train."

This "train" of thought led to a third story in the sequence that began with *The London Crimes*—the Parisian adventure many consider Walter Gibson's most extraordinary mystery, *Zemba.* The London doublet had become a trilogy.

Regardless of distractions, the change of scenery did both The Shadow and his raconteur a world of good. The novels you are about to read number among the most exciting in this long-running series. True to his plan, John Nanovic published them months apart, with *Zemba* separating the British-based tales. Here they are in the order Walter Gibson wrote them, *The London Crimes* and its powerful sequel, *Castle of Doom.*

Will Murray edited The Duende History of The Shadow Magazine, *and posthumously collaborated with Lester Dent on seven Doc Savage novels published by Bantam Books.*

*The Harvester reaps what he has sown, but
The Shadow comes along to check the harvest of*

The London Crimes

Book-length Novel from the Private Annals of
The Shadow, as told to

Maxwell Grant

CHAPTER I
ABOARD THE BOAT TRAIN

DARKNESS had engulfed the English country-side. The special boat train from Plymouth was speeding on toward London, carrying passengers who had landed from the steamship *Patagonia*.

Two men were seated in a well-lighted compartment of a third-class carriage. Though they had crossed the Atlantic on the same liner, they appeared to be unacquainted. This was not

surprising; for the pair made a distinct contrast.

One was a sharp-faced, ruddy-complexioned man whose age was no more than forty. Though restrained in manner, he gave occasional signs of restlessness; this was indicated by the frequent tightening of his lips, and the furrows which sometimes showed upon his forehead.

Upon the seat beside this man was a black leather briefcase. One hand, its fingers powerful in their pressure, was resting on the briefcase. The owner of the bag regarded it as important; and with

The Cast

THE SHADOW

astounded London and confounded Scotland Yard by the daring and ease with which he perpetrated his many crimes on business men of high degree. It is because of this supercrook that

LIONEL SELBROOK, who comes to London broke but with options on valuable oil concessions to sell, is given the protection of Scotland Yard until the deal, which involves the handling of much cash

Continued on pages 18 and 19

THE SHADOW, mysterious being in black, crime fighter extraordinary, master of darkness, whose knowledge of pending crime allows him to lay plans to thwart it before the crime is committed. Feared by the underworld in all crime capitals the world over, it is on a boat train from a transatlantic steamer to London that The Shadow again meets

ERIC DELKA, Scotland Yard operative, who is returning from New York with a briefcase full of crime reports to be delivered to his superiors. It is this briefcase that brings The Shadow into personal contact with Delka and gives him entrée to Scotland Yard, and embroils him with

THE HARVESTER, master of disguise, who because of his many aliases and art of make-up, has

Eric Delka of Scotland Yard

good reason. His identity and his occupation were the explanations.

This sharp-faced man was Eric Delka, special investigator from Scotland Yard. Delka was returning from a trip to New York, where he had acquired important information for the London Metropolitan Police Office. All the facts that Delka had gained were contained in the portfolio which rested close beside him.

The other occupant of the compartment was an elderly gray-haired gentleman. Delka, though he had not met the man, had seen him on the *Patagonia* and had heard mention of his name. He was Phineas Twambley, an American.

Seated catercornered to Delka, Twambley was hunched forward, dozing. His face, though benign of expression, showed weariness. His long, scrawny hands were weakly resting upon the handle of a heavy, gold-headed cane. Delka remembered that Twambley had always needed the cane to hobble about the decks of the liner.

COINCIDENCE had apparently placed Delka in the same compartment as Twambley. A porter at the dock had told the Scotland Yard man that many of the passengers from the steamship were taking first-class carriages, which meant that there would be more space in the third-class coaches.

The porter had also offered to find a vacant compartment, a suggestion that was to Delka's liking. Though the porter had failed to make good his boast, he had done well; for he had managed to place Delka in a compartment that had but one other occupant.

Though Delka would have preferred complete seclusion, he had found no immediate objection to Phineas Twambley as a traveling companion. The only hitch had arrived when Delka had chosen to light a cigarette. Then the old man had burst into a coughing spasm. Delka had desisted without waiting to hear a protest from his fellow passenger.

Two hundred and twenty-five miles to London. Such was the distance of the trip; and the train was due to clip the mileage in less than five hours. A portion of the journey had been covered; but Delka was glum as he considered the annoyance of going without a smoke.

Casually, he eyed Twambley. The old man was dozing more profoundly. Delka produced a silver pocket-case and extracted a cigarette. He saw the old man stir and shift position. Delka smiled wryly and shook his head. He decided that a few puffs of cigarette smoke would probably awaken the old chap.

Quietly, Delka arose and opened the door into the corridor. He stepped from the compartment, eyed Twambley again, then softly closed the door. Striking a match, the Scotland Yard man lighted his cigarette. He felt an immediate appreciation of the first few puffs.

Delka had left his precious briefcase in the compartment; but that, to his mind, had been a wise procedure. Though he kept the briefcase always with him, Delka acted as though it was an item of little consequence.

In a circumstance such as this, the best plan was to let the briefcase remain where it was. Old Twambley was by no means a suspicious character; moreover, the old man had luggage of his own, heaped in a corner of the compartment. If Twambley should awake—which seemed unlikely—he would probably not even notice the briefcase.

So Delka reasoned; but despite his shrewdness, he was wrong. The instant that the Scotland Yard man had closed the door of the compartment, Phineas Twambley had opened one eye. Motionless, he waited until half a minute had elapsed. Satisfied that Delka must be smoking, the old man displayed immediate action.

Dipping one long hand beneath the seat behind his luggage, Phineas Twambley brought out a briefcase that was the exact duplicate of Delka's. With surprising spryness, the old man sidled across the compartment and picked up Delka's briefcase. He laid his own bag in the exact position of the other; then, moving back, he thrust Delka's portfolio out of sight. The exchange completed, Twambley went back to his doze.

A few minutes later, Delka returned to find the old man sleeping. Delka sat down and rested his hand upon the briefcase that was in view. Totally unsuspicious of what had occurred, the Scotland Yard man decided to drowse away the time. Like Twambley, Delka began to doze.

IT was a sudden noise that caused Eric Delka to awaken. Always a light sleeper, Delka came to life suddenly when he heard a *click* from close beside him. Opening his eyes, he caught a glimpse of Twambley, head bowed and nodding. Then Delka swung his gaze toward the door to the corridor.

Delka was nearer the door than Twambley, for the old man had chosen a seat by the window. It was from the corridor door that the noise had come; and Delka, despite his quick awakening, was too late to stop the next event that developed.

The door swung inward; two hard-faced men with glimmering revolvers spotted the Scotland Yard man before he could make a move.

"Up with 'em!" growled one of the arrivals, jabbing the muzzle of his revolver straight toward Delka. Then, to this companion: "Cover the old guy, Jake, in case he wakes up."

Delka's hands went reluctantly upward. The briefcase slid from beside him; half shifting, the Scotland Yard man tried to cover it. His action brought a growl from the man who had him covered.

"No you don't, Delka," snarled the intruder. "We

know what you've got in that briefcase. We're goin' to give it the once-over. An' you'll be a lucky guy if you haven't got the dope you went after. Because if you know too much, it'll be curtains for you!"

Delka stood up slowly, in response to a vertical urge from the rowdy's gun. With sidelong glance, he saw Twambley dozing as steadily as before. The second crook was chuckling contemptuously as he watched the old man.

"He's dead to the world, Pete," informed Jake. "Go ahead with the heat. See what Delka's got in the briefcase. If he starts trouble, I'm with you. The old bloke don't count."

Pete reached forward. With one hand, he started to pull back the zipper fastening of the briefcase. The train was driving forward with the speed for which the Great Western Railway is famous. It took a curve as the crook tugged at the bag.

Momentarily, Pete lost his footing. His shoulder jarred against the wall of the compartment. His gun lost its aim.

Delka, watching Jake also, saw opportunity. With a sudden bound, the Scotland Yard man pounced upon Pete and grabbed the fellow's gun wrist.

Jake swung with a snarl. He could not aim at Delka, for Pete's body intervened. The thug was getting the worse of it. With a quick move, Jake leaped across the compartment and swung to gain a bead on Delka. At the same moment, another roll of the train gave Pete a chance to rally.

The grappling thug shoved Delka back against the wall. Jake shouted encouragement, as he aimed his revolver toward Delka. As if in answer to the call, another pair of thugs sprang into view from the corridor. Like Pete and Jake, these two had revolvers.

Odds against Delka. Murder was due. But into the breach came an unexpected rescuer—one whose very appearance had made him seem a negligible factor. With a speed that would have been incredible in a young and active man, Phineas Twambley launched into the fray.

MAGICALLY, the old man straightened. His right hand swung with terrific speed. That hand gripped the heavy cane; with the swiftness of a whiplash, the stick flashed downward and cracked Jake's aiming wrist. Solid wood won the conflict with bone. The gun went clattering from Jake's fist. The thug sprawled with a howl.

That was not all. As Twambley's right hand performed its speedy action, his left shot beneath the right side of his coat. Out it came—a long, clutching fist that gripped a .45 automatic.

The thugs in the doorway snarled as they aimed to kill. Their revolvers swung too late to match that swiftly whisked automatic.

The first shot boomed for a living mark. One would-be killer thudded forward to the floor. The other, aiming, fired. But Twambley was double quick. Diving sidewise, the old man struck the wall. The thug's hasty aim was wide. The bullet that spat from the revolver cracked the window just beyond the spot where Twambley had been. Then came the old man's second action; another roaring shot from his automatic.

Flame spurted. The thug in the doorway staggered, then went diving out into the corridor. Jake, springing upward, had grabbed his revolver with his left hand, anxious to get new aim at Twambley. A sidewise swing from the cane sent the fellow sprawling back to the floor. This time, Jake's head took the crack.

Delka had gained Pete's gun. He had twisted the crook about. With one fierce drive, the Scotland Yard man rammed his adversary's head against the wall. Pete slumped. Delka, staring, saw a leveled automatic—Twambley's.

THE old man's hand moved slowly downward, following the direction of Pete's sagging form. Not content with disposing of three adversaries, he had gained the aim on the fourth. Had Pete still shown fight, this amazing battler would have dropped him.

Shouts from the corridor. Train attendants had heard the sound of fray. They were dashing up to learn the cause. They had blocked the path of one crook who sought escape. That was the reason for the shouts; but Eric Delka scarcely heard the outside cries.

For a strange sound had filled the compartment, a whispered tone that rose above the chugging of the train. It was a weird burst of mirth, a chilling burst of repressed mockery intended for Delka's ears alone.

Once before, the man from Scotland Yard had heard that taunt, upon a previous time when business had taken him to the United States. Then, as now, Eric Delka had been rescued by the author of that sinister mirth. (Note: See "The Man From Scotland Yard;" Vol. XIV, No. 5.)

Here, in this compartment, stood a man whose lips did not move; yet Delka knew that it was from those lips that the laugh had come. The lips of Phineas Twambley. Delka knew the concealed identity of his rescuer. Twambley was The Shadow.

Strange, amazing battler who hunted down men of crime, The Shadow—Delka's former rescuer—had appeared in England. That Delka might choose the proper course of action, The Shadow had revealed his identity to the man from Scotland Yard.

As Delka stared, the long left hand unloosened. The automatic dropped from The Shadow's clutch,

The old man straightened. His right hand swung with terrific speed ... Cracked Jake's aiming wrist ...

to fall at Delka's feet. In a twinkling, that long, firm hand seemed scrawny. The Shadow's form doubled; hunched, it sought the support of the heavy cane. Then, with a shudder, The Shadow sank back to the seat where he had been. A quavering figure, with a face that wore a senile grin, he had resumed the part of Phineas Twambley.

Eric Delka understood. Quickly, he grabbed up the gun that The Shadow had let fall. Train guards were already at the door of the compartment. It was Delka's part to take credit for having won this battle, alone. Such was The Shadow's order.

To that command, Delka had responded without question, even though no word had been uttered. Whispered mirth had carried the order; and its tone had borne full significance. Eric Delka could only obey.

He had heard the laugh of The Shadow!

CHAPTER II
AT SCOTLAND YARD

THE Great Western train was a few minutes late when it reached Paddington Station, its London terminus. Seated in the cab of the gaudily painted locomotive, the engineer eyed two men as they walked along the platform.

One was Eric Delka; the engineer had heard about the Scotland Yard man when the train had been held at Taunton. Delka was the chap who, single-handed, had crippled a crew of murderous attackers. Those thugs had been turned over to the authorities at Taunton.

With Delka was a gray-haired, stoop-shouldered companion who hobbled along at a spry pace. The engineer had heard mention of his name also. The man was Phineas Twambley, who had been in Delka's compartment during the battle.

According to report, however, Twambley had figured in the fray only as a spectator. The engineer was not surprised, once he had viewed Twambley. Delka's companion looked too old to have been a combatant in active battle.

That opinion was shared by everyone who had come in contact with Phineas Twambley, except those who had been participants in the fight. The crooks whom The Shadow had downed were in no condition to talk, while Eric Delka was tactful enough to keep his own conclusions to himself. His first commitment came when he and The Shadow had walked from the train shed. Then Delka cagily addressed his companion.

"I should like to have you accompany me to the Yard, Mr. Twambley," vouchsafed Delka. "Perhaps you would be interested in my report to Sidney Lewsham. He's acting as chief constable of the C.I.D. I should like to introduce you to him."

"Very well." The Shadow chuckled in Twambley fashion. "However, I should like to send my luggage to the Savoy Hotel—"

"We can arrange that quite easily."

Delka gave instructions to the porter. The luggage that bore Phineas Twambley's tags was marked for the Savoy. During the process, however, Delka was suddenly astonished to see his stoop-shouldered companion pluck a briefcase from among the stack of bags.

"This appears to be yours, Mr. Delka," remarked The Shadow, in a crackly tone. "I shall ask you to return *my* briefcase."

Half gaping, Delka looked at the bag in his own hand. Hastily, he pulled back the zipper fastenings. He saw at once that the contents consisted entirely of steamship folders and British railway timetables.

As The Shadow took the briefcase from Delka's hand, the Scotland Yard man yanked open the one that The Shadow gave him.

Within were Delka's precious documents—the fruits of his journey to New York. Realization dawned upon Delka; new proof of the protection which The Shadow had afforded him. Had crooks aboard the train managed a getaway, they would have gained nothing. The very bag for which they had battled had not been Delka's! Thinking this over, the Scotland Yard man smiled; but made no comment.

WITH Twambley's luggage arranged for its trip to the Savoy, Delka and his companion descended to the Paddington Station of the Bakerloo Line, the most convenient underground route to the vicinity of Scotland Yard. A dozen minutes after boarding the tube train, they arrived at the Charing Cross underground station. From there, a short southward walk along the Thames Embankment brought them to the portals of New Scotland Yard.

Delka gained prompt admittance to the office of Sidney Lewsham, acting chief of the Criminal Investigation Department. Lewsham, a towering, heavy-browed man, was curious when he gazed at Delka's companion. Briskly, Delka introduced The Shadow as Phineas Twambley.

"Mr. Twambley aided me in subduing those ruffians aboard the train," explained Delka. "He used his stout cane as a bludgeon during the fight. Moreover, he preserved my briefcase, with its important documents."

"How so?" queried Lewsham, in surprise. "I had no report of this by telephone from Taunton."

"I saw that the attackers were striving for the briefcase," chuckled The Shadow, "so I seized it and threw it beneath a seat. The ruffians tried to make away with a similar bag that was lying with my own luggage."

Lewsham smiled when he heard the story. So did Delka; but the investigator suppressed his momentary grin before his chief spied it. Delka knew well that Lewsham was rating Phineas Twambley as an old codger who could have been of but little use. That pleased Delka; for he had no intention of stating who Twambley really was.

For Delka knew himself to be one of a chosen few who had gained The Shadow's confidence. Like Joe Cardona of the New York police, like Vic Marquette of the United States Secret Service, Delka had profited in the past through The Shadow's intervention. His part, Delka knew, was to aid The Shadow; and in so doing, gain a powerful ally. It was best to accept The Shadow in the guise that he had chosen to assume.

"In fairness to Mr. Twambley," began Delka, "I thought that he might be entitled to a partial explanation of the circumstances that forced him into his predicament aboard the train. That is why I brought him here, sir, in case you felt such an explanation permissible."

"Of course; of course." Lewsham nodded, as he seated himself behind his huge mahogany desk. "Well, Delka, there is no reason why Mr. Twambley should not hear the complete story. I intend to make it public within a few days. The whole country shall know of the crimes which balk us."

"You intend to publish the facts about The Harvester?"

"I do. Moreover, our present meeting is an excellent occasion for a preliminary review. I am going into details, Delka, and your friend Mr. Twambley may hear for himself."

LEWSHAM leaned back in his big chair. He thrust out a long arm and began to spin a large globe of the world that stood near to the desk. Stopping the revolving sphere, he leaned forward and folded his arms upon the desk.

"London has become a reaping ground," he declared, "for an unknown criminal, whose methods are unique. We have styled this rogue 'The Harvester,' for want of a better sobriquet. We have no key to his identity; but we do know that he employs crafty men to aid him; also that he controls certain bands of murderers."

Drawing Delka's briefcase toward him, Lewsham opened it and extracted documents. He referred to records that were obviously duplicates of papers on file in Scotland Yard.

"The Harvester," explained Lewsham, "is always preceded by another man. This fellow operated at first under the name of Humphrey Bildon. He first opened an account with a local banking house and established credit there.

"One day, Humphrey Bildon introduced a friend: Sir James Carliff. Because of Bildon's introduction, and because persons present had met Sir James Carliff, the banking house cashed a draft for eight thousand pounds. That sum, Mr. Twambley"—Lewsham smiled, remembering that the visitor was an American—"amounted to approximately forty thousand dollars."

As The Shadow nodded, Delka put in a comment.

"But it was not Sir James Carliff," stated the investigator, "who received the money."

"It was not," added Lewsham, emphatically. "It was an impostor; the man whom we have dubbed The Harvester. He made an excellent impersonator. Those who saw him actually took him for Sir James Carliff."

Referring to his notes, Lewsham brought up the second case.

"Humphrey Bildon appeared again," he stated. "He had the cheek to negotiate with another banking house, immediately after his dealing with the first. He arranged for a loan to be given Monsieur Pierre Garthou, the head of a French mining syndicate. Monsieur Garthou appeared in person and left the

banking office with twenty thousand pounds in his possession.

"Immediately afterward, a fraud was suspected. Bildon and Garthou were stopped by Thomas Colbar, a representative of the banking house, when they were entering a taxicab to leave for Victoria Station. Garthou produced a revolver and riddled Colbar with bullets. The victim died instantly."

"But the murderer was not the real Garthou," reminded Delka. "It was The Harvester, again, passing himself as Garthou."

"Precisely," nodded Lewsham. "That is why we sought both Bildon and The Harvester for murder. But the leopards changed their spots. Up bobbed Bildon, this time under the name of Thomas Dabley. The bounder arranged the purchase of a steamship."

"A STEAMSHIP?" questioned The Shadow, in an incredulous tone that suited the part of Twambley. "For what purpose?"

"I am coming to that," replied Lewsham. "The steamship was loaded with goods for South America. Both the vessel and its contents were in the hands of receivers who wished to make a quick sale. Dabley, otherwise Bildon, introduced an American named Lemuel Brodder."

"I have heard of him. He is a New York shipping magnate. Considered to be very wealthy."

"Exactly. Brodder bought the vessel and its cargo for ten thousand pounds—only a fraction of the full value—and insured both the steamship and its goods for thirty thousand, through Lloyd's."

"Was that the steamship *Baroda?*"

"It was. An explosion occurred on board, before the vessel had passed the Scilly Islands. All on board were lost. Lemuel Brodder appeared to collect his insurance. Fortunately a swindle was suspected upon this occasion. Lloyds had already communicated with New York."

Delka was nodding as Lewsham spoke. The investigator tapped a pile of papers that had come from the briefcase.

"The real Brodder was in America," stated the investigator. "The swindler here in London was none other than The Harvester."

"Impersonating Brodder!" exclaimed The Shadow, in a tone of feigned astonishment. "The Harvester again!"

"Yes," nodded Delka. "That is why I went to New York, to see what might be learned there. The Harvester was shrewd enough to take to cover when he learned which way the wind was blowing. I met the real Brodder. He closely resembled the descriptions that I had of the impostor."

"Rogues had been seen aboard the *Baroda,*" added Lewsham, "while the ship was docked here in London. They were the miscreants who placed the explosives which caused the deaths of innocent crew members. That is how we learned that The Harvester had criminal bands at his call."

"Tonight's attack upon you, Delka, indicates another thrust by The Harvester. Two of those miscreants are dead; I have received that news from the Taunton police. The others know nothing, except that they were to assassinate you and seize your documents."

"So our summary is this: We have an infernally clever rogue with whom to deal; namely, The Harvester. Of him, we have no description, for always, he has appeared as someone else. To reach him, we must first apprehend his lieutenant"— Lewsham paused to emphasize the word, which he pronounced "leftenant"—"his lieutenant, who has appeared under the names of Humphrey Bildon and Thomas Dabley. Who may, in all probability, adopt another name in the future."

Picking up another report sheet, Lewsham read:

"Height, five feet eleven. Weight, twelve stone "

"One hundred and sixty-eight pounds," inserted Delka in an undertone, for The Shadow's benefit. "Fourteen pounds to a stone."

"Military bearing," continued Lewsham, "square face, complexion tanned. Eyes sharp, but very light blue. Hair of light color, almost whitish. Voice smooth, very persuasive and precise.

"There, Mr. Twambley, is a description of Dabley, alias Bildon. Should you meet such a person while in London, notify us at once. For this chap who aids The Harvester apparently possesses none of the chameleon traits which characterize his master. Dabley—or Bildon, if you prefer—lacks the ability to disguise himself.

"Within a few days, his description will be public property. For the present, we choose to wait; in hope that the man may reveal himself. Should new chances for quick swindling reach The Harvester's notice, he might send his lieutenants to sound them out."

THE acting chief arose and bowed to The Shadow, as indication that his interview with Phineas Twambley was concluded. It was apparent that Lewsham wished to confer with Delka, regarding information that the investigator had brought back from New York. The Shadow knew that such facts could not be vitally important; otherwise, Delka would have made an effort to have him remain.

Instead, Delka offered to have someone accompany the visitor to the Hotel Savoy. Chuckling in Twambley's senile fashion, The Shadow shook his head.

"I shall hail a taxicab," he declared. "I doubt that I am in personal danger, gentlemen. Certainly no scoundrels will be about in the vicinity of Scotland Yard."

A few minutes later, the stooped figure of Phineas Twambley stepped aboard an antiquated taxi that stopped for him upon the embankment. The lights of Westminster Bridge were twinkling; other, myriad lights were glowing as the ancient vehicle rattled its way toward the Hotel Savoy. But The Shadow had no thoughts of the great metropolis about him.

A soft laugh issued from the disguised lips of Phineas Twambley, while long, tightening fingers gripped the head of the huge cane. The Shadow's laugh was prophetic. He had learned facts that might influence the immediate future.

For The Shadow had already devised a plan whereby he might gain a trail to The Harvester. Should luck aid his coming effort, he would have opportunity to deal with that murderous supercrook while Scotland Yard stood idle.

CHAPTER III
OPPORTUNITY KNOCKS

TWO days after the arrival of The Shadow and Eric Delka, an unusual advertisement appeared in the classified columns of the London *Times*. The announcement was printed under the heading "Personal" and read as follows:

SILVER MINE: Wealthy American is willing to dispose of his shares in prosperous Montana silver mine. Prefers transaction involving one purchaser only. Apply to H. B. Wadkins, representative, Suite H 2,
    Caulding Court, S. W. 1.

When Eric Delka entered the office of his acting chief, Sidney Lewsham thrust a copy of the *Times* across the desk. A blue-pencil mark encircled that single paragraph, of all the advertisements that covered the front page. Delka nodded slowly as he read the silver mine offer.

"It sounds like The Harvester," said Delka. "But it is not in keeping with his technique."

"Quite true," returned Lewsham, sourly. "That is the only trouble, Eric. I cannot believe that The Harvester would become so bold as to openly flaunt his activities before our faces."

"A 'sucker' game," remarked Delka. "That is what they would term it in the States. This chap Wadkins, whoever he may be, is out to trap some unsuspecting investor."

"Yet he is working blindly," mused Lewsham, "like a spider in the center of a web. I doubt that The Harvester would strive in such fashion, Eric. I can fancy him taking advantage of this announcement, once it had appeared. Yet I cannot picture him inserting the advertisement."

"Suppose I call there this morning," suggested Delka. "A chat with Mr. H. B. Wadkins might prove enlightening."

"Not too hasty, Eric." Lewsham shook his head. "Wait until the day is more advanced. Make your visit shortly before teatime. He might suspect an early caller."

Reluctantly, Delka came to agreement with his chief. Somehow, Delka had a hunch that an early visit to Caulding Court might be preferable to a late one.

In that opinion, Delka happened to be correct. Had he gone immediately from Scotland Yard to Caulding Court, he would have obtained a prompt result.

EXACTLY half an hour after Delka had held his conference with Lewsham, a man of military bearing arrived at an arched entryway that bore the sign "Caulding Court."

The arrival was attired in well-fitted tweeds; he was swinging a light cane as he paused to study the obscure entrance. Tanned complexion, with light hair and sharp blue eyes—Eric Delka would have recognized the man upon the instant. The arrival was Thomas Dabley, alias Humphrey Bildon, chief lieutenant of The Harvester.

Passing through the archway, the tweed-clad man surveyed various doorways that were grouped about the inner court. He chose the one that was marked H 2. Warily, he entered, to find a young man seated in a small anteroom that apparently served as outer office.

"Mr. Wadkins?" queried the light-haired visitor.

"No, sir," replied the young man. His gaze was a frank one. "I am secretary to Mr. Wadkins. He is in his private office. Whom shall I announce?"

"Here is my card." The visitor extended the pasteboard. "I am Captain Richard Darryat, formerly of the Australian-New Zealand Army Corps. Announce my name to Mr. Wadkins."

The visitor smiled as the secretary entered an inner office. The alias of Darryat suited him better than either Bildon or Dabley, for he looked the part of an ANZAC officer. Seating himself, Darryat inserted a cigarette in a long holder. Scarcely had he applied a match before the secretary returned.

"Mr. Wadkins will see you, Captain Darryat."

Darryat entered the inner office. Behind the table, he saw a hunched, bearded man, whose hair formed a heavy, black shock. Shrewd, dark eyes peered from the bushy countenance. Half rising, H. B. Wadkins thrust his arm across the desk and shook hands with Captain Darryat.

"From Australia, eh?" chuckled Wadkins, his voice a harsh one. "Well, Captain, perhaps you know something about silver mines yourself?"

"I do," replied Darryat, with a slight smile. "As much as most Americans."

"Wrong, Captain," Wadkins grinned through his heavy beard. "I am a Canadian. Spent a lot of time, though, in the States. That's how I became interested in Montana silver. I hail from Vancouver. Hadn't been in London long before an old partner of mine wrote me and sent along his shares in the Topoco

Mine. Told me to sell out—so I did."

"Do you mean that you no longer have shares to offer?"

"That's about it, Captain. They were snapped up pronto, all except a few thousand dollars' worth. Here is what I have left."

WADKINS drew a batch of stock certificates from a desk drawer and showed them to Darryat. The fake captain's eyes lighted. Darryat knew mining stocks. He had recognized the Topoco name.

"Seven thousand dollars' worth, to be exact," remarked Wadkins. "Sixty-seven thousand was what I had for a starter. One customer took sixty thousand, cash and carry."

"Who was he, might I ask?"

Darryat's question was casual; but it brought a shrewd look from Wadkins. Then the bearded man shook his head.

"I don't even know the chap's name," he declared. "He dealt through a solicitor, who arrived here bright and early. Sorry, but I can't state the name of the solicitor. All I can do is offer you the seven thousand dollars' worth of remaining shares."

"Hardly enough," mused Darryat. "I, too, represent a prosperous client. I suppose you have no other offerings, Mr. Wadkins?"

"None at all. If I fail to sell these, I shall purchase them myself. I intend to leave London shortly; in fact, I may close the office after today, should I make no sale."

"And if you make a sale—"

"I shall close the office, anyway. By the way, Captain, would you be interested in a large purchase of some Canadian gold mine stock?"

"I might be. Who is offering it?"

"A friend of mine in Toronto." Wadkins was rising, crablike, to hold a hunched position as he spoke. "See my secretary when you leave. Ask him to give you the Toronto prospectus. It may interest you."

Darryat nodded. Rising, he shook hands with Wadkins and walked to the outer office. Wadkins followed him and spoke to the young man who served as secretary.

"Find the Toronto prospectus, Vincent," ordered the bearded Canadian.

"Let Captain Darryat have it. Good-bye, Captain."

Returning to the inner office, H. B. Wadkins closed the heavy door. Stepping to the desk, he picked up a flat suitcase and opened it. His body straightened, as a soft, whispered laugh issued from his bearded lips. With quick, deft hands, he whisked away his heavy black wig and detached the bushy beard from his chin.

The laugh—the action; both were revelations of identity. The so-called Captain Darryat, whatever his impressions, had failed to guess the true personality that had lain behind that disguise.

H. B. Wadkins was The Shadow!

PACKING his discarded disguise, The Shadow donned hat and coat. His countenance, calm and masklike, was one that Darryat would not have recognized. Nevertheless, The Shadow was taking no chances on an immediate meeting with his recent visitor. There was a rear door to the inner office. Opening it, The Shadow threaded his way through a narrow passage that led him to another street.

Meanwhile, in the outer office, the secretary was looking for the Toronto prospectus. In so doing, he was playing a game that bluffed Captain Darryat. For Harry Vincent, agent of The Shadow, had his own work to accomplish. He was rummaging through boxes at the bottom of a closet, giving Darryat a chance to look about the office in the meantime.

Upon Harry's desk was an envelope, one that had been brought by messenger. From it projected a letter. Sliding his body between the desk and the closet, Darryat slid the folded paper from the envelope. He opened it and quickly read the message.

The letter bore the printed heading: "Cyril Dobbingsworth, Solicitor," with an address that Darryat recognized. Dobbingsworth's office was located at the Cheshire Legal Chambers, near Chancery Lane, close to the Temple.

The message, itself, fitted with the story that Darryat had heard. Dobbingsworth had been prepared to buy the silver mine stock for a wealthy client; his note was an announcement of an early call which he intended to make on H. B. Wadkins.

Darryat slid the paper back into the envelope, just as Harry Vincent turned about. The Shadow's agent had the prospectus that Darryat wanted. It was merely a printed folder from Toronto. Darryat scanned the pages, nodded and thrust the prospectus in his pocket. Turning about, he strode out through Caulding Court.

Upon the desk lay the telltale envelope. Harry Vincent had placed it at an exact angle; the projecting message emerging just one inch. Darryat, in replacing it, had not only edged the paper further in; he had also moved the envelope. Harry knew that the bait had been taken.

The Shadow had not only drawn The Harvester's advance man to a given spot; he had also supplied him with a lead to follow. The advertisement in the *Times* had served a purpose that Scotland Yard had not guessed. It was The Shadow's move to reach The Harvester!

CHAPTER IV
THE GAME DEEPENS

Soon after Captain Darryat's departure, Harry Vincent went out to luncheon. He took the front door that led through the court. On his way, Harry made careful observations. From these, he was certain that Darryat had not remained in the vicinity.

When he returned, nearly an hour later, Harry again made sure that Darryat was not about. The double checkup was sufficient. Should Darryat return to find that H. B. Wadkins had gone, he would suspect nothing; for a time interval had occurred wherein Wadkins could have left through the court.

After lingering for an hour in the office, Harry proceeded to close up. He packed various papers in a suitcase; he prepared a small sign that bore the word "Closed." Attaching this notice to the door, The Shadow's agent made his departure. Again, no signs of Darryat. Harry's work was finished.

About half an hour after Harry's final exit, Captain Darryat swaggered along the street that led to Caulding Court. Peering in from the archway, The Harvester's lieutenant eyed the door with the number H 2. He saw Harry's sign and approached. A chuckle came from Darryat when he read the notice.

H. B. Wadkins had cleared out. That fact fitted perfectly with Darryat's plans. After a brief inspection, the tanned man strolled from Caulding Court. Then, of a sudden, he performed a surprising action. Forgetting his swagger, Darryat whisked about and dived into a convenient doorway. A strained, hunted look appeared upon his features; his sharp eyes narrowed as he watched a man who approached alone. The arrival was Eric Delka.

Darryat had recognized the Scotland Yard investigator; and he had been quick enough to slide from Delka's sight. He saw Delka enter Caulding Court; then, satisfied that the investigator was alone, Darryat became bold and stole to the archway.

Peering through, he saw Delka reading the sign on door H 2. He caught a shrug of Delka's shoulder. Then Darryat slid out to the street and returned to his previous hiding place. He watched Delka reappear and walk away.

Obviously, Delka had also read the advertisement in the *Times* and had decided to make a visit to the office of H. B. Wadkins. The bird that Delka sought had flown; and Darryat was sure that Wadkins would not be back. Nevertheless, the chance visit of Delka had produced a definite influence upon Darryat's plans.

Darryat had his own game to further, in the service of The Harvester. He did not intend to alter it; but he did plan to use new precautions—something that he would not have considered had he failed to catch that brief view of Delka.

SOON afterward, Darryat was walking briskly across the vast asphalt spaces of Trafalgar Square. Reaching The Strand, he followed that important thoroughfare until it changed its name and became Fleet Street. There, Darryat sought Chancery Lane and finally located the Cheshire Legal Chambers.

Entering, he discovered a closed door that bore the name of Cyril Dobbingsworth. Darryat rapped. A querulous voice ordered him to enter.

Inside a little office, Darryat came face to face with Cyril Dobbingsworth. The solicitor was an ancient, stoop-shouldered old fellow, who was sipping tea and nibbling biscuits at a decrepit desk. Stacks of law books were all about; the walls were adorned with faded portraits of famous British jurists.

Dobbingsworth apparently fancied himself as a traditional London barrister. Darryat, however, classed him immediately as a weather-beaten fossil.

"Your name, sir?"

Dobbingsworth's crackled query brought a smile to Darryat's lips. The pretended captain extended his card.

While Dobbingsworth was studying it, apparently puzzled, Darryat sat down and stated his business.

"I have come, sir," he stated, "to inform you of a hoax which has been perpetrated against a client of yours."

"A hoax?"

"Yes. In regard to a Montana silver mine."

Dobbingsworth blinked. Darryat could see scrawny hands shake as the teacup jogged in the solicitor's fingers. Dobbingsworth tried to splutter, but words failed him.

"I, too, have met H. B. Wadkins," purred Darryat, in a voice that befitted Scotland Yard's description of him. "He offered me the stock that remained. I wisely refrained from buying it."

"Why so?" queried Dobbingsworth, anxiously, as he pushed back a shock of gray hair from above his withered face. "I have been assured that the Topoco Mine is a sound one. Have you evidence, sir, to the contrary?"

"None," replied Darryat, "but I hold doubts regarding the particular stock that was in the possession of Wadkins. I scrutinized it rather closely. It appeared to be a forgery."

The teacup clattered as Dobbingsworth set it heavily upon the desk. The old solicitor clucked hopelessly. Darryat leaned forward.

"Wadkins has abandoned his office at Caulding Court," he informed. "Fortunately, I learned that you had dealt with him. That is why I came promptly to these chambers."

"This is a case for Scotland Yard!" exclaimed Dobbingsworth, in an outraged tone. "It is, indeed! I shall inform headquarters at once!"

He reached for an antiquated telephone. Darryat stopped him.

"ONE moment, sir," objected Darryat, smoothly. "Would it not be best to consult your client, prior to taking such a step?"

"What purpose would that serve?" demanded Dobbingsworth. "If my client has been swindled—"

"I have no proof of that," interposed Darryat. "I have stated merely that the stock which Wadkins showed me appeared to be spurious. In order to venture a proper opinion, I should have to examine the stock that you purchased from Wadkins."

As he spoke, Darryat eyed a large, old-fashioned safe at the rear of Dobbingsworth's office. The solicitor was not watching Darryat at the time. Instead, Dobbingsworth was shaking his head in most dejected fashion.

"I have delivered the stock," he affirmed. "My client was here, awaiting my return. I cannot show it to you."

"But what of your client?" queried Darryat. "Could we not arrange an appointment with him?"

"He has gone from London for the day. To Kew Gardens, I believe."

"Will he return this evening?"

"Yes. But I have to depart for Sheffield, to attend to a matter which concerns another client."

"Perhaps if you gave me a letter of introduction—"

"To my client?"

Darryat nodded.

"Zounds!" exclaimed Dobbingsworth, pounding the desk with his scrawny fist. "That, indeed, is a timely suggestion! But I can do better, sir. Remain seated, while I call a messenger."

Dobbingsworth picked up the telephone and put in a call. That completed, he took a large quill pen and began to transcribe a message. Darryat noted the long, old-fashioned penmanship that had characterized the letter that he had seen on Harry Vincent's desk.

A boy appeared at the office door. He was attired in the uniform and round hat that symbolized the London messengers. The solicitor handed him the envelope containing the finished letter. He added the fee that was required. The boy left.

"My client's name," informed Dobbingsworth, "is Lamont Cranston. He is a wealthy American. He resides at the old Manor Club."

"Near St. James Square?" queried Darryat, "close by Haymarket?"

"That is the location of the new club," replied Dobbingsworth, with a shake of his head. "The old Manor Club is closer to Piccadilly. It is a club no longer; it has some name which I have forgotten, although I have the actual address. It is a bachelor's apartment; very exclusive—"

"I recall the place. Known as the Moravia, is it not?"

"That is the name. Quite stupid of me to forget it. Very well, Captain. I have written Mr. Cranston to receive you. You will find him there at nine o'clock this evening. I should like to have you discuss the subject of those securities with him in person. If he chooses to communicate with Scotland Yard, he may do so."

"An excellent suggestion. My thanks to you, sir."

"I owe the thanks, Captain."

The old solicitor shook hands and Captain Darryat departed.

WHEN Darryat had gone, Cyril Dobbingsworth sat at his desk, sipping tea, staring out toward the direction of the Temple.

There had been definite significance in the visit of Captain Darryat; points which the smooth swindler had not amplified in his discourse with the solicitor. Darryat had stated that he had visited Wadkins; he had also added that the man had closed his office. Sure proof that Darryat had not come directly to Dobbingsworth's office.

A smile showed upon the withered features of the old solicitor. That expression proved that Dobbingsworth understood the facts. Then, from crackly lips came the soft tones of a whispered laugh—the same that H. B. Wadkins had delivered earlier in the day.

Cyril Dobbingsworth, like H. B. Wadkins, was The Shadow! From one assumed personality, he had gone to another. He had left Caulding Court ahead of Captain Darryat that he might be here at the Cheshire Legal Chambers before the swindler could possibly arrive.

Darryat had been totally deceived. He had never suspected a link between Wadkins and Dobbingsworth; much less that the two could possibly be the same. He had been suspicious of Wadkins; he had been lulled by Dobbingsworth. Believing that one had fled and that the other was going out of town, Darryat would have no qualms about calling on Lamont Cranston.

There, again, he would be due to meet The Shadow. For the personality of Lamont Cranston was one that The Shadow used frequently. Today, he had dropped the guise of Phineas Twambley altogether. After a brief appearance as Wadkins, then as Dobbingsworth, he would be Cranston and would keep that assumed identity. Except for one brief interval, long enough to put in a call to Scotland Yard.

With that call, The Shadow would announce himself as Phineas Twambley, in order to bring Eric Delka to the trail. This evening, he would tell the investigator that he had chanced to see a man answering the description of Dabley, alias Bildon, in the neighborhood of the Moravia Apartments, near St. James Square.

For The Shadow knew that he had hooked more than a little fish. The same bait that had caught Captain Darryat would snag another—and a larger—personage of crime. The lure of sixty thousand dollars, in sound silver securities, would bring more than a lone lieutenant.

Captain Darryat's visit to the residence of Lamont Cranston would be but the forerunner to another arrival. The Harvester, himself, would follow. Tonight, the supercrook was destined to meet The Shadow!

CHAPTER V
THE COUNTERTHRUST

AT precisely ten minutes before nine, Captain Richard Darryat strolled from the subdued glow of St. James Street and arrived at the entrance of the Moravia Apartments. The evening was mild and mellow; Darryat, fashionably attired, looked like a usual habitue of this section where exclusive clubs flourish.

Ascending the steps of the Moravia, Darryat was impressed by the fact that the place had changed but little since the days when it had housed the old Manor Club. The same exclusive atmosphere pervaded the squatty, stone-fronted structure. It was necessary to ring the bell in order to gain admittance.

A uniformed attendant answered Darryat's ring. He asked for the visitor's card. Darryat proffered it. The flunky bowed and conducted Darryat through a mammoth hallway, to an automatic elevator.

"Mr. Cranston awaits your arrival, sir," stated the attendant. "His apartment is on the third floor. Its letter is D. Are you acquainted with this type of lift, sir?"

"Quite," returned Darryat, studying the buttons of the automatic elevator. "I shall proceed to the third floor."

Hardly had the door of the elevator closed before a man emerged from the darkness of a side room. It was Eric Delka; he had seen Darryat's entry. Tensely, the investigator gave instructions to the flunky.

"That is the man," whispered Delka. "Remember: From this minute on, you are to signal if any stranger seeks admittance."

The servant bowed his understanding. He went his way along the hall, while Delka returned to the hiding place. There he spoke to men who were stationed with him.

"Old Twambley had good eyesight," commented Delka, in a tone of approval. "It's lucky he saw that chap standing outside here this afternoon. He guessed correctly when he thought it was Dabley, alias Bildon."

"Which name is the rogue using tonight?" came the query.

"Neither," returned Delka, studying the card. The flunky had given it to him. "He is employing a new alias. He calls himself Captain Richard Darryat. He is bound for Apartment D, on the third floor, to meet a gentleman named Cranston."

"Shall we follow?"

"No." Delka chuckled. "We shall remain here for a short while. Where Darryat appears, The Harvester will follow. It is best to bide our time."

THERE was reason for Delka's chuckle. For the first time, the investigator had learned that a man named Lamont Cranston was residing at the Moravia; that it was he upon whom Darryat was calling. Delka remembered the name of Cranston from the past. He knew that there was some connection between Cranston and The Shadow.

Not for one moment did Delka suppose that Cranston and The Shadow were one. The Shadow's brief appearance in the role of Phineas Twambley had thrown Delka from the track.

Delka thought of Cranston as an adventurous American millionaire; one well qualified to take care of himself in emergency. He believed that The Shadow occasionally shunted desperate characters in Cranston's direction, after due warning to the millionaire. Hence Darryat, alone, did not strike Delka as a threat.

A ring of the doorbell caused Delka to peer out into the hall. He saw the flunky admit a wan, droopy-faced man who nodded and went to the lift. The attendant returned to answer another ring at the door. This time, he admitted a stoop-shouldered man who was carrying a large cane and wearing a heavy overcoat.

Delka caught sight of a face that was conspicuous because of a brown Vandyke beard. The flunky conducted the new visitor to the lift, and pressed the button for its descent. The man with the Vandyke entered and went upward.

The attendant started back toward the door, making a motion with his hand. Delka sneaked out and intercepted him. The flunky spoke.

"Thought I'd better report, sir," he stated, solemnly. "The first gentleman to enter was Mr. Rufus Holmes, who lodges in Apartment A on the fourth floor. The second was Sir Ernest Jennup."

"He resides here?" queried Delka.

"No, sir" was the reply, "but he calls occasionally upon the Honorable Raymond Fellow, whose apartment is on the second floor. I deemed that it would be quite right to admit Sir Ernest without question. The Honorable Mr. Fellow is at present in his apartment."

"Quite all right," agreed Delka. "Carry on."

With that, the investigator returned to the side room while the servant took his place near the outer door.

MEANWHILE, Captain Darryat had gained a cordial reception at Apartment D, on the third floor. His knock had gained him a prompt admittance. He had come face to face with a tall, hawk-faced occupant who was attired in dressing gown.

His host had announced himself as Lamont Cranston. Richard Darryat had accepted the invitation to lay aside his coat, hat and walking stick. He had accepted an expensive panatela which Cranston proffered him.

Both men were seated and were smoking their thin cigars. Cranston, though an American, seemed to have acquired the reserve of a Britisher, for his opening conversation was stilted and formal.

Darryat, eyeing him closely, was impressed by a keenness which persisted despite Cranston's languor. Somehow, Cranston reminded him of someone whom he had met before; Darryat could not recall whom. He did not grasp the truth: namely, that this personage who now passed as Cranston had been both Wadkins and Dobbingsworth. Such was the capability of The Shadow's disguises.

"So Dobbingsworth sent you here," remarked The Shadow, in a calm, leisurely tone that fitted the guise of Cranston. "His note indicated that you wished to speak to me regarding the Montana silver stock. Do I understand, Captain, that you wish to buy some shares?"

"I would like to invest in Topoco Mines," nodded Darryat. "From anyone who has such securities."

"Unfortunately," declared The Shadow, "my holdings are not for sale."

"I doubt that I would buy them if they were," returned Darryat. "That is why I have come here, Mr. Cranston."

The Shadow feigned a puzzled expression. Darryat shook his head dubiously and leaned forward in his chair.

"To be frank, Mr. Cranston," he stated, "I have ventured here on a sad errand. It is my painful duty to inform you that your mining stock is spurious."

The Shadow stared, apparently startled.

"You understand, of course," added Darryat, "that such is my opinion. I saw the remaining shares that Wadkins had to offer. I have learned, for a fact, that Wadkins has left London."

"His office is closed?"

"Yes. Under the pretext that his work is finished. His work, however, was illegitimate. If you would let me glance at that stock, Mr. Cranston—"

"Certainly."

Reaching to a heavy table, The Shadow pulled open a drawer and produced the stock in question. He handed the bundle to Darryat. The pretended captain gave it close scrutiny; then shook his head.

"I doubt the stock's authenticity," he declared. "Quite sorry, old chap, but I am familiar with this sort of thing. However, I do not wish you to go upon my opinion alone. I hope to help you; and I took the liberty of inviting a friend here for that purpose."

"A friend?" queried The Shadow.

"Yes," nodded Darryat. "Sir Ernest Jennup, the well-known banker. Of course you have heard of him; he has offices on Lombard Street."

"I have met him," recalled The Shadow. "A

stoop-shouldered man, past middle age, with a Vandyke beard and—"

"You have described him precisely." Darryat glanced at his watch. "Since Sir Ernest should be here, shortly, I left word with the doorkeeper to invite him up here immediately upon his arrival."

"Of course. I shall be glad to hear Sir Ernest's opinion. A chat with him will be quite in order."

"He will probably suggest that you place the securities in his custody, that he may have them examined by experts who are competent at detecting forgeries."

"An excellent suggestion."

Hardly had Darryat spoken before a rap sounded at the door. The fake captain spoke in an eager whisper.

"It is Sir Ernest!"

THE SHADOW arose leisurely and strolled toward the door to answer the knock. Before he was halfway there, the rap was repeated—this time in sharp *rat-tat* fashion, two strokes at a time.

As The Shadow advanced, a sudden hiss came from behind him. He turned to stare at Darryat. The crook had brought a revolver from his pocket.

Darryat was leveling the weapon with his right hand, while his left clutched the mining stock. In

harsh whisper, Darryat delivered a command.

"Stop where you are!"

The Shadow paused; his hands half lifted, his face showing perplexed concern. Approaching, Darryat sneered.

"The game is up, Cranston," he stated. "That man outside the door is not Sir Ernest Jennup. He is a gentleman whom Scotland Yard has chosen to call The Harvester. He is the chief whom I serve."

The Shadow's face registered bewilderment. Hands rising further, he was backing to the wall beside the door.

"We came here to make you our dupe," jeered Darryat. "We would easily have succeeded. However, this afternoon I chanced to spy a Scotland Yard investigator: one, Eric Delka. I informed The Harvester. He said to be ready for emergency.

"That second rap, delivered in double, repeated fashion, is my chief's signal. It means that Scotland Yard has meddled. We cannot risk the time that we would need to properly induce you to turn over your securities."

Again came the repeated rap. Thrusting the mining stock into his pocket, Darryat sidled to the door; there he gripped the knob with his left hand, while he still kept The Shadow covered with his gun.

"It shall have to be crudely done" was Darryat's

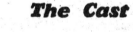

The Cast

Continued from page 6

money, is consummated. Rudlow, Limited, is the banking house handling the deal and it is there that Selbrook meets

JUSTIN CRAYBAW, managing director of the banking house and in charge of the details of handling the oil options and reselling them, making a large commission for his firm. It is at the country estate of Craybaw that most of the details of the deal are worked out. Working along with Craybaw is

SIR ERNEST JENNUP, a London banker of high degree, whose advice adds much to the actions of Craybaw in the transfer of the oil

The Rajah

final jeer. "By seizure, not by strategy. Those Scotland Yard men may be waiting for us. So we will coax them from their nests by starting a rampage. Too bad for you, Cranston; but murder is part of our game, when necessary—"

Darryat had turned the knob and was drawing the door inward. He moved back to admit The Harvester; and in that moment of confidence, Darryat let his right hand turn slightly. In a split second, The Shadow's languid resignment faded. He remained Cranston in appearance, only; not in action.

THE SHADOW'S long body shot forward with arrowlike rapidity. His left hand shot for Darryat's right wrist. His right sped to a deep, inner left pocket of his dressing gown.

Darryat tried to leap away; to aim as he did so. He was too late. A viselike fist caught the scoundrel's wrist. Darryat was whirled about like a helpless puppet.

The crook tugged at the trigger of his gun. His hand, twisted sidewise, no longer held its aim. Spurting flames spat toward the ceiling, where useless bullets found their only target. The Shadow, swinging clear about, had gained the center of the room. Darryat, twisted double by the jujitsu hold, was in his clutch, between The Shadow and the door.

The barrier had swung wide. There, upon the threshold was the figure of a bearded man, stooped no longer. The Harvester still had the facial guise of Sir Ernest Jennup; but he had dropped the pose of the banker whom he was impersonating.

Hissed oaths were coming from the lips that wore the false Vandyke. Savagely, with glaring eyes, the master crook was aiming a revolver of his own.

The Shadow, in turn, had whipped out an automatic with his right fist, while his left hand had hurled Darryat into many gyrations. Sidestepping across the floor with Darryat in front of him, The Shadow was leveling his .45 past the fake captain's shoulder. Darryat was screaming with helpless rage.

The game was really up. Darryat's shots had ended it. Those barks of his revolver had been heard; for shouts were coming from a stairway, far below. Through his hopeless thrust, Darryat had precipitated an immediate duel between The Shadow and The Harvester.

Guns ripped booming shots with simultaneous fury. The Shadow was aiming at The Harvester; the supercrook was firing toward his indomitable foe. But in that battle, both had a different disadvantage. The Shadow's aim was injured by Darryat's struggles. The Harvester's openings were handicapped because The Shadow held Darryat as a shield.

The Harvester's life seemed charmed as the master crook swung back and forth in the doorway.

The Cast

options. Jennup has important dealings with the

RAJAH OF DELAPORE, Indian potentate, whose collection of precious gems is invaluable, and upon whom suspicion is cast as to being The Harvester. Suspicious also are the doings of the rajah's English secretary,

JED RANWORTHY, whose disappearance in answer to a strange telegram throws mystery on his actions and leaves him open to suspicion in the crimes that follow his leave-taking.

DAWSON CANONBY, famous London jeweler, comes into the case as a gem expert on a little matter between himself and the rajah.

Phineas Twambley

Each stab from The Shadow's automatic was jinxed either by a movement of his target, or through a chance twist by Darryat. Yet The Harvester, in his haste, could not find an opening through which to jab a bullet. Each time that the killer fired, The Shadow was making a shift.

Viciously, fiendishly, The Harvester gave up his first tactics and opened a final volley straight for the intervening figure of Darryat.

A hoarse scream came from the helpless hench-man as riddling bullets found Darryat's body. The Harvester hoped to blast the human shield from The Shadow's grasp. He counted upon a sag of Darryat's body to allow a better path toward the fighter in the dressing gown.

The Harvester failed. Not for an instant did The Shadow release his twisting clutch.

Shouts from atop the stairs. With a mad snarl, the false-bearded supercrook dived away from the doorway, just as The Shadow thrust his steadied gun over Darryat's sagged shoulder. The automatic spoke; its tongued barks were too late. The Harvester had plunged from view, diving straight into the arms of Delka and two Scotland Yard men.

DELKA and his companions were aiming, as they shouted a command to halt. The Harvester crossed their expectations. Swinging his gun hand like a bludgeon, he struck down the closest man and hurled the fellow's body at the others. As Delka and his remaining aide swung to take new aim, the fleeing crook leaped down the stairway, four steps at a time.

The Scotland Yard men launched wild shots; then took up the pursuit.

The Shadow, springing from his own apartment, made for the front of the hallway. Reaching the door of an unoccupied apartment, he jabbed a master key into the lock. A few twists opened the door. Dashing to a front window, The Shadow opened it and sprang out upon a balcony.

The Harvester had already reached the street. The Shadow caught a glimpse of the Vandyked face as the crook sprang aboard a moving car. Trees intervened as The Shadow aimed. The Harvester had made a getaway.

Still, there was work for The Shadow to per-form. Delka and the man beside him had reached the outer steps. At Delka's call, other Scotland Yard men were rising from secluded spots across the way. Guns began to boom from another passing car. The Shadow caught the glimmer of a machine gun muzzle. So did Delka; and he cried a warning.

Trapped men of the law were diving for hasty cover; they would have been too late but for The Shadow. Gripping a fresh automatic, he opened a swift downward volley, straight for the portion of the car where he knew the machine gunners must be.

Cries came from within the automobile. The turning muzzle stopped. While revolvers spurted wildly, the driver, stampeded, stepped on the accel-erator. The car sped rapidly away.

Pocketing his automatic, The Shadow strode rapidly back to his own apartment. On the way, he saw the slugged Scotland Yard man rising dizzily from the floor. That chap was recovering. The Shadow's present business was with Darryat. Reaching his apartment, he found the bullet-riddled crook gasping, upon the floor.

Glassy eyes looked up from Darryat's tanned face as The Shadow stooped above the victim whom The Harvester had sacrificed. Though dying, Darryat could see the glimmer in The Shadow's gaze. He recognized the countenance of Lamont Cranston; but his ears caught the tone of a strange, awesome voice.

"Speak!" It was a command, delivered in a sin-ister whisper. "State the identity of your chief. Your life meant nothing to his purpose."

Darryat managed a nod.

"The Harvester," he panted. "The—The Harvester. I—I can name him. He—he pretends to be many—but he is only—only one. I know—I know which one he is. His name—his name—"

DARRYAT'S eyes had focused toward the door. There, his blurred stare saw a moving figure, com-ing closer. It was the Scotland Yard man, groggily entering the doorway to the apartment; but to Darryat's disjointed brain, that shape meant only the person whom he had previously seen at that spot—The Harvester.

A choking gasp from Darryat's lips. Still fearful of his murderous chief, the dying lieutenant stayed his utterance. His lips trembled, closing on the name that they were about to utter. Then they unclamped with a final, spasmodic cough.

Darryat's body slumped. That cough had been his last. Dead weight pressed The Shadow's sup-porting arm. Darryat was dead. Chance had worked against The Shadow. Though victorious, he had not gained the one word that he wanted. The identity of The Harvester remained unknown.

Somewhere in London, a supercrook was still at large, prepared to resume a career of baffling crime. The Shadow, to frustrate The Harvester, must still continue with a blind battle. One more difficult than the first; for tonight, The Shadow had drawn The Harvester through Darryat. Under pres-ent circumstances, Darryat was no more.

Yet the whispered echo of repressed mirth that came from The Shadow's lips was one that fore-boded ill for The Harvester. Unheard by the entering Scotland Yard man, The Shadow had delivered a secret challenge; one which would not end until The Harvester had met with deserved doom.

Boldness was The Harvester's forte. Balked, the crook would stage a comeback, on the rebound. Though The Shadow had not identified The Harvester, he knew the rogue's ilk. He had dealt with others of that sort before.

The Shadow was confident that soon the super-foe would strike again. The Shadow would be prepared for that coming thrust by the master of crime.

CHAPTER VI
THE LAW LEARNS FACTS

"IT'S a jolly deep tangle, Mr. Cranston. If you can produce a clue for us, we shall appreciate it."

Eric Delka made the statement. He and The Shadow were holding a morning conference with Chief Constable Lewsham, in the latter's office at Scotland Yard.

The Shadow, still guised as Lamont Cranston, was seated opposite Lewsham, in the very chair which he had occupied when playing the role of Phineas Twambley. Neither Delka nor Lewsham, however, suspected his doub le identity.

"Regarding my mining stock." The Shadow, rising, paced slowly across the office. "I purchased it from this chap Wadkins, whoever he was. The stock is bona fide. Wadkins, therefore, may be honest."

"Unless he was part of the game," objected Lewsham, promptly. "Wadkins may have been in league with The Harvester."

"Which is why we are still looking for him," added Delka. "Unfortunately, we have found no traces of the fellow, despite your description of him."

The Shadow nodded, as though convinced of a new possibility by the arguments of the Scotland Yard men. He paused by the wide window, where heavy side curtains framed a view of the Houses of Parliament, beside the Thames.

"Darryat spoke of Wadkins," mused The Shadow. He had avoided all mention of the supposed solicitor, Dobbingsworth. "I doubt, though, that he could have been the rogue who showed himself at my doorway. The one you call The Harvester."

"I agree on that," asserted Delka. "The Harvester is the specialist who puts the finishing touches on every game. He was willing even to sacrifice his right-hand man, Darryat."

"Alias Bildon, alias Dabley," remarked Lewsham, referring to a record. "Also alias Darryat. Our fingerprint records show him to be Louis Markin, once incarcerated in Dartmoor Prison. We supposed that Markin had left the country."

"Being dead," stated Delka, "the chap afforded us no new clue. Nor do those thugs who were covering the apartment house last night. They are like the cutthroats who attacked me on the up train from Plymouth. Mere ruffians who serve The Harvester."

Big Ben began to boom the hour of nine. As the strokes came from the great clock near the river, Lewsham and Delka both glanced methodically at their watches. That routine performed, the chief constable picked up a copy of a tabloid newspaper that was lying upon his desk.

"We have issued a complete statement," said Lewsham. "With full particulars and a photograph of Markin, with his aliases. The picture was snapped when the body reached the morgue. The one way to offset The Harvester is to give notoriety to his doings. He may have various irons in the fire.

"Any new intelligence may aid us. We came closer to The Harvester when we learned that he had been seen near the Moravia Apartments. That is why we came there to aid you, Mr. Cranston. By the way, Delka"—Lewsham turned to the investigator—"you have not seen Twambley since yesterday?"

"I did not see him yesterday," returned Delka. "He called me by the telephone, sir. Twambley has left the Savoy. According to the word he left there, he intends to tour the continent."

"A good place for him to be," nodded Lewsham. "Since he provided information against The Harvester, it is wise that he should leave England. Yet this is a wretched business! Wretched, indeed, when I am forced to admit that a man is safer out of London! Nevertheless, it is true. Frankly, we are balked, unless—"

THERE was a knock at the door. Interrupted, Lewsham called to enter. A uniformed constable appeared. The man had an urgent message.

"Two persons to see you, sir," he stated. "Sir Ernest Jennup and Mr. Justin Craybaw."

"Show them in at once!"

All eyes were upon the elder of the two men who entered. This was the true Sir Ernest Jennup. His manner—his carriage—most of all, the appearance of his face were proof that The Harvester's impersonation had by no means been a perfect one. The real Sir Ernest, with his well-trimmed Vandyke, was much more distinguished in appearance than the impostor had been.

The man with Sir Ernest was also possessed of dignity. Justin Craybaw was tall, broad-shouldered and robust of appearance. He was a man not over forty; his face, though tight-skinned, was healthy in its ruddiness. He was clean-shaven with short-clipped black hair, his temples tinged an iron-gray.

Sir Ernest was the first to speak. In precise tones, he took up the matter of The Harvester's most recent exploit. Indignantly, he denounced the impostor.

"I had not visited the Moravia Apartments for weeks," declared Sir Ernest. "Hence I can scarcely accuse the doorkeeper of negligence in believing the impostor to be myself. The hallway at the Moravia is a gloomy one.

"But to think that the scoundrel would have the cheek to impersonate me! Bah! It is outrageous! Last night I was traveling southward from Glasgow, a passenger in a first-class sleeping carriage. Imagine my amazement when I arrived at King's Cross at half past seven this very morning!"

Reaching to the desk, Sir Ernest picked up the tabloid newspaper and spread its pages.

"Fancy it!" he exclaimed. "This sensational sheet flaunted before my nose, with hawkers shouting out my name for the entire depot to hear! I, the victim of a hoax of which I knew nothing! Shocking scandal!"

"My apologies, Sir Ernest," interposed Lewsham, soothingly. "It was not to our liking. Our duty, however, is to further the purposes of the law when—"

"With which I quite agree," broke in Sir Ernest, emphatically, "and for that reason I have no quarrel. Instead, I have come here to congratulate you upon your course. I can overlook the temporary embarrassment which was thrust upon me. You have served the law well."

THERE was significance in Sir Ernest's tone. Keen interest gripped the listeners. Smiling pleasantly because of the surprise which he had created, Sir Ernest leaned back in his chair and waved his hand toward Craybaw.

"Proceed with the details, Justin," he suggested. "Unless you wish a further introduction."

"Such would be wise, Sir Ernest," inserted Craybaw.

"Very well." Sir Ernest nodded. "Mr. Craybaw is the managing director of Rudlow, Limited, a financial concern that is connected with my banking houses. This morning, he called me by telephone, directly after I had reached my Lombard Street office. When I heard the information that he has to offer, I suggested that he accompany me here at once."

"Information about The Harvester?" queried Lewsham, turning quickly to Craybaw. "Or about his lieutenant, Markin?"

"Concerning the latter," replied Craybaw, "under his alias of Captain Darryat."

"You had met Darryat?"

Craybaw shook his head.

"No," he replied, "but I had heard of the fellow; and his ways struck me as suspicious. Suppose I give you a brief sketch of the circumstances."

"Proceed."

"Not more than two months ago," recalled Craybaw, "Rudlow, Limited, was approached by a gentleman named Lionel Selbrock, recently returned from Mesopotamia. Selbrock—whose credentials appeared to be of the highest—made claim that he was the holder of oil options valued at a quarter million in pounds sterling.

"It was his desire that Rudlow, Limited, should undertake the disposal of those options, at the price quoted. Selbrock, in turn, insisted that he would be satisfied to receive two hundred thousand pounds as his payment. This offered an excellent profit, fifty thousand pounds to be exact, for Rudlow, Limited.

"The directors conferred upon the matter and resolved to undertake the sale. An agreement was drawn up with Selbrock. The next process was to discover a suitable buyer."

Craybaw paused. He formed another mental calculation; then resumed:

"Less than a fortnight since—twelve days ago, as I recall it—Lionel Selbrock was approached directly by a man who offered to dispose of his options. That man named a potential buyer: namely, the Rajah of Delapore."

"He is here in London," put in Lewsham, with a nod. "Prepared to sell a large number of valuable jewels. One of my men talked with his secretary, to make sure that the wealth was properly protected."

"Exactly," stated Craybaw. "The rajah's purchase of the oil options was to be contingent upon his sale of the jewels, a point which has apparently been already arranged. But what is most important is the identity of the man who called upon Selbrock to arrange the transaction."

"Was it Darryat?"

"It was. He tried to induce Selbrock to visit the Rajah of Delapore and come to immediate terms. Selbrock refused to do so."

"On account of his agreement with Rudlow, Limited?"

"That was the reason. Selbrock came directly to us, as an honest man should have done. His suggestion was that we negotiate with the rajah."

"Eliminating the so-called Captain Darryat?"

"Entirely. Selbrock reasoned that Darryat was entitled to no consideration, because he had attempted to produce an illegal transaction. A point, however, with which I could not agree."

"So you did not contact the rajah?"

"On the contrary, we did." Craybaw's tone was serious. "Our position was a rather unique one. Since we had agreed to sell Selbrock's options, we could hardly refuse to negotiate with a purchaser whom he suggested. Had Darryat come to us, we would naturally have been forced to consider him; but he had dealt only with Selbrock. Darryat's interests, therefore, were entirely beyond our jurisdiction."

"QUITE so," put in Sir Ernest Jennup. "The course was decided upon by the board of directors at Rudlow, Limited. Against the advice of Mr. Craybaw."

"Not precisely," corrected Craybaw. "I advised that Darryat be consulted, since his name had been drawn into the transaction; for that appeared to me to be the clearer course. The board of directors voted that we first open negotiations with the rajah."

"And you did so?" queried Lewsham.

"Yes," replied Craybaw. "I interviewed the rajah in my office, along with Selbrock and the board of directors. He declared that he had not authorized Captain Darryat to act as his representative. He stated that he knew very little about the fellow. Since Selbrock held to the same opinion, we decided to undertake the complete transaction.

"As it now stands, we are awaiting the rajah's disposal of his jewels. When he assures us that such negotiation has been completed, we shall purchase Selbrock's options at the price of two hundred thousand pounds. We shall then dispose of them to the Rajah of Delapore for two hundred and fifty thousand."

Lewsham had risen to his feet.

"Can this transaction be postponed?" he queried. "Without jeopardizing the interests of Rudlow, Limited?"

"My present belief," replied Craybaw, "is that it should by all means be postponed, until Scotland Yard has had time to fully investigate the possible influence of Captain Darryat."

"A decision with which I fully agree," nodded Sir Ernest. "That is why we have come here so promptly. Furthermore, as a principal stockholder in Rudlow, Limited, I believe that the entire transaction should be supervised by the authorities."

"With reports upon Selbrock," added Craybaw, "and also upon the Rajah of Delapore. For that matter, we shall also insist that you examine the status of Rudlow, Limited."

Sidney Lewsham smiled.

"Very well," he agreed. "We shall commence at once. I shall appoint you, Delka, to the task, with as many competent assistants as you may require."

Handshakes were exchanged. Sir Ernest Jennup departed, accompanied by Justin Craybaw. As soon as the visitors were gone, Lewsham turned to Delka and The Shadow.

"THE fine hand of The Harvester has been at work," declared the chief constable. "Here we have a perfectly legitimate transaction, needing only a move to bring seller and purchaser together. Somehow, The Harvester learned of it. He used Darryat to arrange a shortcut, eliminating the natural intermediary: Rudlow, Limited. Fortunately, the game was stopped."

"It was 'spiked,' as they say in the States," chuckled Delka. "That is why Darryat was sent on a lesser game. Maybe The Harvester has given up hope of getting his fists into either the oil options or the jewels."

"Not The Harvester," returned Lewsham, with a shake of his head. "He is somewhere in the offing. We

have a new lead, also. The rogue must be keeping close watch upon developments in Lombard Street."

"He has done so in the past."

"Yes. Moreover, his impersonation of Sir Ernest shows that he has had contacts among bankers. I wonder"—Lewsham paused musingly—"I wonder if either Selbrock or the rajah ever met Sir Ernest."

"I shall make inquiry of both, when I meet them," stated Delka. "You can ask Sir Ernest, chief. Unless you prefer that I—"

"I shall ask him. Meanwhile, Delka, when you call on Selbrock and the Rajah of Delapore, I would suggest that you have Mr. Cranston accompany you. He can listen and ascertain if their description of the pretended Captain Darryat tallies with your own."

Ten minutes later, Eric Delka left New Scotland Yard accompanied by The Shadow. As the two walked toward an underground station, Delka was delivering brief comments regarding their coming quest. The Shadow, however, was silent.

His thin lips, perfectly disguised, wore a slight, fixed smile that sometimes went with the personality of Lamont Cranston. For where Delka simply hoped for news of The Harvester, The Shadow was already positive that he would have a complete trail, before this work was finished.

CHAPTER VII
THE SHADOW DECIDES

FROM Westminster to Aldgate was a ride of a dozen minutes by the Metropolitan and District Lines, the route which Delka and The Shadow took. This was the circle service of the underground; their train traveled on the "inner rail" to make its rapid journey. When they came up the steps at Aldgate, Delka pointed to a distant sign which bore the name: "Addingham Hotel."

"That is where Lionel Selbrock is stopping," informed the Scotland Yard man. "Justin Craybaw left the address with the chief. Come; we shall see if Selbrock is at his diggings."

Aldgate marked the abrupt limit of the old city; with it, the beginning of the East End, where the most squalid quarters of London are located. Almost on the fringe of a dilapidated district, the Addingham Hotel occupied an unenviable site.

It was a hostelry that advertised bed, breakfast and bath for eight shillings the night, reasonable rates which were determined more by location than by furnishings. For the lobby of the Addingham, though old, proved quite pretentious when Delka and The Shadow viewed it.

At the desk, Delka inquired for Lionel Selbrock and was referred to Room 402. Ascending in the lift, the visitors walked along a well-kept hall until they reached the proper door. There Delka knocked. Receiving no response, he turned the knob. The door opened; Delka and The Shadow stepped into an unlocked room.

Selbrock was not about, so Delka eyed the quarters. The room was comfortably furnished and quite tidy. Upon a writing desk Delka noted a portable typewriter, with a pipe and tobacco pouch beside it. Strolling over, Delka studied the machine.

"An American typewriter," he remarked. "Cavalier Portable, No. 4. A very popular machine nowadays. We have several at headquarters. I wonder whereabouts this chap Selbrock can be? He left his door unlocked; he cannot have traveled far—"

DELKA paused as he saw The Shadow turn toward the door. Someone was entering. The visitors saw a tall, rangy man who appeared youngish despite the gray streaks in his hair. The arrival smiled a greeting.

"Cheerio," he said. "I was informed that I had visitors. Are you from Scotland Yard?"

"Are you Lionel Selbrock?" returned Delka, promptly.

"None other," responded the rangy man. "Your name?"

"Eric Delka, acting inspector. This is Mr. Cranston."

"Jove!" exclaimed Selbrock, as he shook hands. "So you two are the pair who dealt with those beggars at St. James Square, last night. I have just been breakfasting and reading the news at the same time. Congratulations."

"It appears that we encountered a friend of yours," remarked Delka, cagily.

"Captain Darryat?" queried Selbrock. "He was no friend of mine. I suspected that bounder of double dealing. I am not surprised to learn that he was a rogue. I suppose that you have come to question me regarding Darryat?"

"I have," expressed Delka. "We heard of you through Justin Craybaw. He told us of your financial arrangements with Rudlow, Limited. I should like to ask you a few questions, Mr. Selbrock. Perhaps they may strike you as abrupt; nevertheless, I shall appreciate prompt answers."

"Righto," agreed Selbrock.

"First"—Delka looked about him—"just why have you chosen this hotel for your residence?"

"Because of its moderate rates."

"Rather modest quarters for a man worth a quarter million—"

"Not yet, inspector." Selbrock paused to laugh. "My present circumstances are somewhat straitened. I have not yet disposed of my options, old fellow. I am living on hopes."

"I see. But just why do you keep your room unlocked? Have you no fear of thieves?"

"None at all. My valuable documents are already with Rudlow, Limited. They require my signature to complete the transfer of the options. He who robs me gains nothing but a secondhand typewriter and a worn-out tobacco pipe."

Delka nodded. Then he proceeded with a question of a different sort:

"Are you acquainted with Sir Ernest Jennup?"

Selbrock paused; then slowly shook his head.

"That is a poser," he admitted. "I am acquainted with Sir Ernest, yes; because I know him well by sight. I saw him once at his bank; twice at the offices of Rudlow, Limited. But I have never spoken with him."

"Not even when you made arrangements with the directors of Rudlow, Limited?"

"Not even then. Sir Ernest was not present on those occasions. Justin Craybaw serves as managing director. He was in charge of the conferences."

"Very well. Next, what can you tell me concerning the man who called himself Captain Darryat?"

"Only that he learned somehow of my options. He came here and asked me to open negotiations with a friend of his, the Rajah of Delapore."

"And what was your answer?"

"That I could deal only through Rudlow, Limited."

"What was Darryat's response?"

"He was angry when he left. He told me to handle my transactions for myself. He dared me to open negotiations, through Rudlow, with the rajah. He claimed such friendship with the rajah that my cause would prove useless."

"So you took up the challenge?"

"I did. I asked Rudlow, Limited, to communicate with the Rajah of Delapore. His excellency did not rebuff us. On the contrary, he acted quite in opposite to Darryat's prediction."

"You saw Darryat after that?"

"Never. I suppose that the chap had become quite disgruntled. It was cheek that made him hurl his defy. I met the rascal's bluff. Yet I feel sorry for the beggar, now that he is dead."

Selbrock's face had saddened. Delka changed the subject. He felt no regrets for Darryat.

"About these oil interests," remarked the Scotland Yard man. "You have credentials, I suppose?"

"They are with Rudlow, Limited."

"Have I your permission to examine them?"

"Absolutely! You might also interview the Turkish ambassador, to authenticate the seals and signatures. All are quite in order, I assure you."

DELKA appeared satisfied with the interview. He nodded to The Shadow and the two took their leave. Selbrock insisted upon going with them to the lobby. The last that they saw of the man was when he waved a cheery farewell as they stepped to the street.

"A confident chap" was Delka's comment.

"Nevertheless, I shall make close scrutiny of those documents that he brought from Istanbul. Suppose we walk over to Liverpool Street and take the Central London. It will carry us to Mayfair; the trains call at Marble Arch, which is a convenient station."

Mayfair, due west from Aldgate, constitutes the smartest section of London's celebrated West End. Arrived at Marble Arch, the entrance to Hyde Park, Delka and The Shadow traced their way southward along Park Lane, then turned toward Grosvenor Square. They arrived at a palatial, marble-fronted building which proved to be an apartment hotel. Delka glanced at his watch.

"Even with the short wait at Liverpool Street," he chuckled, "and the thirteen minutes' trip to Marble Arch, the journey has taken us scarcely more than a half hour. Unless the Rajah of Delapore is an early riser, we shall certainly find him at his residence."

The Rajah of Delapore was at home. Delka and The Shadow were ushered to his sumptuous second-floor apartment, to enter a living room which was thick with the atmosphere of the Orient. Carved chairs, ornate tapestries, the perfume from silver incense burners—all formed a part of this transplanted room which seemed to have been brought intact from a native province in India.

A tall, sallow-faced man received the visitors. Long-nosed, with sleek, black hair, this fellow possessed a pair of quick beady eyes that had the peculiar faculty of enlarging themselves. The man was smooth-shaven; and the color of his skin seemed almost artificial.

"My name is Ranworthy," said the man by way of self-introduction. "Jed Ranworthy, secretary to His Excellency, the Rajah of Delapore. His excellency has instructed me to discuss matters with you until he can join us in conference. Pray be seated, gentlemen."

Delka decided to quiz the secretary, for a starter.

"Being from Scotland Yard," stated Delka, "I am here to find out all that can be learned concerning Captain Richard Darryat. What can you tell us about him, Mr. Ranworthy?"

"Captain Darryat?" Ranworthy smiled sourly. "I knew the chap for a rogue the moment he introduced himself here. I did not state that opinion to the rajah. I wanted his excellency to form the conclusion for himself."

"I see. How did Darryat happen to come here?"

Ranworthy shrugged his shoulders before replying.

"Like anyone else," he declared, "the man could have learned that a Hindu potentate was residing in Mayfair. There was no deep secret surrounding the presence of the Rajah of Delapore in London."

A turbaned Hindu servant entered the living room while Ranworthy was speaking. Delka watched the fellow stalk quietly across the room and leave by another door. The Shadow, meanwhile, eyed Ranworthy. The secretary paid no attention to the servant's brief visit.

"HIS excellency has been here for nearly two months," continued Ranworthy. "Captain Darryat first appeared during the past fortnight—no, perhaps it was earlier than two weeks ago. Darryat told us about Lionel Selbrock and the Mesopotamian oil holdings."

"Did he suggest terms for their acquisition?"

"No. On the contrary, he acted as a disinterested party. He claimed that he merely wished to be of service to the rajah. Darryat tried to make us believe that he had once served as an officer in the Bengal Lancers. That was when the rajah began to doubt him."

"I see. And after that?"

"We heard from Rudlow, Limited. His excellency went to their offices. He arranged to purchase the monopolies."

"And did Darryat come here again?"

"Yes. The rajah chided him for misrepresenting facts. He told Darryat to render a bill for services."

"Did Darryat do so?"

"No. On the contrary, he acted nastily and departed in a huff. We could not understand his actions, unless—"

"Unless what?"

Delka's question came sharply when Ranworthy paused. The secretary resumed his statement abruptly.

"Unless Captain Darryat was after bigger game and chose therefore to sulk, once his moves were countered. That was the opinion which I shared with his excellency, the rajah."

Ranworthy's tone had become a convincing purr, a smooth manner of talking that matched the persuasive language of the late Captain Darryat. The Shadow alone noted this fact. Delka had never talked personally with the swindler who had died the night before. Ranworthy's tone was paradoxical; it showed that the secretary himself might be a smooth worker, contrarily it lacked his statement that he had been keen enough to see through Darryat.

"By the way," questioned Delka. "Did you ever meet up with Sir Ernest Jennup?"

"The man who was impersonated last night?" queried Ranworthy. "Yes. I met him several times at his banking house on Lombard Street. In connection with money matters that concerned the rajah."

"Was his excellency with you on those occasions?"

"Twice, I believe. Yes, twice. That is correct."

BEFORE Delka could put another question, curtains parted at the end of the long living room and a tall, imposing man stepped into view. It was the Rajah of Delapore, in person. The Hindu nabob was garbed in native costume.

The rajah's attire was a masterpiece of barbaric tailoring. His waist was encircled with a jeweled sash, from which hung a short sword, in golden scabbard. His coat was bedecked with semiprecious stones, garnets and turquoises, with an occasional topaz. His turban, too, was fronted with gems, a large ruby forming the exact center of a cluster.

The rajah's face was a true Caucasian type, with perfectly formed features. The dusky hue of his skin actually added to his handsome appearance; for it formed a relief to the glitter of his attire. The hand that the rajah thrust forward was long and shapely; but the grip that he gave to the visitors was firm.

"Welcome, friends." The Rajah of Delapore spoke in a musical tone. "I have chanced to overhear your conversation; therefore I understand your purpose here. I have read about last night's episode. My congratulations to you, Inspector Delka; and to you, Mr. Cranston."

Delka and The Shadow bowed. The rajah turned to Ranworthy.

"You may leave," he told the secretary. "Inform Barkhir that I wish to speak with him."

Ranworthy bowed and departed. The rajah looked toward Delka with a quizzical gaze, as if inviting questions. The Scotland Yard man had one.

"This secretary of yours," he asked, in an undertone. "How long has he been in your employ, your excellency?"

"Ranworthy joined me in Calcutta," returned the rajah musingly. "I needed a secretary who knew London. Ranworthy had good references. I employed him."

"You came directly to London?"

"No. We stopped for a while in Paris."

"And since your arrival here, have you been busy?"

"Indeed not. Neither myself nor Ranworthy. I require his services only in the mornings. At other times, he is entirely free."

A sudden light showed upon Delka's features. The rajah did not appear to notice it; but The Shadow did. A moment later, a tall, native-garbed Hindu entered the living room. He was not the servant who had gone through previously. This was Barkhir, whom Ranworthy had been told to summon.

The rajah gave an order in Hindustani. Barkhir departed, to return with a trayload of refreshments. The rajah invited his guests to join in the repast. While they ate with him, he made final remarks.

"Ranworthy has told you all that we know about Darryat," he stated. "My opinion is simply that the scoundrel was after my many gems. I have brought them to London, for sale."

"And you keep them here," added Delka. "Such, at least, is the understanding at the Yard."

"The jewels are in this room," smiled the rajah. "Yet they are quite safe. Only I know their hiding place."

"Not Ranworthy?"

"Not even Ranworthy. I would defy him to discover them. That is why I had no fear of Darryat, even after I believed that the man was a rogue. My secrets are my own."

"But Ranworthy is close to you. He might learn facts, your excellency."

The rajah's eyes blazed suddenly; then softened.

"Ranworthy," he stated quietly, "is honest. Such, at least, is my opinion. When I form such conclusions, I am never wrong."

"I meant no offense," apologized Delka. "It is simply my business to check up on every detail."

"I understand," nodded the rajah. "Well, inspector, I can assure you that the jewels will soon be sold. No danger will remain here. I shall return to India with the oil options in their place."

THE interview ended. Ranworthy appeared; the rajah retired and the secretary ushered the visitors from the apartment. When they reached the street, Delka was in a musing mood.

"There is much to be learned," he told The Shadow. "Somewhere amid this mess is a link with Captain Darryat. Do you agree with me, Mr. Cranston?"

"I do," assured The Shadow, quietly. His gaze was upward, toward the rajah's apartment. "Yes, I agree."

As The Shadow spoke, he caught a quick glimpse of a face that drew back from the curtained window of the living room. A brief flash only, but sufficient to identify its owner. The watching man was Ranworthy, whom The Shadow and Delka had left alone in the living room.

"We are near your diggings," remarked Delka, as they turned southward on Berkley Street. "There is Piccadilly, just ahead of us. St. James Square is on the other side."

"I shall drop off there," decided The Shadow. "When shall I see you again, inspector?"

"Tomorrow morning," declared Delka. "No—tomorrow afternoon would be better. At the offices of Rudlow, Limited. By that time, I shall have checked upon all details."

They parted. The Shadow went directly to his own apartment. There he made a telephone call. It was Harry Vincent who responded. The Shadow gave instructions.

One hour later, Harry Vincent checked in at the Addingham Hotel in Aldgate. He obtained a room almost across the hall from the one occupied by Lionel Selbrock. The man from Mesopotamia, though unwatched by Scotland Yard, was to be covered by The Shadow.

Later that same day, an old-fashioned taxicab rolled past the marble-fronted hotel in Mayfair, where the Rajah of Delapore resided. Keen eyes stared from the interior. The cab stopped further on; a keen-eyed personage with a cane alighted and strolled back along the street.

He remained in that vicinity for a while. Later, another individual took his place, this one a hunched man with a cane. After that person had departed, a third took up the vigil. All were one and the same: The Shadow; yet in none would the rajah or Ranworthy have recognized Lamont Cranston.

Scotland Yard had ignored the rajah also; and his secretary, as well. But not The Shadow. He was keeping vigil here until the morrow, when he met again with Delka. There were threads in this skein that needed untangling. The Shadow intended to accomplish such work.

While Eric Delka still suspected a coming move from The Harvester, The Shadow was sure that such a stroke would arrive. His was the task to learn, that he might be prepared.

CHAPTER VIII
DOWN FROM LONDON

IT was three o'clock the next afternoon. Harry Vincent was seated in his room at the Addingham Hotel, hunched in front of a gas-log fire. It was a raw day in London; creeping haze was token that a fog might set in after nightfall.

The transom above Harry's door was open; he was listening for any sounds from across the hall. Yesterday, Harry had entered Selbrock's room while the man was out. Today, Selbrock had not gone out. At intervals, however, Harry had heard brief clicks from the portable typewriter. That was a sound which pleased Harry.

For yesterday, Harry had performed a definite job. He had removed the roller from Selbrock's typewriter. In its place he had inserted a duplicate, of the exact appearance. A roller suitable for a Cavalier No. 4, yet one which had already begun to perform a required function. That substituted roller was a device of The Shadow's recent invention.

Footsteps in the hallway. A knock. Moving to the door, Harry edged it open. He saw a round-hatted messenger tapping at the door of Selbrock's room. Harry watched; the door opened. Selbrock, in shirtsleeves, made his appearance. He was puffing at his briar pipe.

Selbrock received the message, tipped the messenger, and ripped open the envelope. He did not move in from the doorway, hence Harry was able to watch the expression that appeared upon the man's genial face.

Selbrock appeared to be delighted. He waved the message in his hand, then pounced back into the room. Harry saw him open a suitcase and bring out a thick, squatty book with paper covers. It was a Bradshaw, the British railway guide.

Still holding his message, Selbrock consulted the timetables. He tossed the Bradshaw into the suitcase, donned his coat and vest, then thrust his message into his coat pocket. Harry saw him move out of sight beyond the opened door.

Then came rapid *clicks* of the typewriter. Soon Selbrock reappeared, sealing a message in an envelope. He threw a few clothes into the suitcase and hurried from the room. His face still registered an expression of hearty pleasure.

SOON after Selbrock had gone, Harry produced the typewriter roller. Crossing the hall, he opened the unlocked door and went to Selbrock's machine. He removed the duplicate roller and inserted the one that belonged to the typewriter. Returning to his own room, Harry tugged at the end of the duplicate cylinder and pulled it loose.

From within, he brought out a most ingenious device. It was a spiral coil of paper, wound about a central core, that was loosely weighted so that one portion would always keep to the bottom. The roller, itself, was the thinnest sort of metal shell; but at front and back were strips of thicker metal, attached by end projections to the weighted core. Hence these strips always held their position, despite the coiling of the paper within.

The metal strip at the front showed a slight space between itself and a taut line of carbon ribbon. The paper coiled between the ribbon and the strip of metal. Hence, in typing, Selbrock had always had his keys encounter a solid-backed portion of the roller.

Most ingenious was the fact that the paper coil started *beneath* the stretch of carbon; but in uncoiling, it ran *above* it; that is, between the carbon and the shell of the roller. Hence, once a portion of the paper had received impressions from the keys, that part of the coil no longer came under the carbon. New paper replaced it as long as the coil unwound.

Succeeding impressions naturally had to be driven through the increasing thickness of the coils; but that fact was offset by the remarkable thinness of the paper.

Hence Harry, as he unrolled the coil, discovered a complete record of everything that Selbrock had typed since yesterday. All of the man's notes had been brief; most of them were merely to tradesmen, ordering them to hold certain goods until Selbrock had funds available. The final note, however, was more illuminating.

It was addressed to Rudlow, Limited, and stated

merely that Selbrock had received a telegram from an old friend who was in England; that he was leaving London but would be back the next day. The few sentences, however, gave no clue to Selbrock's destination.

Harry brought out his own Bradshaw and began to thumb the pages. Twenty minutes of futile effort soon convinced him that his task was hopeless. There was no way of guessing which of the many London railway depots Selbrock had chosen. Harry's only hope was to reconnoiter.

Leaving his room, he went downstairs. Near the door of the lobby, he encountered one of the Addingham's page boys.

"I am looking for a friend of mine," informed Harry. "A gentleman named Selbrock, who is stopping here. Could you find out where he has gone?" The boy volunteered to gain the information. He returned shortly to state that Selbrock had taken a motorcab, otherwise a taxi. The boy added that he had driven to Euston Station, the terminus of the London, Midland and Scottish Railway. Not an economical course, according to the boy, for his opinion was that Selbrock could have saved cab tariff and traveled much more satisfactorily by the inner rail of the Metropolitan and District Lines.

THAT was a tip to Harry. With the Bradshaw bulging from his pocket, he hurried out of the hotel and headed for the Aldgate Station of the underground. Picturing the circle service of the tube, Harry forgot himself. He fancied the trains running on the right-hand tracks, as in America; for his brief sojourn in London had not sufficed to accustom him to the British system of trains on the left.

Thus Harry took the wrong side of the underground. Boarding a train, he settled back in the comfortable seat and chuckled at the elegance of this line when compared with New York subways. He referred to Bradshaw. Concentrating upon the trains of the L. M. & E., he found that there was a four o'clock Restaurant Car Express, London to Liverpool, with through carriages to Carlisle. Calculating the time from Aldgate to Euston Station, Harry believed that he would make it. Then, glancing from the window of the underground train, he recognized a station and realized his mistake.

He had taken the long route from Aldgate and was already well along the circle! Thirty-five minutes from Aldgate to Euston, by the outer rail, which Harry had taken, instead of a mere dozen which the inner rail required. A glance at his watch told Harry that he would be too late to overtake Selbrock. That quest was finished.

MEANWHILE, The Shadow had encountered an odd situation in Mayfair. He had seen Jed Ranworthy appear suddenly from the apartment hotel, spring aboard a waiting cab and ride away. The Shadow, disguised as a chance stroller, had no opportunity to follow.

The Shadow strolled away. When he returned, it was in the guise of Cranston. He entered the apartment hotel and sent his card to the Rajah of Delapore. Barkhir, the Hindu, admitted him.

A few moments later, the rajah appeared. He seemed cordial, yet puzzled by the visit. In the quiet tone of Cranston, The Shadow explained.

"I expected to find Inspector Delka," he stated. "He said that he might be here this afternoon."

"You will probably find him at Rudlow's," returned the rajah. "I communicated with them, today, making final arrangements for my business. Delka was expected some time in the afternoon."

"I shall proceed there. Very sorry, your excellency, to have disturbed you. I expected to make inquiry from your secretary."

"Ranworthy is not here. He has gone out of London for the night. To Yarmouth, I believe."

"Yarmouth? At this season?"

"It was not a pleasure trip," smiled the rajah. "Word from some relative who is ill there."

After leaving the rajah's, The Shadow returned to his own abode near St. James Square. He consulted a Bradshaw and found that a through train left Liverpool Street Station for Yarmouth, shortly before five o'clock, via the London and Northeastern Railway.

That was the one which Ranworthy would probably take to reach his destination, on the east coast, at eight in the evening. But it did not explain his hasty departure, unless he had intended to do some shopping before train time.

There was not sufficient time to go to Liverpool Street, particularly because The Shadow had a telephone call to make in response to a message that awaited him. His call was to Harry Vincent.

From the agent, he learned of Lionel Selbrock's departure, and of Harry's theories on the same. That call concluded, The Shadow strolled from his quarters, hailed a taxi and ordered the driver to take him to Threadneedle Street, where Rudlow, Limited, was located.

On the way, The Shadow considered the coincidental circumstances that had taken Lionel Selbrock and Jed Ranworthy from London. Each had received an urgent message; one from a friend, the other from a relative.

Selbrock had presumably departed for the northwest; Ranworthy for the northeast. But The Shadow had only Harry's guess concerning Selbrock; and the rajah's statement regarding Ranworthy. It was possible that Selbrock could have bluffed persons at the hotel; that Ranworthy could have deceived the rajah.

What was the connection between these occurrences? The thought brought a thin smile to The Shadow's disguised lips. He was piecing the circumstances that had suddenly caused both himself and Harry Vincent to lose trace of persons whom they had been watching. The best way to find an answer was to study circumstances elsewhere. That was exactly what The Shadow intended to accomplish.

The ancient taxi was passing the Bank of England. The Shadow eyed the structure that housed England's wealth, and the view made him think of The Harvester. Wealth was the super-crook's stake. There might be opportunity for the hidden criminal to gain it, while the transactions of Rudlow, Limited, were in the making.

The taxi rolled along Threadneedle Street, to the north of the Lombard Street banking district. It came to a stop. The Shadow alighted and sought the offices of Rudlow, Limited. He was just in time to enter before the closing hour of five.

ANNOUNCING himself as Lamont Cranston, The Shadow was ushered into a quietly furnished room, where he found three men. One was Justin Craybaw, the managing director; the second, Sir Ernest Jennup. The third was a person whom The Shadow had not expected to find here: Sidney Lewsham, the chief constable of the C.I.D.

It was Craybaw who gave greeting.

"Good afternoon, Mr. Cranston!" exclaimed the managing director. "Your arrival is most timely. We are about to set out for my country residence, near Tunbridge Wells. Can you accompany us?"

"You are going by train?" queried The Shadow.

"By motor," replied Craybaw. "We shall travel in Sir Ernest's phaeton. I should like to have you dine with us."

"Agreed," decided The Shadow. "With one proviso, however. I must be back in London quite early in the evening."

"You may return by train," said Craybaw. "I shall have my chauffeur, Cuthbert, carry you to the station in the coupé. The others will be staying late, since they expect Inspector Delka on the train which arrives at nine o'clock."

"Very well."

The group left Craybaw's office. They went to the street and walked to a garage where Sir Ernest's automobile was stationed. Sir Ernest took the wheel, with Craybaw beside him. The Shadow and Lewsham occupied the rear seat of the trim car.

"A quiet motor, this," remarked Lewsham, leaning half from the car and eyeing the long hood. "Not a sound from underneath the bonnet, despite the high power of the vehicle."

They were crossing a bridge that spanned the Thames. There, thick mist was spreading through the darkening gloom. Every indication marked the approach of a heavy fog. Lewsham looked upward, toward the smokiness that clustered the sky.

"We are in for a pea-souper," prophesied the chief constable. "Fog so thick that one could cleave it with a knife!"

"I noticed those signs this morning," put in Craybaw, from the front seat. "Even when I was coming up to town, riding past Waterloo into Charing Cross Station. You are correct, sir. The fog will prove dense tonight."

Sir Ernest was silent at the wheel, piloting the long car southward toward the open road which led to Tunbridge Wells, some thirty-five miles from London. The Shadow, too, was silent. He was pondering upon a subject of deep concern.

Fog over London. A blanket of haze not unlike the smoke screen which The Harvester had created in regard to crime. Yet, with the coming of one fog, the other seemed to be clearing. Curious events were piecing themselves within The Shadow's keen mind.

Unless previous circumstances were matters of pure chance, the answer to certain riddles would be forthcoming before this night was ended. To The Shadow, past events would control the future. Crime was clearing because the time was near when it would strike. By then, The Shadow hoped to hold the final key.

CHAPTER IX
SOUTH OF LONDON

JUSTIN CRAYBAW'S home was a pretentious country residence, situated close to Tunbridge Wells. Past the suburban belt, it was almost a spot of rural England. The house, though large and modern, had all the isolation of a rustic abode, for it was surrounded by spacious grounds, with high hedges along the traveled roadway.

Long driveway formed entry to the grounds; and on the far side of the house was a conservatory that overlooked a secluded, rolling lawn. It was in this room where the four assembled after dinner, to smoke their cigars and to discuss the matter that was their chief concern.

"Chief Lewsham," began Sir Ernest, "we are exceedingly alarmed by the activities of this rogue you term The Harvester. I, for one, was more than annoyed to learn that he impersonated myself. To me, that fact stands as a warning that we may expect to hear from him again."

"His tool, Captain Darryat, was close to the Rajah of Delapore," added Craybaw, seriously. "For that matter, The Harvester contacted with Lionel Selbrock also. Those facts show us that The Harvester may be planning a new and more potent game."

Lewsham nodded slowly.

"I believe that you are right," he decided. "The Harvester has not reaped sufficient spoils. A rogue of his ilk will never cease until he has gained a final triumph. He is as dangerous as ever."

"Not quite," put in The Shadow, in the easy tone of Cranston. "He is handicapped by his sacrifice of a chief lieutenant, Captain Darryat."

"But he may have others," objected Lewsham. "Someone could work in place of Darryat."

"Hardly so," stated The Shadow. "If The Harvester had possessed another competent lieutenant, he would not have played Darryat as his regular trump card."

The statement impressed Lewsham. It was logical and it came as a ray of hope. The Shadow, however, was prompt to squelch the chief constable's glee.

"The Harvester has become a lone hand," emphasized The Shadow. "He possesses underlings, certainly; but none above the class of thugs. Without Darryat, The Harvester is less dangerous. But he may prove to be more slippery."

"Because Darryat's death has destroyed our only link!" exclaimed Lewsham. "You are right, Mr. Cranston! We shall have no clue to The Harvester until he himself reveals his final part."

"Which he will do," predicted The Shadow, "after he gains the spoils that he is seeking. Yet even after he has struck, he will prove slippery."

SIR ERNEST was tugging at his Vandyke beard, puzzled by words which The Shadow had uttered.

"You speak of spoils," remarked Sir Ernest. "Just what spoils do you mean? Selbrock's options or the rajah's jewels?"

"Either," replied The Shadow, "or both. Perhaps he has designs on other wealth. Suppose you tell me, Sir Ernest, just what precautions have been taken to keep The Harvester from meddling with this coming transaction?"

"Mr. Craybaw can answer that question," returned Sir Ernest. "While I and others are the ones who have financed Rudlow, Limited, we have placed full control in the hands of our managing director."

"A responsibility which I have accepted," smiled Craybaw, "and which I recognized." Then, solemnly, he added: "And my position, moreover, is a matter which must be fully discussed tonight. That is why I wanted you here, Chief Lewsham."

Lewsham nodded. He, too, was serious.

"Let me summarize the situation," continued Craybaw. "Today I talked by telephone with Selbrock. I told him that we were ready to take over his options. Because I had already heard from the Rajah of Delapore. His gems will be sold tomorrow."

Sir Ernest nodded to indicate that he had already heard this news from Craybaw.

"Our agreement with Selbrock," resumed Craybaw, "is a most peculiar one. Many of its provisions are awkward, yet all are clear. Selbrock

appears to be a poor hand at business; hence we thought it best to comply with any oddities that he requested.

"The agreement, for instance, calls for payment in specie. To clarify that condition, I have arranged to pay with Bank of England notes to the sum total of two hundred thousand pounds. That money should be in the office of Rudlow, Limited, by noon tomorrow."

"It will be," assured Sir Ernest, with an emphatic gesture. "It will come by armored vehicle, with guards in attendance. To be placed in the vault which adjoins your office, Craybaw. You will be protected every minute while the money is there."

"A wise procedure," nodded Craybaw. "Wise, for a second reason, also. Since Selbrock was to be paid in specie, the agreement which I drew up with the Rajah of Delapore called for him to pay in similar wise. He is to produce a quarter million of currency."

"Then we must protect him, also?"

"No. The rajah has insisted that he can take measures of his own. It is not our affair, Sir Ernest. If the rajah should ask for protection, it would be our duty to provide it. As the situation stands, we cannot interfere."

A pause; then Lewsham asked:

"Do I understand, Mr. Craybaw, that you also request protection on the part of Scotland Yard?"

"Absolutely," replied Craybaw. "The presence of your competent men will be most welcome. The armored cars will be needed afterward, to carry back to bank the money that we received from the rajah."

"WOULD it be possible," queried The Shadow, "to pay Selbrock with money that the rajah provides?"

"The directors considered that plan," stated Craybaw. "It appeared to be a good one, because it would have obviated the need of bringing our own funds from bank. Unfortunately, the agreements had already been drawn up and signed. Therefore, we could scarcely change our method.

"As intermediaries in this transaction, Rudlow, Limited, must first purchase Selbrock's options in order to make the sale to the Rajah of Delapore. Therefore, to avoid technical dispute, we must show the sum of two hundred thousand pounds. Which means that if the rajah appears at the same time as Selbrock, there will actually be the two sums in our office. A grand total of four hundred and fifty thousand pounds."

"Which The Harvester would like to get," gritted Lewsham. "That is when the danger will arise. Tomorrow, when the deal is made. By the way, who knows about this arrangement, other than the directors of Rudlow, Limited?"

"Selbrock knows," replied Craybaw. "So does

the rajah. And, of course, the latter's secretary, Ranworthy."

"What was it you mentioned about Selbrock this afternoon?" queried Lewsham, as if recalling something that he had heard. "Was he going out of town?"

"For the evening, yes," replied Craybaw. "He will return tomorrow. He sent a brief message from his hotel. He intended to visit some old friend."

"Odd of him to leave London at so vital a time."

"Hardly so. He knows that the transaction will not take place early in the day. The options merely await his signature."

"And what about the rajah?"

"Either he or his secretary can sign any necessary papers. After the rajah has paid the money, the options will be his."

A pause; then The Shadow quietly remarked:

"Ranworthy has gone to Yarmouth."

"To Yarmouth?" echoed Craybaw. "Why there, at this season?"

"To visit a relative who is ill there."

"I see. Then he may not be back tomorrow."

"Possibly not."

The sound of the starting of an automobile motor came from in front of the house. Craybaw glanced at his watch.

"It is Cuthbert, starting for the station," he stated. "To bring back Inspector Delka. The train is due there shortly. It is twenty minutes before nine. I told Delka to leave the train at High Brooms, which is quite as near as Tunbridge Wells. I always have Cuthbert meet the trains at High Brooms."

CONVERSATION was resumed. A clock was chiming the hour of nine when a servant appeared at the door from the house. It was Craybaw's house man, Hervey.

"Nine o'clock, sir," informed Hervey.

"Well?" queried Craybaw.

"You told me to speak to you at nine," replied Hervey. "You did not state the reason why."

"Forgetful of me!" exclaimed Craybaw. "I recall now that I intended to run over to Hayward's Heath in the coupé. To deliver a parcel which I brought from the city. I chanced to remember that it will be my nephew's birthday, tomorrow. After all, the matter is unimportant, unless—"

Craybaw glanced at his watch.

"I have it," he decided. "Your train, Mr. Cranston, leaves High Brooms at half past nine. We shall take the coupé as soon as Cuthbert arrives with Delka. Then I can run to Hayward's Heath and back, after leaving you at the station."

Rising, Craybaw motioned toward the door to the house.

"We must be ready with our hats and coats," he reminded. "Time will be short after Cuthbert returns. We shall join you later, gentlemen."

Craybaw and The Shadow walked through a living room and entered a small study which was equipped with desk, bookcases, and a small safe. Hervey brought the hats and coats, while Craybaw was consulting a road map.

"Not far to Hayward's Heath," he declared, pointing out the road to The Shadow. "To High Brooms; then back again. Hm-m-m. I can have Cuthbert take you to the station, then return and bring the car to me. It would be best for me to remain with the other guests."

Hervey had gone out. He came in to bring word that Cuthbert had arrived with Delka. Craybaw urged The Shadow to hasten; they reached the front door to find Delka alighting with Lewsham and Sir Ernest there to greet him.

Craybaw explained the new arrangement. The Shadow entered the car with Cuthbert and they headed for High Brooms.

IN the dimness of the coupé, The Shadow observed Cuthbert's face. The chauffeur was a methodical, honest-visaged fellow, who stared steadily along the road. They reached High Brooms with minutes to spare, thanks to Cuthbert's capable and speedy handling of the car.

The Shadow alighted. Cuthbert backed the coupé. While he was doing so, The Shadow, pausing in a spot away from the station lights, was quick to open a light briefcase that he had brought along with him from the hotel.

Black cloth came from the case. A cloak slipped over The Shadow's shoulders. A slouch hat settled on his head. His hands stuffed his own light overcoat partly into the briefcase, along with the hat that he had been wearing. With a toss, The Shadow skimmed the burden along the soft ground beneath a clump of hedgelike bushes.

Cuthbert was sliding into low gear, about to drive away from the station. A being in black, his figure obscured by darkness, The Shadow sprang across the gravel unheard by Cuthbert because of the grinding gears. With a quick leap, The Shadow gained the rear of the coupé.

Clinging there, he pressed flat against the cover of the rumble seat, riding unseen on the return journey, through hedge-flanked lanes where traffic was absent. The Shadow was making a prompt return to the home of Justin Craybaw.

Despite the fact that he had claimed an appointment in London, The Shadow had found a reason to remain a while in the vicinity of Tunbridge Wells!

CHAPTER X
PATHS IN THE DARK

WHEN the coupé arrived back at Craybaw's, The Shadow dropped off as Cuthbert took the final curve. A black shape in the darkness, he paused beside a mass of shrubbery to observe proceedings at the lighted housefront. Craybaw had come out, wearing hat and coat, accompanied by the others.

"I shall not be long," assured Craybaw. He was carrying the parcel under his arm. "Make yourselves quite at home, gentlemen. Keep the wheel, Cuthbert. You can drive more rapidly than I. We must make a swift journey."

The coupé pulled away. Sir Ernest went back into the house, accompanied by Lewsham and Delka. The Shadow saw Craybaw give a final wave from within the car. Half a minute later, the light went out in front of the house. Hervey had evidently extinguished it.

Across the driveway, Sir Ernest's phaeton was standing in an isolated spot. The Shadow glided in that direction and slid aboard the trim car. Sir Ernest had not locked it; hence The Shadow saved considerable delay. Nevertheless, he took time to glide down a short slope, not putting the car into gear until he had coasted almost to the driveway entrance.

The Shadow knew Cuthbert for a rapid driver, and the chauffeur had gained a few minutes' start. Nevertheless, his speed could not have matched the rate at which The Shadow traveled, once he gained the road to Hayward's Heath. The Shadow was determined to close the distance between himself and the car ahead.

The smooth motor was noiseless, even at high speed. The phaeton clipped the mileage, for road crossings were few and well apart. Nevertheless, the start that Cuthbert had gained proved a long one. Guided by his memory of the road map, The Shadow arrived at Hayward's Heath without overtaking the coupé.

Wheeling about, The Shadow began to retrace his course. He was working upon a definite conjecture; one that caused him to increase speed after he had ridden a short way. Rounding a curve in the return road, The Shadow gained the answer that he sought.

Right ahead was the coupé, coming back from Hayward's Heath! Yet The Shadow had taken the one road that Craybaw would have chosen and he had not passed the light car on the way. The conclusion was obvious. The coupé had not continued to Hayward's Heath. Somewhere along the road, it had swung off upon one of many side lanes, while on its original journey. That had occurred early in the pursuit.

After a brief pause at some unknown spot, the coupé had begun its return, only to have The Shadow catch its trail.

That much accomplished, The Shadow slackened speed. He let the coupé reach Craybaw's well ahead of him. When The Shadow piloted the phaeton softly into the driveway, he saw the coupé standing by the entrance. Craybaw was going up the house steps with Hervey, who had put on the lights. A moment later, both were inside. The lights went out.

EASING the phaeton past the coupé, The Shadow parked it in the secluded corner of the driveway, confident that no one had detected its absence. Afoot, he circled the house and came to a door that led into the conservatory. The lights were out; apparently all had gone inside to escape the increasing chill.

Softly entering the conservatory, The Shadow found the house door ajar. From the darkness, he peered into the illuminated living room, where Hervey had lighted a fire in a huge grate. Craybaw was standing there, rubbing his hands for warmth.

A definite change had come over the managing director of Rudlow, Limited—one that The Shadow detected promptly, for he could see Craybaw's face against the firelight. His stubbly hair was somewhat tousled; his skin lacked a trifle of its ruddiness. His eyes, moreover, showed an unnatural sparkle against the glow from the fireplace.

Craybaw was a man who appeared slightly shrunken. His manner was nervous and restless; his eyes were quick as they darted sharp looks at the other persons with him. The Shadow caught one puzzled look upon the face of Sir Ernest Jennup. Then Sidney Lewsham registered doubt. Craybaw curbed his restlessness.

"Come, Delka!" he exclaimed, his voice carrying a natural tone. "How is it in London? Any news concerning The Harvester?"

"None," returned Delka, gruffly. "All I can report is a satisfactory check on Selbrock and the Rajah of Delapore."

"And Ranworthy?"

"All right, so far as the India Office knows. I inquired there. They know a few facts about him. All tally."

Sir Ernest and Sidney Lewsham eased back in their chairs. Craybaw's return to natural form had allayed their alarm. Then came an unexpected episode. It began when Hervey entered with a stack of papers.

"For you to sign, sir," stated the house man. "So that Cuthbert can post them in time for the last mail."

Craybaw wheeled angrily. His eyes flashed; almost with a glare.

"Why do you bring the letters here?" he stormed. "I can sign them in my study!"

"But it is customary, sir. You told me earlier that I should bring the letters to you."

"I have changed my mind about it. Take them away."

"You said that two of them were important, sir—"

"Take them away!"

Hervey hesitated; then turned and obeyed. Craybaw's glare ended. He turned apologetically to his guests.

"Hervey's idea of importance is ridiculous," he scoffed. "Important letters! Bah! None of them are of consequence!"

Sir Ernest lifted his eyebrows.

"Not even the letter to the Berlin shippers?" he inquired. "The one that you mentioned at dinner?"

Craybaw did not answer for a moment. His fists clenched; then opened.

"I had forgotten that one," he remarked. "Perhaps I should have it posted. No—on second thought, it needs correction. I shall take it to the office in the morning."

Hervey returned.

"Shall I have Cuthbert put the coupé away, sir?" he inquired. "He is still waiting at the front."

"Cuthbert is not in the car," put in Craybaw, bluntly. "I left him at Hayward's Heath. He asked if he might go into London. I told him he could take the train from there."

"When will he return, sir?"

"In a few days. He needed a short vacation, so I granted one to him."

LEWSHAM was looking toward Delka, who was studying Craybaw. The man by the fireplace produced a handkerchief and mopped his forehead.

"I have acquired a slight chill," asserted Craybaw. "Due, perhaps, to all this worry. You will pardon my actions, gentlemen. Frankly, I am overwrought by worry."

"Perhaps it would be wise for us to leave for London," suggested Sir Ernest. "You must rest, Craybaw. Tomorrow is an important day."

"I shall be quite fit by morning. No, no, gentlemen; I would prefer that you stay here. For the night, if possible. The fog must be thick there; driving would prove abominable. Am I right, Delka?"

"It's turned into a pea-souper," acknowledged Delka. "A bad one. I only hope that it will let up before morning."

"Turning out as you predicted, Craybaw," laughed Sir Ernest. "Remember? At the bridge?"

"What's that?" Craybaw snapped the question. "At the bridge?"

"When you spoke about the fog—"

"Yes. Of course. I did not quite catch your question, Sir Ernest. Gentlemen, I insist that you remain all night. We can drive up to London in the morning, in Chief Lewsham's car."

"In my car?" queried Lewsham, surprised.

"Do you mean my phaeton?" queried Sir Ernest.

"Of course," replied Craybaw, in an annoyed tone. "What has come over me? Really, I am not myself since this chill struck me."

He turned to Hervey, who was standing in the doorway. The house man looked perplexedly toward his master.

"Scotch and soda," ordered Craybaw. "It should prove a remedy for the chill. Fetch it, Hervey, with tumblers for all of us. Cigars, gentlemen? Hervey, where is the box of cigars?"

"You never keep boxes of cigars, Mr. Craybaw. I can bring some coronas from the humidor—"

"That is what I meant. The coronas. I thought I had left some loose ones about. Very well, Hervey. Bring us a supply."

Seating himself, Craybaw regained composure by half closing his eyes. Sir Ernest decided to remain at the house; Lewsham and Delka also agreed, after the latter had added a few details about the heaviness of the evening fog.

Hervey arrived with drinks. Craybaw came to life and ordered him to put away the coupé and the phaeton. Hervey requested the keys to the garage; Craybaw fumbled in his pocket, produced a bunch and told the house man to pick out the right ones.

Lewsham mentioned that he and Sir Ernest had talked to Delka about tomorrow's plans. In so doing, the chief constable reviewed some of the conversation that had been held earlier in the evening. Craybaw, sipping at his drink, warmed up to the discussion. His manner became more natural. He decided that his chill was passing.

A clock was chiming half past ten. Lewsham, noting the time, began to reconsider his decision. He asked when the last train left; Craybaw shifted the question to Hervey. The house man stated that the last up train departed from High Brooms at two minutes after eleven.

"We could still make it," mused Lewsham. "Fog seldom delays the railways."

"Stay here," insisted Craybaw. "Sir Ernest will see to it that you reach your office at the accustomed hour."

"Very well," agreed Lewsham, in a tone of final decision.

SILENTLY, The Shadow moved from the sun porch. Gaining the lawn, he took a shortcut past the house, across to a gate. From there, he strode briskly in the direction of High Brooms station, sensing his direction, choosing paths that he knew must be shortcuts.

By the time he neared the station, he was divesting himself of cloak and slouch hat. Reaching the shrubbery, he regained his briefcase. He drew out his overcoat and his fedora hat; then stuffed the other garments into the bag. A few moments later, he was hurrying to the station platform, just as the up train for London made its arrival.

It was Lamont Cranston who soon was seated alone in the seclusion of a smoking compartment, riding into London. The whispered laugh that came from the lips of the American millionaire was, however, a reminder of his true identity. The Shadow had reason to be mirthful.

The Shadow had divined The Harvester's game. He knew where the master crook could be found. He understood the new part that the superman of crime had chosen to play. There were details, however, to be settled. The Shadow preferred to wait.

For The Harvester was shrewd. Too clever to wither if confronted with accusations. Moreover, he was the central figure of a dangerous crew. Small-fry though his henchmen were, they had proven themselves murderers in the past. They should not be allowed to remain at large.

Even before his first skirmish with The Harvester, The Shadow had decided that the master crook should be delivered to the law, under circumstances which would leave no doubt as to his ways of crime. The Harvester had nearly been trapped in the perpetration of a criminal act at the Moravia. The Shadow intended to give him new opportunity to thrust his head into a tightening noose.

The oddity of Justin Craybaw's strange behavior was no riddle to The Shadow. The change in Craybaw had taken place during that trip from Tunbridge Wells to Hayward Heath, a journey which had never been completed. Something had happened upon the road before The Shadow could arrive to prevent it.

There was a chance that new murder had entered the game. If so, it could not be rectified. But if The Harvester had chosen to spare life, the rescue of any innocent person could wait until the morrow.

For The Shadow, to be sure of positive success, had one more task to perform tonight; and duty lay in London. That accomplished, the last vestige of The Harvester's deception would be ended.

The Shadow knew.

CHAPTER XI
AFTER MIDNIGHT

IT was a few minutes past midnight when The Shadow reached Charing Cross Station, the London terminus of the Southern Railway, which line he had taken in from High Brooms. He went directly west from Charing Cross, riding in the Piccadilly Line of the underground. His only pause between the railway station and the tube was when he stopped to make a brief telephone call.

After a short trip via underground, The Shadow emerged from a station near the southern fringe of the Mayfair district. He stepped immediately into a fog so thick that the shop fronts were scarcely visible from the curb of the sidewalk. Delka had been right when he had stated that a real "pea-souper" had set in over London.

Late traffic was almost at a standstill. Wayfarers were few. Fog had stilled London, like a living hush settling over a doomed city. Sometimes fogs like these persisted for days; and always, with each new advent, London became stalled. The first nights were the worst, for it was then that citizens lacked the "fog-sense" that they always regained when a pea-souper continued its clutch.

Depending upon his keen sense of direction, The Shadow headed in the direction of Grosvenor Square. Choosing a parklike stretch, he crossed a strip of dampened grass, to pause when he reached the side of a bulky building that loomed suddenly from the darkened mist. He had arrived at the apartment hotel where the Rajah of Delapore dwelt.

The side of the squatty building lacked the smooth marble that characterized its front. Moving along a roughened wall, The Shadow paused at a definite spot. Despite the darkness and the mist, he had gauged the exact place he wanted. He was directly below a window of the rajah's living room.

Standing in a narrow space, The Shadow was between the wall and a terraced embankment. Had he taken to the soft earth of the bank, he could have gained a height that would give a slanted view toward the windows of the rajah's apartment. That, however, was insufficient. Looking upward, The Shadow could see blackness only. There was no chance to peer into the rajah's curtained abode.

The Shadow donned cloak and slouch hat. He laid his coat and fedora against the terrace, with the briefcase upon them. They marked the right location, and would prove useful later; for The Shadow had ordered an aide to join him here. His telephone call from Charing Cross had been received by Harry Vincent, at the Addingham Hotel.

Harry's job was to watch the front of the building, to see if persons entered. If they did, Harry was to come to the side and signal from the spot where he found the hat and coat that The Shadow had worn as Cranston. For The Shadow intended to pay a visit to the rajah's sumptuous living room. He could take care of himself within; but he needed to avoid intrusion from outside.

BY this time, Harry must have arrived, despite the thickness of the fog. The Shadow decided not to linger. Pressing close against the wall, he gripped the roughened stone and crept upward like a mammoth beetle. His toes dug into depressed surfaces during the climb. Though the course would have been precarious for the average climber, The Shadow proved himself a veritable human fly. He reached a window of the second floor.

A catch yielded as The Shadow probed between the sections of a heavy sash. The window slid upward, noiselessly. High and old-fashioned, the opened window provided a four-foot space. With gloved hands, The Shadow slowly reached through and parted the thick, velvet curtains that hung within.

The living room was bathed in mellow light that came from table lamps. Those fixtures were the only modern fittings in an Oriental room. The place was empty, yet its subdued glow seemed foreboding. Nevertheless, The Shadow entered. He let the curtains close behind him.

The end door was provided with draperies; it was behind those hangings that the rajah must have stood when he heard Delka question Ranworthy. Gliding in that direction, The Shadow peered through the curtains and spied an empty, dimly lighted hall. No one was about; neither the rajah nor his Hindu servants.

The Shadow stalked back into the living room. He eyed the outer door that led in from the outer hall. After that glance, he began to look about him. The Shadow had not forgotten the veiled challenge issued by the Rajah of Delapore. The rajah had mentioned jewels, hidden somewhere in this room. The Shadow had caught a peculiar note in the rajah's expression of self-confidence. It had been enough to arouse his doubts. There was a chance that the rajah had no jewels. That constituted an important point in the present issue. Hence, The Shadow had come here to learn the exact state of the rajah's wealth.

Keen reasoning backed the method which The Shadow used in his prompt search for a hiding place. He was confident that there could be no hidden wall space, for the rajah had merely rented this apartment. Similarly, The Shadow rejected the many Oriental objects that stood about the living room. Those were the obvious furnishings that an intruder would search.

INCONSPICUOUS about the room were the lamps that provided the mild illumination. These were useful, rather than ornamental. They were objects that no thief would want. For that very reason, The Shadow studied the table lamps. He spied one that was not illuminated. Approaching the lamp, The Shadow discovered that its cord was not attached to the wall.

The lamp had a wooden base; set upon that was a brass ball, some four inches in diameter. The sphere supported a miniature lion, upright, with its paws upon a brass shield. A rod straight up from the lion's head supported a lamp shade that resembled an inverted bowl of glass.

The lower ball was flattened at the top, to serve as a level base for the ferocious-looking brass lion. Eyeing that portion of the fixture, The Shadow became immediately active. Gripping the lion with one hand, the sphere with the other, he began a reverse twist.

His assumption was that the portions of the fixture screwed together; that the thread would be a left-hand one, to deceive anyone who guessed the fact. The surmise proved correct. The lion came free from the brass ball.

Glimmers showed within the sphere. Tilting the lamp base, The Shadow caused the contents to trickle to a thick pad which rested on the table. A shimmering array of jewels spread about. The Shadow had uncovered the rajah's cache.

Examining the jewels, The Shadow saw stones of red, others of blue. Rubies and sapphires. Then he spied glittering gems of green; large emeralds among the other stones. Carefully, The Shadow dropped some of the gems back into the spherical container. They landed without noise, for the interior was padded.

There was a dullness about the stones that another investigator might have attributed to the gloomy light. Not so The Shadow. He knew why these gems lacked lustre. The final proof came when he had completed the operation of replacement. The gems bulged from the ball; it was necessary to press them into packed formation in order to screw back the upper portion of the lamp.

These reputed jewels were paste, imitation stones that had been provided in proper quantity to jam tightly in the container, so that they would not rattle. The Rajah of Delapore had bluffed about bringing jewels to London; yet he had been wise enough to back that bluff with these false treasures that would deceive the average person who viewed them.

WHAT was the rajah's game?

The Shadow replaced the upper portion of the table lamp; then began a brief consideration of the factors. There was more to this than the present bluff. If the rajah wanted to impress persons with the fact that he had jewels, he would have logically exhibited the false stones; at least, with caution.

Instead, he was guarding these fake gems as carefully as if they were real ones. Upon making that discovery, The Shadow had been faced with an entirely new problem that concerned the motives of the Rajah of Delapore.

While The Shadow still pondered, a sound came to his ears. It was from below the opened window—a low, subdued whistle. Harry Vincent's call. The agent had arrived; he must have seen someone enter the front of the building. It was time for The Shadow to leave.

At present, The Shadow was at the innermost corner of the room. To reach the window, it was necessary for him to pass in front of the curtained doorway that led to the inner apartments. The Shadow started his journey; then stopped suddenly. A key was clicking in the outer door. It was too late to depart.

Quickly, The Shadow stopped by the hanging draperies of the inner doorway. They were thick curtains like those at the window, double in their formation. Opening the front portion of a curtain, The Shadow edged between. He stopped when his body was half obscured. He did not want to allow a bulge that might be seen from the inner hall, should a servant appear from that direction.

The door had opened. The Rajah of Delapore appeared and closed the barrier behind him. He was clad in Oriental attire; but his present garb was quiet, rather than resplendent. It lacked the decorations of the clothes in which The Shadow had previously seen him.

Looking about the room, the rajah gave a frown; then clapped his hands. The sound must have carried, for The Shadow immediately heard footsteps in the inner hall. Barkhir came past the curtains, not noticing The Shadow. The servant salaamed when he saw his master.

"You have been keeping watch, Barkhir?" queried the rajah, his tone severe.

"Yes, highness," assured Barkhir. "Soon Sanghar will replace me."

This reference was to the other servant. The rajah put an immediate question:

"Where is Sanghar?"

"He sleeps," replied Barkhir. "Shall I awaken him, highness?"

"Not at present. First, tell me if Mr. Canonby called by the telephone."

"He did, highness. One hour ago. He said that he would expect a return call from your highness."

"Good. I expected to be here, but the fog delayed me. Remain here, Barkhir, while I call Canonby. He is at home, I suppose. He would not be at the jewelry shop at this hour."

"He is at home, your highness."

Barkhir had opened the front of a boxlike stand that was near the outer door. From this teakwood container he removed a telephone and handed it to the rajah. The latter raised the receiver and put in a call.

The Shadow listened intently. He had recognized the name of Canonby.

Among the jewelers situated in Old Bond Street, none was better known than Dawson Canonby. The fact that the rajah had dealings with a man of such repute was a significant point indeed. Whatever the game of the man from India, The Shadow was about to gain an inkling of it.

Harry Vincent, groping through the fog, had been delayed with his signal. That delay had served The Shadow for the present. Though his hiding place was precarious, he had gained an opportunity to learn the final details that he sought.

CHAPTER XII
THE SHADOW DEPARTS

THE Rajah of Delapore received a prompt answer across the wire. Scarcely had he dialed before he began his conversation. Dawson Canonby had evidently been waiting close to his home telephone. The Shadow could hear the sound of a voice across the wire. Then the rajah spoke.

"Good evening, Mr. Canonby." The tone was musical. "Yes, this is the Rajah of Delapore... Yes, of course... The final arrangements... Tomorrow...

"At some time in the afternoon... I shall call you when I am ready... Yes, be prepared to bring the money... Of course... Be sure that you are well guarded...

"The armored lorry?... Does it carry the name of your jewelry house?... Excellent!... Use that vehicle when you come to Rudlow's... Yes. I shall have the false stones with me...

"Do not be perturbed, Mr. Canonby. There is no reason. This transaction lies between us... No, no. It will be unnecessary for you to express an opinion regarding the false stones. You can indicate that you have seen them previously...

"Certainly... The very fact that you accept them will prove sufficient... Let the witnesses form their own conclusions... Come, Mr. Canonby! This is no time to have qualms... Ah! You will carry through as I desire?... Excellent!... Yes, of course it is purely a protective measure... You understand the circumstances..."

While the rajah was talking, The Shadow had moved back further between the door curtains. Barkhir's assurance that Sanghar was asleep gave indication that no danger lay from within the apartment. The Shadow expected the rajah and Barkhir to come through the doorway. That would leave the living room empty, with opportunity for prompt departure.

The Shadow had already formed a possible theory regarding the rajah's possession of the false gems. The telephone call to Canonby had been a final enlightenment. The Shadow had come to a full conclusion regarding the motives that actuated the Rajah of Delapore.

The main problem had become departure. The only hazard that appeared imminent was a possible inspection by Barkhir. Should the servant part the thick curtains by the window, he would discover that the sash was open. That might cause a search about the living room.

In anticipation of such a possibility, The Shadow was ready to glide back into the inner rooms the moment that Barkhir made a move toward the window. He felt confident that he could find some quick means of exit before being discovered.

Sanghar's knife skimmed the folds of his cloak and pinned a portion of it to the paneled wall.

"Lock up, Barkhir," ordered the rajah. "Then summon Sanghar and tell him to relieve you. It is wise that someone should be up and about during the entire night."

Barkhir moved toward the window. It was The Shadow's cue. He knew that Harry Vincent, stationed below, would draw back into the fog if he heard sounds from above. The Shadow's immediate task was to find a new exit. He glided from beyond the curtains, moving backward in the dim inner hall.

A sudden sound warned The Shadow. Quickly, he wheeled toward the rear of the little hall. His move was timely. A lunging, white-clad form had launched itself in his direction. Brown hands were driving for his throat, above them a vicious face beneath a turban.

Sanghar had awakened. The servant had come to relieve Barkhir. He had spotted The Shadow!

GLOVED fists were quick enough to catch Sanghar's wrists. The servant's drive, however, was sufficient to fling The Shadow hard against the wall. Sanghar wrenched one hand free. From his sash he whisked a knife and drove the blade hard for his adversary's body.

The Shadow twisted; Sanghar's knife skimmed the folds of his cloak and pinned a portion of it to a paneled wall. The knife drove halfway to the hilt when it struck the woodwork.

The Shadow bounded sidewise. His cloak ripped by his left shoulder, where Sanghar's thrust had pinned the cloth. With a sudden turnabout, The Shadow gripped the Hindu and hurled him, spinning, clear across the hall. Sanghar sprawled. The Shadow wheeled directly toward the curtained doorway to the front room.

Again, he was just in time. The rajah had heard the commotion, and so had Barkhir. The latter had drawn a knife; he was driving through to aid Sanghar.

Had The Shadow hesitated, the second Hindu would have been upon him. But instead of pausing, The Shadow plunged straight against Barkhir, to meet the servant's drive.

Smashing forms collided at the doorway. The Shadow's ramlike shoulder sped under Barkhir's thrust. Clamping hands caught the servant's waist. With the fury of his plunge, The Shadow drove Barkhir clear back into the living room and sent him rolling, tumbling across the floor.

One more adversary—the rajah, himself. He was across the room, almost by the telephone. He had paused there to gain a revolver from the teakwood box. The rajah started to take aim; he barked a command to halt. The Shadow, whirling toward the window, came to a momentary pause.

He had guessed that the rajah would hesitate if he stopped. The rajah's desire was to trap the intruder; by feigning a willingness to parley, The Shadow saw a chance to outguess him. But the rajah's action changed suddenly into a ruse, when he saw a new opportunity.

Both Sanghar and Barkhir had recovered themselves, despite the vehemence of the flings that The Shadow had given them. Sanghar, knife regained, was bobbing in from the curtained doorway; Barkhir, still clutching his blade, was coming up from the floor.

The Shadow was trapped—the rajah straight before him, Sanghar at one side and Barkhir at the other. The servants had paused, seeing that the rajah held their adversary covered. Then came the rajah's command in rapid Hindustani—words that The Shadow understood.

The order was for the vassals to spring in and capture their cloaked antagonist.

The Hindus lunged with surprising swiftness, their knives ready for fierce strokes if The Shadow struggled. But The Shadow had a counter move. An instant before the men came upon him, he wheeled toward the curtained window, a few feet behind him.

With harsh cries, Barkhir and Sanghar converged to pounce after their quarry. Their white-clad forms came between the rajah and The Shadow, forming a temporary screen. The rajah could not fire for the moment; glowering, he waited until his servants gripped their foe. That moment never came.

Hard upon his whirl toward the window curtains, The Shadow gave a mammoth bound toward the sill. Launching himself headlong, he dived squarely into the heavy draperies, half spreading his arms as he flung his full weight forward.

Like a living arrow, The Shadow's form sped clear of wild knife thrusts delivered by the Hindu servants. With a rip, the velvet curtains snapped loose from flimsy fastenings. A diver enveloped in a curtained shroud, The Shadow plunged out into space, carrying the velvet draperies with him.

Harry Vincent saw the plunge from below. Looking straight up, he saw a zooming form shoot out into the fog, a figure that formed a huge, spreading mass of indefinable shape. The Shadow's dive was one of great proportions. It carried him—curtains and all—clear of the narrow space between the building and the terrace.

A dozen feet through midair; but it was a drive, more than a fall. For The Shadow, by the very power of his dive, reached the soft ground of the terrace six feet above the spot where Harry stood. The rajah's window was only a dozen feet above Harry's head. The Shadow had fallen less than half that distance.

The long plunge would have crippled him, nevertheless, had it not been for the curtains. Sweeping those draperies before him, The Shadow landed, completely wrapped in velvet. Jarred, but uninjured, he came rolling free, just as Barkhir and Sanghar began mad shouts of angered frustration.

Then came shots from the window. The rajah had arrived; he was stabbing bullets toward the mass that he could dimly discern upon the terrace. While flashes jabbed through the fog, a tall figure unlimbered beside Harry Vincent and gloved hands caught the agent's arm.

The Shadow had cleared in time. Lost in this lower darkness, he was dragging Harry toward the house wall. The rajah's shots had ended. His first ire finished, he had evidently decided that it was folly to dispatch new bullets toward an outsprawled foe.

FROM somewhere close by came the shrill blast of a whistle. An answering note trilled. Some police constable had heard the shots and was signaling to a comrade.

The Shadow had whisked off his torn cloak. He was stuffing it into the briefcase, which lay close to the wall. Along went the slouch hat and the gloves. The Shadow was donning coat and fedora. He gave a warning whisper to Harry.

Footsteps clattered on paving from in front of the apartment hotel. Harry expected that The Shadow would start for the rear; instead, his chief dragged him forward, then pushed Harry up a lesser slope of the embankment. Together, they reached the projecting shelter of a widespread bush, just as a London bobby, armed with torch and truncheon, appeared on the soft ground beside the building.

Another officer had come from the rear of the apartment hotel, a fact which proved The Shadow's wisdom in taking this middle course. The two were flicking their lights upward, calling to those above. They could see the dim glow of the living room, now that the curtains were cleared away. It was the rajah who answered them. He gave his identity.

"Look upon the terrace," called the rajah. "You will find the thief there. He leaped from the window. It was I who fired the revolver."

Warily, with ready clubs, the constables moved upward. Their lights glimmered upon the curtains. They began an examination of the bullet-riddled velvet.

"No one here, your excellency," called one constable. "Nothing here but curtains, sir. The blighter must have scrambled away somewhere."

"He cannot have gone far," returned the rajah.

"We shall rout him out, sir," promised the second bobby. "Trust us to find him if he is still about."

Each bobby started in a different direction. New whistles were sounding; they called to new constables who were arriving in the fog. To Harry Vincent, crouched by The Shadow, the officers seemed everywhere about. They were forming a cordon; and these London policemen were used to searches in the midst of fog.

Nonetheless, The Shadow outguessed them. Rising from beside the bush, he whispered for Harry to follow. He began to thread a course through the parklike sector, changing direction with uncanny ability. At times, The Shadow paused and held Harry back, while a searching bobby lumbered by. Then they were on their way again, unnoticed.

The Shadow took an inward course, back toward the spot where they had started; then reversed the trail. He and Harry emerged upon a sidewalk. The Shadow led the way across the street, to a narrow side thoroughfare which he located perfectly despite the fog.

Harry lost all sense of direction as he walked along with his silent companion. It was not until they reached the vicinity of St. James Square that he began to gain an inkling of their location; even then, Harry was somewhat confused.

The Shadow stopped near a street lamp. Harry viewed the features of Lamont Cranston, masklike in the mist.

HARRY had met his chief in this guise, before. He knew, of course, that The Shadow was not the actual Lamont Cranston. The real Cranston was a globe-trotter, who cooperated with The Shadow by allowing the latter to assume his guise.

The Shadow had not originally asked such permission; Cranston had once balked about the matter. Subsequent events, however, had caused the globe-trotter to agree upon the procedure. The real Cranston had found it wise to accept The Shadow's friendship.

"Facts are complete," remarked The Shadow, quietly, to Harry. "Various persons are concerned, among them one who is playing a double game. That one is The Harvester."

Harry nodded.

"Lionel Selbrock left London today," resumed The Shadow, in Cranston's level tone. "So did Jed Ranworthy. A strange change has come over Justin Craybaw. The Rajah of Delapore has no jewels of value. Instead, his gems are false. He has arranged a bogus sale that will take place tomorrow. The purchaser of the fake gems will be Dawson Canonby."

Harry blinked in wonderment at the completeness of The Shadow's information.

"Sometimes," resumed The Shadow, "it is best to add new complications to those that already exist. Particularly when a new riddle may allow an opportunity to accomplish something of importance. Therefore, Lamont Cranston will disappear temporarily, before tomorrow morning."

Harry nodded slowly.

"My absence," added The Shadow, "will prevent

me from being at the offices of Rudlow, Limited. You must go there in my stead. Wait until the morning is well advanced; then call at Rudlow's and ask for Inspector Eric Delka.

"Tell him that you are a friend of Lamont Cranston's; that you have learned that I am absent from London; that you are concerned over my disappearance. Use every possible pretext to remain with Delka."

"I understand," said Harry.

"It is most essential," concluded The Shadow, "that Justin Craybaw should be watched. Something has occurred that concerns Craybaw; something that Delka does not fully understand. He may suspect, however; therefore it should prove unnecessary to prompt Delka. I feel confident that he will watch Craybaw of his own accord.

"Should he show signs of omitting such duty, it will be your part to inform Delka that the last you heard from me was at midnight, tonight; that I told you to pass the word to him that Craybaw needed observation.

"Do not, at any time, express too much anxiety for my safety. Just use enough to establish yourself with Delka. No more. My instructions should be plain."

"They are," nodded Harry. "You can be sure that I—"

An almost inaudible whisper from The Shadow. Harry broke off his sentence. Footsteps were approaching; a friendly looking bobby loomed from the fog and stared from beneath his helmet.

"Good evening, constable," greeted The Shadow, in Cranston's quiet style. "You are just the chap to aid us. We have lost ourselves in this beastly fog. I am trying to locate St. James Street; my friend wants the underground to Aldgate."

The bobby grinned until his lips matched the curve of his chin strap.

"You are not the first wayfarers who have asked for directions," declared the officer. "Well, sir, you have as good as found St. James Street for a beginning. You are on Charles Street, just east of St. James Square. If your friend will walk east to Haymarket, he may turn north, straight to Piccadilly Circus."

"You can find your way to Aldgate easily enough," remarked The Shadow to Harry. "Good night, old chap. Ring me in the morning."

As Harry strolled away, The Shadow thanked the officer, who tipped his fingers to his helmet and resumed his beat. As soon as the bobby had pounded from sight, The Shadow chose his own direction through the fog.

Harry Vincent, groping on toward Piccadilly Circus, remained bewildered as he considered the facts that The Shadow had stated. Harry's duty was plain; still, it did not explain the circumstances that foreboded coming crime.

Selbrock, Ranworthy, and the Rajah of Delapore—all three seemed oddly concerned. The Shadow had named another: Justin Craybaw; and he had specified that the managing director of Rudlow's was the chief one to watch.

Why?

Harry could not answer the question. He realized, however, that a game was afoot; that already, a crook known as The Harvester had gained first innings. Four men were involved; one of them must be the master hand of evil.

Such was Harry's final conjecture as he neared the lights of Piccadilly Circus and headed for the immense underground station. He was still perplexed when he had stopped before a slot machine to buy a ticket that would carry him to Aldgate. Harry's only consolation was that on the morrow, he might find someone more baffled than himself; namely, Inspector Delka of Scotland Yard.

For Harry Vincent was sure of one fact only. He was positive that The Shadow, alone, could have revealed the depth of the coming game. Only The Shadow, master sleuth, could fathom the ways of so insidious a supercrook as The Harvester.

CHAPTER XIII
THE SHADOW BY DAY

DAWN showed lessened fog in London. The threat of a prolonged pea-souper had been banished by spasmodic breezes in the final hours of night. The mists, however, had not lifted from the neighborhood of the Thames when an early morning train crossed the railway bridge outside of the Cannon Street station.

Aboard that Southern Railway local was an outbound passenger, the same who had come up by last night's train from High Brooms. The Shadow, garbed in walking clothes, was riding southward. With him, he was carrying a knapsack. Anyone who claimed an acquaintance with Lamont Cranston would have been surprised to observe the adventurous millionaire bound on so plebeian an excursion.

The Cannon Street train required a change of cars at Tunbridge, three miles before High Brooms. Rather than wait for the connecting local, The Shadow left Tunbridge station as soon as he had arrived there. Provided with a map of the terrain, he chose a cross-country route toward Craybaw's. It was not quite eight o'clock when he arrived at the back of the country estate.

Passing through a wicket, The Shadow took a circuitous course that brought him to a cluster of trees close by Craybaw's conservatory. Parking his knapsack, The Shadow approached the high side of the porch; pausing beneath the windows, he caught the tones of cautious voices.

"Odd about Craybaw." The comment was in Lewsham's voice. "He has been behaving differently, Delka, ever since he took that short journey last night."

"He appears to be irritable this morning," returned Delka. "Why should he have quibbled so much with that chap Hervey?"

"About the landscape gardeners?"

"Yes. Hervey reminded him that he had already contracted for workmen next week. Yet Craybaw insisted that a new lot should begin here today."

"Where is Craybaw now?"

"In his study, mulling about. When I was there, he thrust away some papers in a lower drawer of the desk."

"Letters or documents?"

"Nothing but penciled notations. He pulled them out later, crumpled them and tossed them back."

"Probably something inconsequential. Nevertheless, Delka, you are to take complete charge of Craybaw. Do not let him out of your sight until this spell has ended. Should he become ill, stay with him."

"Do you think that some threat has been made against him?"

"Possibly. Or it may be something more serious. I have been wondering about that chauffeur of his, Cuthbert. By the way, Delka, it is time for us to be starting. Better jog inside and find out what arrangements have been made."

Delka went into the house. The Shadow was about to move away when he heard a new voice. Sir Ernest Jennup had come out to the conservatory and was speaking to Sidney Lewsham.

"Craybaw's condition troubles me," declared Sir Ernest. "Unquestionably, the man is no longer himself. He acts as though a huge burden lies upon his shoulders."

"Does he appear ill?"

"Yes and no. He insists that he must go into the office; yet he says he is willing to relax after this business is finished."

"Should he summon a physician?"

"He will not hear of it."

The conversation ended. Delka was coming directly to the conservatory. The Shadow could hear Craybaw's voice. The man's mood had certainly improved, for his words were cheery.

"I have come out of the doldrums," declared Craybaw. "Nothing like fresh country air for a tonic, provided it is in the morning. Night is bad, when the atmosphere chills; particularly at this season."

"You feel improved?" queried Sir Ernest.

"Positively," returned Craybaw. "If you are agreeable, Sir Ernest, we might start for the city at once. I feel sure that we are all desirous of a prompt arrival."

THE four men left the conservatory. The Shadow moved back to the clustered trees. From among the trunks of the tiny grove, he saw the Londoners emerge from the front door and enter Sir Ernest's phaeton. The long car rolled from the driveway.

Finding a path to the front road, The Shadow took it and soon reached the highway over which he had driven the night before, when following the coupé to Hayward's Heath. Carrying knapsack and swinging his walking stick, The Shadow had no reason to avoid the notice of passers. No one would have recognized him as a recent guest at Craybaw's.

Glancing at a road map, The Shadow paused to make a final estimate of distances. All along the edge of the map were computations that he had completed during the morning's railway journey. The Shadow had calculated with exactitude.

He had known the average speed at which Cuthbert drove, for he had watched the speedometer when the chauffeur had taken him to High Brooms. He knew also the speed with which he, himself, had driven from Craybaw's home to Hayward's Heath. Furthermore, he had gauged to a matter of seconds the amount of start that the coupé had gained over the phaeton.

Since he had not passed the coupé on the road, The Shadow knew that it had left the route at some unknown point. That point, according to his computations, must lie within three miles from Craybaw's house. The map showed only five logical lanes within that space.

The Shadow rejected the first, which lay fairly close to Craybaw's; also the second, for it was beyond this lane that The Shadow had picked up the coupé's trail on the return trip. The possibilities had been definitely reduced to three.

The Shadow was walking along the right side of the road, against the traffic. This was hardly necessary, for no cars had appeared upon the road. He reached the third lane, more than two miles from Craybaw's. He paused there. This was the first of his three possibilities.

The road widened somewhat at the lane; and a curve made the crossing dangerous. It was a spot at which Cuthbert would necessarily have slowed the coupé, when turning left.

At the side of the road, The Shadow found deep dust, scruffed by footmarks. At one spot, he located tire tracks that could have been from the coupé. These formed an inverted V—a proof that the car had stopped at the very entrance to the lane; then had backed.

MOVING along the lane, The Shadow found similar tracks in the dust. While he was examining the marks, he heard the rumble of an approaching motor. Turning about, The Shadow hurried back to the main road. He was walking along it when the roar of the car came from the mouth of the crooked lane.

Turning about, The Shadow came strolling toward the lane, like a chance pedestrian bound upon a hike. A light truck rolled from the lane; aboard it were half a dozen workmen, who were clad in old clothes. They eyed The Shadow as the truck turned in the direction of Craybaw's. In stolid fashion, The Shadow kept on walking.

The rumble of the car faded. The Shadow stopped his stroll. He knew that he had quelled any suspicions on the part of the men in the truck; but he had formed his own conclusions about their identity. They were the workmen expected at Craybaw's; but they were not local rustics. The Shadow knew faces when he saw them.

Despite their garb, those men were thugs of the type that The Harvester had used before. They were of the same ilk as the ruffians who had been aboard the up train from Plymouth. They matched the crowd that had backed The Harvester on his raid at the Moravia.

Between the dust and the truck, The Shadow had the complete story. Last night, the coupé had been waylaid. Cuthbert had been halted by men at the lane entrance. They had forced the chauffeur to drive the coupé down the lane, carrying Justin Craybaw with him.

The map showed the lane to be one mile in length. Somewhere in that stretch, these minions of crime had their headquarters. After they had captured the coupé, The Harvester himself had driven back to the house. At present, he was being accepted as none other than Justin Craybaw.

Taking to the lane, The Shadow strolled along, watching for new signs of interest. At the end of a half mile, he passed an elbow in the road and came to the front of a tumbledown cottage. The gate was broken; an old beagle saw the stroller from the porch. With a bound, the dog jumped to the path and set up barking.

An old woman appeared at the door. Wagging a broom, she cackled at the dog; then came down to the gate. The beagle subsided; wagging its tail, it came to make friend with the tall stranger at whom it had barked.

"It's good morning to you, sir," greeted the old countrywoman. "'Tis not often that Pauper here sees wayfarers along this road. Ah! 'Tis a bad dog he is, at times."

Pauper was apparently impressed by the criticism, for he sniffed at The Shadow's hand and stood quiet while the stroller patted him.

"But it's harmless he is, at heart," added the woman, looking at the dog. "Not like the hounds that dwell at the end of the lane. I'd advise ye, sir, to be cautious when you have gone further. The old cot below here is not a good place to venture."

"Merely on account of the dogs?" inquired The Shadow.

"And the men what own them," confided the woman. "A bad sort, they are. It was up to devilment they were, last night; and this morning some went past here. Just a little time ago, sir. Peacefullike, in their motor wagon; but it's not my way to trust them."

The Shadow thanked the woman for the advice. He was about to proceed, when she offered him a bottle of milk for tuppence, to carry with his lunch kit. The Shadow made the purchase and gave the woman a silver half crown, adding that he expected no change. He left the gate, with the woman still gasping her thanks at such surprising generosity.

NEARING the end of the lane, The Shadow left the road and climbed a little hummock. From the slight hill, he gained the view that he wanted. Secluded from the end of the lane, because of intervening trees, was a fair-sized cottage. A path through a side glade offered a convenient means of approach.

The Shadow took the path. He had neared the cottage when he encountered the dogs of which the woman had spoken. Two large hounds began to bark; then they bounded through the furze and came upon the intruder.

The Shadow stood motionless; the hiss that came from his lips was like a compelling command. The dogs stopped short.

Speaking in a low, strange tone, The Shadow approached. In the gloom beneath the trees, his eyes burned with a fiery glow that the dogs discerned. One hound whimpered; the other tried to bay, but no sound came from its quivering throat. Both beasts cowered when The Shadow reached them.

The Shadow's manner changed. Walking stick tucked beneath his arm, he stroked a dog with each hand, treating them in the same friendly fashion that he had shown the beagle. The dogs ceased their cringe. They accepted The Shadow as a master.

A whistle from the cottage. Then a gruff voice; one man speaking to another.

"Where did them hounds go?"

"Into the thicket. Started up a fox, maybe."

"A fox? There's none of 'em hereabouts. They turned up a grouse, more likely."

Again the whistle. The hounds were loath to leave. They gazed at The Shadow, with inquiring eyes. He gave a low command: "Home." The dogs hesitated. The Shadow made a gesture with his hand. Quietly, his canine friends trotted back toward the cottage.

"Here they come" were the words that reached The Shadow. "Couldn't have been any prowler in there. The hounds would have tore him to ribbons. Go tell Dokey that it was a false alarm."

"Where is he? In the kitchen?"

"Sure. Cooking lunch for that bloke upstairs. We'll have our own grub later."

The voices faded. The Shadow returned through the thicket. Skirting back to the lane, he plucked the brambles from his knickers. A smile showed on his masklike features. The Shadow had found out details that he wanted. He knew that there were still three men at the cottage; that the place was serving as a prison, due to the reference to "the bloke upstairs."

HALF an hour later, The Shadow arrived back at Craybaw's. From the trees beside the conservatory, he spied the pretended landscape gardeners at work near the rear of the grounds. They were trimming hedges, while Hervey, the house man, watched them.

The Shadow took this opportunity to enter the conservatory. He went through to Craybaw's study. There he opened the desk drawer and found some crumpled sheets of paper. He studied them and found penciled comments, arranged in schedule formation.

One name on the paper was "Twin Trees," the name of the lane where The Shadow had been. Other words were "London" and "Rudlow's," with hours and minutes checked after them. Some notations had been crossed out; others had question marks beside them. The last references stated: "Twin Trees, 2 1/2; cottage 1"; these were references to the mileage.

A soft laugh from The Shadow's lips. He dropped the crumpled papers in the drawer; then turned to the old safe in the corner. After brief experiment, he opened the strong box, finding the combination with ease. Inside were bundles of papers and filing boxes that contained various documents.

A brief inspection showed that none were important. The opened safe, however, inspired The Shadow to another idea, for he sat down at the desk and inscribed a note, which he sealed in an envelope. He went to the safe and picked out a filing box. He removed the papers, put his envelope at the bottom, then replaced them.

Closing the safe, The Shadow turned the dial, then started from the study. He heard Hervey entering from the conservatory, so he stepped into a nook beneath the main stairs, just outside the study door.

Hervey went past; The Shadow continued through the living room. He went out through the conservatory and reached the tiny grove.

Comfortably stretched beneath the trees, The Shadow indulged in another smile. It was not yet noon; there was time to rest and gain a doze to make up for a night of very little sleep. For, The Shadow was prepared for developments that would not take place until later in the day.

He had guessed the key to crime; he had divined where the final stroke would come. Here at the home of Justin Craybaw; there was no need to travel elsewhere.

Often The Shadow sought action, and was forced to set out to find it. Today he was confident that action would be brought to him.

A curious turn of events; but one that fitted with The Shadow's knowledge of The Harvester.

CHAPTER XIV
EVENTS IN LONDON

SHORTLY before noon, Harry Vincent arrived at the offices of Rudlow, Limited. He paused outside the building in Threadneedle Street, to watch the unloading of a bank truck. Harry was but one of many curious observers who saw four uniformed men march into the building with an object no larger than a small satchel.

There were others about, whom Harry took to be Scotland Yard men. They followed the bank guards into the Rudlow office; but the armored truck remained. Two constables moved the crowd along. Harry decided to go into the building.

The outer office occupied by Rudlow, Limited, was fenced off in one corner to form a waiting room. This was where Harry entered. At the gate, he inquired for Inspector Delka. A boy was sent into a suite of private offices. He returned, followed by Delka.

Harry introduced himself. When he stated that he was an American, and a friend of Lamont Cranston's, Delka became keenly interested. He told Harry to follow him. They went through to the private offices; there they entered a conference room, beyond which was a door marked with the title: "Managing Director."

Both Sidney Lewsham and Sir Ernest Jennup were seated in the conference room. Two bank guards were at a table in the corner, with revolvers ready in their holsters. Between them was the precious bag that had been brought in from outside.

Delka introduced Harry to Lewsham and Sir Ernest. Both eyed him with a trifle of suspicion. Harry stated himself.

"Cranston called me shortly after midnight," he explained. "He had come up to London and was at Charing Cross, so he said. He told me that he would be at the Moravia all day; but that he would be busy and would prefer to see me later."

"Yet you went to the Moravia?" queried Lewsham.

"Yes," acknowledged Harry, "because another

matter came up this morning. I wanted to talk with him about my passport. But Cranston was not at the Moravia."

"How did you happen to come here?"

"I made inquiry to the Moravia. They suggested that I communicate with Scotland Yard and ask for Inspector Delka. I did so and learned that he was here."

Harry's tone was a grave one that showed deep concern. It passed muster, especially because the others began at once to wonder about The Shadow's whereabouts.

"The last we heard of Cranston was when he left Craybaw's," mused Lewsham. "But if anything has happened to him, we can now trace from Charing Cross."

"Not necessarily," put in Delka, with a shake of his head. "The call could have been from somewhere else. It came at midnight, you say, Mr. Vincent?"

Harry nodded.

"Why was Cranston at Charing Cross as late as midnight?" queried Delka, suddenly. "His train arrived there long before that. Unless he missed it and took a later one."

"Cuthbert would have mentioned it," remarked Sir Ernest. "Or he might have brought Cranston back with him."

"And there would be no reason for Cranston staying at Charing Cross," insisted Delka. Then, to Lewsham: "This may be another development, chief."

Harry was relieved when Lewsham shook his head.

"Forget it for the present, Delka," decided the chief constable. "Since Cranston said for Vincent to wait until evening before calling at the Moravia, there is a chance that Cranston had alternate plans for the day. Let us wait until nightfall before we press this matter."

HARRY had apparently established himself because of his claim of friendship with Lamont Cranston. No one urged him to leave, so he quietly seated himself beside Delka. Lewsham made a cryptic comment to Delka.

"Remember about Craybaw?"

Delka nodded. Harry smiled to himself. He understood that Lewsham meant for Delka to watch Craybaw. There was no need for Harry to bring up the emergency warning.

The door of Craybaw's office opened and a small group of men filed out. These were evidently the directors. One remained and shook hands with Sir Ernest Jennup. He was a portly, pleasant-faced man, who wore pince-nez spectacles. Craybaw introduced him to Lewsham.

"Mr. Thaddeus Blessingwood, the comptroller for Rudlow, Limited."

Blessingwood bowed pompously and adjusted his spectacles. He talked with Sir Ernest and it became evident that Blessingwood was the official who acted as contact with the banking house that had financed Rudlow's. Finally, Sir Ernest ended the conversation and pointed to the moneybag in the corner.

"Two hundred thousand pounds are waiting," he stated quietly. "It would be best to place the funds in the vault."

"At once!" agreed Craybaw. "Through my office, please. The vault connects with it."

Blessingwood went with Craybaw, followed by the guards who carried the money. Lewsham also went to see the installation of the funds. Delka spoke to Harry.

"I am lunching with Mr. Craybaw," stated the Scotland Yard man. "If you wish to remain in case we hear from Mr. Cranston, you are quite welcome to come with us."

"Thank you," rejoined Harry. "I appreciate the invitation."

When Craybaw returned, Delka introduced Harry and mentioned the matter of The Shadow's absence. Craybaw started to express concern regarding his friend Cranston; but Delka assured him that all was probably well. They went out to lunch, leaving Chief Lewsham in charge of the office. Sir Ernest and Blessingwood went out together.

It was after one o'clock when they completed luncheon. Harry had gained a chance to chat with Craybaw; he noted that except for short spells of absentmindedness, the man seemed to behave in normal fashion. It was plain, however, that Delka intended to stay close to Craybaw.

Craybaw had taken Delka and Harry to a restaurant close by Piccadilly Circus. When they came out, they walked through Piccadilly and Craybaw stopped in front of a shop that advertised travel goods. He suggested that they enter.

"I am going to the Riviera," Craybaw remarked. "I need a rest for my health. New luggage is the first requisite toward correct travel. I shall need a steamer trunk and a stout pigskin kit bag."

Craybaw purchased both articles. He ordered the salesman to ship the steamer trunk to Tunbridge Wells. The pigskin kit bag, however, was another matter.

"A masterpiece in leather!" expressed Craybaw. "We shall carry it with us in the motor cab. Sir Ernest shall see it; and Blessingwood, also. Gad! They will be envious!"

WHEN they reached Rudlow's, Craybaw strode into the conference room and proudly exhibited the pigskin bag. He classed it as a bargain at ten guineas, a price which Sir Ernest agreed was reasonable. When Craybaw went into his private office, he carried the bag with him and placed it on a corner table, beyond his desk.

Delka had made inquiry to learn if word had come from Lamont Cranston. Learning that none had been received, the C.I.D. man made a suggestion to Harry Vincent. He decided that it would be best for Harry to go back to the Addingham Hotel and await word there.

Before Harry could produce a pretext for remaining at Rudlow's, an interruption came to save him the trouble.

Two Scotland Yard men entered the conference room, accompanying a stocky, nervous-faced man who was carrying a satchel. Introduced to Sidney Lewsham, this arrival expressed relief. He was glad to see the chief constable of the C.I.D.

"I am Dawson Canonby," he explained. "My own conveyance is outside; and my guards were with me. I left them on the street when I met your men, chief."

"You have brought valuables with you?"

"Yes. Currency. A quarter of a million, in this bag. As purchase money for the gems owned by the Rajah of Delapore."

Justin Craybaw had come from his office. He had heard the final remarks. His eyes gazed sharply toward Canonby's satchel.

"Money for the gems?" queried Craybaw. "But where is the Rajah of Delapore?"

"He will be here shortly," replied Canonby. "He called me from his hotel."

A boy was knocking at the door of the conference room to announce that the Rajah of Delapore had arrived.

Dressed in Hindu attire, the rajah made his appearance, followed by his two servants. He bowed in greeting; then beckoned to Barkhir, who produced a small package.

"The jewels," explained the rajah. "You have seen them before, Mr. Canonby."

"Of course," returned Canonby, his tone nervous.

"But you must see them again," assured the rajah. He opened the package and showed a square teakwood box. "They are here for your inspection."

Canonby opened the box and began to count over the gems, mumbling as he did so. The others looked on, wondering somewhat about the jeweler's haste. None, however, recognized that the jewels might be imitations, with the possible exception of Justin Craybaw.

The managing director was eyeing the jewels keenly and Harry noted it. Canonby completed his inspection, dumped jewels back into the box and closed the lid. He lifted the satchel and handed it to the rajah.

"Not heavy," remarked Canonby, with a wan smile, "but that is because I acquired notes of high denomination. A quarter of a million, your excellency. Shall I count the money in your presence?"

"Mr. Craybaw can do that," returned the rajah, indifferently. "The money will soon belong to Rudlow, Limited."

Canonby turned to Lewsham.

"My men will guard my return journey," said the jeweler. "If your officers will accompany me to the street, I shall not be in danger."

Lewsham gave an order to two Scotland Yard men. They went out with Dawson Canonby.

CRAYBAW and Blessingwood were counting the money while Sir Ernest watched them. The bundles of crisp notes totaled two hundred and fifty thousand pounds. The count finished, Craybaw turned to the Rajah of Delapore.

"Your excellency," he stated, "when I called you this morning, I supposed that we would have heard from Lionel Selbrock before noon. Unfortunately, we have not. Therefore, we must hold the transaction until we know where he is."

"The delay will not matter," returned the rajah.

"It might so far as this money is concerned," objected Craybaw, seriously, "unless you wish me to place the funds in the vault. Rudlow, Limited, is willing to assume responsibility. We can give you full receipt for two hundred and fifty thousand pounds."

"That will be satisfactory."

Craybaw went into his office and produced a receipt form. He sent it to be typed; it came back a few minutes later. Craybaw passed it to Blessingwood.

"You may sign it," he said.

"But I am not the managing director," exclaimed Blessingwood. "That is your office, Craybaw."

"This blank bears the name 'comptroller,'" stated Craybaw. "I meant to bring one of my own; but I picked out this disused form instead. You are the comptroller, Blessingwood. You have sufficient authority to sign. Others will witness the receipt."

Blessingwood nodded and picked up a pen. He sat down at the table and signed the receipt. Sir Ernest Jennup was nodding, apparently decided that the procedure was in order. He took the pen to affix his signature as a witness.

Craybaw remarked that he would place the money in the vault. In casual fashion, he picked up the satchel and walked from the conference room into his office. He let the door swing shut behind him. Other witnessing signatures were needed, so Lewsham ordered Delka to add his name below Sir Ernest's. Lewsham, himself, signed third.

While the ink was drying, Craybaw returned from his office. He began to chat with the rajah; then suddenly returned through the door to the other room. He came back, carrying the pigskin bag that he had purchased. He was holding it between both hands, in front of him, to give the bag better display.

"Look at this sample of British workmanship," remarked Craybaw, proudly. "Have you ever seen its equal, your excellency? This is the finest pigskin you—"

The rajah stepped back, withdrawing his hand before he touched the bag. His action was as quick as if he had encountered a flame. Barkhir and Sanghar dropped back toward a corner. Craybaw stood still.

"We are Mohammedans," explained the rajah, politely, "myself and my servants. To us, the pig is unclean. I admire the bag, Mr. Craybaw, but I cannot touch it."

"My apologies—"

"They are unnecessary. You did not know the circumstances."

Craybaw placed the offending bag on a table in the corner of the conference room. The rajah picked up the receipt from Rudlow, Limited, and folded it. Craybaw sat down in a corner by the table. Lewsham opened conversation with the rajah.

"There was a report at the office," said Lewsham, "concerning an attempted robbery at your apartment. I understand that nothing was taken, however."

"We thwarted the intruder," declared the rajah, with a smile. "Unfortunately, he escaped us. He was probably seeking my jewels. He did not find them."

"You have no clue to his identity?"

"None whatever."

HARRY was facing Craybaw while the others talked. He saw the managing director open the door and carry out the pigskin bag. He placed it in the custody of an office boy. Delka glanced toward the door and noticed Craybaw returning. Meeting Delka's gaze, Craybaw half closed his eyes.

"I feel the chill returning," he said to Delka. "I feel that the strain is becoming too much for me. I should not have come in town at all. I dread the train trip back to Tunbridge Wells."

Sir Ernest overheard the remark.

"I shall carry you there in my car," he declared. "The motor trip may improve you. The day has turned mild; and we can make a rapid journey in the phaeton."

Craybaw nodded his thanks. He steadied himself, for the rajah was preparing to leave.

"I shall return," declared his excellency, "as soon as I have heard from you, Mr. Craybaw."

"That will not be necessary," stated Craybaw. "When Selbrock arrives, we shall have him sign the documents at once. We shall bring the options to your apartment."

"Very well."

The rajah left with his servants. Craybaw walked slowly back into his office, then slumped into the chair behind the desk. He had left the door open; the others saw his action. Sir Ernest entered the inner office.

"You are ill, Craybaw," insisted Sir Ernest. Delka and Lewsham had joined him. "Come. You must return to your home."

"But if Selbrock comes!" gasped Craybaw. "His options must be attested—"

"I can take charge of that," inserted Blessingwood, who had also entered. "As comptroller, the duty comes within my province."

Craybaw nodded. Reaching for Delka's shoulder, he drew himself up from the desk. Sir Ernest added support. Craybaw steadied and walked slowly through the conference room. Delka stopped to speak to Harry.

"I must go with Mr. Craybaw," said the C.I.D. man. "I shall call you at the Addingham, when we hear from Mr. Cranston."

There was only one alternative. Harry took it. He left the office and preceded the others to the street. But when he had crossed Threadneedle, he waited and watched. He saw Craybaw come out with Delka and Sir Ernest.

The phaeton had been summoned from the garage. The three men entered it, Delka going in back with Craybaw. Then the office boy appeared, lugging Craybaw's newly purchased pigskin bag. Harry watched him place it in the front seat beside Sir Ernest.

Something in the boy's action caught Harry's eye. The hoist when the bag went over the door seemed more than necessary for so light an object. Just as the phaeton pulled away, the answer struck Harry. Chance had given him a thought that had occurred to no one else.

That bag was not empty! Craybaw had carried it as though it was. He had said nothing, however, to the office boy regarding emptiness. True, the bag had been empty when Craybaw had carried it to the office; but it was empty no longer. Harry knew what it contained.

Two stores of wealth! Cash intended for Selbrock; funds brought by the Rajah of Delapore! There was only one explanation. The Harvester, clever at disguise, was playing the part of Justin Craybaw! He had taken the place of the managing director of Rudlow, Limited.

The Harvester had not placed the money in the vault. He had put it in the bag. He was making away with it, deceiving Sir Ernest Jennup and Eric Delka.

Harry's course was to call The Shadow; he realized suddenly that it would be impossible. He did not know where The Shadow was.

One other possibility, only. That was to inform Sidney Lewsham, in hope that the chief constable might act. First a call to the Moravia, in the wild hope that The Shadow might be there. Then back to Rudlow's, to see Lewsham.

Such was the course that Harry Vincent took as duty, not knowing whether or not he would injure The Shadow's plans. But in this emergency, he could think of but one purpose. That was to defeat the game that The Harvester had played.

CHAPTER XV
SCOTLAND YARD MOVES

BACK in the Rudlow offices, Thaddeus Blessingwood had solemnly taken the place of Justin Craybaw. The pompous comptroller had decided that it was his duty to occupy the managing director's office. He had invited Sidney Lewsham to join him; and the chief constable had accepted. They were sitting opposite each other, across Craybaw's big desk.

"It is serious business, this," remarked Blessingwood, solemnly. "I cannot blame Mr. Craybaw for weakening beneath the burden that was placed upon him. Frankly, I would lose my own confidence were it not for your presence, Chief Lewsham."

"Because of the half million in the vault?" queried Lewsham, with a smile.

"Yes," nodded Blessingwood, "when I consider the crimes that have electrified London. The Harvester is a desperate criminal."

Blessingwood had opened the desk drawer in front of him. He brought out some printed sheets; then clucked his puzzlement.

"Odd," he remarked, "that Craybaw should have found one of my receipt blanks. There are many of his own here. Hah! What is this? A telegram!"

Blessingwood unfolded a paper. His eyes popped behind his pince-nez spectacles as he thrust the sheet across the desk.

"From Lionel Selbrock!" he ejaculated. "Dispatched from Carlisle this morning! Craybaw must have received it, yet he did not mention it. What in the world is Selbrock doing in Carlisle?"

Lewsham snatched the telegram. He scanned its lines. The message had been sent from Carlisle prior to noon. It stated simply that Selbrock could not arrive at Rudlow's before the next morning. Lewsham recalled suddenly that Craybaw had received several envelopes during the morning. The telegram must have been in one of them.

"Something is vitally wrong," decided Lewsham. "Why did Craybaw insist that Selbrock would be in town today? He must have read this telegram. Let me have the telephone, Blessingwood."

The comptroller passed the instrument across the desk. Lewsham put in a call to the Rajah of Delapore. It was answered. The rajah had just returned to his apartment. Lewsham explained matters; then hung up.

"He knows nothing about Selbrock," assured Lewsham. "But the rajah is coming over here to confer about the matter. By the way"—he studied the telegram—"this distant trip to Carlisle is odd on the part of Selbrock; but I recall also that the rajah's secretary, Ranworthy, made a trip to Yarmouth. I wonder if there is a connection?"

"Yarmouth is not on the way to Carlisle," reminded Blessingwood.

"I know that," snapped Lewsham. "But we have no proof that either man went to the destination that he claimed."

"We have this dispatch from Selbrock—"

"A telegram with his name attached. Anyone could have sent it. What ails Craybaw, for not mentioning this matter? The man is ill; but certainly rational enough at intervals to have remembered this telegram."

"Craybaw was lost in enthusiasm over his pigskin bag. That was unusual. I never saw him so intrigued before over a ten-guinea purchase—"

"THE pigskin bag!" A connection struck Lewsham, suddenly. "What became of that bag, Blessingwood?"

"Craybaw took it into the conference room—"

Lewsham bounded to the door. He saw no sign of the bag. He started to the outer door, to be met there by an entering boy.

"Mr. Vincent is back, sir," informed the office employee. "He says that he must see you at once. It is something about Mr. Craybaw—"

"Bring Vincent here!" ordered Lewsham.

Harry arrived. Lewsham hurried him into the inner office, where Blessingwood was standing, puzzled.

"What do you know about Craybaw?" demanded Lewsham. "Is it anything that concerns his pigskin bag? Did he have it with him when he left here?"

"One of the boys was carrying it," explained Harry. He realized now that his return had been wise. "I saw it go into Sir Ernest's phaeton. The bag was heavy—not empty, as it was when Craybaw purchased it. I decided to inform you—"

"Blessingwood," broke in Lewsham, "open the vault at once. Look for the money that you put there."

"I did not place the funds in the vault," reminded Blessingwood, as he hurried to the vault room. "I came in here and opened the vault, to save Mr. Craybaw trouble. You were with me—so were others; but we left while he was putting the money in the proper place."

"So we did," exclaimed Lewsham, while Blessingwood worked at the dials. "Then Craybaw came out afterward. At least, that was the way I recall it. But that was with the funds intended for Selbrock—"

"And Craybaw came in alone when he brought the rajah's money," added Blessingwood. "He must have opened the vault himself; for I did not come with him."

"If he opened the vault at all!"

The grimness of Lewsham's tone made Blessingwood turn about in alarm; just as he swung open the door of the vault, Lewsham pounced forward.

"Show me the money!" he cried. "Find it, Blessingwood! Do not stand there useless! You know this vault is—"

Blessingwood pawed through the vault. His search became excited. His spectacles tipped from his nose and hung by their cord. Speechless as he ended the hunt, he stood panting, with face purpled.

"The money!" demanded Lewsham. "Four hundred and fifty thousand sovereigns!"

"Gone!" gasped Blessingwood. "It is nowhere in the vault!"

"Nor was it ever placed here!" shouted Lewsham. "Craybaw has tricked us! No—not Craybaw—it was The Harvester!"

"The Harvester?" echoed Blessingwood. "But it was Mr. Craybaw. At least—at least—"

"You suspect something?" demanded Lewsham. "Something in the man's action, aside from his withholding of the telegram?"

"Yes." Blessingwood found his answer. "The matter of the signature. Craybaw would not have brought out the wrong receipt slip. He would not have turned that signing over to me, as comptroller. Not under ordinary circumstances."

"But The Harvester would!" ejaculated Lewsham. "In order to avoid writing a signature that was not his own; one that would have been suspected. Craybaw's! He passed that issue last night, as well, when he refused to sign letters that Hervey brought to him!"

SPECULATION ended as Lewsham suddenly remembered the great task at stake. Nearly half a million pounds had been gained by a master crook. That, to Harry Vincent, meant the staggering sum of close to five million dollars.

Lewsham went for the telephone in Craybaw's office. He put in a telephone call to the managing director's home in Tunbridge Wells. The reply came that the line was out of order. Lewsham hurried through the conference room. He called to men outside. Half a dozen C.I.D. operatives came at his command.

"Fifteen minutes ago," announced Lewsham, studying his watch, "Inspector Delka and Sir Ernest Jennup left here with a man whom they thought was Justin Craybaw. It was not Justin Craybaw. That man was an impostor. He was The Harvester."

The Scotland Yard men stared in amazement.

"The Harvester carried a pigskin traveling bag," added Lewsham, grimly. "It probably contains nearly half a million pounds. Sir Ernest and Inspector Delka do not know of the bag's contents. They are taking The Harvester to Tunbridge Wells. They will be there within the next thirty minutes.

"Their destination is the home of Justin Craybaw, where The Harvester will still continue to pose as the owner. Our one hope is to arrive there before he learns that we have uncovered his game. We cannot rely upon the local authorities at Tunbridge Wells. The Harvester would outmatch them.

"I shall ride in the first of three swift motors, leading the way to Craybaw's. We shall deploy about the grounds and close in to trap The Harvester. You, Tunning, and you, Dawsett, arrange for the cars at once."

Two men hastened to call Scotland Yard. Lewsham paced the conference room, then delivered a new order:

"Parkins, you will call Tunbridge Wells from here, immediately after my departure. Do not call Craybaw's home; that would be useless, for the telephone is out of commission. Communicate with the local authorities. Tell them to meet us on the road this side of High Brooms. Do not name our destination; otherwise they might blunder. Say that I am coming. That should prove sufficient.

"Keep Blessingwood and Vincent here with you. We shall need their testimony later. Also that of the Rajah of Delapore. Have him remain after he arrives. Wilton will stay with you. Summon more men from headquarters should you need them. Another call, also. To Croydon Air Field. Have planes set out for Tunbridge Wells in exactly"— Lewsham paused to glance at his watch—"in exactly forty minutes after my departure. They must not arrive overhead until we have formed a cordon.

"Blessingwood will give the location of Craybaw's home, to identify it for the airmen. Procure a map at once, Blessingwood. We must ensnare The Harvester should he attempt to escape by air."

Lewsham paused, breathless. He glanced from the window. It was slightly foggy still, here in London; but the visibility would be good, south of the city. It lacked a full hour until dusk, even though the afternoon had waned.

"Duties for you two," announced Lewsham, turning to the last pair of subordinates. "Burleigh, you are to apprehend a man named Lionel Selbrock. You will find complete data concerning him in my office at headquarters. He is presumably in Carlisle, a fact of which we have no proof other than a telegram.

"Nevertheless, watch the proper railway stations. Also his hotel. Have all the motorized units of the Flying Squad ready to arrest the man on sight. Cover his hotel, the Addingham. Spare nothing in this duty, Burleigh. Here, I shall give you a written order."

Lewsham pulled a pad from his pocket. While he was scrawling the order, he gave similar instructions to the last of his six men.

"Layton, you have a man to trap. His name is Jed Ranworthy, secretary of his excellency, the Rajah of Delapore. Question the rajah about Ranworthy, who is supposed to be in Yarmouth. Whatever the rajah's opinion of the man's honesty, do not shirk your duty. Data on Ranworthy will be found at my office. Use it."

Lewsham scrawled a second order. Hardly had he finished before news came that the motorcars were in Threadneedle Street. With Tunning and Dawsett, each delegated as a car commander, Lewsham made haste to reach the street.

HARDLY had the chief gone before the Rajah of Delapore arrived. Scotland Yard men informed him of the circumstances. Questions were asked concerning Ranworthy. The conference room was in a buzz. Harry Vincent walked into Craybaw's office to cheer up Blessingwood, who was slumped behind the managing director's desk.

"It will be a terrible blow to Sir Ernest Jennup," groaned Blessingwood. "To him and the other financiers who control Rudlow, Limited. Poor Craybaw; his plight must be terrible, for he is either dead or a prisoner somewhere. But neither Justin Craybaw nor myself are owners in Rudlow, Limited. We shall suffer when the concern goes into bankruptcy, but we may find placement elsewhere.

"Who can The Harvester be? This man Selbrock? Or Ranworthy? Could he be"— Blessingwood lowered his voice to a whisper— "could he be the rajah? Or that jeweler, Canonby? Deuce take me!" The comptroller banged the desk with his fist. "I am mistrusting everyone!"

Harry Vincent restrained a grim smile. He was pleased, at least, that he had declared himself. Otherwise he, too, would have been under immediate suspicion. Harry saw Blessingwood glance at his watch and shake his head, troubled. Harry knew the man's thoughts.

Blessingwood was considering the start that The Harvester had gained. Fully thirty minutes, by the time that Sidney Lewsham had managed to give orders and begin pursuit. Time to be more than halfway to Craybaw's home near Tunbridge Wells.

But Harry Vincent did not share Blessingwood's apprehensions. Harry was thinking of another factor in the case: The Shadow. The light had dawned. Harry knew where The Shadow must surely be. At Craybaw's. For Harry's remembrance of The Shadow's final words last night came as proof that the master sleuth had dug deeply into The Harvester's game.

The trail, Harry was sure, was leading to some spot where The Shadow waited. Sir Ernest Jennup could remain a dupe; Eric Delka could continue to be deceived by The Harvester's game. The Shadow knew the truth. He would meet the rogue who posed as Justin Craybaw. The Harvester was playing into The Shadow's hands.

Yet in his confidence, Harry still had one bewildered phase. Who was The Harvester? That, Harry decided, was a question that could be answered by only one person other than The Harvester himself.

The Shadow!

CHAPTER XVI
THE HARVESTER REAPS

THE time element had been figured closely by Sidney Lewsham. The chief constable had known, when he left Rudlow's, that The Harvester would reach Tunbridge Wells within twenty minutes after men from Scotland Yard had started their pursuit from London.

Almost at the exact minute of Lewsham's calculation, Sir Ernest Jennup's long phaeton nosed into the driveway of Justin Craybaw's country home. Sir Ernest's toot of the horn brought Hervey to the front steps.

It attracted other attention also—that of distant gardeners about the hedgerows. Furthermore, it drew the keen gaze of a solitary watcher who still rested in the little grove beside the conservatory. As if in answer to an expected signal, The Shadow arose and dropped aside his knapsack. It fell, opened, to the grass.

The car was obscured by the corner of the house. The workmen could not see the inner fringe of the trees. Quickly, The Shadow gained the conservatory and entered the house through the living room. He had found a hiding place before the arrivals entered from the front.

The voice of Justin Craybaw sounded from the doorway. The tight-skinned man was calling over his shoulder to Hervey, who had remained by the phaeton at his order.

"Bring in that pigskin bag, Hervey" was the order. "Take it to the study. Leave it beside my desk."

Eyes watched as the supposed Craybaw and his two companions went into the living room. The Shadow was obscured behind a corner of the niche beneath the stairs. He saw Hervey go into the study,

lugging the pigskin bag. The house man dropped the burden and came out again.

Hardly had he reached the main hall before The Harvester met him. The man who passed as Craybaw gave an order which both Sir Ernest and Delka could hear.

"Scotch and soda to my guests," stated The Harvester. "Tell them that I shall return promptly, Hervey. I am going to the study for a few minutes."

Stepping into the study, The Harvester closed the door behind him. The Shadow, peering from his darkened hiding place, could see a cunning gleam upon the features of Justin Craybaw. The door, when it closed, did not come tightly shut. The Harvester left it ajar.

The Shadow edged forward from his hiding place. He gained the door and peered into the study.

While he watched The Harvester, he heard footsteps. Hervey was coming with tray and glasses. The Shadow moved back into the stairway niche.

He had no need to spy further. He had seen sufficient. Indeed, The Shadow had hardly regained his hiding place before the study door opened and the figure of Craybaw emerged. This time, The

Harvester was carrying the pigskin bag. He took it into the living room.

GLASSES were clinking when The Shadow moved toward the base of the stairs. From beside a huge newel post, he could hear the conversation in the living room. Hervey had gone. Craybaw's voice was sounding with a note of harshness.

"Suppose we step out to the conservatory" were the words. "The fresh air benefited me during the ride in the phaeton. It will be cool in the conservatory. By the way, Sir Ernest, would you be kind enough to carry this new bag of mine?"

Sir Ernest's voice responded. The Shadow heard the men move to the conservatory. He followed into the living room. Peering from a vantage point, he could see beyond the windows. Gardeners were moving in from the hedges.

The Shadow's right-hand automatic blasted from above the shoulder of The Harvester's dying henchman.

"Do you find the bag heavy?"

The query came in Craybaw's tone. Sir Ernest replied.

"Amazingly so," he affirmed. "I could not believe that it was an empty bag, had you not just bought it."

"Lift it, Delka," suggested The Harvester. "Place it upon the wickerwork table."

Delka did so. He gave a surprised exclamation.

"That bag is not empty!" expressed the C.I.D. man. "I saw and handled it at the luggage shop. Did you have some other purchases put inside it?"

"In a sense, yes."

The Shadow had come closer at The Harvester's words. The living room was gloomy, for it was nearly sunset. Unseen, he eyed the group upon the porch. He could observe the evil curl that had formed upon The Harvester's lips. The rogue's face looked different from Craybaw's.

"Yes," hissed Craybaw. "That pigskin bag is well-filled. With spoils! To the value of four hundred and fifty thousand pounds!"

Sir Ernest came to his feet with Delka. Both were too late. From his hips, The Harvester had yanked forth revolvers. In the light of the glass-paned conservatory, he was covering his companions. Slowly, their hands came up. Delka gasped his understanding.

"The Harvester!"

A LAUGH from twisted lips.

"Yes," gibed The Harvester. "In a new disguise. One that you all suspected; but did not fathom. I play the part of Justin Craybaw better than I imitated you, Sir Ernest. This was a role which I had been practicing for a long while.

"You thought that I was in the game. No wonder. My lieutenant, Markin—otherwise Captain Darryat—had made good progress in his various interviews when he mixed into the affairs of Rudlow, Limited. Darryat had told me all I needed, before he failed me in another issue.

"The part of Justin Craybaw was the one I chose to enact. It gave me access to the total funds— moneys, that never went into Rudlow's vaults. Cash for which I purchased the pigskin bag. The Harvester has gained his final triumph. I have reaped my greatest crop."

Sir Ernest Jennup was trembling with rage and chagrin. Eric Delka was taut, ready to spring upon The Harvester should occasion offer. The super-crook divined the intention. He snarled a warning:

"If you want death, Delka, you can have it! But if you stand where you are, you will not suffer. I have no intent to kill. Why should I?" The tone became one of contempt. "The pair of you are beggarly fools! I shall not fear you in the future.

"Look from the windows. See the men about the lawn. They are henchmen, ready at my call. Two have already bound Hervey, back in the kitchen. They have joined the others.

"I tried to kill you once, Delka. That was before I understood your full stupidity. I do not murder for love of it. Why should I waste bullets upon idiots?"

Delka's face was angered, like Sir Ernest's. Nevertheless, the C.I.D. man had been impressed by The Harvester's words. Delka's tenseness had lessened.

"You will be bound, but not gagged," promised The Harvester. His face was distorted; but his manner calm. "You can shout your bloody heads off. It will not serve you. No one lives hereabouts. The telephone wires have been cut at my order.

"I shall have ample time to make my departure before you are discovered. Scotland Yard will arrive here later; probably not for several hours. Yet I would not care if it was this very minute. My plans are made.

"Before my men enter, let me mention a minor matter." The Harvester edged to the conservatory window. The Shadow could see men moving up from the lawn. "It is about Justin Craybaw. He is still alive; so, for that matter, is Cuthbert. I had no need to dispose of them.

"That will be a task for you, Delka, to find those whom I have left behind. Prisoners of The Harvester, the reaper of the spoils. Too bad my hands are filled. I would open the bag for you and let you see what compact bundles those banknotes form.

"Unmarked money. Good anywhere. I saw to that, gentlemen. Remember"—The Harvester chuckled—"I was Justin Craybaw. Ah! Your jailors are arriving. Turn about, gentlemen, and face them. I bid you farewell."

DELKA turned with Sir Ernest. They saw two men coming up to the rear door of the conservatory, each carrying a ready revolver. But Delka spied something else. One corner pane of glass, set against an outside shrub, served as a mirror because of its darkness. Through that reflected pane, Delka caught a glimpse of The Harvester behind him.

The man who looked like Craybaw had pocketed his guns. With leering face, he was reaching for the pigskin bag. An interval had come; a moment when Delka and Sir Ernest were uncovered by weapons. Delka grabbed the opportunity.

With a cry to Sir Ernest, the Scotland Yard man spun about. He launched himself for The Harvester, pulling a revolver as he did so. Sir Ernest, after an instant's falter, made a similar swing and sprang behind the man from Scotland Yard.

The Harvester saw it coming. With a quick fling, he sent the pigskin bag skidding to the front door of the conservatory. Yanking out a revolver, he twisted away from Delka; as the Scotland Yard man aimed,

The Harvester clipped his chin with a free fist. Delka had forgotten that the rogue's illness was feigned. The Harvester had outmatched him.

Delka sprawled upon the floor. Sir Ernest, coming into the fray, went staggering from a second punch. Their bodies had intervened between The Shadow and The Harvester. There was another reason, also, why The Shadow did not fire.

That concerned the two men from the rear door. They had reached the conservatory. Viciously, they were aiming for Delka and Sir Ernest, when they heard a fierce laugh from the door of the living room. They wheeled to see The Shadow, framed in the portal.

A roar rattled the conservatory window as guns blasted in simultaneous fray. Revolver bullets whizzed wide, from muzzles that were rapidly aimed. But the slugs that sped from automatics were straight and withering. Crooks staggered as they leaped forward to fight The Shadow.

One man toppled; the other still kept on. He grappled with his foes as The Shadow swung out to meet him. Gun dropped, the rogue had gained a dying grip. That did not help The Harvester. He had bounded to the front of the conservatory. Looking back, he saw two forms locked in fray. He did not recognize Lamont Cranston.

Nor did he have time to wait, to deal with this foe. He did not even have opportunity to aim at Sir Ernest or Eric Delka, who were rising groggily from the floor. The Shadow's right-hand automatic blasted from above the shoulder of The Harvester's dying henchman.

It was like that fight at the Moravia; but on this occasion, The Harvester did not choose to wait. Bullets were cracking glass panes all about him, as The Shadow's shots sped close. Like Darryat, The Harvester's dying minion was serving his chief.

Moreover, The Harvester had gained his swag. Shouting a wild order to others on the lawn, he snatched up the pigskin bag and dived off for the cluster of trees beyond the conservatory.

The Shadow wrested free of the man who clutched him. Leaping over the body of the other, he sprang out through the rear door to deal with a new quartet of fighters.

The men were scattered on the lawn. They saw the figure that appeared by the house wall. Dropping behind terracelike slopes, they opened long-range fire. The Shadow's responses zipped the turf beside them. One man was hit; he writhed and rolled to better cover.

Delka, on his feet, was still "punch drunk." Yet he managed to shove a revolver into Sir Ernest's fist and point to the door through which The Harvester had fled. Together, they took up the chase. They spied their quarry; he had ducked past the clump of trees and was dashing for the front road. "The phaeton!" cried Sir Ernest.

THE HARVESTER must have heard the shout. Pausing suddenly, he ripped quick shots at the car, which was scarcely twenty paces from him. Front tires delivered answering explosions. The Harvester had found the broad treads of the wheels.

Savagely, Delka and Sir Ernest opened fire. The range was too great; The Harvester was nearing the front hedge. He must have scrambled through a thicket opposite, for when they reached the roadway, he was no longer to be seen.

Shots still roared from behind the conservatory. Delka remembered the lone fighter. He decided that it must be Hervey. He told Sir Ernest to come back with him. Reluctantly, the latter agreed.

As they turned, a car roared into view. It wheeled into the driveway. From it sprang Sidney Lewsham and a squad of Scotland Yard men.

Delka gave quick explanation. Lewsham ordered his men to scour for The Harvester. Delka and Sir Ernest dashed back toward the house. Already a sudden change had marked the fray upon the lawn. The Harvester's four minions, including the wounded man, had risen and were taking to mad flight.

Other cars had appeared beyond distant hedgerows. Through gateways were pouring new reserves from Scotland Yard. The sun was down beyond a wooded hill; revolvers were stabbing wildly from the darkened streaks of the rolling lawn.

The Shadow had ceased fire. Crouched by the house wall, he watched the spreading fray. The Harvester's tools were too desperate to risk capture. They were fighting to the death, unwilling to surrender. Shooting point-blank at the Scotland Yarders, they gave the latter no alternative. Riddling bullets sprawled the thugs in flight.

The Shadow moved quickly from the wall. He hurried past the conservatory. Approaching men spied him as he circled for the trees. Delka and Sir Ernest heard their shots. Cutting through the conservatory, they watched the Scotland Yard men begin new chase. They caught but a fleeting glimpse of a figure that reached the trees.

The Shadow had found his knapsack. From it, he tugged his black cloak and slouch hat. With a slinging toss, he sent the knapsack up into the trees, where it clung, lost among the boughs. Donning the cloak, he seemed to dwindle in the gloom of the tiny grove. His figure had faded toward a hedge before the Scotland Yard men arrived.

Airplanes were coming from the sky, circling low about the lawn. One swooped downward and made a landing on a level stretch of lawn. Sidney Lewsham, arriving from the front, dashed over to talk with the pilot.

Dusk was settling, with searchers everywhere. Yet

The Harvester had made a getaway with the pigskin bag. The hunt was becoming fruitless. Nor could men with flashlights uncover that other unknown whom they had seen heading for the tiny grove.

Yards from the house, resting by a hedge where searchers had just scoured, The Shadow stood enshrouded in his cloak of black. The twilight breeze caught an echo of his whispered laugh. That tone denoted satisfaction, even though The Harvester had fled.

For The Shadow knew more than did those frantic hunters. He knew that The Harvester's game was not yet through. Too bold to risk mere oblivion, The Harvester would return. Then would The Shadow seek the final laugh.

CHAPTER XVII
DELKA FINDS A CLUE

IT was a gloomy group that assembled in Justin Craybaw's study, a half hour later. Sidney Lewsham was the man in charge. He listened to the story told by Eric Delka and Sir Ernest Jennup. Then came the reports of others.

Cruising cars had found no one near the vicinity of the house. Airplanes had lost out through poor visibility. The one that had landed had risen again to lead the others back to Croydon. Darkness had covered The Harvester's flight.

"We have facts," decided Lewsham, "but they are not sufficient. Our only hope is this: The Harvester may have some hideaway close by. It is our task to find it."

"I agree, chief," put in Delka. "It is likely that swift work was done last night, when The Harvester supplanted Craybaw. Crooks must have been close. What is more; those gardeners came from somewhere near at hand."

Upon sudden impulse, Delka went to the desk drawer. Yanking it open, he found crumpled papers. With a chuckle, he spread them upon the desk. Here were the notations that he had seen that morning.

"The Harvester wrote this!" exclaimed Delka. "Look! It's like a schedule. What's this? Twin Trees, two and one half; cottage, one."

Looking about, Delka spied Hervey. The house man had been loosened from bondage in the kitchen. Delka showed him the notes. Hervey's eyes lighted.

"Twin Trees is a lane!" he exclaimed. "Two and one half miles from here. Let me see—the lane— yes, it is nearly a mile in length, with a cottage at the end of it."

"Take us there," ordered Lewsham. "At once."

Leaving a few men at the house, the squads set out.

AS they passed along the road that led toward Hayward's Heath, keen eyes spied the motor cars.

The Shadow was counting the vehicles. He knew which must be the last, for he calculated that one car would be left at Craybaw's.

The final car slowed for a turn. The Shadow gained the rear bumper. He rode along until the car had passed midway along the Twin Trees Lane. There The Shadow dropped away. Soon the automobile stopped.

Lewsham was spreading his men about, their object to surround the cottage. When the men deployed, The Shadow moved forward. He had an objective which he knew the others would skirt— the glade where he had met the dogs that morning.

By taking a direct course, The Shadow was first to reach his vantage point. He waited under cover of the trees. He was listening for the hounds, ready to draw them should they begin to bark. Near to the cottage, he saw one of the dogs. The Shadow approached.

Luck spoiled the game. From somewhere in back of the cottage came a muffled grunt. One member of the closing cordon had stumbled into a ditch. The hounds began to bark. Quickly, The Shadow issued a low, eerie whistle. The dogs stood still; then moved toward the glade.

The Shadow had curbed the hounds; but they had given the alarm. Searchlights gleamed suddenly from windows of the cottage. The glares revealed the officers from London, amplified by local constables. Shouts from within the cottage; men sprang out into the darkness.

Under the searchlights, these defenders were in darkness. They began an unexpected fire from the edges of the front porch. The Shadow heard the starting clatter of a submachine gun. He saw the flashes as bullets streamed from the muzzle.

The Shadow's automatics roared from the glade, while the hounds quivered at his feet. An oath came from the porch as the machine-gun fire ceased. Then a groan. Men deserted a crippled companion and dashed beyond the cottage.

A motor roared. A swift sedan sped suddenly out from an old driveway, to run the gauntlet of the lane. This time, the Scotland Yard men were behind stone walls. The Shadow's timely fire had saved them from one machine-gun barrage. They expected another; it blasted uselessly from the sedan.

Again, The Shadow's guns were speaking; but trees forestalled his efforts. Like grim sentinels in the darkness, they received the bullets intended for the sedan. The car sped onward, followed by shots along the line. Scotland Yard men were starting a pursuit.

Up the lane, the other cars formed a partial barricade, which fleeing crooks avoided by a sharp half circuit. The men in the cars had dropped away for shelter. Their revolver shots spurred the sedan to swifter flight. Leaping back to their cars, officers wheeled the machines and began chase.

The Shadow's automatics roared from the glade, while the hounds quivered at his feet.

Their swift cars contained machine guns also. Chances were that they would overtake their prey. Roaring through the night, pursued and pursuers whizzed in the direction of Hayward's Heath.

Meanwhile, those about the cottage invaded. The Shadow watched from darkness; for the glitter of the searchlights was lost when it struck the thick-treed glade. He could see lights within the cottage. Then came exclamations. Through the window of an upstairs room, The Shadow saw men raising a figure that was bound and gagged. Cloth was ripped from the rescued prisoner's face. The light showed the pale face of Justin Craybaw.

Rescuers helped the prisoner down to the porch. Others appeared, guiding another released captive. This was Cuthbert. The chauffeur had been found in a room on the opposite side of the house. The Shadow watched the Scotland Yard men take the prisoners toward the lane. One car had remained there.

Officers remained at the cottage. The Shadow spoke to the dogs and the hounds roamed gingerly forward to make friends with the newcomers. The Shadow skirted back through the woods. He heard the last car rumble toward the main road. He circled to the lane.

WHEN he neared the outlet, The Shadow paused. A local constable had remained on duty, beneath a light that marked the main road. While The Shadow waited, the sound of approaching cars was audible. One machine rolled up and stopped. It was a Scotland Yard car.

"Back to the house," stated the constable. "That's where Chief Lewsham has gone. The cottage is in the hands of the law. The prisoners are freed."

"They found Justin Craybaw?" The eager voice from the car was Tunning's.

"They did that," replied the constable. "And they have rescued his man Cuthbert, the chauffeur."

"We have news, too," stated Tunning. "Dawsett's car bagged the one that sped away. Fairly cluttered it with bullets."

"And the men in it?"

"We found two of them. The sedan was stalled at Hayward's Heath. But neither was The Harvester."

"What became of him, inspector?"

"We don't know," growled Tunning. "He could have dropped off somewhere, to gain a car of his own. Or he might have boarded a train somewhere in or around Hayward's Heath."

"Deuce take the rogue!"

"The blighter is incredible. Sergeant Dawsett reported up to London after he found the dead men in their car. But The Harvester has slipped us."

A second car had come up behind Tunning's. It was Dawsett's. The two vehicles moved onward. The constable began a steady pace, shaking his head. Stopping, he stared speculatively in the direction of Hayward's Heath.

He was thinking of The Harvester, and his opinion was that Scotland Yard had failed when the crook had managed to slip away after the chase. The constable's decision was that the job should have been left to the local forces that patrolled and knew the vicinity of Tunbridge Wells.

Yet while he mused, the constable was revealing his own inefficiency. Directly behind him passed a black-clad shape that he would have seen had he thought to turn about. Yet the constable's inefficiency was excusable. This passer was a personage far more incredible than the elusive Harvester.

The Shadow was gaining the main road. He passed from the lamp glare before the constable wheeled. He was gone when the man resumed his pacing. The Shadow's destination was the one that the cars had chosen. He was going back to Justin Craybaw's.

ALL patrol had ceased about the grounds when The Shadow arrived there. Nearing the trees, The Shadow moved beneath them and risked a flashlight glimmer in an upward direction. He spied his knapsack, one strap dangling. Reaching for a bough, he drew himself upward and regained the knapsack.

Stowing away cloak and hat, The Shadow rested the knapsack upon his arm. He retrieved his walking stick from beneath the steps to the conservatory. His shoes crunched the gravel as he walked toward the front door of the house.

Lights were burning above the doorway. The Shadow was challenged when he came within their focus. A Scotland Yard man demanded to know the visitor's identity. The Shadow looked curiously about, then smiled in the characteristic manner of Lamont Cranston.

"I presume that Chief Lewsham is here?" he questioned. "And Inspector Delka?"

"They are," returned the man at the door. "Do you have business with them?"

"I should like to speak with them. My name is Lamont Cranston."

The guardian had evidently heard mention of the name, for his eyes opened. He nodded and motioned toward the door.

"You may go in, sir," he declared, "and announce yourself. I believe that they were about to begin a search for you."

The Shadow entered. As he crossed the threshold, he still wore his quiet smile. He had reason to believe that his entry would cause surprise—a conjecture that was to prove correct, particularly because of his costume.

But that surprise, The Shadow knew, would prove mild when compared to one that might occur before he left. For The Shadow had reason to believe that The Harvester, himself, would be revealed within these walls before the evening had ended.

Boldness was The Harvester's forte. In keeping with his game, he would have reason to return to a scene of final crime. That, The Shadow knew.

CHAPTER XVIII
CRIME REVIEWED

EIGHT o'clock was chiming when The Shadow entered Justin Craybaw's study, to find a group assembled. Lewsham and Delka stared in surprise when they recognized the tall form of Lamont Cranston. A conference was interrupted while Lewsham put a question.

"Where have you been, Cranston?" he asked. "We were alarmed about your safety. A friend of yours informed us that you had gone from London."

"Was it Vincent?" inquired The Shadow, with a slight smile.

"Yes," nodded Lewsham. "He had an appointment with you."

"Not until this evening," explained The Shadow. "Since I did not expect my friend Vincent during the day, I decided to leave foggy London and seek the countryside. I chose this terrain because I wanted to see what it was like by day.

"Unfortunately, I hiked further than I had expected. Coming back toward Tunbridge Wells, I decided to stop here and see if Craybaw chanced to be at home. Being late, I should like to telephone to London.

"I see that I have intruded upon a conference. If I might be allowed to make a telephone call, I shall then take the next train up to London—"

"Not at all!" interjected Lewsham. "We shall need you here, Mr. Cranston. Serious events have taken place today. Join us and listen. Your own testimony may be required."

The Shadow seated himself. His face showed a puzzled expression, a well-feigned registration. Lewsham turned to Craybaw, who was seated in an easy chair. Lewsham's nod indicated that he wished Craybaw to proceed with a story that he had begun.

"It happened near the entrance to Twin Trees Lane," explained Craybaw. His tone was wearied. "When Cuthbert slowed for the crossing, men leaped upon the running board of the coupé. They thrust revolvers against our faces. They ordered Cuthbert to reverse the car; then drive down the lane.

"We reached the cottage. We were bound and gagged; then separated. I saw Cuthbert dragged to one room. I was taken to another. We remained as prisoners, without chance for communication. Our captors were rough fellows; but they treated us with some consideration. At least, I can so testify. Meals were brought to me during my imprisonment."

When Craybaw paused, Lewsham looked toward Cuthbert. The frank-faced chauffeur was seated on the other side of the room.

"Your story," ordered Lewsham.

"Three men captured us," corroborated Cuthbert. "I saw them bind Mr. Craybaw while others were doing the same with me. Then they dragged us apart. I was well treated. They saw to my wants. With one exception." The chauffeur stroked a stubbly growth upon his chin. "I was not allowed to shave."

"What of The Harvester?" queried Lewsham. "Did you meet him?"

Cuthbert shook his head.

"I heard the coupé drive away soon after I was bound and gagged," said the chauffeur. "I suspected that something must be up. That was all, however."

"Did you encounter him, Craybaw?"

"Not precisely," stated Craybaw. "After I was bound, I was placed in a room that was quite dark. Men entered and focused a lantern upon my face. I heard whisperings; I expected to be questioned."

"But you were not?"

"No. The men with the light went away."

LEWSHAM pondered. At last, he spoke.

"The Harvester was overconfident," he decided. "He slipped when he played his game here. He would have done better to question you, Craybaw; but it is apparent that he must have known a good deal about your affairs.

"I fancy that he knew he would have to use his wits, no matter how well prepared he chanced to be. His feigning of illness was a clever stroke. It was the one point that lulled our doubts as to his identity.

"Various persons knew that you were entertaining guests last night. The Harvester could easily have ascertained facts. It seems apparent, however, that he must have been quite close to the game all along. That may enable us to trap the rogue."

Methodically, Lewsham began to calculate the time element.

"It was approximately half past five when The Harvester was last seen here," he asserted. "Dusk was settling. It was dark by half past six. That was when our search of the grounds was completed; and also when Delka found the clue that led us to the cottage.

"At seven o'clock, we attacked. A motorcar ran the gauntlet and was found later at Hayward's Heath. There is a possibility that The Harvester was in that motorcar; that he escaped alive. If so, he has had but an hour's leeway. But I doubt emphatically that The Harvester was aboard that car."

"By George!" exclaimed Sir Ernest Jennup. "You have struck it! Perhaps the rotter did not return to the cottage at all!"

"Precisely," nodded Lewsham. "Why should he have necessarily gone there? His men were stationed on guard, ready to clear away when they received the order. We anticipated their move. There is likelihood that The Harvester had chosen his own course, meanwhile."

"Which would mean that he had two hours!" exclaimed Delka. "Longer than that, chief! He might have cut across to High Brooms station; or he may have had a motor of his own, somewhere."

"The Harvester could have been in London long ago," stated Lewsham, moodily. "He has had ample opportunity, whatever means of conveyance he may have chosen. The more that I consider it, the more I doubt that he would have risked carrying his spoils to the cottage.

"Tell me one thing, Craybaw"—he turned to the rescued prisoner—"something most important. Did you hear any sounds about the cottage that would have indicated The Harvester's return?"

"Men were moving about," recalled Craybaw. "I heard their muffled conversation. There was nothing, however, to indicate that an outsider had arrived."

"And you, Cuthbert?" quizzed Lewsham.

"I noticed no unusual sounds," responded the chauffeur. "Nothing more than Mr. Craybaw has mentioned."

"The Harvester could have taken to the cottage," put in Delka. "But he could have left from there prior to our arrival. That would have been good strategy; for he could have notified his men to dash away on a false trail."

"Quite possible," agreed Lewsham. "That may explain why they were so prompt to run the gauntlet. Zounds! I wish that we had not annihilated those beggars!"

"None would have talked if captured," reminded Delka. "The Harvester is too cagey to permit such fellows to learn his full plans. I would guess that The Harvester made for the cottage to begin with."

"And he would have reached it before six o'clock," assured Lewsham. "Through prompt departure from there, he would still have had the two-hour start which I have conceded him."

Gloomy silence pervaded the group. Justin Craybaw looked toward Sir Ernest Jennup.

"I suffered agony, Sir Ernest," declared Craybaw, choking. "I realized what lay at stake, once I had been captured. I realized the loss that your banking house might suffer through the failure of Rudlow, Limited. My own loss—of position and repute—that is but little compared to your plight."

"You are not to blame," stated Sir Ernest. "You bore up stoutly, Craybaw. Why should I cast blame upon you? The Harvester impersonated me, only recently. Jove! The scoundrel has the quality of being everywhere—anywhere—"

A sharp rap at the door. It was Tunning, announcing arrivals. Parkins and Wilton had come from Rudlow's. They were bringing persons with them. Lewsham ordered prompt admittance.

THE first to enter were Blessingwood and Harry Vincent. The comptroller hurried over to confer with Craybaw and Sir Ernest.

The Shadow rose in leisurely fashion to shake hands with Harry, who showed a glad expression at meeting his supposed friend, Cranston.

Then came the Rajah of Delapore, his face emotionless. Behind him, with Parkins and Wilton, was another man: Dawson Canonby. The jeweler's expression was strained. Chief Constable Lewsham noticed the fact at once.

"What is this?" he exclaimed. "Why have you brought these men out here, Parkins? How does Canonby happen to be with you?"

"An idea struck me, chief," explained Parkins. "You had ordered a complete roundup; but you had left Canonby out of it. I called the Yard and ordered headquarters to fetch him to Rudlow's."

"Which was done," added Wilton, "and Mr. Canonby desires speech with you, chief. He insisted that he could talk only if all of us came here to Tunbridge Wells."

"That is what I declared," expressed Canonby, in a shaky tone. "I said that we must be brought here, under guard. I made that statement, once I had heard of the robbery."

"You have information for us?" demanded Lewsham. "Come! Speak quickly, man!"

Puzzled looks were everywhere; but neither The Shadow nor Harry Vincent shared them. Nor did the rajah of Delapore. He was standing by the desk, his lips curled in a contemptuous smile. He was watching Canonby. Again, the jeweler trembled. Then, finding his tongue, he pointed an accusing finger straight at the rajah.

"There he stands!" exclaimed Canonby. "He is the thief you seek! He is The Harvester! Yes, The Harvester—this man who calls himself the Rajah of Delapore!"

CHAPTER XIX
THE RAJAH PASSES

COMPLETE hush followed Canonby's accusation. Men stared rigidly when they heard the jeweler's words. Yet listeners were impressed; for they knew The Harvester's incredible ability to change his guise at will. It was not inconceivable that the Rajah of Delapore should be the culprit.

Sidney Lewsham sat motionless. It was Sir Ernest Jennup who found voice. He looked from Canonby to the rajah; then back to the jeweler. In firm tone, Sir Ernest gave an order:

"State your reasons, Canonby, for this accusation."

"I shall," nodded Canonby. "When his excellency arrived in London, he came to me at my shop in Old Bond Street. He was accompanied by his secretary, a man named Ranworthy.

"The rajah wished me to be party to a curious transaction. He showed me false jewels, which were of fine appearance, though manufactured of paste. He declared that he intended to arrange their sale.

"I was puzzled, until he explained his purpose. He produced a large sum in Bank of England notes—a quarter million, sterling—and requested that I keep the money in my vault. He declared that on a specified date, he would request me to appear with the money. At that time, my duty would be to buy the false gems from him."

"Was that time today?" put in Lewsham.

"It proved to be," stated Canonby. "Last night, his excellency called me by telephone and told me to bring the money to the offices of Rudlow, Limited. Today, I did so. Here are the false gems, which I purchased."

Canonby tugged two bags from his coat pockets. Opening them, he flung a glimmering clatter of false stones that rolled about the blotting pad on Craybaw's desk.

"Just paste!" denounced Canonby. "Worthless glass—"

"One moment," interposed Sir Ernest severely. "Tell me, Canonby, why you made yourself party to this arrangement which you now denounce?"

"I was paid for it," replied the jeweler. "Two thousand pounds was the amount that I received for storing the rajah's money in my vault."

"A trifling amount," remarked Lewsham, "when one considers that you risked the keeping of a quarter million."

The Shadow saw Canonby blanch.

For a moment, the fellow faltered; then his color returned.

"I was duped," he stated. "The rajah asked for no receipt. He affirmed that he would rely upon my integrity. I am honest, gentlemen. I can prove that I had those funds in my possession; that I preserved them faithfully. That should be evidence that I was no party to any vile scheme."

Listeners seemed convinced. Lewsham turned promptly to the Rajah of Delapore.

"You had some purpose in placing these funds with Canonby," expressed Lewsham. "We await a sufficient explanation, your excellency."

"I SHALL supply one gladly," purred the rajah, with a pleased smile. "Had Canonby spoken of this at Rudlow's, I could have settled the question before our arrival. I am not The Harvester. It is folly for anyone to believe so.

"I am actually the Rajah of Delapore. I came from India with gems which I valued at a quarter million, sterling. When I arrived in Paris, I transacted with the jewelry firm of *Fréres Francine.* They purchased my gems. Here are the receipts."

Calmly, the rajah drew forth folded documents and placed them in the hands of Lewsham.

"The purchasers specified, however," resumed his excellency, "that I should not reveal the fact that I had sold my jewels on the Continent. They were perturbed by thoughts of criminal attempts in Paris. They provided me with imitation gems, which I brought to London.

"I kept the false stones hidden, guarding them as carefully as if they had been genuine. I went to Dawson Canonby and arranged the sale of the false gems. He is right when he states that I trusted his integrity. He was recommended to me by *Fréres Francine.*"

"A firm with which I deal!" exclaimed Canonby. "You should have told me of the arrangement, your excellency."

"I would have done so," assured the rajah, "had it proven necessary. However, since you accepted my proposition without question, I decided not to state the circumstances. I knew that I would not place you in jeopardy. Jewel thieves have avoided England recently; moreover, they would gain nothing if they sought to wrest these false stones from your possession.

"The payment of two thousand pounds to you, Canonby, was shared equally by *Fréres Francine* and myself. Peruse the contract, Chief Lewsham. You will learn all the particulars, attested by Paris notaries."

Sir Ernest was on his feet. He was not convinced by the rajah's smooth tone.

"You say that you are not The Harvester!" stormed Sir Ernest. "What evidence do we have to that fact?"

"What more do you require?" laughed the rajah. "I understand that you encountered The Harvester here. That took place while I was still in London."

"He abducted Justin Craybaw!" accused Sir Ernest, indicating the managing director. "And after the abduction, he took Craybaw's place. The Harvester could also have kidnapped the Rajah of Delapore."

"At what hour?" inquired the rajah.

"At any time after six o'clock," decided Sir Ernest. "By such a process, he could have assumed a new identity when—"

"Not in my case," interrupted the rajah. "It was considerably before six that I arrived at the office of Rudlow, Limited. I have been there since, until I was brought here. I have not left the sight of the Scotland Yard men who had me in their keeping."

Tunning and Wilton nodded their agreement. Sir Ernest subsided. The Shadow, watching the rajah, awaited new arguments. They came.

"WHY should I have placed a quarter million with Canonby?" he queried. "It would not have been necessary for a criminal to do so. Nor would the act have given me status. On the contrary—Canonby himself bears witness—my action has caused me embarrassment.

"If The Harvester, that rogue, had possessed a quarter million, he would not have placed it in the keeping of a jeweler with orders to keep the matter secret. Instead, he would have used the money to establish himself.

"The Harvester may be wealthy. If so, he is keeping it a secret. He may have ability at disguise; but he would not impersonate myself. Nor could I have impersonated Justin Craybaw. Look at my skin. It is dark—not dyed. How could I have passed myself for an Englishman?

"You seek The Harvester, the man who sent Captain Darryat to me. I believe that I can name him; for I have been wary of recent circumstances. Last night, in fact, an attempted robbery took place at my abode. That made me think more deeply; for I believed that The Harvester might be in back of it.

"The Harvester, gentlemen, is a man close to this game. One who left London yesterday; who has hoaxed us with false pretensions. I can name him; it is your task to capture him. The Harvester is Lionel Selbrock!"

Almost with the rajah's words, the door swung open. Turning, those in the room saw two men upon the threshold. One was a member of the C.I.D.—Burleigh—while the other was the very person whom the rajah had just denounced. Lionel Selbrock, pale and staring, had arrived to hear the accusation.

He was Burleigh's prisoner; for the Scotland Yard man was holding a revolver muzzle against Selbrock's back. No more dramatic entry could have been arranged. The very circumstances were an echo of the rajah's words; they stood as proof of Selbrock's guilt.

To Harry Vincent, the answer was plain. Selbrock was The Harvester. Yet when Harry glanced toward The Shadow, something made him wonder. There was a smile upon the lips of Lamont Cranston; one that meant to wait for further judgment.

Did The Shadow believe Selbrock innocent? Or was his cryptic smile an indication that he expected the man to confess guilt? Harry could not answer. Yet he was sure that The Shadow must know all.

CHAPTER XX
TWO PLEAS ARE HEARD

"WHERE did you trap Selbrock?"

The query came from Sidney Lewsham. It was addressed to Burleigh as the C.I.D. man pushed the prisoner to a convenient chair. Burleigh answered, watching Selbrock as he spoke.

"At the Addingham," he said. "How he slipped in there, I can't guess. We were watching every terminus."

Selbrock heard the statement. He leaned back and delivered a guffaw. He followed by looking straight toward Lewsham.

"Don't let this chap excuse his own inefficiency," he said, with a gesture toward Burleigh. "We have debated that point all the way out here. He swears that he had every terminus covered. He is wrong. If his men had been properly placed at Euston Station, they would have arrested me when I arrived aboard the *Royal Scot.*"

Burleigh looked troubled. Selbrock grinned.

"The *Royal Scot* drew in ahead of schedule," he remarked. "I understand that it does so quite frequently. We covered the three hundred miles from Carlisle in less than five hours and a half. We departed from Carlisle at ten minutes after twelve. We reached Euston Station at half past five."

"Is this correct, Burleigh?" demanded Lewsham. "Were your men negligent in meeting the *Royal Scot* at Euston?"

"They may have been," admitted Burleigh, in a sulky tone, "but I doubt it, sir. If this chap came from the *Royal Scot,* he must have dashed from the gate in a great hurry."

"I was aboard one of the front carriages," assured Selbrock, promptly. "That is probably why I escaped observation. But I did not rush from the gate."

"What time did Selbrock reach the Addingham?" quizzed Lewsham.

"Not until half past seven," replied Burleigh. "That was when we apprehended him."

"I was dining in the meantime," put in Selbrock. "I tell you, I have been hoaxed. Badly hoaxed! Look at this telegram that I received yesterday. Wait—Burleigh has it."

"Here it is, sir," informed Burleigh. "The slip was in Selbrock's pocket."

Lewsham received the paper. The Shadow, standing nearby, could read the message. It was signed "Dorcus" and it called for Selbrock to meet him at Abbey Town, by the earliest train possible.

"Who is Dorcus?" questioned Lewsham.

"An old schoolmate," returned Selbrock. "We were friends at Rugby. I have not seen him for years. Inquired everywhere for him. Then came this telegram, which I received yesterday. That is why I took the four o'clock afternoon express to Carlisle."

Harry Vincent looked toward The Shadow. He saw the latter's smile. Selbrock was claiming that he had taken the very train which Harry had picked from the pages of his Bradshaw.

"THREE hundred miles north to Carlisle," resumed Selbrock, "arriving there at ten-fifty. I had just time to catch the last local for Abbey Town, at ten minutes past eleven. Twelve miles to Abbey Town; I reached there at eleven thirty-eight."

"And met Dorcus?" queried Lewsham.

"No," responded Selbrock, sourly. "That was the catch to it. Dorcus was not there at Abbey Town station. Someone had spoofed me. I stood there, gawking, upon the platform of the station. The last train had gone down to Carlisle. No one was about.

"Anyone will attest my statement when I say that a provincial town becomes quiescent after nightfall. The passing of the last train is heard by no one; for all are asleep. There was I in Abbey Town, with no place to spend the night.

"My only opportunity was to walk five miles to the end of the line at Silloth, where I knew that I should find a hotel; for Silloth is close to the shore of Solway Firth. I arrived there after midnight; so I slept amid the West Coast breezes. The hotel register at Silloth will testify to the fact that I was there."

Lewsham nodded doubtingly. Selbrock became indignant.

"I have been hoaxed, I tell you!" he exclaimed. "When I left Silloth by the morning down train, I did not reach Carlisle until half past eleven."

"You slept too late for the early train?"

"Yes. I dispatched a telegram from Carlisle. Then I took the *Royal Scot* at ten minutes past noon. It was the logical train, under the circumstances. Rudlow, Limited, must have received my telegram. I addressed it to Justin Craybaw."

"The telegram was received," admitted Lewsham, "but Craybaw was not at Rudlow's to make it public. Our question, therefore, is whether or not you actually dispatched the message from Carlisle."

"I was in Carlisle—"

"A burden of proof lies upon you."

Selbrock came to his feet, his face savage. Burleigh stood ready with revolver, in case the accused man made trouble. Selbrock stormed his challenge at Lewsham.

"Your blind stupidity is the cause of this!" he exclaimed. "If the men you sent from Scotland Yard had been on the job at Euston, they would have met me at half past five! That would have supported my alibi! Burleigh has admitted negligence. The burden lies upon you. Prove that I was in Carlisle!

"Send to the town of Silloth. Find my signature upon the hotel register there. Examine those ticket stubs that Burleigh took from my pocket along with that spoofing telegram. They prove that I traveled up to London, aboard the *Royal Scot*.

"Call the Wildersham Cafe, in Piccadilly. Ask for Lester, the headwaiter. He will say that I arrived there at six; that I talked with him while I dined."

IT was the Rajah of Delapore who answered Selbrock's outburst. He had passed the accusation along to the man from Mesopotamia; hence the Hindu potentate took it upon himself to attack Selbrock's rebuttal.

"Lies, all these," denounced the rajah, in his well-toned voice. "The Harvester has tools everywhere. It is no use, Selbrock. Someone was in Silloth, to inscribe your name there. That same person must have sent the telegram from Carlisle. Lester, the headwaiter at the Wildersham, may be in your pay. It would be wise to apprehend him also. *You* are The Harvester, Selbrock. Your game was to gain my quarter million—"

"Absurd!" interposed Selbrock. "My Mesopotamian oil options were worth two hundred thousand pounds alone. Why, when I had such a fortune coming to me, would I have risked a career of crime?"

"The options may be false—"

"False? They satisfied you."

The rajah had no reply. Lewsham introduced a nod.

"Quite correct," he said. "The oil options have been thoroughly investigated."

"They have," added Justin Craybaw, from behind the desk. "Yes, the options are quite in order. As a matter of fact"—he paused, seriously— "Rudlow, Limited, is still responsible to you for purchase. Unless we declare a bankruptcy"—he turned to Sir Ernest—"we shall have to buy those oil holdings at the price established."

"So that is why you have come here!" stormed Sir Ernest, convinced that Selbrock must be The Harvester. "Your bold game is to mulct us of another fortune!"

"You are wrong," rejoined Selbrock. "Unless the Rajah of Delapore has committed himself to purchase, I shall reclaim the oil options."

"Then we owe the rajah a quarter million!" exclaimed Blessingwood. "I signed his receipt! He is the one who can demand money. *He* must be The Harvester!"

Selbrock grinned as he gazed toward the rajah. Luck had turned the tide. The burden was tossed back upon the man who had passed it. That, however, produced a lull, for the rajah had already cleared himself. Sidney Lewsham called for silence.

"One thing is certain," decided the chief constable. "Your trip to Carlisle, Selbrock—or your claim to such a journey—is part of The Harvester's scheme. If you are The Harvester, the situation fits. A confederate could have sent you the telegram yesterday. He could have sent that wire this noon, the one which The Harvester received when pretending himself to be Justin Craybaw.

"Assuming you to be The Harvester, Selbrock, I can see purpose in both telegrams. Assuming that you are not The Harvester, I can see no purpose. If anyone can cause me to change this position, I shall harken gladly. Otherwise, I shall arrest you as The Harvester."

"And let the crook make good his escape?" demanded Selbrock. "One more mistake on your part—"

He paused, as a voice intervened. The Shadow had stepped forward. He was picking up the telegram, studying it in Cranston's leisurely fashion.

Lewsham produced the other wire. Harry Vincent watched. Apparently, The Shadow had some defense for Selbrock.

"THE HARVESTER'S scheme, yes," assured The Shadow. "But one that he would never employ as an alibi. A freak trip to Carlisle; then to Abbey Town, dependent upon a telegram from a friend that cannot be produced. It is too flimsy, Chief Lewsham.

"Let us assume that Selbrock is *not* The Harvester. Why, then, did the master criminal induce him to leave London? Particularly with this telegram, which close inspection shows to be doubtful?" The Shadow passed both messages to Lewsham, who compared them. Each was marked as being from Carlisle; but the one which Selbrock had received did not quite match the one that he swore he had dispatched today. There were minor differences. Lewsham's eyes narrowed as he studied them.

"I can answer the questions," assured The Shadow, quietly. "The Harvester realized that he could not incriminate Selbrock. Hence such a step was not his initial purpose. He merely desired to remove Selbrock from London; and with good reason.

"The Harvester knew that funds were coming to the offices of Rudlow, Limited—funds that Selbrock could claim by merely signing over the options. The Harvester wanted to hold those funds until the rajah arrived with another supply of wealth. Then he would have access—as Craybaw—to both.

"There was one step necessary; namely, to send Lionel Selbrock so far from London that he could not return until late today. The very schedule that Selbrock had given us is proof that such was the purpose. The Harvester arranged that Selbrock would not reach London until nearly five o'clock—too late to reach the offices of Rudlow, Limited, before the closing hour. Too late, in any event, to arrive before the double wealth was stolen."

The logic of The Shadow's quiet tone was impressive. Listeners nodded in spite of themselves. The Shadow added a final clincher.

"Had The Harvester felt that he could throw the blame on Selbrock," he added, "he would have hoaxed him further—to some place in Scotland. But The Harvester knew that Selbrock could stand the test. To accuse Selbrock is a folly, which is merely lengthening the short space of time which still belongs to The Harvester.

"For I assure you that the master criminal can be unmasked. Once his name is known, with his true identity, he can be taken. Cold logic should make his name apparent—"

"Jed Ranworthy!"

THE exclamation came from Justin Craybaw, who rose from behind his desk. Sir Ernest Jennup also sprang to his feet. Sidney Lewsham gave a quick nod. He turned to the Rajah of Delapore.

"Your secretary!" exclaimed Lewsham. "We are seeking him, your excellency. Can you help us?"

"He said that he was going to Yarmouth," replied the rajah, slowly. "He was to return tonight. If only I had known; if I had but suspected—"

Someone was rapping at the door. Delka opened it. An outside man was there, with new information:

"Layton is here. He has bagged the bounder whom he was set to trap."

"Jed Ranworthy?"

"Yes. Layton is bringing him into the house."

Footsteps followed the announcement. All gazed expectantly toward the door. They were not disappointed. Layton and another Scotland Yard man arrived, a prisoner between them. The man whom they had captured was nervous in his manner, blinking his dark, beady eyes.

There was no doubt as to the prisoner's identity. That long-nosed, sallow face beneath the sleek black hair, characterized a countenance that was quickly recognized. Hard upon The Shadow's statement; immediately after Justin Craybaw's declaration of Ranworthy's name, the secretary had been brought before this board of inquisition.

Again, Harry Vincent discerned a firm smile upon the masklike lips that were The Shadow's. This time, Harry was convinced that the game had found its end. The Harvester was here within this very room. Under the master quizzing of The Shadow, The Harvester's machinations would be revealed.

But Harry Vincent did not realize the strange, crosscurrent of events that was to ensue before the game was finally completed. Only The Shadow knew!

CHAPTER XXI
THE SHADOW'S TURN

JED RANWORTHY stood before the tribunal which had sought his presence. Flanked by Scotland Yard men, he heard the outpour of accusations. Nervously, the sallow secretary twitched, while he waited for a chance to speak. When it came, Ranworthy could not have claimed ignorance of the charges against him. Everything had been said.

"You were close to the Rajah of Delapore." The final summary came from Lewsham. "You could have been the one who brought Captain Darryat to the rajah's attention. Through Darryat, you met Selbrock, although your knowledge of his options may have begun previously.

"You came in contact with Justin Craybaw and had every opportunity to examine his affairs. You met Sir Ernest Jennup, which would have enabled you to impersonate him that night at the Moravia. This business is your doing, Ranworthy. Yet we shall allow you opportunity to speak."

Ranworthy licked his manila-hued lips.

"I admit my position," he declared, in a voice which quivered despite his attempt at smoothness. "Nevertheless, I am not The Harvester. Someone is plotting to destroy me. My case is like Selbrock's."

"No similarity whatever," interjected Lewsham. "Selbrock was duped. You were not."

Lewsham looked toward The Shadow as he spoke, as if seeking corroboration from a keen brain like Cranston's. The Shadow made no statement. He was waiting to hear Ranworthy out.

"Quite like Selbrock's," insisted Ranworthy. "I, too, was duped—by a telephone call which I thought was from Yarmouth. I believed that I was summoned there to visit a sick relative. I made inquiry at Yarmouth last night, with no success.

"Today, I remained there; and did not give up my inquiry until this afternoon. Then I returned to London. When I reached his excellency's apartment, I was arrested."

Ranworthy turned to the rajah.

"I had intended to discuss this matter with your excellency," he declared, "because it involved factors that might indicate some plot against yourself. Particularly because I read of an attempted robbery at your hotel. My assumption was that I was drawn away to make the task an easier one."

"You cannot avoid the issue, Ranworthy," asserted Lewsham, annoyed by the secretary's attempt to shift the subject. "Selbrock's story carries logic. Yours does not. You held a key position. You could well be The Harvester."

"You take me for a criminal?" scowled Ranworthy. "Ask his excellency if that is a just opinion. Had I chosen to become a thief, I could long ago have purloined the jewels which his excellency possessed."

Lewsham pointed to the baubles that Canonby had thrown upon the desk.

"These stones are false," declared the chief constable. "They were not worth stealing; and you knew that fact, Ranworthy."

"I refer to the real gems," persisted the secretary. "The ones that his excellency sold to *Frères Francine,* in Paris. I had access to those valuables.

I could have stolen them while on the Continent. My escape would have been simpler in France. But I am not a criminal."

"You restrained yourself," put in Justin Craybaw, "because you saw an opportunity for double gain. You wanted the money that should have gone to Selbrock."

"THAT is preposterous!" argued Ranworthy. His tone had steadied; his logic was shrewd. "I knew nothing of Selbrock's options until after the Rajah of Delapore and I had arrived in London."

"That is true," recalled the rajah, suddenly. "We arrived in London in advance of Selbrock. There was no way in which Ranworthy could have produced those arrangements which involved Rudlow, Limited.

"Chief Lewsham, I must appeal to you in behalf of an innocent man. My trust in Ranworthy has not been destroyed. Were he The Harvester, he would not have passed the opportunity to steal my gems in Paris.

"True, I intended to convert the jewels into cash. I did that, however, in Paris—not in London; and when we brought the money with us to England, it remained in Ranworthy's keeping. That would have been his final opportunity for criminal gain.

"My original intention was to invest the money in securities. This matter of the oil options, with the contracts which called for cash, was something in which Ranworthy had no hand. Ranworthy is honest; moreover, he is innocent."

Ranworthy was encouraged by the rajah's plea. Quickly, the secretary strengthened his position.

"Were I The Harvester," he declared shrewdly, "and had I posed as Justin Craybaw, I would never have played the fool by returning to a trap. What would I have had to lose by flight? Nothing. Absolutely nothing!

"Suppose my story of a trip to Yarmouth had been a pretext. Suppose that I had gained nearly half a million, here at Tunbridge Wells. I would have let the search go on, in London and in Yarmouth. I would no longer have had need to serve as secretary to his excellency, the Rajah of Delapore.

"That makes my case stronger than Selbrock's. He might have had reason to return to London; to face it out brazenly. Not I, however. If I am The Harvester, I am also a fool. Since The Harvester is no fool, I cannot be The Harvester."

Ranworthy had drawn himself upward, to launch his statement with the skill of an orator. Harry Vincent saw The Shadow smile in satisfaction. Apparently, he had been ready to take Ranworthy's part, but had found the task unnecessary.

Huge bewilderment gripped Harry Vincent. This sequel was contrary to his expectations. The rajah; then Selbrock; finally Ranworthy—all had presented clearing arguments. Was the accusation to be thrust back upon Lionel Selbrock?

BEFORE Harry could decide what was due to follow, the unexpected came. Ranworthy was speaking again. Confident that he had proven his own innocence, the secretary was paving the way to a new consideration. One that came swiftly.

"What is The Harvester?" cried Ranworthy. "I shall tell you. He is an opportunist! A criminal who has masked himself as a man of importance. One who has had access to large dealings. One who has covered himself and trusted to confusion among those who seek him.

"How and when he learned of the transactions at Rudlow, Limited, I cannot state. I only know that he must be a man who has little to lose and much to gain. One who would remain close by only if it should be essential to his purpose."

"Which it might well be," added The Shadow, during the sudden pause that followed Ranworthy's words. "You have spoken well, Ranworthy. You have stated facts which I, myself, would have given, had you not done so. With this addition: The Harvester not only would remain close by. He has actually done so."

The steady tones of The Shadow's speech brought final impressiveness to the scene in Craybaw's study. His pause came as a challenge—as if he believed that the logic of his words would bring a prompt opinion from some other quarter.

Tense, breathless moments. Then the bombshell dropped. Justin Craybaw, his face regaining its ruddy color, was the man who rose and lifted an accusing finger.

"The Harvester is here!" pronounced Craybaw, solemnly. "Bold to the end, cunning as a fox, he has seen trapped men clear themselves from false blame. Ensnared at last, he has played his final card; his last stroke of daring by which he hopes to save himself.

"He has appeared in many disguises; but always has he failed to fully cover the measures that he has taken. At last I know him; he imprisoned Cuthbert and myself, after our abduction. I shall point him out; for he is here—the only man who could be The Harvester. Stand ready to seize him; for he may attempt flight."

All eyes were upon Craybaw's uplifted hand. It descended, leveling firmly as it pointed. Like the others, Harry Vincent turned to eye the direction of the accusing forefinger. A startled gasp came from Harry's lips.

Justin Craybaw's finger had stopped. His eyes were glaring straight toward the object of his accusation, squarely toward a silent personage who met his gaze unflinching. Those who followed the direction saw the immobile features of Lamont Cranston.

Only Harry Vincent realized the astounding circumstance. The person whom Craybaw termed The Harvester was The Shadow!

CHAPTER XXII
THE FINAL VERDICT

HARRY VINCENT'S brain was drumming. Grim doubt had seized him at this moment. Through his mind was passing a whirl of confusion that produced ill thoughts. No matter what the outcome, he saw trouble.

It was possible that The Shadow had met with evil; that The Harvester had donned the role of Lamont Cranston.

Yet that seemed incredible. Harry felt sure that such circumstance could not exist.

This was The Shadow, this visitor who wore the guise of Cranston. That fact, however, made the situation even more alarming to Harry. He knew The Shadow's ways. To cope with such crooks as The Harvester, The Shadow, too, was forced to bury his identity.

To prove that he was not The Harvester would be a task. For The Shadow—as Harry well knew—had veiled his own whereabouts during the past night and day. Others had come through with alibis. The Shadow could not.

To Harry's ears came fateful words. Justin Craybaw, looming above the desk, was pouring forth words that bespoke a righteous indignation. Past accusations forgotten, the managing director of Rudlow's was summing a new theory that made all others fade.

"You, Cranston, are the one who entered unforeseen," denounced Craybaw. "It was at your apartment that Captain Darryat was slain. Some tool of yours masqueraded as Sir Ernest, to add strength to your claims. But you were The Harvester!

"You disposed of Darryat, whom you no longer needed, for he had blundered and made the game unsafe. As a man who had been threatened, you took up the work yourself. You gained close contact with everyone concerned."

"Right!" exclaimed Sidney Lewsham. Then, turning about: "Remember, Delka, how Cranston went with you to visit Selbrock and the rajah?"

Delka was weak. He could not even nod. He had trusted Lamont Cranston, believing him to be identified with The Shadow.

"Last night you came here!" roared Craybaw. "You saw your way clear to deal a cunning stroke! You started back to London; but you did not go there. Instead, you called your henchmen. You waylaid me, with Cuthbert, upon the road to Hayward's Heath!

"You, alone, knew that I was bound there. Returning, you took my place. That masklike face of yours"—Craybaw leaned forward to eye The

Shadow closely—"is one well suited to disguise.

"And yet you failed." Craybaw's face was fixed in a grim smile. "Trapped in this terrain, you were forced to emergency measures, once you had finished your impersonation of myself. Boldly, you walked into this house, pretending that you had been on a walking trip past Tunbridge Wells.

"You are The Harvester. I defy you to deny it! You remained unseen, unheard of, from the time that you left this house. Forced to disappear that you might pass yourself as me. Tonight, bold to the finish, you have stood by in hope that others would be denounced. All have proven alibis—except yourself."

Pausing, Craybaw wagged his finger with finality.

"There," he asserted, firmly, "stands The Harvester!"

SCOTLAND YARD men closed in, covering The Shadow with their revolvers. Sidney Lewsham, inspired by one last possibility, turned to Harry Vincent.

"When did Cranston call you?" asked the chief constable.

"At midnight," replied Harry, "from Charing Cross."

"That call was from here," accused Craybaw. He turned to Sir Ernest. "At what hour did you and the others retire?"

"At half past eleven," replied Sir Ernest. "Am I not correct, Chief Lewsham?"

"You are." Lewsham turned to Delka. "Inspector, this man Cranston is The Harvester. All doubt is ended."

Delka arose. He knew that it would be his duty to remove the prisoner to Scotland Yard.

"Wait."

The Shadow spoke quietly, despite the four gun muzzles that were jabbing his ribs, beside the knapsack which he still wore. The firmness of his tone brought a pause.

"I am not The Harvester." The Shadow spoke directly to Lewsham. "I demand the right to furnish my proof to the contrary."

"Later. At headquarters."

"The proof lies here."

Lewsham looked startled. Then, with challenge, he ordered:

"Produce it."

The Shadow turned to Justin Craybaw.

"Before your abduction," he told the managing director, "we entered this study. That was prior to my departure for High Brooms, in the car with Cuthbert. Do you remember it?"

"Certainly," acknowledged Craybaw.

Sir Ernest and Lewsham nodded their corroboration.

"While we were here alone," affirmed The Shadow, seriously, "I gave you a sealed envelope. I asked you to keep it for me, Craybaw. You opened the safe"—The Shadow nodded toward the corner—"and placed the envelope somewhere therein."

"This is outrageous!" ejaculated Craybaw, to Lewsham. "This rogue gave me no envelope!"

"You said something about a filing box," recalled The Shadow. "I think that you said you would place the envelope in it. This matter is important. Surely, Craybaw, you have not forgotten the envelope?"

Craybaw spluttered. The Shadow turned to appeal to Lewsham. The chief constable, anxious to end the matter, put a demand to Craybaw.

"Have you a filing box in the safe?" he asked.

"Of course!" returned Craybaw. "Every safe of this type has filing boxes supplied with it. There are several in my safe."

"Then one must hold the envelope," assured The Shadow. "You locked the safe afterward, Craybaw."

"Let us settle this," decided Lewsham. "Open the safe, Craybaw. We shall examine the filing boxes."

CRAYBAW arose reluctantly. He went to the corner, motioned others away and turned the combination of the safe. The steel door opened. Craybaw picked out filing boxes and handed them to Lewsham. Standing in front of the opened safe, he awaited the return of the boxes. His lips showed assurance that none would contain the envelope.

The Shadow was watching Sidney Lewsham. He spoke when the chief constable was examining the papers in one filing box. Lewsham's fingers were upon an envelope.

"That is the envelope," remarked The Shadow, quietly. "Open it, Chief Lewsham. Read the message within it."

Craybaw stepped forward indignantly. He stared at The Shadow, then eyed the envelope.

"Another hoax," he snorted. "Do not be tricked, Chief Lewsham. This man Cranston—The Harvester—did not give me that envelope."

The Shadow had turned his eyes toward Delka. The Scotland Yard inspector noted a singular keenness in the gaze.

"Look in the safe," suggested The Shadow. "Examine those packages in the back corner at the bottom—"

Delka hesitated; then realizing that he was not needed to cover the prisoner, he stepped toward the safe. Justin Craybaw had caught the words; he spun about to make a protest. Lewsham, meanwhile, had ripped open the envelope and was reading the first lines of an unfolded paper.

"Away from there, Delka—"

As Craybaw cried the words, Lewsham sprang to his feet. Paper in left hand, he whipped out a revolver with his right. He covered Craybaw pointblank.

"Proceed, Delka!" snapped Lewsham. "Craybaw, stand as you are!"

Delka had gained the packages. Loose paper wrapping fell away. The investigator's eyes were popping as crisp banknotes tumbled from their stacks.

"The money!" gasped Delka. "All of it! The Harvester's swag! Here, in the safe—"

"Where Craybaw placed it," added The Shadow, "while you and Sir Ernest were in the living room."

Lewsham had barked a new command. Scotland Yard men turned their revolvers toward Craybaw. The Shadow stepped away, no longer covered. As his men closed in on Justin Craybaw, Lewsham passed the paper to Sir Ernest, who read its words aloud.

"'Justin Craybaw is The Harvester,'" read Sir Ernest. "'His game is to feign his own abduction. He and his chauffeur will be seized; but he will return. Tomorrow, he will leave his office, carrying funds that are in his keeping.

"'He will reveal himself after his return, pretending that he is an impostor. He will take to flight, carrying a bag of worthless papers. He will be found, a prisoner, to prove his innocence.'

"'His spoils, which he will trust to himself alone, will be found within this safe. The money will prove that Justin Craybaw is The Harvester.'"

SIR ERNEST dropped the paper. He stared incredulously at The Shadow.

"How did you guess this?" he queried. "Why did you not inform us of this ruse, last night?"

"It was guesswork," replied The Shadow, "inspired by my observation of Craybaw and his anxiety to set out for Hayward's Heath."

"Then you were not positive?"

"Not quite. I chose to leave the envelope for future reference. I could not condemn a man until his guilt was proven."

Justin Craybaw was glaring from the wall. He knew that The Shadow must have entered here today, to place the envelope in the safe. But his denial of The Shadow's statements would have served him naught. Instead of such procedure, Craybaw snarled his known guilt.

"Yes, I am The Harvester," he sneered. "I disguised myself as others; so why not as myself? I let my men fake an abduction, so that Cuthbert would testify that it was genuine.

"I came back. I acted oddly for your benefit." He glared from Sir Ernest to Sidney Lewsham. "I wanted you to believe afterward that I had been kidnapped on that trip to Hayward's Heath. That an impostor had come here in my stead. Then this morning—"

"You made the mistake of shaving," interposed The Shadow. "Odd that no one noticed it tonight."

Cuthbert, in the corner, rubbed his stubbly chin and blurted a surprised cry. The others realized that they had missed a perfect clue. It was proof, in itself, of Craybaw's ruse. His beard had not begun to grow during his supposed imprisonment.

"We know the rest," snapped Lewsham, angered by his own slip of previous observation. "You went to your offices and behaved oddly there. You refused to sign a receipt; as you had refused to sign letters last night, when Hervey brought them to you."

"All part of the game," smiled The Shadow, "to build up your illusion that The Harvester must be someone other than Craybaw."

"And you came out here with Delka and myself!" exclaimed Sir Ernest, facing Craybaw. "You had Hervey bring in the bag. In this study you transferred the money to the safe—"

"And put some form letters into the bag," interposed The Shadow. "One bundle of them; after that, two bundles of pink blanks; then one of green, to add the final weight—"

He stopped. Craybaw was staring in astonishment. So was Sir Ernest.

"I chanced to be close by," remarked The Shadow. "I came into the house and watched the operation from outside this door. You see, Sir Ernest, I was concerned about your money. That was why I took a walking trip today, so that I might make positive that Craybaw—if he gained the funds—would place the money here in the safe."

Eric Delka, too, was staring. He realized, at last, that Lamont Cranston was the rescuer who had come out to the conservatory. He saw also that Justin Craybaw's escape had been permitted by that rescuer.

Delka was right. Once Craybaw had deposited the money, The Shadow had preferred to let him flee. Not only had that process exposed the full game, it had also assured Cuthbert's safe release. For Craybaw needed the honest chauffeur as an alibi witness.

Moreover, it had given Scotland Yard a chance to deal with those ruffians who had occupied the cottage. Knowing the ways of Justin Craybaw, alias The Harvester, The Shadow had divined that he would sacrifice his last henchmen to the law.

MEN were moving from the study, at Sidney Lewsham's order. All were to leave except those who represented the law. Delka had bundled up the money. He was coming along with Sir Ernest Jennup. Justin Craybaw snarled a parting as he stood guarded.

"You'll find the pigskin bag in the well behind the cottage," he sneered. "Covered with a blanketing of stones, that we threw down after it."

Delka grinned.

"Cheeky chap," he remarked. "Bold to the finish."

"Quite," rejoined Sir Ernest.

Harry Vincent and others had followed; all were going to the living room. The Shadow did the same; but while the crowd was clustering about the money, he strolled through the doorway to the darkened conservatory.

From there, he saw the Rajah of Delapore, Lionel Selbrock and Jed Ranworthy, exchanging congratulations in the living room. Dawson Canonby was apologizing to the rajah. Thaddeus Blessingwood was helping Sir Ernest Jennup count the recovered banknotes.

In the darkness of the conservatory, The Shadow opened his knapsack. Laying it aside with the walking stick, he donned his cloak and slouch hat. Peering from darkness, he saw Sidney Lewsham and a squad of Scotland Yard men conducting Justin Craybaw out through the front hallway.

The Shadow waited; then stole softly forward, to the front door of the conservatory. From that vantage point, he heard voices about the cars out front. The Harvester was being thrust aboard an automobile.

Then came a snarl that only Justin Craybaw could have uttered. Shouts from the C.I.D. men; a high-pitched call from Craybaw as he scrambled free from captors. Before the Scotland Yard men could down him on the gravel, shots echoed from the trees past the house.

The Harvester had ordered reserves to be present here tonight. Thugs down from London, they were ready. As their guns flashed, they came charging forward. Scotland Yard men dropped to cover. Massed foemen ripped to the attack.

The Shadow had drawn automatics. With pumping jabs, he opened a flank fire. Fierce shouts changed to wild yells as The Harvester's crew received the fierce barrage. Figures tumbled to the turf, while others scattered.

Flashlights gleamed. Gaining their torches, ready with their guns, the C.I.D. men swooped upon the spreading crooks. Lewsham shouted orders. Two of his men—Turning and Burleigh—had grabbed Craybaw and were dragging him, writhing, into the house.

The law had gained the edge. Turning, The Shadow moved back through the conservatory. There, he heard a shout from the front hallway. Thudding sounds as overpowered men sprawled to the floor. Then, into the living room, came The Harvester.

With final frenzy, Craybaw had thrown off Burleigh, gaining the man's gun. He had slugged Tunning. Free, he was leaving the outside battle to his henchmen, while he dashed in, alone, upon the men in the living room.

DESPITE their number, The Harvester was not facing odds. Only one man was armed. That one was Eric Delka.

While others dropped for cover of chairs and tables, Delka whipped out his revolver. One hand against the table where the money was stacked, the Scotland Yard investigator was making a belated draw. The Harvester, gun already aiming, could have dropped him where he stood.

A laugh changed Craybaw's aim. It came from within the door to the conservatory. Its fierce burst made The Harvester swing in that direction. Upon the threshold, Craybaw saw The Shadow. In a trice, the master crook recognized that this must be a guise of the supersleuth who had unmasked him.

The Shadow, too, was aiming. His cloaked shoulders dipped as he pressed the trigger of an automatic. Craybaw, his hand moving, fired simultaneously. Tongues of flame stabbed across the room. A snarl came from Craybaw as his right hand drooped. A crash of glass resounded from beyond The Shadow.

The cloaked fighter had clipped The Harvester's wrist. Craybaw's bullet, singing past The Shadow's shoulder, had ruined another pane of glass in the much-damaged conservatory.

Despite his wound, Craybaw rallied. Dropping back, he tried to aim again. Then, springing in his path came Eric Delka, snapping the trigger of his revolver. Flame thrusts withered the murderous Harvester, thanks to the bullets that issued with them. Delka, with other lives at stake, had taken no chances.

The Shadow, ready with new aim, could have dropped Craybaw but for Delka's intervention. Wisely, he stayed his trigger finger when the Scotland Yard man blocked his path. From the doorway, he saw Delka stop short; then stoop above the caved body of Justin Craybaw.

The Harvester was dead.

Harry Vincent, first to stare toward the door to the conservatory, was the only one who caught a fleeting glimpse of a vanishing form in black. But others, wondering, heard the sound that followed—a strange, uncanny tone that crept in from the night.

Shots had ceased about the house—for the law had won the outside battle. The Harvester was dead; that sound, despite its taunting echoes, might have been a knell. It was a strident, eerie peal of mirth that rose to shivering crescendo, then faded as though passing into some sphere that was unearthly.

The triumph laugh of The Shadow. The mirth of the departing victor, who had dealt with his insidious foe, The Harvester. To The Shadow belonged the last laugh.

THE END

SHADOWS OVER ENGLAND by Anthony Tollin

During the late 1930s and 1940s, The Shadow enjoyed international popularity. American radio scripts were rebroadcast with Australian, Mexican and Brazilian casts, while pulp novels were reprinted in a number of foreign editions, including a long-running Canadian series and Spanish-language editions published in Spain, Mexico and Argentina.

Perhaps the most intriguing reprints appeared in England's *The Thriller*. The Shadow made his British debut in the March 29th, 1938 issue and quickly became one of *The Thriller*'s most popular series, often awarded the cover spot over such established features as The Saint. Published by The Amalgamated Press, the "bedsheet"-sized weekly had debuted in 1929 with its first three issues showcasing Edgar Wallace mysteries, and soon became the home of Leslie Charteris' Saint novelettes.

The Thriller Shadow reprints came about through Walter Gibson's earlier newspaper work for the Ledger Syndicate. Colin Turner, representing London's Literary Features Ltd., was negotiating European reprint rights to American syndicated features including Gibson's quizzes and puzzles. During a luncheon meeting with Gibson and the Ledger Syndicate's George Kerney, the Scotsman expressed an interest in the Shadow stories, adding "Street & Smith would be a plum for us, but we can't get it!" Turner explained that the publishing house was already represented in England by the Curtis Brown Agency. However, when apprised of the situation, S&S circulation manager Henry Ralston revealed that the Curtis Brown Agency had no exclusive on the Shadow rights, and entered into a contract for British reprints that same afternoon.

The Shadow novels underwent severe cutting to fit in *The Thriller*'s 24-page format, while the settings were transported to England. Clyde Burke became a reporter for London's *Morning Sun,* while Commissioner Weston headed Scotland Yard, aided by Inspector Joe Carton (an Anglicized Joe Cardona). Lamont Cranston was recast as a British sleuth with a new origin most likely inspired by *The Count of Monte Cristo:*

> Mystery shrouds the personality of the Shadow. The police know him as a gallant ally and welcome his aid in their eternal war on crime. Detective-Inspector Joe Carton is aware that the Shadow's cloak hides the person of Lamont Cranston, millionaire.

THE THRILLER LIBRARY 2ᵈ WEEKLY

The SHADOW— the world's mightiest crime avenger, in a powerful, long complete story.

The SHADOW—internationally famous as the greatest mystery character in modern fiction—on the screen—on the air—and NOW in The THRILLER Library.

ENTER the SHADOW BY MAXWELL GRANT

Meet the Phantom Sheriff before he Vanishes!

Who is this will-o'-the-wisp Western lawman who wages war against big-city crime barons? Why has he left the ranges to round up ruthless crooks in the East? What chance have his Colts against mobsters and their machine-guns? You'll find the answers in "The Phantom Sheriff's Fiery Trail," the thrilling yarn appearing today in WILD WEST WEEKLY. This man-sized paper features a full programme of super-stories of Western adventure .. yarns of the cattle country, range wars and rustlers, bandits, marshals and Mounties who always get their man. Ask today for

WILD WEST WEEKLY 2ᵈ

Every Thursday, at all Newsagents.

SINISTER BROADCAST By Maxwell Grant

There was no way of smashing the most deadly efficient crime-ring ever to loot London, no chance to unmask the "brain" behind it ... until The SHADOW'S inspiration devised that brilliant trap by radio

A MASTERPIECE OF THRILL-STORIES —— WITH "THE SHADOW"

But even he does not suspect that the name of Lamont Cranston is also assumed by this mysterious being.

Years ago dire tragedy entered the life of the Shadow. He was then a flourishing solicitor. A frame-up by a man he trusted threw him into a felon's cell, from which he escaped as a fugitive from justice. He then discovered that the same ruthless criminal who had wronged him had also claimed his only son as a victim. Together, this ill-matched pair had vanished into the underworld.

Heartbroken, embittered, a price on his head, the escaped convict vanished completely from the ken of man. At the self-same moment Lamont Cranston, reputed millionaire, appeared and the Shadow began his war on crime. The Shadow has a dual motive in all his exploits. He seeks to exterminate such menaces to society as the man whose victim he was. He seeks knowledge of the whereabouts of his son and to rescue him from the snares of evil men.

In *The Thriller* stories, The Shadow's secrets are known only by aide Richard Burbank, who relates:

I believe I am the only man who knows his tragic history, for I knew him long before he took the name of Lamont Cranston—when his name— his true name—was John Harverson.... Joe Carton, the Scotland Yard detective, knows that Lamont Cranston and the Shadow are one and the same person; but he does not guess that beneath those two distinct personalities, lies another—that of John Harverson, escaped convict. If he ever finds that out his duty will be to arrest the Shadow!

Shadow novels like Tinsley's *The Fifth Napoleon* featured distinctive American locales that couldn't be transformed into English settings. Since British readers knew The Shadow and his aides as London-based crimefighters, the Dark Avenger and his allies underwent name changes in stories that remained set in America. Burbank was rechristened Langley and Joe Cardona became Chief-Inspector Benny Goodfellow, while Lamont Cranston was reborn as Colorado's Kit Halsam who battled American crime as the Phantom Sheriff:

Beside him stood the Phantom Sheriff. From the top of his ten-gallon Stetson to the heels of his Coffeyville boots, the man was clad in dead black. A mask covered most of his face. Black-gloved hands rested easily on the butts of twin Colts.

Kit Halsam's voice came from behind the mask, a voice which had chilled the blood of many an evildoer when the Phantom Sheriff had been on the warpath.

Like The Shadow, the Phantom Sheriff terrorized criminals with his haunting mirth:

His laughter made eerie echoes in the empty garage. Many of the toughest crooks in far-off Colorado would have recognized that sound. Hearing it, they would have cringed. For the mirth that bubbled from those grim lips was the ominous laughter of the Phantom Sheriff.

The Phantom Sheriff's exploits appeared in both *The Thriller* and *Wild West Weekly*.

The Shadow's excursion as a British crimebuster became a casualty of war when *The Thriller* was revamped in March 1940 as the shortlived *War Thriller.* During the next decade, British readers would experience The Shadow's adventures only via imports of unsold American pulps, often transported to Great Britain aboard ships as ballast.

Chuckling evilly, the Fifth Napoleon forced Benny back towards the open well. When Benny had nearly lost hope, a black figure appeared from the shadows behind the master crook, a gleaming black Colt in his hand.

CASTLE OF DOOM

Lone and grim it stood there, a landmark of feudal warfare centuries old. But when rifles cracked within its grim old walls, The Shadow knew it was the beginning of a modern battle of crime!

A Complete Book-length Novel from the Private Annals of The Shadow, as told to

Maxwell Grant

CHAPTER I
CRIME OVER LONDON

THICK, smoke-laden fog had gained its grip on London. Night, descending like some black umbra through the mist, had added sinister gloom. Street lamps, their rays cast back upon them, were nothing more than blurred orbs of illumination that seemed to hang in midair.

Silence was heaviest upon a narrow street not far from Piccadilly Circus. This thoroughfare lay somewhere between the huge stores of Regent Street and the quality shops of Bond Street. The very obscurity of the section added to the lull; but with it, the unnatural calmness was foreboding. Stilled air seem to be waiting for some startlement. It came.

The shrill sound of a policeman's whistle cleaved the fog. Shouts came in muffled utterance. Harsh oaths were rasped in challenge. Then came the scurry of footsteps upon paving; after that, the heavy pound of pursuing feet. Other whistles trilled; then clatter faded.

Rogues of the night had countered with the law. Ghoulish plunderers, creeping out from hiding places, had been scattered back to cover. Patrolling policemen had converged, were staying close to the vicinity. Heavy, methodical footsteps were proof that the law remained.

Close by one of Piccadilly's corners, a stalwart uniformed figure loomed into the light. Steady eyes peered from beneath a helmet. Then the London bobby raised his arm as a pedestrian approached.

"Better not go through that way, sir," informed the officer. "There are prowlers about. They may be footpads, for aught that we have learned."

"Thank you, officer."

THE man who spoke was nattily attired. He was wearing a light-gray topcoat and a trim bowler hat. His face showed him to be no more than thirty years; and his features carried an aristocratic mark. High cheekbones, sharp nose and gray eyes that were dreary despite their friendly gaze. The bobby took mental note of that distinctive countenance.

"It's a bad night, sir," reminded the officer.

The young man nodded. He was nervous as he tightened the fawn-colored gloves that he was wearing. Then his jauntiness returned; he drew a light walking stick from beneath his elbow and swung it rakishly to indicate that he had at least a slight measure of protection should he encounter danger.

"I am going to the Acropolis Club, near St. James Street," he told the bobby. "Since I can reach there by continuing along Piccadilly to my turning point, I shall do so. Good evening, officer."

Fog swallowed the well-dressed young man as he swaggered along his way. The bobby resumed a short-paced patrol.

New footsteps clicked. A well-dressed young man came into the hazy light. The officer surveyed a clean-cut face; then took note of the arrival's attire. This passer stopped of his own volition. He addressed the bobby in American fashion.

"Hello, officer," he said, with a friendly smile. "I'm lost in this plagued fog. I wonder if you could give me directions?"

"Certainly, sir," acknowledged the bobby, "but first I must warn you to be careful hereabouts. There have been suspicious lurkers in this neighborhood."

"The newspapers have agreed upon that," laughed the American. "They claim that the mysterious burglars have accumulated everything that is worthwhile taking in this section and others. Rather an exaggeration, to my way of thinking."

"Quite right you are, sir." Ending his discussion of recent crime, the bobby changed the subject. "About your directions, sir. You are in Piccadilly, walking westward. What destination have you chosen, sir?"

"I should like to reach the Acropolis Club, in St. James Street."

THE officer stared, momentarily dumbfounded by the coincidence. Then, politely, he covered his surprise and gave careful directions. The American set out upon the route that the previous man had taken.

Another bobby approached from the side street. He came with information from the restricted area.

"We have scoured the neighborhood," he stated. "The rogues have scattered back to shelter. The orders to warn wayfarers are ended."

"No vans seen about?" questioned the first bobby.

"None," replied the second. "These were—"

The speaker paused. A pedestrian was strolling from the mist. He was a man of military bearing, that appearance being increased by his attire. He was wearing a khaki-colored overcoat; his felt hat was set at a slight tilt. His greeting was cheery as he approached the officers.

"Hello, there!" he exclaimed. "Trouble hereabouts?"

The first bobby stared. He had seen coincidence in the fact that two passers had been going on foot to the Acropolis Club. But that had been nothing when compared to the present puzzle.

The officer had remembered the first man's face. High cheeks, sharp nose and gray eyes. A voice that was brisk; but well accented. To his amazement, the bobby was staring at that face again, listening to the same voice!

Yet this could not be the identical Englishman. The first had worn a light-gray topcoat and bowler hat. This man was clad in a khaki coat and soft hat. The first had worn gloves and carried a walking stick; this man had neither.

Moreover, the first man had continued west. This chap had come from an easterly direction. Brief minutes had separated their arrivals. Yet, as he stared, the bobby realized that the first man might have stopped somewhere close by, changed his hat and coat, and then circled back.

"Beg pardon, sir," questioned the bobby. "Were you not the gentleman who passed by a short while ago?"

"I?" queried the sharp-faced young man, in apparent surprise. "Not at all. I have been strolling in this direction from The Strand. Enjoying London after a long absence."

"You have lost your way, sir?"

The bobby's query was cagey. It was an effort to learn the new arrival's destination. Gray eyes flashed.

"Ah! I have it!" The wayfarer's tone was jesting. "Some other chap, dressed like myself, strolled by here in the fog. Well, I must grant that my attire is a bit unusual for a Londoner. You see, I am just home from India."

THE bobby had stepped a trifle to one side, to gain a better view of the man's face. The wayfarer noticed this effort at closer scrutiny.

"You are wondering about India?" he laughed.

"Wondering why my face is not a tanned one? That is because I came home on sick leave. I lost two stone in weight, thanks to the beastly fever spell that I experienced in Bombay. I turned as white as a ghost."

"It was not that, sir," confessed the bobby, stepping back. "It was your face, not your attire that made me believe you were the other gentleman returned. But I see that I am wrong, sir."

"Ah! My face is not the same?" The question was quick. "Perhaps you did not observe the other chap closely, then?"

"Your face is the same," expressed the officer, slowly, with a deliberate nod of his head. "Quite the same, sir, except for one difference."

"And what is that?"

"Your paleness. Once you mentioned it, sir, I realized the truth of it. Had I been asked to choose which one of you had come from Bombay, I would have picked the previous gentleman."

"How was he dressed?"

"In the best Bond Street fashion, sir."

"Indeed. I suppose he was on his way to some club?"

"He was, sir. Quite swanky with his light-gray topcoat, his bowler and his walking stick."

"Ah! A walking stick!" The man in the khaki coat took up a bantering mood. "I fancy that he carries it quite rakishly, as though ready to cane any bounder who might disturb his passage."

The bobby had no reply. The description was so perfect that he again stood dumbfounded, able only to nod.

"And, of course, he was going to his club," resumed the young man from the fog.

The bobby found words.

"Yes, sir. The Acropolis Club."

"That was it, sir," added the second bobby. "There was another man also going to the Acropolis Club; but he passed by a trifle afterward. He was an American."

"And did he look like me also?"

"Not at all, sir."

The young man laughed heartily, while both bobbies smiled. Then, with a slight click of his heels, the wayfarer gave a friendly half salute. With that, he strolled away into the fog.

TRAMPING footsteps faded as the bobbies resumed their beat. Crime had been a false alarm tonight. The wave of robbery that had been discussed was rightly classed as something of the past. Yet crime had not been banished from London.

It hovered still, as menacing as the fog; and, singularly, that first bobby at the corner had come in contact with three men whom crime would soon concern. Grim events would involve those Englishmen who looked alike; the swanky Londoner and his double back from India.

Into that same picture would come the man who had appeared between; the American who had been directed to the place that the other two appeared to know more perfectly—the Acropolis Club near St. James Street.

CHAPTER II
CRIME DISCUSSED

CRIME talk was heavy at the Acropolis Club. It was the only subject among the members who had gathered in the smoking lounge. Fog had not kept these gentlemen from their accustomed meeting place; and in their discourse, they could find but one theme.

"Outrageous!" Such was the opinion given by a dignified man with a drooping, white mustache.

"Scotland Yard is not idle, however, Dunbarth," objected a roundish-faced club member. "Those audacious crimes were committed one after the other, with such expedition that the law could not keep pace with them."

"Quite so, Rutherwaite," acknowledged Dunbarth. "Nevertheless, crime may begin again. Mark my words!"

"What is your opinion, Cranston?" queried Rutherwaite, turning to a tall, calm-faced personage who was seated nearby. "Do you not agree that the miscreants will be content with the hauls that they have made?"

"Quite probably" was the quiet response, "so far as London is concerned. Their booty has been estimated at three hundred thousand pounds, I understand, and—"

"More nearly half a million," put in Rutherwaite, "according to the latest estimate of the *Daily Sketch*.".

"The *Sketch!* Bah!" Dunbarth gave an indignant ejaculation.

"What of the American journals?" queried Rutherwaite. "Have they exaggerated the news from London?"

The question was addressed to Cranston. He made a quiet reply.

"I left New York," he stated, "two days after the crime wave began. At that time, the American newspapers estimated that half a million dollars in valuables had been taken. While I was making the voyage to England, the wave continued, to reach three times its original toll. A million and a half dollars would coincide with Dunbarth's estimate of three hundred thousand pounds."

"Precisely," nodded Dunbarth. "The Duke of Clandermoor's gold plates; the portraits from the Earl of Kelgood's gallery; the two jewelry shops on Bond Street; the jade vases housed in storage, that awaited shipment to the British Museum—"

"And the jeweled tiaras," added Rutherwaite,

"that belonged to Lady Darriol; to say nothing of the Smith-Righterstone tapestries—"

"Which I intended to include," interposed Dunbarth, testily. "But why quibble over estimates? The vital point is: what has Scotland Yard learned through its well-known Criminal Investigation Department? Only that the robbers used motor vans in every expedition, to aid their entry and speed their departure."

"You term them robbers," observed Cranston. "I should deem them murderers."

"Quite right," agreed Rutherwaite. "A servant was slain at the Duke of Clandermoor's town house. An officer was shot in cold blood when the robbery was done at Pettigrew's shop in Bond Street."

"And new crime will come," began Dunbarth. "Mark my words. New robberies—"

"Not in London." The words were Cranston's, delivered in a tone of finality. "Murder, perhaps, in London. Robbery, perhaps, elsewhere."

THERE was an almost prophetic note in the speaker's voice, as though he had coolly calculated the future. There was reason why that should be. For this American who had arrived in London was not a chance visitor as the club members supposed.

He was a master sleuth, The Shadow. Learning of swift, mysterious crime in the British capital, The Shadow had taken on the guise of Lamont Cranston, for a prompt trip to London.

"That is it," nodded Rutherwaite. "Why should the bounders resort to further crime? They have made their haul. The proper course—the one that the Yard has taken—is to watch every port and every vessel leaving England and—"

"It will be useless," injected Dunbarth.

A young man had entered the lounge while Dunbarth was speaking. Rutherwaite waved a greeting. This arrival was the very man who had first met the bobby at one of Piccadilly's corners. Rutherwaite made the introduction.

"This is Geoffrey Chiswold," he told The Shadow. "Jeff, this is Lamont Cranston, recently arrived from New York."

They shook hands. The Shadow spoke.

"You are one of several Londoners whose names have attracted my attention," he told Chiswold. "Are you not the Geoffrey Chiswold who recently sold your property to a man named Barton Modbury?"

"Yes," acknowledged Geoffrey, with a nod. Then, bitterly: "It had been in the family for more than three hundred years. I was sorry to dispose of the old place."

"Why did you do so?" queried Dunbarth.

"The place had become a burden," explained Geoffrey. "The upkeep and maintenance of servants would have driven me into debt. I wanted to make

RUTHERWAITE—member of the Acropolis Club.

journeys, particularly to Canada. I invariably lacked a sufficient surplus."

"I suppose the situation has changed," inserted Rutherwaite. "You should find present circumstances an improvement."

"I have," acknowledged Geoffrey. "I am prepared for my voyage. I sail tomorrow for Canada."

"I hope that you made out well with your sale of the castle?"

"I did quite well. Modbury is wealthy. He was willing to pay the price that I asked."

"Modbury is an Australian?"

Geoffrey shook his head.

"No," he replied, "Modbury is a South African from the Kimberley region. He is a specialist in the choice of gems. He particularly favors uncut diamonds—"

Geoffrey stopped abruptly. His face became troubled. Then, in a confidential tone, he added:

"That fact must not be mentioned, gentlemen. It is the reason why Barton Modbury chose to purchase Chiswold Castle. He wanted to be far from London."

"On account of the robberies?" queried Rutherwaite, in an undertone.

GEOFFREY nodded.

"Then," queried The Shadow, "Barton Modbury purchased Chiswold Castle because of the protection it offered?"

"He did," nodded Geoffrey, "and he has reopened it. He wanted me to be his guest there, for he is entertaining some of the finest folk to whom I introduced him. However"—Geoffrey smiled regretfully—"I could not fancy myself occupying a place in Chiswold Castle while I was no longer the owner. That is why I decided upon my trip to Canada."

Geoffrey Chiswold arose and shook hands in parting. He strolled away to chat with other friends. The Shadow, still standing, turned about as an attendant approached and handed him an envelope. The Shadow opened it.

"The gentleman is waiting at the door, sir," stated the attendant. "Will there be a reply?"

"Yes." The Shadow smiled slightly as he wrote a note of his own and folded it. "Give this to Mr. Vincent."

BARTON MODBURY—new owner of Chiswold Castle

The attendant departed. When he arrived at the door of the club, he gave the message to a young man who was standing there. This arrival was the second passer whom the bobby had encountered in Piccadilly; the American who had inquired the way to the Acropolis Club.

He was Harry Vincent, agent of The Shadow. He, too, had come to London, to aid in the tracking down of criminals. Harry had brought in a report of certain investigations which he had conducted at The Shadow's order.

The message that Harry read at the door of the Acropolis Club referred to Geoffrey Chiswold. It gave the club member's name, described his appearance and attire with exactitude. It told Harry to wait until Geoffrey Chiswold came from the Acropolis Club; then to take up his trail through the fog and report where Geoffrey had gone.

For in Geoffrey Chiswold's mention of Barton Modbury, the South African diamond king, The Shadow had found cause for prompt investigation. Though The Shadow agreed with Scotland Yard upon the point that successful criminals intended to remove their swag from England, he also held to theories of his own.

He had heard of Chiswold Castle previously. Tonight, he had met Geoffrey Chiswold and had listened to brief statements from the former owner concerning Barton Modbury, the diamond king who had bought the old castle that stood far from London.

In picturing the coming trail, The Shadow had seen Chiswold Castle as a possible goal for men of crime. That was why he had deputed Harry Vincent to the task of learning all he could concerning Geoffrey Chiswold.

CHAPTER III
TWISTED TRAILS

THE SHADOW had expected Geoffrey Chiswold's stay to be a short one at the Acropolis Club. His calculation was correct. Within twenty minutes after his arrival, Geoffrey made his departure.

When Geoffrey Chiswold stepped from the Acropolis Club, Harry spotted him immediately.

He took up the trail. An easy one, at first, for Geoffrey's footsteps were a half shuffle from the sidewalk. As the trail continued, Harry allowed more leeway. At times, he loitered, then made swifter pace to draw close to his quarry. Guided by sound, Harry gained confidence, except when other passers added their gaits to Geoffrey's.

Then came the incident that threw Harry off the trail. They had passed a side thoroughfare where Harry had been out of touch with the footsteps. As Harry closed in again, he saw the blurred light from a restaurant window, a place which offered him a chance to check upon the trail. He closed in upon the man whose footsteps he could hear. At the lighted spot, Harry stopped dead short.

He had caught sight of his quarry, but the man was no longer Geoffrey Chiswold. Though Harry could only see his back, he knew that the man was the wrong one. Footsteps had been deceiving; the light proved the fact. The man just ahead of Harry was not wearing a gray topcoat and Derby hat. Instead, he was attired in khaki coat and soft hat. Moreover, he had neither cane nor gloves.

Where had the trail been lost?

Harry could think of but one logical spot; the last street that they had passed. Turning, The Shadow's agent made as much haste as possible in the opposite direction. He still had hope to pick up the lost trail. Odd circumstance had tricked Harry Vincent. The other was the man who looked like Geoffrey Chiswold, a fact that Harry had not discerned by the lights of the restaurant, for he had seen the man's back and not his face. The chief deception lay in the fact that the man who intervened was walking in exactly the same fashion as Geoffrey. Harry had taken the second man's footsteps for the first.

UP ahead, Geoffrey Chiswold had maintained his pace. As he continued, he became conscious of a sound behind him; one that resembled an echo. He paused by a doorway and listened. The shuffling echo sounded from the corner; then stopped.

His right hand clutching his walking stick, Geoffrey edged back toward the light. He fancied that he heard sounds creeping toward him from the fog. He caught a momentary glimpse of a stocky form. Swinging the cane, Geoffrey bounded forward. As he did, the other man sprang from the opposite direction.

They met in the lighted patch. A khaki-colored arm shot forward and caught Geoffrey's wrist. As the young man writhed, unable to swing his cane, he came face to face with his antagonist. Geoffrey's struggle ceased. His lips phrased a name of recognition:

"Nigel!"

The other laughed harshly and thrust away Geoffrey's wrist.

"The Chiswolds meet," remarked Nigel, in a tone which was similar to Geoffrey's. "Two cousins reunited after an absence of five years. Well, Jeff, are you glad to see me?"

"I thought you were in India," replied Geoffrey, coldly. "What brings you back to London?"

"The call of home," returned Nigel, "plus a Bombay fever. Well, old chap, the prodigal has returned. As my only relative, you might provide the fatted calf."

"I suppose so." Geoffrey seemed reluctant.

"What do you want, Nigel? Money?"

Nigel laughed. Nigel's laugh was not pleasant. Then his manner changed.

"Let us drop it, Jeff. Money does not matter; I changed my spendthrift habits while in India. I have gained a disappointment; one for which you are responsible."

"And what may that be?"

"About Chiswold Castle. Why did you sell the place, Jeff?"

"Chiswold Castle was my property, Nigel. It was part of my inheritance. You had no share of it."

"I shared memories of the place."

"Then you can keep them. That is what I have chosen to do. I am leaving for Canada tomorrow."

"So soon?" Nigel was studying his cousin closely. "Well, since you will be absent, do you think that Modbury would welcome me if I dropped out there and introduced myself?"

GEOFFREY'S fists clenched.

"So that is it!" he accused. "You wish to profit by my friendships. To use our relationship as a method of imposing upon wealthy persons, such as Modbury. You have heard about him, I suppose—"

This time, Nigel showed anger. Then, restraining himself, he questioned:

"Just what do you take me for, Jeff?"

"A rogue," returned his cousin. "One who was a black sheep when he left England. Whose return can be but a single indication. You are here to get money —by any means. I would put you above none."

"Burglary? With murder perhaps?" Nigel's query was sharp.

Geoffrey found difficulty in stammering a reply. Before he could become coherent, Nigel sneered contemptuously.

"I'm glad I located you," he scoffed. "I could not learn what club you belonged to, in the short while I have been in London; but a bobby saw you tonight and told me where you had gone.

"That's why I waited for you; to find out how much you knew. Well, Jeff, your mind sees possibilities, doesn't it? As soon as you encounter your cousin Nigel, your thoughts go back to the past. You see in me a potential criminal; one who has grown, magnified, enlarged; until now you connect me with actual crime—"

"I do!" challenged Geoffrey. "So will others, when they come to investigate you. They will realize what I realized; that every recent crime here in London involved places and spoils that you might know about.

"The gold plates at Clandermoor's! You dined off it ten years ago! The Kelgood gallery! We played hide and seek in there when we were youngsters! The jewelry shops, where our grand-aunt used to take us! The tiaras—the tapestries—"

"I have seen them all," interposed Nigel, "and so have you, my dear cousin. What would Scotland Yard say, should I tell them that?"

"You—you rogue—"

"And should I prove to them that I was aboard a P and O liner at the time of the robberies? Then whom would they question? Have you thought of that, cousin Jeff?"

GEOFFREY'S lips were twitching; he was gasping indignant words.

"Whether you did or not," remarked Nigel, "it does not matter. As for Modbury and his diamonds, I shall find out regarding them. Perhaps his wealth has been overrated. Possibly"—Nigel paused and curled a disdainful smile—"possibly Modbury merely wanted seclusion and sea air. On the contrary"—Nigel's tone was reflective—"he may really be a chap of unusual wealth.

"If so, he may have possessions with which he can well dispense. If so, I shall learn. Because, Jeff, I intend to go to Chiswold Castle. If you refuse to introduce me to Modbury, I shall go there on my own initiative."

Geoffrey Chiswold had regained a grip upon himself. He was firm as he met his cousin's steady, narrowed gaze.

"One move, Nigel," he warned, "and I shall denounce you to the law. It is only to protect the Chiswold name that I restrain myself."

"The Chiswold name," snorted Nigel. "You always were hypocritical about it, Jeff. Go on. Denounce me to the law. It will prove a boomerang, if you do.

"Since you are leaving England, I shall make no trouble for you. Ah! You are eyeing me! You are pleased to see that I am down to your weight at last. You would like to thrash me.

"Why not try? I shall grant you privilege to use your cane. That would make a proper handicap. But remember, it might bring us to a police court. The Chiswold cousins would come into prominence. It would be better to restrain yourself, Jeff. Say nothing. Sail for Canada. Be away when scandal breaks."

PRODUCING a pencil and a card, Nigel passed them to Geoffrey. Calmly, he ordered:

"Write the address of your diggings. I may be calling there tomorrow, to see if you have left. Do not hesitate—I want the correct address."

Quivering with both fear and rage, Geoffrey scrawled the address and thrust the card into Nigel's hand. His own face pale, Geoffrey stormed:

"You are the one who should be leaving England. Heed my advice—"

"I never take advice," interposed Nigel. "I give it. Take mine and go to Canada, or else jump into the Serpentine. You never were a good swimmer, Jeff."

With that, Nigel Chiswold turned on his heel and strode away through the fog; leaving his cousin Geoffrey white-faced and quivering, like a man who had seen a ghost.

CHAPTER IV
THE HOUSE IN WHITECHAPEL

HARRY VINCENT, in his effort to regain Geoffrey Chiswold's trail, had run into various difficulties. Not only had he failed to pick up sounds of footsteps along the side street; he had run into an obstructing block that forced another choice.

A street ran left and right. Neither direction seemed the more likely. Finally, however, Harry had decided on the left, in the hope that he might regain the corner where he had first lost the trail.

A low-built corner light afforded a chance to locate himself. Harry made in that direction; then paused, confused. He saw a long, narrow street stretching away into a path of murky gloom; but he could not decide whether or not it would lead him from this puzzling region. It was while he chided himself upon his bewilderment that Harry heard the shuffling gait of a walker.

The footsteps were quicker than Geoffrey's; but they bore a resemblance. Harry drew back into a doorway and waited. A man came into the range of the light, then stopped there. Harry stared completely amazed.

This was the man who had led him from Geoffrey's trail; the walker in the khaki topcoat. But as the man paused in the light, Harry caught a complete glimpse of his features. Like the bobby at the Piccadilly corner, The Shadow's agent mistook Nigel Chiswold for Geoffrey.

Watching, Harry saw Nigel draw a card from his pocket and study it as though memorizing something written there. Then, with a slight laugh, Nigel tore the card into eight pieces and tossed the bits of pasteboard to the sidewalk. Turning, he strode off through the fog.

Harry hurried forward. He scooped up the pieces of the card, but made no attempt to put them together. Instead, he hurried after Nigel. Soon, he was again on the trail of elusive footbeats. Nigel, however, proved too difficult a quarry.

His speed changed; his footsteps turned a corner, then faded. Following, Harry decided that the man must have changed his gait. Then he realized that he was following no one. Nigel must have guessed that he was being trailed and worked the trick of ducking into a doorway.

Harry's only clue was the torn card. Reaching a main thoroughfare, he found a hotel. He went into the lobby, sat at a writing desk and pieced the card together. It gave him the address of a flat in the Belgravia section, near Belgrave Square. Harry made a telephone call to The Shadow, at the Acropolis Club. He was told to investigate further, then report again.

MEANWHILE, Nigel Chiswold had arrived at an obscure hotel, not far from Soho, that foreign corner so curiously wedged into West End London. Ascending by a lift, Nigel went along a darkened hall and knocked softly at a door. The barrier opened; he stepped into a lighted room.

A huge, dark-skinned man greeted him. The fellow was a veritable giant who looked ill at ease in his English clothes. Had he been in native costume, he might have been taken for a Hindu; but he was not of that nationality. The man was an Afghan.

"Greetings, Amakar," stated Nigel. "I have good news."

"You have found the man?" queried the Afghan, slowly. "The one that you did seek?"

"I found my beloved cousin," laughed Nigel, "and that means a task for you. He says that he is going to Canada, Amakar."

"Canada is a place far away?"

"Too far away; and yet not far enough. What is more, the beggar does not trust me. After we had parted, he followed me. I ended that little game. It made me feel sure, though, that he had given me his correct address."

Nigel produced a map of London. He pointed out Belgrave Square while Amakar, looking over his master's shoulder, nodded his understanding.

"Do you remember Sannarak?" questioned Nigel, looking up. "The chap who made so much trouble for us at the Khyber Pass?"

"I remember Sannarak."

"And what you did to him?"

"I remember."

"Do the same tonight. To my cousin, Geoffrey, when he has left the place where he lives. He will have to go to the London docks." Nigel pointed out the spot beside the Thames. "Therefore, you may arrange the ambush in that vicinity. Do not take men with you to Belgrave Square.

"Speak to them in Soho, before you leave. Tell them to be ready near the docks. When they see you, they can follow. Use no more than necessary, Amakar. I rely upon your wisdom."

Amakar bowed.

"As for my cousin," smiled Nigel, wisely, as he stuffed a briar pipe with tobacco, "you will know him when you see me. Do you understand, Amakar?"

"I understand," replied the Afghan. "The face that will seem to be my master's will be the face of his cousin."

"That is the correct assumption. Afterward, Amakar, come back here and give me all the details. Then I shall decide upon our next step."

Nigel arose and opened the door. The Afghan went out into the hall. Nigel saw him go down a flight of rear stairs. Returning to the hotel room, Nigel stared from the window.

Below, dulled by the fog, lay a hazy spread of illumination that represented Soho. That section, with its varied flood of humanity, had been Amakar's habitat since he and Nigel had been in London.

It was a place where those of many nations rallied. Soho, where an Afghan might pass as a Hindu and where Hindus were not uncommon. Like other portions of London—the others in the East End—Soho was a spot where lurkers flourished. Amakar, the Afghan, had friends in Soho, who were not of his own nationality.

NOT long after Amakar had left the hotel, Harry Vincent arrived at Belgrave Square. Harry could actually discern the fronts of staid, old-fashioned buildings that loomed indefinitely up into the blackness. They were four-story structures; but the fog magnified them to gigantic proportions.

One of these houses bore the address number that Harry had pieced together from the card. From the outlet of the little cul-de-sac, Harry could see lights in the windows of the second-story rear.

He recalled that the card had borne the reference "2 B"; and that fact proved that the building contained flats. Two to a floor, as Harry estimated; which meant that someone was at home in the place for which he had searched. Harry's next problem was to learn who lived there. While he was pondering upon some plan, the upstairs lights went out.

Harry circled to the front of the building, keeping far enough away to be obscured. While he was watching, a taxicab chugged up and parked in front of the house. The driver alighted and stood waiting upon the curb. The door of the house opened and a young man appeared.

It was Geoffrey Chiswold, wearing his gray coat and bowler. Geoffrey was carrying a huge suitcase, which he turned over to the taxi driver. He went back into the house and reappeared with a second suitcase of similar proportions to the first.

HARRY turned up his coat collar and shuffled into the light. With shoulders slightly stooped, he approached Geoffrey with the manner of a hang about who knew this neighborhood. Obsequiously, Harry tipped two fingers to his hat and asked:

"Help you with your luggage, sir?"

"Very well." Geoffrey nodded as he handed the suitcase to Harry, who carried it to the cab. "Wait here, my man, and you may help me with some satchels."

The taxi driver glowered at Harry's interference; but The Shadow's agent made no comment. He shuffled back to the door of the building, relieved Geoffrey of two smaller grips and took them to the cab. He held the door open for Geoffrey to enter the vehicle. The taxi driver shrugged and took his place behind the wheel.

"Here is a shilling, my good fellow," said Geoffrey, passing a coin to Harry. Then to the taxi driver: "Take me to Liverpool Street Station. I must pick up a parcel that is checked there."

"Righto, sir," returned the driver.

Harry slammed the door of the cab.

"Thanks for the bob, sir," he said to Geoffrey. "Good luck to you, sir."

The cab swung around an isolated lamppost and the driver slowed to take directions. Harry, sauntering away, caught a last glimpse of the vehicle. Had the cab not been there, he might have spied a man who had stepped out from the sidewalk. This was a new arrival who had come up through the fog.

Amakar, the Afghan, had made good speed from the neighborhood of Soho. He had come by underground, arriving just as the taxi was pulling away from the house. Too late to hear Geoffrey speak to the driver, Amakar had moved swiftly when he saw the cab stop.

SIDLED UP beside the cab, Amakar peered into the interior. Geoffrey had turned on the dome light. In the feeble glow, Amakar spied the features that resembled those of his master, Nigel. His own dark features almost out of sight, Amakar watched and listened while he heard Geoffrey address the driver.

"Why the delay?" queried Geoffrey. "I am in no hurry; but I expect progress."

"Choosin' my way, sir," returned the driver. "There's roads as is better on a blarsted night than this one. Goin' to Liverpool Street is somethin' as needs a bit o' thinkin', sir.

"As for harfterward, sir, where is it that you'll be wantin' to go? If I knows as where to tyke you, when you 'ave picked up the parcel—"

"After Liverpool Street," interrupted Geoffrey, "I am proceeding to London docks. To go aboard the Steamship *Borealis*. But I shall walk from Liverpool Station, through Aldgate and east to the docks. It will be preferable to riding at a snail's pace, once I have obtained my package."

"A good plan, sir. I'd bet me last bob that you'd be reachin' the docks afore I'll be comin' with the luggage. This bloody pea souper is thick by the river—"

"Enough, driver. Choose your route and proceed."

The cab moved onward. Harry Vincent was out of sight in the fog. Amakar, stepping back from the lighted island, was seen by no one. The Afghan was gulped by the blackness, vanishing like some fabulous, gigantic jinni that had been summoned elsewhere.

Belgravia was a secluded island in the midst of London; but it was not far from that section to the jumbled hubbub of Victoria. It was thither that

Harry Vincent had headed, knowing that he would find two requisites—a telephone and an underground station. Despite the shortness of the walk, he had trouble finding his destination; but at last he emerged from the fog and located his surroundings.

From one of the railway stations, he called the Acropolis Club and spoke to The Shadow. Harry informed his chief that the Belgravia address had been Geoffrey's. This was information, for Geoffrey's only known London address had been the club itself.

Then Harry added that Geoffrey was bound for Liverpool Street Station, which formed a terminus of the London and Northeastern Railway. He mentioned that Geoffrey had gone by cab. Beyond that, Harry knew nothing else. He had not overheard the final conversation between Geoffrey and the driver.

The Shadow's order was to go to Liverpool Street. Taking the underground, Harry was soon speeding on his way. He was confident that he would reach the L.N.E. depot ahead of Geoffrey; he knew also that he would arrive there before The Shadow, who intended to join him there.

REACHING Liverpool Street, Harry began to watch for incoming cabs. This was a puzzling task, for it took him several minutes to determine where Geoffrey's taxi might arrive. At last Harry stationed himself at the right spot and was immediately rewarded. A cab pulled into view and Geoffrey alighted.

The taxi driver must have known streets where fog had thinned, for he had made surprisingly good time on the journey. Light traffic had unquestionably aided him along his course. So Harry thought as he followed Geoffrey into the railway station and watched while the young man reclaimed a light but bulky package from the parcel room.

Geoffrey went back to the cab with Harry following. He put the parcel aboard with his luggage and spoke to the driver. Then, instead of entering the cab, Geoffrey turned and walked away. For a moment, Harry stood rooted. Then, resolving upon the only course, he followed.

The taxi driver was ready to pull out. Another cab blocked his passage. He climbed out angrily to start an argument with its driver. The other driver gave a good-natured guffaw, delivered in cockney fashion.

Geoffrey's cabby could see no joke about the matter. He was about to force a quarrel with the jester when the other cabby himself brought an end to the forthcoming quarrel. Turning, he happened to see a tall arrival who had stepped quietly into view at the moment when Geoffrey's cabby had climbed out of his cab.

"Taxi, guv'nor?" queried the driver of the blocking cab.

A quiet reply in the negative. The tall stranger turned and strolled away in the direction of Houndsditch Road, the direct path to Aldgate. Quickening his pace to a long, easy stride, he set his lips in a thin, fixed smile as he fathomed the path of Geoffrey Chiswold.

This arrival at Liverpool Street was The Shadow. Still in the guise of Lamont Cranston, wearing a light cape and high silk hat, he had covered his evening clothes when he had left the Acropolis Club.

Reaching his goal just before Harry Vincent's departure, The Shadow had divined that the disputant with the luggage-filled cab was the driver who had brought Geoffrey Chiswold here. He had learned which way Geoffrey had gone; and he knew that Harry must be on the trail.

AT Aldgate, the eastern limit of the old city, Harry was close upon Geoffrey's heels. He was taking no chances upon losing his quarry. From Houndsditch Road, Geoffrey turned east into Aldgate High Street, as Harry had expected. Lights showed him hazily in the fog. A short walk carried Geoffrey to Whitechapel High Street. There Harry saw the young man hesitate. After a brief pause, Geoffrey suddenly started into the Whitechapel section.

Once again, Harry was trailing by footsteps; and as he muffled his own tread, he fancied that he caught slight, scuffling sounds from across the fog-laden street. It seemed as though some heavy, long-pacing walker was keeping on a line with him.

Geoffrey turned a corner. So did Harry. Geoffrey's pace had quickened. The sound of the footsteps was decreasing. Harry hurried forward. Through blackened gloom, he caught other sounds, like voices engaged in muttering.

He lost the sound of Geoffrey's footsteps; then paused. Edging in from the curb, he thrust his hand through the solid murk and touched the dampened corner of a building.

No sounds of footsteps. Harry knew the answer. Geoffrey Chiswold had stopped in front of this house in Whitechapel. There was no noise ahead; that tread from across the street had ended. All that Harry could hear for the moment was the semblance of a sound in back of him, like a low, whispered hiss in the blackened fog.

THEN, before Harry could turn or answer, a buzz began ahead. Voices snarled; there was a protesting cry; then a wild, shrill scream that rent the fog-filled atmosphere. A responding shout broke automatically from Harry's lips.

The Shadow's agent sprang forward on the instant. He knew the author of that scream, the reason for its utterance. Geoffrey Chiswold had met with disaster at the hands of lurkers in the fog. The shriek that he had given could only have come from a man who had felt the arrival of doom.

Here, upon this squalid street in Whitechapel, in front of an obscure and crumbly East End house, murder was being done. To Harry Vincent, agent of The Shadow, belonged the duty of driving off those attackers who had set upon Geoffrey Chiswold.

CHAPTER V
DEATH AND STRIFE

IN his forward spring, Harry Vincent came suddenly into light. Like an oblong shaft that cleaved the solid darkness, the glow stretched from the rectangular opening of a doorway in the house itself. Beginning from a lighted hallway, the rays produced a square upon both the sidewalk and a short flight of steps that led into the house.

Struggling men half blotted the steps. Half a dozen rough-clad thugs had fallen upon a lone opponent. Some had sprung up from darkness; others had plunged out through the doorway. In the center of that vicious throng was Geoffrey Chiswold.

As Harry leaped upon the group, the whole mass shifted to meet him; not face to face, but sidewise, lurched through some fierce impetus from the opposite direction. Harry's mind caught an instant flash: Geoffrey, in his struggle, must have hurled off some attackers. Then Harry had no time for other impressions.

A sprawling hoodlum twisted toward The Shadow's agent. With a mad yell, the rogue flashed a knife blade that was dripping crimson. Harry swung a sidewise stroke that sent the fellow against the house wall. Then he gripped another dirk-laden killer who dove headforemost toward him.

The whole surge carried Harry with it. Thrust backward, Harry saw four blades above him. Then, into the twisting throng came a driving battler, who arrived within three seconds following Harry's spontaneous attack.

IT was The Shadow. From beneath his cape, he had whipped an automatic; but he was not using the weapon as a firearm. Instead, he was delivering hard sweeps with his gun hand, while he used his other fist to pluck down hands that bore dripping knives.

With one hard jolt of his shoulder, The Shadow propelled Harry toward the curb, clearing his agent from the midst of battle. He wanted none but enemies about him; and his flaying fist sent ruffians scudding. Harry, stumbling as he reached the curb, managed to turn about in time to see this outcome.

The Shadow had met the heaving mass of fighters and had actually pitched the tribe back to the steps from which the lunge had begun. Then, with his plucking, swinging method, he had sent ruffians rolling everywhere.

One wild battler alone had gripped The Shadow. Upon the lowermost step, they formed a tableau. The Shadow's free hand held the ruffian's wrist, to withhold the knife stroke. In turn, the foeman was clutching at The Shadow's gun hand.

With a twist, the pair whirled away. Harry, coming in to aid, saw them clear his path. Rogues, coming to their feet, were ready to again wield knives; but they had no opportunity. The Shadow's .45 began to blast.

He was firing despite the man who clutched him, speeding bullets during the mad whirl. Like a turning turret, he swung from left to right, jabbing shots toward scattered thugs.

One rogue spat an outcry as a bullet clipped him. Another shouted a mad warning as a slug singed past his ear. Then, abandoning the foolhardy ruffian who was wrestling with The Shadow, the rogues took to their heels. They wanted the safety of the Whitechapel fog.

All this had happened in quick, amazing seconds. Harry Vincent, rallying, had first tried to aid The Shadow; then had gone toward free attackers only to see them scud like rats. He made a turn to come back toward The Shadow. His chief and the tenacious thug had already reeled beyond the steps.

To reach them, Harry's best course was to clamber over the steps themselves. He wheeled to do so; then stopped short. Before him, blocking his view of The Shadow's struggle, was a new adversary whom he had not seen until this very moment.

A DARK-FACED man was crouched upon the steps. He had been in the midst of that murderous group, obscured at the moment when Harry had driven into the fray. He was rising from his position and his glare was fixed upon Harry.

This last challenger looked like a Hindu, though not attired in Oriental garb. Harry had mistaken him for one of the Whitechapel ruffians, for he had not seen the man's dark face until this instant. Nor had he guessed at the man's titanic size. The fighter on the steps was rising; he loomed like a giant, towering above.

It was Amakar, the Afghan, huge and menacing; the very sight brought a gasp from Harry's lips. But with Amakar's rise came another view. The Afghan, rearing up from his half-seated posture had revealed another figure on the steps. There, sprawled face upward, lay Geoffrey Chiswold.

To Harry's staring eyes came the answer that explained the bloodstained knives. Geoffrey, lengthwise on the steps, was lifeless. His shirtfront was dyed red. Projecting from above his heart was the handle of a dirk. One deep-thrusting assassin had left his knife in the victim's body.

Amakar, in rising, had pressed his upper hand upon the stone step by Geoffrey's motionless shoulder. The Afghan's huge fingers were but inches distant from the knife itself. They possessed the strength required to wrest that blade from its lodging. A weapon lay almost in Amakar's grasp!

Harry Vincent came to double action. To offset Amakar, he sprang forward, bounding up the step edge to encounter the half-risen giant. At the same time, he yanked his own automatic from his pocket. The only way to deal with so formidable a foe was to gain the first advantage.

Amakar did not finish the rise. With a fierce cry in his native tongue, the dark-faced Afghan dived sidewise from his crouch. His long arms, shooting forth like grappling hooks, were instantaneous in their action. Bearing down from the steps like a toppling tower, Amakar caught Harry in his grip.

Harry had no chance to fire. His arm was trapped half lifted. Mammoth arms encircled him. As he went rolling backward, pinned to helplessness, Harry felt those engirding arms hoist him clear of the sidewalk. Then Amakar delivered a twisting heave, in the fashion of a discus hurler.

Harry Vincent cleared the curb in midair. He had reached the center of the narrow street when he struck, shoulder first. The power of the fling carried him onward.

Harry rolled over three times in quick succession before he finally stopped. Even then, it was the presence of the opposite curb that halted him. Harry's head cracked the edge of the sidewalk with a jarring velocity.

HALF dazed, Harry tried to rise, his only thought to get back into the fray. Hemmed in by the fog, he could see only that lighted stretch directly in front of the doorway across the street; against its background, he spied the looming bulk of Amakar. The big man was turning; apparently looking for another prey.

To Harry's dazed senses came the trill of police whistles. The Shadow's shots; the flight of vanished thugs—both had been heard by constables in the district. Harry tried to rise and failed. His right shoulder sagged; his right knee gave with his weight.

As Harry made the effort, a muffled gunshot sounded from the haze. The direction of the report told Harry that it must mean the finish of the fight that The Shadow was having with one lone assassin. Harry was right. Amakar, too, had heard the sound. The big Afghan had located someone in the fog.

Harry saw Amakar leap past the steps. At the same instant, a figure charged forward to meet him. It was The Shadow, hatless, his cape half torn from his shoulders. Despite his tallness, The Shadow looked pygmylike as he plunged toward Amakar. His lithe form looked slender enough for the Afghan to break in two.

A wreath of smoke was curling from above The Shadow's hand. The coil came from his automatic, its curling twist blended with the murkiness of the fog. Then Amakar met the advancing figure. Harry saw The Shadow's hand jerk backward.

Amakar had plucked The Shadow's gun hand while it was on the aim. He had gained the same advantage that he had with Harry. The Afghan's gripping arms surrounded Harry's chief. The Shadow's body was hoisted high in front of the patch of light which formed the background for the scene.

Harry's own gun was gone. It had spilled far from his hand during his long pitch. Helplessly, Harry could only watch; he saw The Shadow whirling like a straw puppet as Amakar prepared to fling him against the house wall.

Whistles were shrilling close by at both ends of the street. Would the law arrive before Amakar could crush The Shadow into senselessness; perhaps do him to death?

Hoarsely, Harry shouted for aid, hoping to bring the officers in his direction. Answering whistles sounded; yet they seemed faraway. All the while, Harry stared; to his amazement, The Shadow did not hurtle on a headlong trip into space. Instead, he was clutching Amakar, choking the Afghan's throat with agile fingers while the big man vainly sought to heave his tenacious adversary to the house wall.

Pounding feet upon the pavement. Shouts from arriving officers. Harry gave an answering cry. At the same moment both The Shadow and Amakar roused to fuller effort. The big Afghan jolted his shoulders upward. His head went back as The Shadow's clutch tightened. Then the two went sprawling sidewise, to slump at the steps.

Amakar's great bulk obscured The Shadow. For an instant, Harry thought that his chief had been crushed by the side of Geoffrey Chiswold's body. Then came the finale; so surprising that it seemed to be a move by Amakar alone.

The Afghan rolled sidewise toward the edge of the steps; then his body snapped upward and performed a tremendous somersault. Like an acrobat missing his cue, the big Oriental landed thwack upon the sidewalk, face upward.

THE SHADOW had gained a jujitsu hold. He had thrown all his strength into a scientific twist. His stroke had hoisted Amakar headforemost into such a sudden dive that the Afghan had turned completely over.

The Shadow, too, had lost his balance in the finish of the flip. Carried by his own impetus, he sprawled from the edge of the steps and landed on hands and knees.

Amakar was rising; The Shadow likewise. Six paces apart, they had a chance to come to grips again. It was Amakar who passed up a renewal of the duel. The reason for the Afghan's action was the sudden appearance of a helmeted officer who came jogging into the circle of light from out of the fog.

The bobby was beyond the steps; he was swinging a truncheon with his right hand while his left pressed a whistle to his lips. He halted momentarily at the sight of Amakar. The Afghan heard the whistle's blast and whirled about. Before The Shadow could leap forward to restrain him, Amakar had plunged into the mist.

Heavy footsteps beat a hard tattoo. Others sounded, coming toward them. There was a shout; a hoarse roar from Amakar; then the Afghan's pace was resumed, while a clattering sound reechoed in his wake. Amakar had encountered another bobby in the fog. He had sprawled the officer and was keeping on his way.

Harry saw The Shadow settle back beside the steps. For a moment, he thought that his chief had been worsted in the fight; that he could not have resumed the fray with Amakar. Then, as he himself crawled laboriously forward, Harry realized that The Shadow's action was a bluff for the bobby's benefit.

Pursuit of Amakar was useless; for the fellow had made a timely flight. The Shadow could only remain and tell his story, along with Harry's. Both would describe the struggle in the fog; with their chance arrival that had come too late to save Geoffrey Chiswold.

For the sprawled man upon the steps had never budged since Harry had first spied his prone form. Death had been swift, hard given upon the sound of his first outcry. Geoffrey Chiswold was dead; his assassins, like ghouls of the night, had scattered through the blanket of the midnight fog.

CHAPTER VI
AT CHISWOLD CASTLE

LATE the next afternoon, two passengers alighted from a branchline train of the London and Northeastern Railway.

The name of the station was Yarwick; and the train was losing no time to move away from it. The engineer seemed to begrudge the halt that he had made. The guard, peering from the rear window of the final carriage was looking back curiously when the train took the bend. A passenger let off at Yarwick was a rarity indeed. Two such curios, seen together, were worth a prolonged survey.

One of the two who had alighted at Yarwick was The Shadow, still in the guise of Lamont Cranston. The other was a keen-eyed, sharp-faced man, whose gaze roamed everywhere. He was Inspector Eric Delka, from the Criminal Investigation Division of Scotland Yard.

A one-horse carriage had creaked up to the station. The coachman who held the reins was eyeing the two potential customers. Even the worn-out steed that drew the rickety victoria looked hopeful as it turned its head toward the platform. The rig looked like a specter from the past; a coach that had met trains before the advent of the automobile age.

The coachman clucked to attract attention. Then, as Delka looked his way, he spoke in crackly, plaintive fashion:

"Carry you to the old Prince William Inn?" he queried. "A shilling apiece, your worships, and the luggage goes to boot."

"We do not want the inn," said the Scotland Yard man. "Our destination is Chiswold Castle. Do you know the place?"

"Chiswold Castle!" croaked the driver, turning about in his seat. "'Tis nigh a half league from here, your honor. 'Twill come high to ride that distance."

"How high?"

"A crown for the pair of you, gentlemen. With the luggage to boot."

"The price is suitable. Take us to the castle." Together The Shadow and Delka embarked.

THE driver lashed with the reins. The creaky victoria rumbled toward the town of Yarwick. A quarter of a mile produced a sleepy village, with a small tavern that carried a weather-beaten sign showing the likeness of Prince William of Orange. Eric Delka smiled as the carriage rolled by.

"A historic place, Yarwick," he told The Shadow. "In the seventeenth century, it was a meeting spot for Jacobites. That was when the inn took on its name. The proprietor was anxious that the authorities should know that he was not one of the plotters."

"What of those who lived in Chiswold Castle?"

"They were strong Jacobites, particularly in the time of Bonnie Prince Charley. They supported the Pretender's claim; and legend states that Prince Charley stayed at times within the castle. That, however, is doubtful. It is more likely that the only visitor was the faithful Ned Burke, the servant who stood so close to the bonnie prince.

"But we have talked enough of the past, Mr. Cranston. Let me ask you a question that concerns the present."

The Shadow displayed a slight smile.

"Sometime ago," recalled Delka, "you were present in London at the time when we were troubled by a notorious rogue known as The Harvester. You were instrumental in the exposure of that dangerous criminal. Am I right in assuming that your presence then was due to more than pure chance?"

"In a sense, yes."

"I believe I understand. Another question, Mr. Cranston. Last night, you and a friend happened to arrive in Whitechapel too late to save young Geoffrey Chiswold from death. Am I correct again in assuming that it was not luck that guided you there?"

"You are right."

"I thought as much," remarked the C.I.D. man. "That is why I saw to it that you and Vincent were relieved from too much questioning."

"Vincent needed rest and medical attention. He was badly bruised during the fray."

Delka nodded; then returned to his theme.

"Also," he reminded, "I asked you to visit Chiswold Castle with me. But before we enter, I should like to have your opinion regarding the unfortunate death of Geoffrey Chiswold."

"I have formed no full opinion," returned The Shadow, in the quiet tone of Cranston. "Last night, I chanced to learn that Geoffrey Chiswold was walking to the London docks. Having met the young man at the Acropolis Club, I felt some responsibility for him. It is not always healthy to venture too near the Thames, alone and afoot, in foggy weather."

DELKA nodded his agreement.

"Vincent and I followed after Geoffrey," resumed The Shadow. "He started at Liverpool Street; we traced him through Aldgate; then into Whitechapel. The last was hardly on his route."

"Young Chiswold probably lost himself in the fog," Delka said. "A pea-souper throws a man off course in unfamiliar territory."

"Perhaps you are right," said The Shadow. "However, Geoffrey was attacked and murdered. The question, therefore, is whether the deed was done by chance or by design."

"We may find out when we reach Chiswold Castle," decided Delka. "Here is the proposition. Geoffrey Chiswold gained money by the sale of his castle. He was close to debt when he did so. Apparently, he saw no danger to himself. If he had, he would have stayed away from Whitechapel.

"Therefore, his death was due to chance; unless we can learn that he had enemies. If such were the case, those of the castle would know of it. Or there might still be personal effects—letters, perhaps—which would give us clues."

"What of Geoffrey's relatives?" queried The Shadow.

"He had none in England," replied Delka. "All are dead, except his cousin Nigel, who went to India and stayed there. The matter of family, however, is entirely absent from this case.

"Geoffrey Chiswold had no remaining estate after he sold the castle. None except the money that he received from Barton Modbury and most of that was spent. Less than a thousand pounds remain to Geoffrey's bank credit. Not a sufficient sum to show a profit to a murderer."

"No. Unless we find direct proof that Geoffrey Chiswold had enemies, I shall investigate no further. I doubt that Modbury can tell us much; for he has known young Chiswold but a short while. Visitors at the castle, however, may give us facts."

"Who are the visitors?"

"Friends who knew Geoffrey Chiswold. One is Sir Rodney Ralthorn, who has firm hold upon one corner of the beet-sugar industry. His daughter, the Honorable Gwendolyn Ralthorn, is another guest at Chiswold Castle.

"Also, her fiancé, Lord Cedric Lorthing, who is a wealthy Londoner. The last of the guests is a Spaniard, Francisco Lodera. Although he has no title, Lodera belongs to a family that held high rating during the days of the Spanish monarchy. He has money, though he is not wealthy."

A brief pause while the carriage rounded a wooded stretch; then took a straight road through the glade.

"How well protected is Modbury?" inquired The Shadow.

"Quite well," replied Delka. "He has a retinue of half a dozen servants, in addition to his secretary, a man named Luval. Moreover, Modbury has kept in close touch with the local police—"

DELKA paused. The carriage had rolled suddenly from the trees. It was skirting a level stretch of cleared land. Beside the field, a tiny white cottage nestled against the green trees; while in the center of the broad open area was an airplane, its metal wings glistening in the late sunlight.

"Lodera's plane," remarked Delka. "A swift one. That must be his pilot, standing beside it. The pilot's name is Dufour."

Another stretch of woods. The carriage came to a spot where the trees opened at the left. A tang of sea breeze was apparent. Delka pointed to a rocky gulch that curved its way between craggy walls of cliff. Blue water showed in the distance.

"Castle Cove," said Delka. "I saw it marked on the map. That crag far beyond is Parrion Head. A few miles along the coast lies Darban-on-Sea, which used to be a popular resort along the drier side."

The Shadow smiled at the reference. This eastern section of England, served by the L.N.E. Railway, was commonly termed the "drier side," due to its greater prevalence of fair weather.

Trees again. The old victoria was swinging a long circle that tended directly toward the coast. A mile would have carried to the shore; but the trip was interrupted in less than half that distance. The carriage clattered to a stop in front of a massive iron gate that hung between pillars of stone.

The road had twisted full about. The Shadow and Eric Delka were coming in by the front gate that led to Chiswold Castle, which, in turn backed upon Castle Cove.

"Hello, Jeremy," greeted the driver of the carriage, as a stoop-shouldered man hobbled from a gatekeeper's lodge. "Visitors to see the folks."

"Welcome to you, sirs," acknowledged Jeremy, tugging the gate inward. "Drive to the castle, itself."

BENEATH spreading trees; past shady nooks; finally the carriage rolled out into the final opening. There, framed gray and solemn against the setting sun stood Chiswold Castle, a massive bulk of masonry that looked its full age of three hundred and fifty years.

Centuries had mellowed the edifice, taking away its prisonlike appearance. Lower windows were grated throughout the ground floor; but ivy vines had entwined about the edges, to produce a pleasant, welcoming appearance.

The corners of the castle were rounded and topped by stone bulwarks; but these portions of the building afforded the most pleasant views. Their windows showed that the rooms within must gain their full share of sunlight.

In front of the castle, where a moat had once been, was a stretch of stone porch, with short steps leading to it. Back of the porch was a massive door; above it, an iron-railed balcony that paralleled the steps below. Broad windows behind the balcony marked a front room on the second floor.

One oddity alone stood out. This was a single turret that rose higher than the third story of the castle. The turret was thin; it was set off center, for it began at the left edge of the central wall wherein the door was set. The turret had no windows; merely slits that appeared just below the circling rampart which served it as a roof.

That turret was as useless as the forgotten moat. Once it could have served as an archer's tower. Now it was no more than an ornamental relic of the past.

Shade enveloped the carriage as it rolled up to the portal of Chiswold Castle. Gloom enclosed the visitors, for the building blocked the rays of the setting sun. There was something somber about the atmosphere that chilled Eric Delka.

The Shadow did not feel the same sensation. Instead, the smile reappeared upon his lips. This was an atmosphere of mystery that carried the touch of darkness. Such elements were to The Shadow's liking.

CHAPTER VII
THE SHADOW'S CHOICE

THE door of the castle opened as the carriage arrived before the porch. A bulky servant studied the victoria; then turned and spoke to someone within. A long limbed man with spectacles stalked out on to the porch, craned his neck, then advanced to the halted carriage.

"Good afternoon," he said, in a brisk voice. "Are you visitors to see Mr. Modbury?"

"My name is Delka," informed Delka.

"Inspector from Scotland Yard. This is Mr. Lamont Cranston. He came with me from London. Yes, we should like to see Mr. Modbury."

"Who is it, Luval?"

The query boomed in a bass voice from the doorway as a heavyset, baldheaded man stepped into view. This individual was wearing knickers. He looked the part of a country gentleman.

"Visitors, Mr. Modbury," replied the spectacled man. "Inspector Delka from Scotland Yard, and Mr. Lamont Cranston."

"I've read about both of you," rumbled Modbury, picking Delka and The Shadow, in turn. "The London newspapers arrived two hours ago. Told all about that affair in Whitechapel. Dark news to us, it was. Geoffrey Chiswold was a likable young chap, with great promise."

"Have the others heard the news from London?" inquired Delka.

"You mean my guests?" returned Modbury. "No. They have not been about since luncheon. Sir Rodney Ralthorn and Lord Cedric Lorthing are hunting grouse. Gwendolyn Ralthorn and Senor Lodera are at the tennis courts."

Modbury turned to the servant who was standing at the door. The man went back into the castle and reappeared with a stack of deck chairs. He set them upon the porch; Modbury invited his new visitors to be seated.

They had hardly taken their chairs before the sound of voices came from close by. A blonde-haired girl in tennis clothes appeared from a corner of the castle, followed by a tall, slender man who was carrying tennis racquets.

The men on the porch arose. Barton Modbury was prompt in his introductions. He presented Delka and Cranston to the Honorable Gwendolyn Ralthorn and Senor Francisco Lodera.

GWENDOLYN RALTHORN was a girl who possessed a naive charm. Her attractive face lighted when she heard that Delka was from Scotland Yard. Her blue eyes enlarged with enthusiasm. Apparently, she linked Scotland Yard with adventure.

The Shadow saw a different reaction on the part of Francisco Lodera. A frown appeared upon his sallow face. The Spaniard's dark eyes narrowed; The Shadow saw him dart a glance past Barton Modbury, who was talking to Gwendolyn and Delka.

The only possible recipient of that glance was Luval, the secretary. The Shadow saw the spectacled man look quickly to see if Modbury was watching; then Luval made a motion of his hand that Lodera detected.

Neither Modbury nor Delka noticed the move. Only The Shadow saw. Lodera's response was a friendly smile that proved his immediate relief.

Then, as he heard what Delka was saying, Lodera drew closer and his face took on a look of sorrow.

"It was murder." Delka was soberly referring to the death of Geoffrey Chiswold. "Foolhardy, indeed, for him to have ventured into Whitechapel in a thick fog. Prowlers had been about in many parts of the city—"

"Poor Jeff," choked Gwendolyn. "He was so likable. I have met him frequently in London. It was through Jeff that you met father, Mr. Modbury."

"I know," nodded Modbury. Then, to Delka: "Tell me, Inspector, does there appear to be some enmity behind this foul play?"

"That is what I wish to learn," replied Delka. "You saw Chiswold recently, Mr. Modbury. Did he ever speak to you of enemies?"

"Never," said Modbury, with a shake of his head.

"Poor Jeff," murmured Gwendolyn.

"I have talked with his creditors," acknowledged Delka. "They could not help me. Nor could members at his club. He seldom talked of personal matters. I wanted to meet those who were close friends to him."

"He was a real friend to father and myself," announced Gwendolyn. "We thought that everyone liked Jeff. Didn't you, Francisco?"

The girl had turned to Lodera. The Spaniard shook his head.

"I do not recall meeting Geoffrey Chiswold," he replied. "In fact, I scarcely ever heard his name mentioned except as the former owner of this castle."

"Don't you remember meeting Jeff?" exclaimed Gwendolyn. "Twice in London. Once right here—"

"Yes," added Modbury. "You met Chiswold here, Lodera. The day before he left."

LODERA chewed his lips. It was Luval who came to his rescue. The bespectacled secretary was quick and tactful.

"I do not believe that you introduced Mr. Chiswold to Senor Lodera," he reminded Modbury. "Therefore, it is not surprising that Senor Lodera should not remember him."

Lodera smiled suavely. The Shadow saw him flash a glance of thanks to Luval. The secretary's statement passed with Modbury.

"That was deuced stupid of me," stated the deep-voiced man. "I recall it, now that you have mentioned the circumstances, Luval. I thought that Chiswold and Lodera had met—"

"And so they had!" injected Gwendolyn. "Surely, you must remember it, Francisco! Once at Lady Allerton's you—"

"Please, Gwendolyn," protested Lodera. His tone sounded pleading. "I knew of Chiswold, certainly. I did regard him as a friend. His unfortunate death distresses me. Probably, I have met him. I begin to place the man, now that the occasions have been enumerated. But I knew nothing about his business, save that he sold his castle."

"That is all I need to know," declared Delka. Lodera's sudden appeal had sounded genuine. The Spaniard actually looked distressed. "I should like, however, to make inquiry of Sir Rodney and Lord Cedric."

"Which you may do," promised Modbury, "as soon as they have returned. Meanwhile, I shall expect you and Mr. Cranston to remain here for dinner. You are also quite welcome to stay overnight, if you so desire."

IT was dinner time when Sir Rodney Ralthorn and Lord Cedric Lorthing came in from hunting.

The news of Geoffrey Chiswold's demise came as a shock to both Sir Rodney and Lord Cedric. When Delka asked them about the dead man, the two agreed immediately that Geoffrey had lacked enemies.

"Preposterous!" was Sir Rodney's opinion. Tall, red-faced, with gray hair and side whiskers, he looked emphatic when he gave it. "That young man had no enemies. His one fault was that he sometimes proved himself a gadfly. A lightweight, when judged by brain capacity. But a gentleman, always, and well liked."

"Quite so. Quite so." Lord Cedric drawled approval. He was a middle-aged, long-faced man, who wore a monocle. "I knew Geoffrey well. He could not have had enemies."

Eric Delka was impressed. Barton Modbury, however, was not entirely convinced.

"Apparently so," boomed Modbury, "but in a case like this, no stone should remain unturned. When Geoffrey Chiswold left here, I told him that I would keep some trunks that contained his personal effects. Perhaps there may be letters among them."

"Where are they?" queried Delka.

"In one of the rooms upstairs," stated Modbury. "I shall have Luval go through them thoroughly with you. Moreover, it might be well to look elsewhere, in some of the rooms which have not yet been refurnished."

"I shall have Mund show us about, sir," put in Luval. "He knows every portion of this old castle."

"Mund is one of the former servants," explained Modbury. "Very well, Luval. How long should it take?"

"A few hours at the most, sir."

Delka turned to The Shadow.

"That means we cannot catch the early train," said the man from Scotland Yard. "At least I cannot. You will have to return to London alone, unless you care to wait."

"I must go back to London," stated The Shadow. "In fact"—he glanced at his watch—"I must leave shortly after dinner."

"I shall have a car for you," said Modbury.

"No, no," returned The Shadow. "There will be moonlight tonight. I would prefer to walk. I noticed shortcuts as we rode here."

"Very well," smiled Modbury. "It is not more than a few miles. I think you will find the walk a pleasant one."

Then, glancing at his own watch, he added:

"You must stay long enough, however, to glance about the ground floor and see some of the furniture that I have installed."

THEY adjourned to a great room across the spacious hall. Here a crackly fire threw its light and drew the slight chill from the musty walls. The Shadow admired the furniture of which Modbury had spoken.

"These have added to the older furniture that was already in the castle," explained Modbury. "Later, I shall install a grand piano. That will help to reduce the mammoth proportions of this room. But I see that the time is passing. It would be best for you to start your walk to the station, unless you will alter your decision and ride back in one of my motors."

"I have made up my mind to walk," declared The Shadow. "I must thank you for your hospitality, Mr. Modbury."

Delka had gone with Luval to make his thorough check on all of Geoffrey Chiswold's remaining effects. The Shadow said good-bye to the others; and a servant ushered him to the door. The moon had risen; its silver glow produced a new beauty to the premises about Chiswold Castle.

Strolling down the driveway, The Shadow reached the fringe of the woods. There, he paused just beneath the trees to look back toward the vast building. Gray walls held a sheen tonight; a veritable reflection of the moonlight that came from stretches where ivy streaks were thin.

Quiet persisted, except for the faint murmur from the sea. Waves rolling against the English coast; a reminder of the days when bold boatmen had brought the young pretender and his followers to these shores.

The Shadow stepped farther beneath the trees. The distant tone of breakers faded. Instead, a sinister whisper crept amid the darkness; a sibilant laugh that issued from The Shadow's lips.

Circling, The Shadow came from the woods near a corner of the castle. He approached the porch. There, from an obscure spot, he produced his bag.

The coachman had left it, along with Delka's. But The Shadow had placed his own grip to one side, before following the others into the house. No servant had spied it. Thus The Shadow had regained it from its niche beneath the wall.

Back toward the woods. There, stooping, The Shadow opened the bag. From it, he produced cloak and hat of black. Obscuring garments enshrouded his head and shoulders. Garbed in this attire, The Shadow could move abroad tonight. Here, perhaps, he would find clues—clues that he would prefer to trace alone.

WHEN Delka arrived outside two hours later, he paused to say good-bye to Barton Modbury. A servant was carrying Delka's bag, to place it in the car. Delka had forgotten about The Shadow's piece of luggage.

Both Delka and Modbury expressed themselves upon one point; namely, that the search through Geoffrey Chiswold's trunks had produced no documents of importance. That fact served as final proof that murder could not have been prearranged.

Sir Rodney and Lord Cedric were also present; but both Lodera and Luval were within the castle. Delka stepped aboard the car; it headed back toward Yarwick. When the purr of the motor faded, only the faint sound of the sea remained. The door of the castle had closed; the men on the porch had gone inside.

Then, again, came the whispered laugh. Closer—so close that it was almost from the porch itself. After that, a streak of blackness moved— scarcely visible—toward the front trees between the house and the lodge keeper's gate.

The Shadow had seen; The Shadow had heard. The Shadow had remained.

CHAPTER VIII
THE MAN AT THE INN

AT about the time when The Shadow was observing Eric Delka's departure from Chiswold Castle, the evening down train had pulled into the little station of Yarwick. Singularly enough, the branchline local had discharged a passenger.

The local cabby with the old victoria was waiting by the station. His luck during the afternoon had brightened him. The arrival of another fare upon the evening train was something that he had not anticipated, yet which he accepted with relish.

"Carry you to the inn, your worship?"

At the coachman's conventional greeting, the arrival turned about beneath the dingy glow of a platform light. For the first time, the coach driver discerned him clearly. He gripped the reins and stared.

Viewed from the back, the passenger had made a huddled figure, for his shoulders had held a definite stoop. When he turned, he produced a muffled sight, for the collar of his old overcoat was turned high above his chin, while the brim of his battered felt hat pointed almost perpendicularly downward.

He was making an effort to hide his face; yet the driver of the victoria spied it, thanks to the angle of the light. The features that he saw were waxlike; broad, yet expressionless, with lips that held a fixed position.

THE man on the platform must have noticed the coach driver's start, for he hastily closed the front of his coat collar with one gloved hand. When he spoke, his voice was gruff; it was also muffled deeply within the protecting cloth.

"Take me to the inn," he ordered, approaching the victoria. "To the Prince William Inn."

"A shilling's the fare," announced the driver, dubious about this odd-looking customer, "and the luggage goes to boot."

"I have no luggage," growled the muffled man.

He stepped aboard the old carriage. The driver clucked to the horse and the rubber-tired wheels jounced over the ruts of the old station road. They rolled through darkness; the coachman urged his horse to greater speed.

The dim lights of the little town came as a relief to the old coachman. He slackened his tiring horse and drew up in front of the Prince William Inn. When he did so, he nervily chose a spot close by one of the few lampposts; then turned about to announce the destination. It was then that he saw the passenger's face again.

It no longer looked like wax. It was more like parchment, smooth and fixed. The eyelids appeared to be the only live portion of the rider's countenance. From beneath them, the coach driver caught a sharp, questioning gaze.

"Here we are, your honor—"

The passenger grunted something; then alighted from the victoria. He handed the driver a shilling and a sixpence for a tip. He managed the matter clumsily, for his hands were still gloved. Then, turning on his heel, the newcomer went into the inn.

THE Prince William Inn boasted a main room that might once have been occupied by its royal namesake, for the place looked to be three hundred years old. It was illuminated by kerosene lamps, plus a sparkling log flame in the grate. One corner formed a sort of desk; by that counter was a doorway that led into a small barroom, which was well lighted by lamps.

The proprietor, a man with a heavy black mustache, was behind the desk when the muffled guest approached. He eyed the stranger suspiciously; then brought a lamp from a ledge beside him and placed it upon the counter. The new guest shied away.

"How much are your rooms?" he inquired, gruffly, holding his coat collar more tightly to his chin. "By the week, I mean?"

"Two and six the night, sir," responded the proprietor. "Twelve and six by the week. A guinea for a fortnight—"

"By the week will suit me," gruffed the stranger. "Twelve and six, you say?"

The proprietor nodded.

"I have no luggage," stated the new guest. "I shall pay you in advance."

He drew a crumpled ten-shilling note from his pocket and thrust it across the counter. Then, clumsy with his gloved hand, he produced some silver and clattered a half crown in front of the proprietor. This coin, the equivalent of two shillings and sixpence, made up the necessary difference.

"Show me to the room."

As the guest spoke, his collar slipped slightly. The proprietor, for the first time, gained a fair view of his visage. The mustached innkeeper drew his breath with a sharp whistle. Then, as the guest moved toward a flight of stairs, the proprietor arose from behind the counter.

There was a registration book upon the desk; but the stranger had not signed. Nor did the proprietor care to press the matter upon this occasion. The face that he had seen might have been a plaster death mask, with coloring that looked like flesh-tinted grease paint!

Taking a pair of candlesticks from a corner of the counter, the proprietor lighted the wicks and led the way upstairs. The stranger followed him; the proprietor nudged open a door that stood ajar and placed the candles upon the mantel of a small room. He turned about and saw the guest staring toward the window. Gingerly, the innkeeper sidled to the door.

Leaving the room, the proprietor closed the door behind him, then moved slowly toward the stairs. Immediately, he heard the click of a key in the lock. The new guest apparently did not wish to be disturbed.

THE proprietor was nervous when he reached the desk. He heard voices from the barroom and went in there, anxious for company. By the bar, he saw the coachman who had driven the victoria. The fellow was holding a huge mug of ale.

"'Twas a great day," he was bragging. Then, seeing the proprietor, "Aye, a great day, Mr. Mullock. Comes two passengers to Yarwick platform and asks to be carried to Chiswold Castle. A crown is the cost, says I, with the luggage carried to boot."

"And this man tonight?" queried Mullock.

Chauncey spluttered; then coughed as he set his mug aside.

"'Twere different tonight," he confided. "'Twas only one fare that I brought from Yarwick platform. Not like their worships. 'Twas the face of him I did not like—"

The sound of a stopping motor came from outside the inn. A big Humber had halted; its chauffeur, a stocky man, was peering in at the door. Mullock and Chauncey recognized him as one of the new retinue at Chiswold Castle.

"When does the up train depart?" asked the chauffeur. "I have a gentleman here for Yarwick platform. He has noted that our timetable is an old one."

"One up train has gone," informed Chauncey. "'Tis an hour yet before the last will call at Yarwick platform."

Another man had appeared at the door. It was Eric Delka, in time to hear the coachman's statement. Delka turned to the chauffeur who had brought him in Modbury's car.

"Ride back to the castle," said Delka. "There is no need for you to wait. I can use this man's victoria to reach the station."

The chauffeur nodded and departed. Delka strolled past the bar and saw the door into the main room. He was about to enter there when he heard Mullock speak to Chauncey.

"The face of the man upstairs," queried the proprietor, in an anxious tone. "You saw it, Chauncey?"

"Aye," nodded the coachman, gripping the mug handle as he spoke. "Aye. Nor was it human; unless 'twas the face of a corpse."

Delka paused to listen.

"I saw the face, too," remarked the innkeeper in an awed tone. "It might have been wax, or plaster."

"'Twas like parchment," protested the coachman. "Save for the color of it. The cheeks were ruddy; the lips were straight."

"But did they move?"

"Nay. Nor could I see them. 'Twas close about his chin that he kept the collar of his coat."

Mullock raised his hands for silence. Footsteps were coming from the stairs, a steady, descending beat. Chauncey shifted along the bar and gripped his mug more tightly. Nervously, he began to gulp his ale.

Mullock withdrew. The barmaid looked frightened. Delka, fully stirred by these odd actions, decided to wait where he was. He edged back from the door. He heard the approach of footsteps; then saw the man who had been mentioned.

THE new guest was still wearing his hat and coat. From the position that he took in the doorway, he faced Mullock, Chauncey and the barmaid; and kept his features well hidden. He must have felt searching eyes upon him, for he pressed his collar to his lips before he spoke.

"I am going out to view the moonlight." The stranger spoke mechanically. "I shall return presently."

Delka, from his point of observation, caught a better glimpse of the man's face than did the others. Remembering their statements, the Scotland Yard man was able to note the parchment-like features, from the half-face view that he gained. They were right. The lips did not move!

Turning about, the mysterious guest stalked out through the main room. They heard the front door close; then his footsteps vanished as they struck soft turf.

"'Tis a ghoul, he is!" breathed Chauncey. The coachman's hand was trembling. "A werewolf that seeks the moonlight. If we hear strange howls on this night, 'twill be the foul fiend in him—"

The barmaid uttered a half shriek. Mullock tremblingly moved forward and gripped Chauncey's arm.

"Hush!" he whispered to the coachman. "Would you drive all guests from my inn?"

Eric Delka spoke to the proprietor.

"Have you a room for the night?" queried the Scotland Yard man. "I believe that I shall not go up to London. The Yarwick air is healthy at this season."

The innkeeper looked grateful. The barmaid suppressed another shriek. Chauncey stared; then let his mug jounce empty from his hand. He watched Delka go with Mullock into the large room. Then, with an air of satisfaction, the coachman nodded and spoke to the barmaid.

"'Tis a fine gentleman," he affirmed. "This one comes from London. 'Twas he that I took to Chiswold Castle, with a friend, this very day."

DELKA did not hear the approval. He was making his arrangements for the night. He signed the register. Mullock carried his bag upstairs, holding one lighted candle while Delka carried another. Delka saw the proprietor glance anxiously at a closed door; they passed it and came to another across the hall.

This was to be Delka's room; and the C.I.D. man knew that the other guest must be occupying the one where the innkeeper had shown anxiousness. Delka waited until Mullock had gone; then he snuffed out the candles and drew a large chair to the window.

From this seat, Eric Delka could see the front street outside the inn. He watched Chauncey come from the barroom and drive away in his clattery victoria. Silence lay outside the Prince William Inn.

Dim lamps still laid a glow beneath unstirring trees. Beyond, where branches thinned, patches of moonlight whitened the ground. Eric Delka gazed, a man on vigil.

He was waiting here to spy the return of the stranger with the wax-made face.

JEREMY—gatekeeper of Chiswold Castle.

CHAPTER IX
JEREMY MEETS A GHOST

BACK at Chiswold Castle, the last light had blinked out shortly after the return of the big Humber landaulet. The chauffeur had driven the automobile into an ancient stable off from the castle; then a light had appeared in upstairs quarters above the improvised garage. Soon after, that light had been extinguished.

Moonlight still remained, and its mellow glow showed a rising shape that came from a narrow fringe of trees behind the castle. There, The Shadow had delved among the craglike rocks that topped the gorge called Castle Cove. He had returned toward the castle when he had heard the car return.

Moving between the castle and the stable, The Shadow followed a circling, well-planned course. He was keeping his tall figure inconspicuous, against the background of shadowy trees. There were spaces, however, where he was forced to come into the open. At those stretches, his glide became more rapid.

Nearing the front corner of the castle, The Shadow came to a sudden pause. He had caught a sound from above: the swinging clatter of a casement window. Halted, The Shadow became a blackened statue in the moonlight. His keen eyes peered upward from beneath the brim of his slouch hat.

Someone was at the second story, looking downward. Someone whom The Shadow could not discern. That person, however, had gained an opportunity to spy the blackened figure on the lawn. The Shadow had stopped because he knew that a moving shape would more probably attract attention than a stilled one.

Behind The Shadow, away from the castle, was the protecting shade of a large tree. Slowly, almost imperceptibly, he began a backward course. He was sure that eyes were watching him; that some wondering observer could not quite identify his shape as a human one. Hence The Shadow was deliberate in motion.

Branches, stirred by a slight sea breeze, were flickering their shaded mass upon the moonlighted turf.

The Shadow, too, was wavering. His own shadow formed a blackened streak that extended forward from his figure. The staring person from the second-floor window would have difficulty in determining whether or not The Shadow's form was solid.

Then, when The Shadow had eased back into shelter, all chance was ended. His own shadow withdrew a bit more rapidly, until it was blended with the streaky darkness from the boughs. Gliding deeper into blackness, The Shadow heard the casement window close.

Keeping to new patches of blackness, The Shadow rounded the front of the castle and held close to trees and shrubbery that formed a helpful line. He was nearing the woods about the front drive when he came to another pause.

The new reason for a halt was the bobbing of a lantern that came from between the castle and stable. The light was approaching the spot where The Shadow stood.

OBSCURED by darkness, The Shadow waited. The light drew nearer. By the lantern's glow, The Shadow recognized old Jeremy. The gatekeeper was carrying the lantern in his left hand; over the crook of his right elbow, he held an ancient fowling piece that looked like the modern replica of a blunderbuss.

The Shadow waited until Jeremy had passed; then followed. The gatekeeper kept on until he reached his lodge. The Shadow saw the lantern bob from view. He spied a gloomy window and approached it, to look into the main downstairs room of the gate lodge. Thanks to a broken, unpatched pane, The Shadow could hear as well as see.

Jeremy's wife had been seated by the firelight. Jeremy, entering, had kept the lantern lighted. He was placing it upon a table when The Shadow observed him. Holding close to the window, The Shadow saw Jeremy shake his head and pick up a clay pipe.

"Ill news, good wife," announced the gatekeeper, in a sorrowful tone. "'Twas in the castle that I heard it, from Mr. Modbury's own lips, ere I began my rounds of the castle ground."

"Ill news?" queried the woman, in a tired tone.

"Aye," nodded Jeremy. "Ill news from London town. Our good master, Geoffrey, was done to death last night."

The woman delivered a sad sigh.

"'Twas on his account that the gentlemen came down from London," concluded Jeremy. "Friends they were to Master Geoffrey, in hope that they might learn who did ill to him."

"Did they learn aught?"

"Nay. 'Twas bad men who roam through London that did the evil. They fell upon poor Master Geoffrey, amidst a great fog."

"'Twas good to us he was, young Master Geoffrey." The woman arose and took the lantern from the table. "Ah! 'Tis an ill world, Jeremy. May naught come to hurt the new master at the great castle. 'Tis he that we serve now."

Jeremy puffed sourly at his pipe.

"Mayhap if Master Geoffrey had held more money, he could have done better with us," observed the old gatekeeper. "'Twas kindness alone that he could give. 'Twould be a sin, Katrine, to think less of him than our new Master Modbury. Ah, Peace be to our dead Master Geoffrey."

The woman had started up the stairs, leaving old Jeremy mumbling and shaking his head. It was obvious that the bad news had hurt him more deeply. That was natural, for the gatekeeper was in closer touch with matters at the castle than was his wife.

The firelight showed old Jeremy seated with bowed head, puffing his pipe in disconsolate fashion. So deep was he in meditation that a new sound did not at first attract his attention. The Shadow heard the noise before Jeremy. It was a cautious tapping at the front door of the lodge.

JEREMY heard it at last. Watching from the side window, The Shadow saw the gatekeeper arouse himself and look toward the fowling piece. Then, disregarding the old gun, Jeremy went to the door and opened it. A man stepped into the darkened fringe of the room.

The newcomer was muffled, coat collar high and hat pressed low. His eyes sparkled in the dim light; but his face was difficult to see. As he stepped toward the fire, The Shadow caught an earlier glimpse than Jeremy.

The stranger's face was lifeless, almost waxen. His lips did not move when he mumbled a greeting; and gave the excuse of being cold, as a pretext to step past Jeremy and approach the fire. The late visitor to the gatekeeper's abode was the mysterious man who had recently left the old Prince William inn.

Jeremy followed the man and watched him peel off his brown kid gloves. The gatekeeper became suddenly suspicious. He reached for the fowling piece. The man at the fireplace stepped back and saw the action. He hissed for caution; the order made Jeremy act more stubbornly. The gatekeeper yanked up the gun.

As counter move, the man by the fireplace threw back his coat collar and whipped away his hat. Seeing the solidified features for the first time, Jeremy became more antagonistic. He thrust his finger to the trigger of the gun; then uttered an incoherent gasp.

The man by the fireplace had pressed both hands to his cheeks; then dropping them, he had carried away his face! In place of that mask that he had worn, he revealed pallid features that Jeremy recognized. Dropping his gun, Jeremy quivered. His lips blurted an awed whisper:

"Master Geoffrey!"

Another hiss for caution. The man at the fireplace stepped toward Jeremy. The gatekeeper tried to back away.

"Nay! Nay!" gasped Jeremy. "'Tis no ill that I have spoken! Nay! Do not haunt me! May your spirit rest—"

HANDS clutched Jeremy's arm. The gatekeeper's face became distorted. He thought that he was viewing a ghost; he expected a clammy, unearthly touch. Instead, this man whom he took for Geoffrey Chiswold was seizing him with the firm grip of a human being.

"'Tis alive!" panted Jeremy. "'Tis Master Geoffrey, in living flesh! Dead, you were—so they said—"

"Geoffrey Chiswold is dead."

The words were cold as they came from slowly moving lips. Once again, Jeremy trembled, for he was staring at a whitish face. This was a ghost, he was sure—a specter that had gained power to enter its forgotten corpse.

Too scared to even mutter, Jeremy sagged to his knees, his hands raised pleadingly. The Shadow, watching steadily from the window, saw a smile appear upon the face of the man from the night.

The Shadow waited, never stirring. Strange though this scene might be, he had divined the outcome. He was ready for the explanation that was due to come.

CHAPTER X
THE MASK CHANGES

"GEOFFREY CHISWOLD is dead."

Again, the pallid man repeated his statement; and Jeremy's hands raised farther as they trembled. Then came added words:

"But I am not Geoffrey Chiswold."

Jeremy blinked and stared upward.

"Not Geoffrey," repeated the supposed ghost. "Look closely, Jeremy. You will remember me."

Thus encouraged, Jeremy arose. In the flicker of the firelight, he stared, still quivering. Then sheer puzzlement enabled him to speak.

"'Tis the face—the face of Master Geoffrey," stammered the gatekeeper. "'Tis the nose—the eyes—but—"

He paused; then, half questioning, he gasped:

"Master Nigel?"

The pale-faced man broadened his wise smile.

"Yes," he affirmed. "I am Nigel Chiswold. I am back from India. I have come to find you, Jeremy, as one would seek an old friend."

"Master Nigel! And 'tis cold you be, and pale from it. Warm yourself by the hearth, sir. 'Tis a nip I can find for you, against the cold—"

He was moving toward the stairs. Nigel stopped him.

"Wait. Never mind that, Jeremy. No one must know that I am here. Do not go upstairs until I have left. You would arouse your wife. Come! Sit beside the fire and hear what I have to tell you."

NIGEL sat down upon a three-legged stool and Jeremy chose a similar resting place. The gatekeeper watched his visitor shed his coat and throw it beside his hat. He saw that Nigel was heavily clad, wearing a sweater beneath the coat of his thick suit.

"I have come here alone," declared Nigel, eyeing Jeremy carefully, "because I must avenge the murder of my cousin. That is my mission, Jeremy."

"The murder?" echoed Jeremy.

"Yes," nodded Nigel. "Geoffrey was murdered. Those who slew him may be here, in Chiswold Castle."

Jeremy blinked; then shook his head emphatically.

"Nay!" he objected. "'Tis an honorable man, is Master Modbury. Nor was he in London, last night. 'Twas a good friend he was to Master Geoffrey—"

"I said nothing of Modbury," put in Nigel, quickly. "There are others here beside him."

"Good people all. Folk who would do no ill to anyone. Nor have they come or gone—"

"I understand. But you must listen, Jeremy. Geoffrey was killed by men in London. Someone dispatched them to that work. Those who ordered them to slay—whether one or many—are to be held responsible.

"I did not know that you had learned about Geoffrey's death. That is why I came here as I did, thinking that you would take me for Geoffrey, but not as his ghost. So you have learned, eh? At the castle, I suppose?"

Jeremy nodded and mumbled: "Aye."

"And upon whom did they place the blame?" queried Nigel.

"Upon no one," returned Jeremy. "So Master Modbury told me. Upon no one who sought Master Geoffrey's life. 'Twas bad men, roaming the fog, who slew him in London town."

"Footpads, eh?"

"Aye."

Nigel smiled and looked relieved. Then his tone became shrewd as he began new argument.

"That is the story that would be told," he declared. "Perhaps it is true. Yet there is a chance that someone in the castle knew that the attempt would be made."

"I cannot believe that to be so, Master Nigel—"

"Remember, Jeremy, that I talked with Geoffrey only an hour before he died."

The man by the fireplace had pressed both hands to his cheeks; then dropping them, he had carried away his face.

"He feared ill?"

"He did. From the way he spoke, I decided that his life must be in danger."

"He spoke of those in the castle?"

"He warned me not to come here."

JEREMY pondered, puffing his clay pipe as he stared at the fire. The Shadow, watching Nigel's face, gained a full explanation of varied circumstances. First, he knew how Harry Vincent had happened to lose Geoffrey's trail; the agent had followed Nigel instead. Second, he had the answer to the strange puzzle of Geoffrey's change in attire. Yet The Shadow had already anticipated these discoveries. Delka had mentioned Geoffrey's cousin, Nigel.

A third point, however, was clear to The Shadow. He knew why Nigel Chiswold had become relieved when Jeremy had attributed Geoffrey's death to persons unknown. Nigel had feared that his own name might have been mentioned in connection. Learning that it had not, Nigel felt secure.

As a trump card, Nigel had told of his meeting with Geoffrey, an encounter which The Shadow had already pictured. The Shadow had thought it likely that Nigel would bob up. He had picked the gatekeeper's lodge as the point of contact; and had followed Jeremy for that reason. Nigel's visit had taken place sooner than The Shadow had believed it would.

"I came to Yarwick." Nigel was speaking again. "I wore hat, coat and mask, when I stopped at the Prince William Inn. I told them I would remain there for a week. That was in case I could not find a friend here. You, Jeremy."

The gatekeeper looked up curiously.

"We owe it to Geoffrey," persisted Nigel, smoothly. "I, his cousin; you, his faithful gatekeeper. We must learn all that goes on within Chiswold Castle. We must be sure that no guilty person is staying there."

Jeremy was nodding. Nigel's tone was convincing, and the gatekeeper was recalling that the castle harbored several persons other than his new benefactor, Barton Modbury.

"Where will you stay?" queried Jeremy. "The gamekeeper's cot, would it do? 'Tis but half a mile along the path that leads from the castle drive. 'Tis the only place, for the cottage beside the distant field is taken. 'Tis there that the airman stays."

"The airman?"

"Aye. The one named Dufour, who guides the plane owned by Mr. Lodera."

"Francisco Lodera, the Spaniard? Is he a guest at the castle?"

"Aye."

"I have heard of him. He belonged to Geoffrey's set. But never mind Lodera for the present. I shall not stay at the gamekeeper's cot. I shall enter the castle."

"The castle!"

JEREMY looked astounded. Nigel smiled; then spoke after a moment's hesitation.

"There are secrets to the castle, Jeremy," he explained. "Secrets known to the Chiswolds alone. One is the old spy room in the turret. It can be reached."

"From within the castle?"

"Yes. From the large room on the second floor."

"But 'tis a task to enter there—"

"I know another means of entrance. The one used by the friends of Bonnie Prince Charley, when they came by sea. The way that Ned Burke used. Through the chamber where there was space for a hundred men should they be needed—"

Nigel broke off abruptly, as if telling Jeremy too much. He put a question.

"Who of the old servants are at the castle?"

"Only Mund," replied Jeremy. "'Twas one by one they left, when money came hard with Master Geoffrey."

"Mund would have been the last," nodded Nigel. "He could not have found position elsewhere. Dull and stupid, he would serve anyone who paid him."

Jeremy nodded in agreement.

"Since you know nothing of the spy room," chuckled Nigel, "I doubt that Mund does. Well, Jeremy, I shall depend upon you. I have food for a while"—he patted the stuffed pockets of his coat—"and when I need more, I shall signal."

"From the turret?"

"Yes. With blinks of a flashlight, at night. I shall let down a cord that I have with me, together with notes. You can send up provisions, unless you feel that it would not be safe."

"'Twould be safe enough, Master Nigel. 'Tis my task to make the rounds at night."

"Good. And later, Jeremy, you may expect a visitor; I do not know what night he will arrive; but you will know him by his password. It is 'Khyber.' Can you remember it?"

"'Khyber,'" repeated Jeremy.

Nigel arose from the stool.

"Take those clothes," he said, pointing to his hat and overcoat. "Hide them somewhere at once—outside this lodge. So that your wife will not find them. Put the mask with them, Jeremy.

"And remember"—his tone was low and emphatic—"I trust in you. Breathe no word of this meeting. Tell no one that I am here. No one, except the friend who says the one word: 'Khyber.'"

JEREMY nodded firmly. Nigel studied him shrewdly; then clapped a friendly hand upon the gatekeeper's shoulder. With that, Nigel turned and left the cottage. The Shadow heard him go along the driveway, through the darkness; but The Shadow did not stir. He was watching Jeremy.

The old gatekeeper was standing stolid, holding

his clay pipe. Minutes passed; then Jeremy came to life. He bundled the coat and hat and gingerly added the mask to them. He opened the door and tiptoed out into the darkness.

The Shadow moved to the corner of the lodge. He saw Jeremy moving toward the high picket fence that led from beside the gate. The Shadow followed.

Jeremy stooped in a patch of moonlight. He moved about; then arose without the bundle and went back into the lodge. The Shadow waited a few moments, then approached the spot where the gate-keeper had been. He found the hat, coat and mask wedged deeply into an abandoned drain pipe that was almost obscured by overhanging turf.

Carrying the bundle with him, The Shadow returned to the edge of the driveway and started toward the castle. He was too far behind to pick up Nigel's trail. He had another objective.

He stopped amid the trees, blinked a tiny flash-light and found his bag at a place where he had stowed it. Taking the bag with the bundle, he continued, giving new blinks cautiously until he found the path that Nigel had mentioned.

He followed this course until he had gone nearly half a mile. Then he used the flashlight regularly until he picked out an obscure building deep in the trees. It was the gamekeeper's cot; a tiny, one-room structure. The Shadow entered.

He found loose boards in the bare floor and pried them upward. Beneath them, The Shadow stowed his bag. He slid off his cloak and slouch hat, to put those garments in the same hiding place. Then he used the flashlight on the bundle that he carried.

A WHISPERED laugh stirred strange echoes within the narrow walls. A slight sound followed; then the flashlight blinked finally upon the barren boards. The bundle was gone; a huddled figure stalked from the little cot. It turned along the path, taking a shortcut toward the town of Yarwick.

Moonlight from amid the trees showed a duplicate of the figure that had entered Jeremy's lodge. The glow revealed the same expressionless face that Nigel Chiswold had worn, held in place by the same coat collar and the identical felt hat.

The mask had changed. It was worn by a different person than the one who had first used it. The mystery man with the corpselike face was due to return to the Prince William Inn.

But the stranger who returned would not be the one that had left. The Shadow had replaced Nigel Chiswold.

CHAPTER XI
TRAILS DIVERGE

IT was morning. All was peaceful about the Prince William Inn, so far as external appearances were concerned. But the three men who occupied the lobby room were holding secret thoughts of their own.

One was Mullock, the innkeeper; he was solemn behind his counter. The second was Chauncey, the coachman. He was just within the door, toying with his whip, but anxious. The third, apparently the least concerned, was Eric Delka. All were waiting the descent of the mysterious stranger.

Mullock had heard him come in late last night. Chauncey had only guessed that the stranger had returned. But Delka had seen and heard. Watching from his front window, the C.I.D. man had once again observed the man with the mask.

He had listened while the curious visitor had come upstairs and unlocked the door of his room. He had heard him lock the door from within. Then Delka had napped until morning. He had come downstairs as early as the proprietor.

IN his upstairs room, The Shadow was seated before a mirror. Propped against the wall was Nigel Chiswold's mask, a piece of workmanship that commanded admiration. Nigel had certainly bought it in London. Made of a flexible composition, the false face formed an excellent replica of a human visage.

Except that it was lifeless. The mask maker had not prepared this device to serve the use to which Nigel had put it. That was why Nigel had made every effort to cover his lips while speaking. A bad feature of his impromptu disguise. One which The Shadow intended to remedy.

Upon the table lay two objects. One was the key to the room. The Shadow had found it in the pocket of Nigel's discarded overcoat; it had the door number, and because of that, The Shadow had experienced no trouble in locating Nigel's room. The other object on the table was a small, flat box.

A portable makeup kit. One that The Shadow had expressly carried for this journey. He had opened it; his nimble fingers were at work. They were kneading The Shadow's own visage, changing it from its former appearance—the features of Lamont Cranston.

Puttylike substance dabbed from fingertips. Grease paint was drawn from the box. Eyebrows changed their shape. The Shadow's countenance took on an amazing change, yet a swift one. The final touches were slower, with daubs of paint. Then the hands dropped; The Shadow stared at the mirror.

His face was the absolute image of the mask that rested against the wall!

A soft laugh from new lips. A slow, lifelike smile. A few more touches; The Shadow held the mask beside his own countenance, to compare both at the mirror's range. The job was perfect.

The Shadow donned hat and overcoat; he tucked the mask out of sight, beneath his coat. Rising, he pocketed the makeup kit; then unlocked the door of his room and went downstairs. Solemn of expression, he pulled his hat a trifle forward when he saw the three men who looked in his direction.

Delka's presence was a surprise to The Shadow. One that thrust him into a campaign of strategy. He had suspected that persons at the inn would be doubtful about Nigel Chiswold. It had become his purpose to end that feeling, in order that no one might guess that the stranger was here for a secret purpose. But The Shadow had not known that Inspector Delka had chanced across Nigel's path.

His reasons for pretense had become much greater, now that The Shadow knew. For it was essential that the law should remain away from Chiswold Castle until after The Shadow had studied matters there. The Shadow knew that he must deal with Delka.

In muffled tone, The Shadow gave a good morning. He strolled to the fireplace and studied the dying embers. Then, with his back to all three men, he let his coat collar fall.

"Will you have breakfast, sir?" queried Mullock, suddenly.

The question was loud; intended to make The Shadow turn. As if startled, he swung about, groped at his coat collar but failed to raise it. Then, with a slow nod, he replied:

"Yes. I shall breakfast here."

THREE men gaped; Delka was as astounded as his provincial companions. The Shadow, in speaking, had moved his lips. His countenance, seen by daylight, lacked the lifelessness of the face that they had seen the night before!

Having decided to breakfast at the inn, The Shadow discarded his hat and coat. In removing the latter, he folded it so that the mask was lost beneath the coat. The proprietor called a servant; a table was laid in a corner of the main room.

Delka had not breakfasted. Strolling over, he introduced himself to The Shadow, who, in turn, announced himself as Professor Roderick Danglar, of Cambridge. In manner, in tone of voice, The Shadow's present guise differed from that of Lamont Cranston. Delka, when they ate together, did not suspect that this pretended professor was his companion of the day before.

He did, however, gain the impression that Professor Danglar would be a man worth watching. The Shadow, in fact, tried to convey that thought to the C.I.D. man; and he succeeded. As the meal progressed, Delka became more and more determined upon a duty; namely, to trail Professor Danglar wherever he might go.

The Shadow's breakfast discourse concerned the fenlands, which bordered on this district. His comments, delivered in the dry way of a pedagogue, brought Mullock over to listen.

NIGEL CHISWOLD—who has just come back from India.

"The fen region," stated The Shadow, "consists of an area which was once a bay from the North Sea. The estuary called The Wash is the last remaining portion. The silt-filled lowlands which have replaced the former bay now compose the fens.

"Originally, the fens were boggy. Since dikes now protect them from the sea and the rivers which flow through them, the fens are fertile land, much akin to the lowlands of Holland. Imagine it! Half a million acres of English soil, that match the famous Netherlands!"

"I have traveled across the fens," remarked Delka, "but I have seen nothing of great interest in the district."

"Because you have not studied it. The fens are interesting because of the old ruins. The Romans made efforts to drain the lowlands. So did the early British and the Danes. Ancient embankments and causeways still survive."

Mullock was nodding as he listened.

"Later," continued The Shadow, "windmills were used to pump water from the fens. Attempts at reclamation were conducted on a large scale; but at one period—during the time of Cromwell—they met with stiff opposition."

"From whom?"

DELKA made the query in a tone of real

surprise. He had not studied the past history of the fens.

"From the fen dwellers," clucked The Shadow. "Rough men who preferred to walk about on stilts through the marshy land. These native fenmen had rights of commonage, fishing and fowling; also the privilege of turbary—otherwise turf-cutting."

"Aye." The statement came from Mullock. "And there are places where the fens are still wild, where men dwell yet—"

"I know," interposed The Shadow. "Those are the lands which I have come to visit. I wish to study the so-called islands of high ground that exist among the marshes. To search for Roman ruins and to hear the primitive dialect, speech of the fen dwellers."

Finishing his bowl of strawberries and clotted Devonshire cream, The Shadow arose and picked up hat and coat. He strolled from the inn so briskly that Delka could find no immediate excuse to follow. It was several minutes before the C.I.D. man could determine upon a purpose. Then he decided to go to the station.

Walking to that destination, Delka found a station agent on duty. The C.I.D. man dispatched a long telegram to Scotland Yard, asking for information concerning Professor Roderick Danglar of Cambridge. That done, Delka went back to the inn, hoping that his quarry had returned.

Hardly had Delka left the station before a figure stepped from a furze which formed a thicket near the road. It was The Shadow, no longer wearing coat and hat. Instead, he was carrying a package wrapped in a newspaper that he had purchased.

The Shadow entered the station and sent a telegram of his own. He left the package in the agent's keeping, to be delivered to a Mr. Ralph Jamison, whenever he should inquire for it.

The Shadow's telegram was addressed to Ralph Jamison, in London; and it mentioned the package at Yarwick. Hence the agent took the whole matter as one of mere routine.

BACK at the Prince William Inn, Eric Delka waited for half an hour. Then Chauncey appeared. The coachman had left while Delka and The Shadow were eating breakfast. He had come back with news. He spoke to both Mullock and Delka.

"'Tis a message I bring," declared Chauncey. "It comes from Professor Danglar. He is tramping off to Highchurch, nigh a league from here. From Highchurch, he will fare to the fens, another two leagues beyond."

Delka calculated in terms of miles. Three miles to Highchurch; six more to the border of the nearest fenland. Delka decided to hire Chauncey's victoria. Soon he was riding toward Highchurch over rough ground where progress was slow.

At Highchurch, Delka made inquiry. He learned that Professor Danglar had gone on to a hamlet where there were persons who knew the fens. Delka took up the trail by carriage; but he realized that the old victoria, following rough, twisty roads, could not beat the speed of a man on foot, who chose shortcut bypaths.

Reaching the hamlet, Delka talked with the natives. He found out that Professor Danglar had obtained a pair of stilts and had gone to visit the wooded Isle of Dean, close to the watery marshes of The Wash. Delka learned also that the Isle of Dean could be reached by boat, should anyone choose to take a roundabout route.

Delka paid Chauncey and sent the carriage driver back to Yarwick. Then he set out on foot, to take a ten-mile hike that would bring him to the channels where the boatmen dwelt. Chauncey started back along the road to Highchurch.

After one league, he heard a hail. Chauncey stopped and gaped when he saw a tall figure stepping from a path. It was The Shadow, still guised as Professor Danglar, carrying a pair of long stilts. He put them aboard the victoria, stepped into the carriage and ordered Chauncey to take him into Highchurch.

"I shall stop there for the day," The Shadow told Chauncey. "Tonight, I may walk back to Yarwick; or else remain in Highchurch. At any rate, I shall leave these stilts at Highchurch. They are a burden and I am already tired from my walk. It would be too great an effort to visit the fens today."

Chauncey no longer feared the stranger, particularly during daylight. As they rode into Highchurch, he told The Shadow of Delka's expedition. A smile appeared upon the lips that had failed to move last night.

Leaving the carriage at Highchurch, The Shadow went to a tiny inn for lunch. Chauncey drove back to Yarwick; hence he was not present to see The Shadow start out on another hike, without his stilts. This time, The Shadow again moved in the direction of the fens; but soon he altered his course. He took a short cross-country route in the direction of Chiswold Castle.

Trails had diverged. Eric Delka had gone off on a blind course. The Shadow, with mid-afternoon approaching, was returning to his only goal, Chiswold Castle.

CHAPTER XII
NIGHT BRINGS ITS SHADOW

DUSK had settled about Chiswold Castle. Heavy clouds had obscured the setting sun; though they did not threaten rain, those clouds predicted that moonlight would be absent. A huge lull had settled along the fringes of the woods. The only spot where light remained was in the broad clearing that served as a flying field.

Dufour, the pilot, was standing beside Lodera's monoplane. Puffing a cigarette, the airman showed a furrowed face as he looked toward the roadway that led from Chiswold Castle. Dufour had been staring frequently in that direction, during the last hour.

There was another person present near the plane, one whom Dufour had scarcely noticed. This was an old rustic, stooped of shoulders and dull of eye, who leaned upon an improvised cane that had recently been a tree bough. The fellow's face was fringed with a round rim of tangly whiskers. He was puffing at an old clay pipe.

Such visitors were not uncommon. They came at intervals to gawk at the plane. When children appeared, Dufour usually ordered them from the premises; but he never bothered about the older persons of this district. They could stand and gawk for hours, for all Dufour cared.

A clatter from the road. Dufour nodded to himself. The beat of horse hoofs thudded from dried ground. A trio of riders approached and drew rein. They were from the castle; and the group consisted of Lord Cedric Lorthing, Gwendolyn Ralthorn and Francisco Lodera.

The latter alone dismounted. Gwendolyn reached out and held the horse's bridle, while Lodera spoke with Dufour.

"You are to fly to London, tomorrow," Lodera told the pilot. "Take off at dawn. After you have reached Croydon, go at once to the city."

Dufour nodded. Lodera pulled a letter from his pocket and was about to hand it to the pilot when he noted the old rustic standing by.

"Who is he?" queried Lodera, in a low tone.

"Only a gawker," replied Dufour. "You can't keep these countrymen away during the daytime."

"Do they ever come about at night?"

Dufour shook his head. Lodera appeared relieved. Nevertheless, he made a gesture toward the cottage.

"You have pen and ink inside?"

Dufour nodded.

"Come along then," decided Lodera. "I shall give you another note of introduction. One that will make your task easier when you arrive in London. Remember: you must be back before nightfall."

"Quite a simple matter."

LODERA and Dufour went toward the cottage. The old rustic remained, smoking his pipe. Gwendolyn spoke to Lord Cedric.

"Really," declared the girl, nervously, "we should be riding back toward the castle. I hope that Francisco hurries."

"Bother the haste!" drawled Lord Cedric. "Why should we be troubled by a bit of darkness?"

"Because of what I saw last night. That weird figure, almost enshrouded by the trees near the castle."

"Come, come, pet!" Lord Cedric seemed annoyed. "You are too imaginative. You saw nothing from the casement. Nothing but a shadow."

"It was a shadow that lived!" persisted the girl, tensely. "It was like a ghost, Cedric—"

"It was old Jeremy, making his round. Gwendolyn, you must cease this childish chatter. I have no tolerance for such fanciful beliefs."

"Francisco was disturbed when I spoke to him about the matter."

"Lodera? Bah! He comes from a credulous, superstitious race. All Spaniards are alike!"

Gwendolyn was biting her lips. Lord Cedric leaned forward.

"I do not like these conferences between you and Lodera," he warned. "Remember, Gwendolyn, our marriage shall take place in the near future. I have allowed you to make friends as you chose; but when you become Lady Lorthing—"

"I never shall," blurted Gwendolyn. "I have told you that, Cedric. You know that I do not love you; that I agreed to marry you only to appease my father."

"Then why not speak to him?" queried Lord Cedric. "Sir Rodney still accepts me as your fiancé."

"I have spoken to him," retorted Gwendolyn. "He says that I cannot break the engagement, without your approval. That is why I am stating plainly that I do not love you. It is you who should speak to my father."

Lord Cedric laughed indulgently.

"You will change your mind," he drawled, "and I shall wait until you do. Love is not all that counts in marriage. Think of the station that you will hold when you share my peerage, as Lady Lorthing."

"That means nothing," protested Gwendolyn. "I warn you, Cedric, I shall never marry you. My mind is firm."

"Your mind is unsettled. Your talk of ghosts is proof that you are distraught. Come, pet; be wise—"

Lord Cedric broke off. Lodera and Dufour were returning. The Spaniard mounted his horse and the three riders started back toward the castle road. Lord Cedric proudly rode ahead, to show the way; while Lodera brought his horse close beside Gwendolyn's.

Dufour chuckled as he watched the departing cavalcade. A knowing grin appeared upon the pilot's hardened features. Then he suddenly remembered the old rustic. He swung about in the dusk, to look for the fellow. The stooped man had gone

DUSK had settled more heavily in the clearing; and it was pitch-black beneath the trees that fringed the field. In that darkness came the blink of a tiny light, which Dufour could not see because of the thick tree trunks. The person who carried the flashlight had penetrated deep into the glade before he brought his torch in action.

His path was leading toward the tiny cot off in the woods. When he reached the little one-room building, the light carrier entered. He wedged his flashlight across a nail in the wall, then stepped into the glow. His features were those of the old rustic who had listened at the flying field.

False trimmings came away. The face looked like that of the so-called Professor Danglar. Then molding fingers worked to produce a more familiar visage; that of Lamont Cranston. The Shadow had no need for other disguises.

Garbed as a rustic, he had wandered near the castle during the late afternoon. He had finally reached the airport; there he had noted Dufour's impatience. The Shadow had expected arrivals from the castle. They had come.

The Shadow had learned useful facts. Dufour was flying to London in the morning, to carry out some business for Lodera. Gwendolyn did not intend to marry Lord Cedric; and that fact also concerned Lodera. The Shadow knew that the girl loved the Spaniard.

Discovery of these facts was sufficient, particularly since The Shadow had also learned that it was Gwendolyn who had seen him from the casement. The girl's story of a ghost had gained no credence with Lord Cedric, although she believed that it had impressed Lodera. That, however, mattered little. Gwendolyn's description of the "ghost" had been sketchy at best.

Night had brought new opportunity. By moonlight, the evening before, The Shadow had investigated the grounds about Chiswold Castle and had seen Nigel contact with Jeremy.

By day, this afternoon, The Shadow had made further study of the outside situation. He was, at least, prepared for a visit within the castle itself; one that would allow him more scope than had his open entry in the guise of Cranston.

Hence The Shadow chose his invaluable cloak of black. The folds came from the suitcase beneath the floor. They slipped over his shoulders. He added the slouch hat; then donned thin gloves and plucked the flashlight from the wall. The glow clicked off; an invisible being glided from the gamekeeper's cot.

From the abandoned shack to the castle, The Shadow took the course that he had already followed. His flashlight blinked intermittently; its flashes became less frequent. At last, he reached the open grounds and glided toward the castle itself. Tonight, since moonlight was absent, the gray walls loomed like a shapeless hulk, to form a perfect covering for The Shadow's approach.

Barred windows blocked a ground-floor attempt; but The Shadow had already picked another spot for entry. Moving directly to the front door of the castle, he edged to one side and gripped the heavy ivy vines that fronted the wall. Slowly, noiselessly, he ascended to the long balcony above the door.

The Shadow was outside the windows of the front room. They, in themselves, were formidable barriers; for the sashes were of metal and the windowpanes were small. To break a glass would be an unwise step; one that The Shadow chose to avoid.

PRODUCING a thin, wedgelike piece of steel, The Shadow pried it beneath a window edge. These windows were of the casement type; they swung outward and they were affixed inside by clamped metal rods. The Shadow, by a levering motion, engaged a knob at the end of one rod. Inch by inch, he pried the fastening outward.

It was a difficult task, for The Shadow was dealing with a clamped device that yielded stubbornly. It would have taken a full hour, or longer, to have completely opened the window by this method.

The Shadow, however, gained his objective after a dozen minutes. He had the window wide enough for his hand to enter. He reached the stubborn clamp and loosened it. Then he opened the window without trouble.

Moving from the darkened front room, The Shadow reached a lighted upstairs hall. All was silent on this floor. Modbury and his guests were at dinner. A black shape that cast a silhouetted streak, The Shadow slowly descended the great stairs. As he neared the bottom, he heard the sound of voices. People were coming from the dining room.

Pausing in the blackness of an alcoved landing, The Shadow observed Barton Modbury stopping near the foot of the stairs. Sir Rodney Ralthorn and Lord Cedric Lorthing joined their host. Modbury boomed a cheery invitation.

"Come to the great room across the hall," suggested Modbury. "I shall have Tyson kindle the large fire, for this cloudy night may soon turn chilly. We can chat in comfort and plan for the coming fox hunt that will be held at Brindley Manor. When is the hunt to be?"

"Tomorrow," observed Lord Cedric.

"No, no," corrected Sir Rodney. "It will be upon the day after. Today is Thursday. The hunt is to be held Saturday."

Luval, the secretary, had approached. He spoke to Modbury just as the baldheaded host was starting toward the great room.

"Shall I complete the typing of those letters, sir?" queried Luval. "There will be time for Hasslett to carry them to Yarwick and catch the late post."

"Very good, Luval."

THE SHADOW had withdrawn from the niche upon the stairs. He was moving upward; and the act was timely. Luval had started toward the stairs. But when the secretary had reached the top, he saw no sign of The Shadow.

Luval opened the door of a side room. The Shadow, peering from the darkness of another doorway, saw the interior. The room was fitted like a small office; but it also had a partial atmosphere of a study. A desk occupied the center. Beyond was a safe, set in an alcove. To one side was a bookcase.

Luval closed the door behind him. The Shadow waited, expecting a new development. It came. Footsteps sounded from the stairway; a cautious, ascending tread. Then a man came into view and sneaked across the hall to tap at the door of the study.

The hall light showed the features of this visitor who had stolen up to talk with Luval. The arrival was Francisco Lodera. Here, in Chiswold Castle, intrigue was in the making.

The Shadow was prepared to become its secret witness.

CHAPTER XIII
THE CASTLE

LUVAL answered Lodera's soft knock. Opening the door, the secretary beckoned the Spaniard into the study. Lodera entered; but Luval did not close the door entirely. He left it ajar, as a guard against intruders.

That fact was to The Shadow's liking. Softly, he crept forward, his black form spectral in the dim light of the hall. A blotting shape, he peered past the lighted crack of the door edge. With keen eyes, he saw both Luval and Lodera.

The two men were facing each other across the desk. Luval was gazing wisely through his spectacles. He was looking toward The Shadow; but he did not discern those eyes at the door. Luval was too interested in his study of Lodera.

The Shadow, in turn, was viewing the men at Modbury's desk; but he was also discovering the possibilities of the room. Because of its mingled furnishings, it offered various nooks. The best was a darkened spot beyond a deep bookcase, where the slope of the roof forced the shelves to end.

That hiding place was more to The Shadow's liking than this doorway. He would have chosen it, had he known that this was the room to which Luval was coming. As it was, The Shadow could only keep his present position.

"I spoke to Dufour." It was Lodera who spoke. "He leaves for London at dawn. He will return before evening."

"Good," chuckled Luval. "Then you will be able to leave here tomorrow night."

"If I receive the money."

"You will have it."

Luval had drawn a card from a desk drawer. He arose and went to the safe in the alcove. He turned the combination, opened the front and drew out a folio which he tossed upon the desk. Then, turning back to the safe again, he lifted a fat bundle and tapped it with his finger.

"The money," he said wisely.

LUVAL replaced the package in the safe, closed the door and returned to the desk. He tossed the little card back into the desk drawer.

"Yes," he affirmed, "the money will be yours tomorrow. But remember"—he looked up and chuckled—"the money is not all that you intend to take with you."

"The rest is arranged," returned Lodera, suavely. "It is the money, alone, that troubles me."

"You have just seen it—"

"Yes. But it is not yet mine. Unless Barton Modbury likes the Spanish jewels—"

"They will satisfy him. I know his likes."

Lodera leaned back at Luval's words. His profile turned toward the door. The Shadow saw a keen gleam upon the Spaniard's handsome face.

"About Modbury," queried Lodera, "do you suppose that he has begun to suspect my game?"

"Not at all," returned Luval. "My only doubts concern Sir Rodney and Lord Cedric."

"They know nothing. Sir Rodney is a blundersome old tyrant; while Lord Cedric is a conceited dolt. The only person who might have made trouble for us was that Scotland Yard chap, Delka."

"Or his friend, Cranston."

"Agreed. You don't suppose that either will be back, on account of Geoffrey Chiswold?"

"No. They will not return. Wait a few minutes, Lodera, while I go over these letters from the folio. Then we can discuss the Scotland Yard angle."

The Shadow was still watching from the door. But with the pause of Luval's voice, he detected a new sound; one that came from elsewhere than the study. The Shadow edged back into the hall. He looked toward the front room. The sound was from there.

Cautious footsteps told of an approaching intruder; and The Shadow had seconds only to avoid discovery. Quickly, he glided back to his obscure doorway near the front of the hall. Immediately afterward, a man came creeping from the front room.

IT was Nigel Chiswold. Face strained, but alert; hands extended before him, like menacing cudgels, Nigel looked prepared for any encounter. The Shadow saw him glance toward the stairs. Then came the faint, indistinguishable buzz of voices from the study. Nigel heard and turned. He stole to the very listening post that The Shadow had so recently occupied.

Luval and Lodera had resumed their discussions; but this time it was Nigel Chiswold, not The

Shadow, who was hearing the details. One interloper had replaced the other. The Shadow had no alternative; he was forced to leave the field to Nigel.

Yet the gleam of The Shadow's eyes was indication that he had heard enough for the present. He was willing to let Nigel listen. The Shadow knew that this episode would cause one cross-purpose to meet another.

Nigel had carried through his plan. He had come down from the spy room in the turret, to study matters in Chiswold Castle. The shrewd smile on his face showed that he was learning facts that suited him. Whatever Nigel's purpose was here, he was gaining results.

New footsteps. The Shadow heard them; but Nigel did not. The tread, though unguarded, was a soft one, coming up the stairs. The Shadow knew that it must be Gwendolyn Ralthorn. The girl's room was on the other side of the hallway. Chances were that she would not glance in the direction of the study.

Gwendolyn appeared at the top of the stairs. As The Shadow expected, she started in the direction of her own room. It was Nigel who spoiled his own chances of escaping discovery. He heard the footsteps in the hall. He spun about, alarmed.

The slight sound of Nigel's move caught Gwendolyn's ear. The girl stopped short. She looked squarely toward the door of the study. Against its background, she saw Nigel's pallid face. The girl quivered in terror; then gasped, aloud.

"Geoffrey!"

Like old Jeremy, Gwendolyn had mistaken Nigel for his cousin; and her reactions were the same. She thought that she was viewing the ghost of Geoffrey Chiswold. But Gwendolyn had greater reason to be horrified. Not only was the apparition inside the castle itself; but the appearance of the supposed ghost came as an added shock to one that she had already received.

Gwendolyn had not forgotten the blackened shape that she had seen upon the lawn in the moonlight. Despite Lord Cedric's skepticism, she had retained her qualms. Upon spying Nigel and taking him for Geoffrey, Gwendolyn had immediately connected this appearance with that of last night's.

"Geoffrey!"

GWENDOLYN'S second cry was a half shriek. With it, Nigel bounded forward, hissing for silence. Gwendolyn dropped back, burying her face in her hands; trying to scream, but failing. As Nigel reached her, she crumpled in a faint.

There was the sound of commotion in the study. The Shadow heard the muffled shove of chairs. Luval and Lodera had heard the noise in the hall. Alarmed, they were coming out to learn the trouble. Nigel heard their suppressed tones. He dived away toward the front room

A creak of the stairs had passed unnoticed; but now it turned to sudden footsteps. As Nigel headed for the front room, a bulky man sprang up to stop his flight. The arrival was a hard-faced servant, whose eyes glinted with determination.

Nigel wheeled at the man's approach. With a scientific jab, he drove his fist to the big fellow's chin, sent the man sprawling against the wall. Madly, Nigel precipitated himself through the doorway of the front room.

Gwendolyn, opening her eyes, caught a blurred glimpse of his departure. She saw the big servant coming up from the floor; then gasped again. As she sagged backward, Lodera and Luval reached the hall.

The Shadow remained an unseen witness to the scene that followed.

"Gwendolyn!" It was Lodera who spoke the name, his suave manner changed to one of dismay. "Gwendolyn!" Then, to Luval. "She has fainted! Come—we must carry her!"

"Not into the study," warned Luval, peering anxiously toward the stairs. Then, seeing the servant by the wall: "Ah! Here is Mund. Help Senor Lodera, Mund."

The servant nodded. Lodera pointed to the front room. Mund balked for a moment; then helped the Spaniard carry Gwendolyn in that direction. Luval looked sharply from the stairs. Those below had heard no sounds, for the great room was distant. The secretary saw where Lodera and Mund had gone. He followed into the front room.

The Shadow moved forward. He reached a spot outside the door; but did not peer into the front room, for those within were using the light from the hall. Gwendolyn was reviving. The Shadow could hear the girl's words.

"The ghost!" The words were a gasp. "I saw it! The ghost of Geoffrey Chiswold! It came in here—it may still be here—"

Lodera was trying to calm the girl. Luval had lighted a candle; he was swinging the candlestick about the room. The flame threw long, grotesque streaks against the wall. Gwendolyn restrained herself with difficulty. To her startled gaze, every shadow looked like a solid thing of life.

"There is no one here," declared Luval, smoothly. "See for yourself. The room is empty. Try the windows, Mund."

The servant did so. He found none loose. The Shadow had reclamped the one by which he had entered.

"Mund must have seen it, too," expressed Gwendolyn, tensely. "I saw the ghost pass him. He had come from the stairs. When I saw you, Mund, I did not recognize you at first."

"Did you see anything, Mund?" queried Lodera, anxiously.

"Of course, not," put in Luval, eyeing the servant steadily. "There are no ghosts about the castle."

Mund shook his head.

"I saw no one," he said in a husky tone. "I heard her ladyship scream, while I was coming from the stairs. Nobody was in the hall."

GWENDOLYN gasped; then shook her head. Mund's testimony had left her speechless. Luval turned to Lodera.

"None should know of this occurrence," he said, cautiously. "Come, Mund. I have some letters that I wish you to take downstairs to Mr. Modbury."

The secretary set down the candle. He left the front room, with Mund following stolidly at his heels. They went into the study; the door closed behind them. The Shadow, drawn back from the doorway of the front room, heard Gwendolyn speak pleadingly to Lodera.

"Mund must have seen it," persisted the girl. "Why did Luval insist otherwise?"

"I don't know," replied Lodera, slowly. Then, in a troubled tone: "Luval is right, however. No one must know that you have seen a ghost. Your father might wish to leave the castle."

"But I cannot remain here, Francisco! Not while Geoffrey's ghost is still about—"

"Only tonight, Gwendolyn. You can make an excuse to stay up until dawn. I shall do the same. I have it! I shall say that I wish to make sure that Dufour takes off for London!"

"If we remain in the great room downstairs—"

"That is exactly what we shall do. Your father is a night owl. He will stay up, also. But say nothing about Geoffrey's ghost."

"But then tomorrow night—"

"We shall be gone tomorrow night."

Another gasp from Gwendolyn; but this was a happy one. Lodera laughed softly and the girl joined. She wanted to ask more questions, but Lodera calmed her.

"Go downstairs," he whispered. "Act as if nothing had happened. I shall talk with Luval. Leave all to me, Gwendolyn."

They came from the front room, just as the study door opened. Luval appeared with Mund. The servant started downstairs, carrying the letters that Luval had given him. The Shadow, black in a darkened corner, saw Lodera gesture for the girl to go down also. Gwendolyn followed Mund. Lodera and Luval descended a few steps to listen for results below.

WHILE the pair stood with heads together, a singular phenomenon occurred in the upstairs hall behind them. Blackness moved forward from a corner. It left a dull, dimly lighted patch of wall at the spot where it had been. Solidified, that shape became a living form; one that either Lodera or Luval might have taken for a ghost, had they chanced to turn and see it.

Weird was The Shadow, as he silently crossed the hall to the opened door of the study. His form made a mammoth blot against the light from the room. Then it faded from view, leaving only a streaked silhouette upon the floor.

Even the floor patch shrank as The Shadow moved into the hiding place he wanted. He was beyond the bookcase, merged with blackness. The burning gaze of his eyes was lost beneath the sheltering brim of his slouch hat.

Footsteps. Lodera and Luval were returning. The Shadow had chosen the vantage point from which he could view the sequel to Gwendolyn's experience with the supposed ghost of Geoffrey Chiswold.

CHAPTER XIV
THE FINAL VIGIL

FRANCISCO LODERA wore a strained countenance when he entered the study with Luval. The secretary motioned him to the chair before the desk; then took Modbury's chair for his own. Lodera was prompt with a statement.

"Gwendolyn saw something," he told Luval. "What could it have been? Do you think that Geoffrey Chiswold is alive?"

"Geoffrey is dead," returned Luval, seriously. "That much is certain, Lodera."

"Then was it a ghost?"

Lodera's face had lost its darkish hue. The Spaniard had been impressed by Gwendolyn's story.

"It was not a ghost," replied Luval, "nor was it a human being. No one could have escaped from that front room."

"What did Mund tell you?"

"He swore that he saw nothing. He would have spoken differently if he had seen. Mund tells the truth to me."

Luval smiled wisely as he spoke. Lodera nodded, relieved.

"Of course," agreed the Spaniard, "he is the man whom you bought when you first came here ahead of Modbury. You told me about that, Luval. Gwendolyn imagined something; that was all. Of course, it could not have been Geoffrey Chiswold. He is dead, as you say. And if it were someone else—"

"Since Miss Ralthorn could not have seen Geoffrey," interposed Luval, blandly, "we have proof that her imagination tricked her. Ghosts are not real, Lodera. It was a hallucination; that is all."

"But if she mistook someone for Geoffrey—someone who was outside this door—then that person might have listened—"

"There was no one. Forget the matter. All will be well; you can trust me for that, Lodera. Keep your mind centered upon tomorrow night."

"That is best." Lodera arose. "I must go downstairs. They will be wondering about my absence. Gwendolyn, too, is down there. I should be with her."

Luval was rising. He held up a warning hand as a cautious tap sounded at the door.

"It is Mund," declared the secretary. "He has come to tell me that Mr. Modbury wishes me downstairs. You must wait"—he glanced at a desk clock—"yes, wait for a full ten minutes before you come down."

LUVAL opened the door. Mund was standing there. The secretary spoke to the servant. Luval told Mund to station himself in the front room. The bulky man nodded his acknowledgment. The two departed, Luval pulling the door almost shut behind him.

Lodera began a troubled pacing back and forth in front of the desk. The Shadow, watching, knew that he was still thinking about the ghost; and Lodera's face showed deep perplexity. Five minutes passed. Lodera began to show restlessness. At the end of two minutes more, he had tilted his head to one side, as if listening.

Suddenly, Lodera made a dart for the door. He was too late; he stepped back from the threshold as the barrier opened. He was faced by a trio of men: Barton Modbury, Sir Rodney and Lord Cedric. Lodera chewed his lips for a moment; then gave a slight laugh that sounded hollow.

"I thought you were in here," he said to Modbury. "The light was on and the door ajar. I stepped in to look for you."

Modbury's face showed anger. Lord Cedric and Sir Rodney eyed Lodera suspiciously.

"Not finding you here, Mr. Modbury, I was about to come downstairs—"

Modbury cut Lodera short. Apparently, his anger had subsided. Modbury went behind the desk, sat down heavily in his chair. He motioned to the others to be seated.

"Quite all right," he told Lodera. "A bit unusual, to find someone in the study; but I suppose Luval's neglect to turn off the light is a sufficient reason. Since we had hoped to find you anyway, it is just as well that you are here."

Lodera smiled in a suave fashion. He produced a cigarette and placed it in the end of an amber holder. His nonchalance had returned. Modbury started to open the desk drawer; then changed his mind.

Going to the safe, he used the combination from memory. He brought out a chamois bag and a package. The latter was the one that The Shadow had seen before.

Back at the desk, Modbury opened the package.

Crisp currency came into view. Modbury counted Bank of England notes; then replaced the money in the safe.

"Ten thousand pounds," boomed Modbury. "More than the price of your rubies, Lodera."

"Yes," acknowledged the Spaniard, with a smile. "My price is six thousand. By the way, Mr. Modbury, Dufour will have the gems here tomorrow. I thought it best to complete our transaction before the day of the fox hunt."

"Very well." Modbury paused and opened the chamois bag. He poured a mass of uncut diamonds upon the desk. "Here are my rough beauties, Sir Rodney. Worth twenty thousand pounds, at a conservative estimate."

Sir Rodney's eye lighted. His gaze was that of a connoisseur. Lord Cedric, too, was interested. He knew the worth of these rough stones.

"Egad!" exclaimed Sir Rodney. "I should like to purchase the lot. This one"—he held up a single stone—"will prove a beauty after it is fashioned."

"As a wedding present for your daughter," suggested Modbury.

"Excellent!" agreed Sir Rodney. "You heard that, Lord Cedric?"

LORD CEDRIC nodded. His dryish features showed a pleased smile. The Shadow's gaze centered upon Lodera. He saw a sudden tightening of the Spaniard's lips.

"I say, Modbury," drawled Lord Cedric, "how can you afford to part with these fine stones? What use have you for rubies such as Lodera's?"

Lodera darted an angry look toward Lord Cedric; then his eyes lost their irate flash as he steadied himself.

"Just this," explained the diamond king. "Uncut diamonds are plentiful in South Africa. The price that I ask for these stones is a normal one, judged by the local market. Moreover, my collection is sufficient. These are but a few of the stones that I possess. That answers one question, Lord Cedric.

"As for the other, rubies are much esteemed, at present, in South Africa. I am quite willing to pay a good price for Lodera's Spanish gems, because I can easily dispose of them when I return to Johannesburg.

"I am a business man from first to last. I shall show a fair profit on each transaction. Among friends, a reasonable profit is all that I expect. Well, Sir Rodney, our business can wait until after my deal with Lodera. We can forget gems until tomorrow night."

Replacing the diamonds in the chamois bag, Modbury put the latter in the safe. He closed the door; then spoke to his companions. His heavy tone carried a chuckle.

"Quite a fortune here," said Modbury. "My

uncut diamonds, at twenty thousand pounds; my banknotes totaling ten more. When Lodera's rubies arrive, we shall have six thousand pounds more in value to protect.

"That is why I have chosen trustworthy servants. To a man, all are competent. All my own servitors—with the exception of Mund—who came with the castle. But both Luval and I deem him reliant."

The group went from the study; and Modbury turned out the light. The Shadow came from his hiding place and moved toward the door. He listened there. Soon he heard footsteps coming up. Luval appeared and called softly to Mund. He spoke to the servant in a whisper. Mund went downstairs.

Luval waited. Soon Lodera appeared, coming cautiously from below. Luval drew him toward the door of the study. They stopped in the hallway; The Shadow heard their whispers.

"I had no chance to warn you," stated Luval. "Mr. Modbury told me to remain downstairs. You were out of here, I hope?"

"No," replied Lodera, softly, "but I managed to cover it. They were suspicious at first. I had better be on my way downstairs, Luval."

The secretary nodded. He followed Lodera to the stairs and descended almost to the alcove. The Shadow made a swift exit from the study; he reached the front room just as Luval gave a low call. Then came the secretary's footsteps; after that, Mund's.

The Shadow had no time to reach the window. Instead, he chose a corner of the darkened front room. Mund entered; then went out again. It was plain that he intended merely to keep guard over the door that led from the front room into the hallway.

TEN minutes passed. Luval had gone to the study. The Shadow heard someone else come up. It was Modbury. The diamond king walked into the study and closed the door. Soon Luval came out and beckoned to Mund. The servant approached from the door of the front room.

"Kindle the fire in the study," ordered Luval, in a low tone. "I shall keep watch here while you are busy."

Mund nodded and went into the study. It was ten minutes before he reappeared. When he came out, he was carrying a batch of sealed letters.

"For Hasslett to take to Yarwick?" questioned Luval.

Mund nodded and went down the stairs. Luval peered into the front room; then, hearing someone on the stairs, he sauntered back into the study. This time the arrival was Lord Cedric Lorthing going toward his own room. Luval had hurried into the study rather than have Lord Cedric see him here.

The Shadow went to the front window. Carefully, he unclamped it; then eased out upon the balcony. He closed the casement behind him, jamming it so tightly that it would pass ordinary inspection, yet would open again when necessary.

Mund's returning figure appeared in the hall light, just as The Shadow crossed the side rail of the balcony. Unseen by the servant within, the black-cloaked intruder descended the thick ivy stems and reached the portico below.

From then on, The Shadow was part of the night itself. The big Humber left for the village, to return a half hour later. Old Jeremy went his rounds with swinging lantern. Lights went out in Modbury's study; but they still remained in the great room downstairs.

INVISIBLE in the darkness, The Shadow circled the castle. He stopped beside the crags to listen to the roar of sea that came up through the hollow of the cove. He passed the windows of the great room, where flickering firelight joined the mellow glow of electric illumination, to throw forth shaded outlines of the window bars.

At intervals, The Shadow returned to the front of the gloomy, blackened building. From long perspective, he gained occasional glimpses of Mund's head and shoulders beyond the lighted inner doorway. At times, The Shadow saw lights go on and off in various rooms.

Francisco Lodera and Gwendolyn Ralthorn had gone through with their plan to stay up until dawn; and they had talked Sir Rodney and Lord Cedric into the same proposition. Hence The Shadow had an all-night vigil of his own; for he expected no move until all had retired. Frequently, The Shadow noted the barren blankness of the lone turret above the wall that edged the front door of the castle.

There were questions that might have perplexed an investigator other than The Shadow, had anyone else been able to learn as much as had the cloaked intruder. They formed an interesting medley.

Why had Mund said that he had seen no one, despite the fact that he had struggled with Nigel Chiswold? Why had Luval insisted that Mund had clung to his story; then kept watch, along with the servant, over the front room? Besides these questions, there were incidents that had a bearing. One—the most important—was the entry of Modbury, Sir Rodney and Lord Cedric before Lodera had gained time to leave the study.

Diamonds, cash—soon rubies as well. The Shadow could see reason for coming crime at Chiswold Castle. But he could see other reasons more important than the fact that wealth was stored there. Reasons for cross-purposes; for deeds of violence.

The Shadow had ferreted the answers to the medley concerning all, including Nigel Chiswold. He knew that his vigil would end before dawn.

CHAPTER XV
DEATH AT DAWN

IT was the hour of dawn, yet darkness still reigned about Chiswold Castle. Clouded skies gripped the east and blocked the rays of the early, rising sun. The cover of night still served The Shadow as a deep-veiled shroud.

Long hours had brought no change to the castle until this very end of night. Then The Shadow had watched the lights blink out within the great room. Other lights had appeared in upstairs windows; but not for long.

Gwendolyn Ralthorn had evidently lost her fear of ghosts, with so little night remaining, or else the others had decided upon sleep while darkness still persisted. Whichever the case, all had retired; and the upstairs lights soon gave way to darkness.

At almost the same time, gray streaks appeared upon the horizon past the trees in front of the castle. While The Shadow kept vigil, hazy dawn widened, crept up through the sky to barely outline the grim shape of Chiswold Castle. Gray stones, however, caught no rays. The massive building still remained a blotting hulk.

Suddenly tiny blinks appeared out of the darkness. They were coming from the slits in the tall turret. Nigel Chiswold was using a flashlight, signaling to old Jeremy, to draw the gatekeeper on his early inspection. Blackness clung heavily to the ground; Nigel still had time for final contact.

THEN The Shadow discerned a new phenomenon hard on the finished blinks of Nigel's flashlight. A wavering glow appeared in the front room on the second floor. Grotesque splotches flickered past the windows. Someone was moving in that room—someone, who carried a lighted candle in its stick.

The Shadow moved forward from a range of fifty yards. The candle light had sidled to an inner corner of the room. Keeping on, The Shadow gained the porch. Completely concealed against the darkened front of the castle, he climbed up by the ivy. The candle was muffed out just as he reached the balcony.

Softly The Shadow drew the casement window outward. He slid into the front room and blinked his tiny flashlight. He found exactly what he expected. Emptiness. Just as Nigel Chiswold had vanished, so had this new intruder. But it could not be Nigel again. The blinks from the turret had been almost simultaneous with the candle flickers from this room.

The Shadow went to the corner beneath the turret. His blinking flashlight picked out smooth surfaces of paneling. The Shadow saw the streaks of fingerprints that had slid along the woodwork.

Using them like arrow points, he pressed upward; then to the side, for the horizontal streaks had crossed the vertical.

Without a click, the wainscoting opened. The Shadow stepped into a musty, tomblike well. His flashlight showed a tiny landing with an opening that led to a spiral staircase. The steps came from deep below. They went corkscrewing upward into the turret itself. The Shadow pulled the panel shut by an inner catch. Extinguishing his flashlight, he ascended the spiral stairs.

They ended with a hinged trapdoor, which The Shadow pressed upward, inch by inch. Peering, he saw the interior of a rounded room where gray light penetrated through slits in the wall and from an opening in the ceiling.

Nigel Chiswold had gone up to the roof of the turret. The slits were too narrow to serve in sending a cord down to Jeremy. Nigel must be calling for a basket in return; hence he had chosen the turret top. But The Shadow was not the first to learn that fact.

A ladder had been placed from the floor to the ceiling; and another man had arrived to use it without Nigel's knowledge. The man was Mund. The Shadow saw his bulky figure at the ladder's top. It was Mund who had used candlelight to open the panel of the lower room.

The Shadow opened the trapdoor swiftly. He came into the spy room just as Mund reached the roof. The bulky servant did not look below. He was too intent upon the work that lay ahead. The Shadow delivered a low, hollow laugh, that came like a menacing taunt from within the spy room.

INSTANTLY, two sounds responded from above. One was a harsh growl from Mund; the other, an exclamation that was Nigel's. Both had heard the weird strain of The Shadow's mirth; they had swung about, to come face to face with each other.

A scuffle began as The Shadow gained the ladder. A snarled oath from Mund; a savage retort from Nigel. Whipping forth an automatic as he climbed, The Shadow projected his head and shoulders from the opening in the turret roof.

He was a witness to the opening of a vicious struggle. Nigel had locked with Mund. The two had ample space in which to fight, for the top of the turret widened above the secret room; and the opening from which The Shadow peered was located at one side of the flat roof

A parapet protected the fighters as they swayed back and forth across the turret top. This parapet was the ancient battlement itself, a wall that was nearly three feet in height.

Its castellated crest was topped by solid posts called merlons, with cutout sections in between—

Mund twisted backward, both hands dropping to his side ... His bulky shoulders poised; then slid from the parapet.

the embrasures, or crenelles, through which bowmen had discharged their arrows in bygone days.

The crenelles were narrow, too small for a body to squeeze through. Hence Nigel and Mund, in their struggle, were protected by the full height of the merlons. Realizing that, each man fought to beat down his antagonist.

Nigel had been forced into a prompt clinch by Mund. Wiry of frame and limb, the man from India had gained a strangle hold upon his foe. Mund, grunting like a choking bull, was bobbing his head back and forth. Meanwhile, he used his powerful arms to shove his antagonist away.

As they twisted, Mund gained the upper hand. Nigel's choking measures failed. The pair staggered against the parapet. Mund then drove Nigel downward and wedged his left arm in a crenelle. Then, as Mund twisted away, Nigel lost his grip on the bulky servant's throat.

LEVERING himself by gripping a postlike merlon, Nigel came up as Mund charged him. He clipped a savage uppercut against the bulky fellow's chin. Mund staggered backward. Nigel, steadying, pounced toward him. Mund swung his back to the wall and whipped out a long-bladed knife.

Evidently, he had not anticipated the need for this weapon; but had changed his mind in the fury of the fray. Nigel, seeing the dangerous dirk, was quick to clutch Mund's wrist. They locked and whirled about like dervishes, while The Shadow followed them back and forth with his moving automatic.

No one could have told which fighter was The Shadow's target. The cloaked watcher was deliberate, for the fray was even. Mund had no chance to use his knife; but Nigel, in clutching the fellow's wrist, could not repeat his choking tactics.

Increasing dawn revealed this vivid scene; a battle to the death. One man was sure to gain a kill.

Once, The Shadow's finger was almost ready to press the trigger, for the pair had leaned half across the parapet; and neither fighter had sure footing. Then the two sagged back. The Shadow was waiting until they broke.

That moment came in a startling fashion. Nigel, still attacking Mund's wrist, had jammed the stolid servant back to the parapet; but was still caught in his grasp. Wrenching his other hand free, Mund drove his heavy fist to Nigel's twisting shoulder. The blow was a lucky one. It sent Nigel sprawling.

Twisting, Nigel caught his footing and dived for the wall. He clamped hold of a merlon, then came up as Mund was turning. Nigel was ready for a long, diving drive.

Mund was still swinging outward as he turned to meet the edgewise attack. The Shadow's gun hand tightened. He was prepared to decide the fray. Then came a finish which anticipated his deed.

From the darkness beyond the front of the castle, a sharp crack resounded. Deep from the lower gloom it came; the report of a powerful rifle.

MUND fumed an oath and let his right hand drop. His knife clattered into a crenelle; then plopped to the turret top within the battlement. Mund twisted backward, both hands dropping to his side.

As Nigel plunged toward him, Mund went over backward. His bulky shoulders poised; then slid from the parapet. Headforemost, while he gasped a gargly cry, Mund went plunging clear of Nigel's clutch, to the stone portico fifty feet below.

Nigel paused to watch the finish of the fall. His hands clutching separated merlons, he stared into the blackened depths. Groggily, he turned about. The Shadow saw his shrewd eyes narrow. Nigel had recognized the sound of that distant shot; and The Shadow, too, could have defined it. The sharp crackle of an Afghan rifle.

A marksman, hidden almost at the verge of the front trees, had witnessed the struggle on the turret top. Amakar, the Afghan, had contacted Jeremy, with the password: "Khyber." He had accompanied the gatekeeper in answer to Nigel's blinks. The dusky sharpshooter had picked Mund from the struggle at a range of more than two hundred yards.

The Shadow had dropped from view, his own plan useless. He had been ready to save one fighter; but the fray was ended. Amakar's stroke had roused those in the castle. Departure was The Shadow's immediate course.

The Shadow was gone before Nigel had turned to the opening in the turret roof. By the time that Nigel had clambered down into the slitted spy room, The Shadow was through the trapdoor. Nigel did not see it lowered from beneath. It was solid floor when he reached it and began to pound wooden wedges into the cracks.

The Shadow, on the spiral staircase, heard the sounds. He knew that Nigel was preparing to offset new invaders. The Shadow continued his descent. He unlatched the panel at the landing and stepped into the darkened front room.

People were pounding down the stairway of the castle; none had stopped to survey the front room. The Shadow gained the window and jammed it tight as he departed. Over the rail, he reached the ivy vines and fairly dropped to the ground below. Obscured by the total darkness that clung to the indentations of the lowered wall, The Shadow still preserved the secrecy of his presence.

Doom had struck at dawn. The Shadow intended to learn its aftermath.

CHAPTER XVI
OLD JEREMY'S STORY

THE great door of Chiswold Castle had been flung open. A flood of excited persons—guests and servants—had arrived to learn the cause of the gunshot and the succeeding clatter of Mund's fall. When they reached the right side of the porch, they saw a bobbing lantern.

Flashlights glimmered. The added glare revealed Mund's crumpled, lifeless body, with old Jeremy beside it. The gatekeeper was pale and shaky. His fowling piece was resting loosely in his hand.

Luval, half dressed, was the first to recognize the dead man's face. The secretary blurted the name: "Mund!"

"Aye," old Jeremy spoke weakly, "'tis Mund. Nor ill did I intend to do him."

The Shadow, twenty paces distant, could hear the gatekeeper's words. He saw the looks of astonishment that appeared upon surrounding faces that clustered in the light.

"'Twas yonder he was," lied Jeremy, pointing toward the windows of the front room above the door. "When I spied him, I laid aside my lantern at this very spot where now I stand. 'Twas a warning—aye, a warning that I called to him."

"What is this?" The question came from Barton Modbury, who had arrived in a dressing gown. "Mund? Dead? You killed him, Jeremy?"

"'Twas I who fired the shot, sir, with this fowling piece that I bear. But 'twas a warning that I first did give him."

"That is right, Mr. Modbury." The statement came from Hasslett, the chauffeur. "I heard some shouts from the castle; then the sound of a gun."

"I spied him at the window" went on Jeremy. "'Twas whilst I was straight before the castle door. I saw the shape of him; and when he came to clamber on the vines, I called to him. 'Twas my duty to fire when he did not halt."

"Of course." Modbury was bending over Mund's body. "Hmm. He's badly racked. It's difficult to tell where the ball struck him. Where was he when you fired, Jeremy? By the front window?"

"Aye, Master Modbury."

"Then how does he happen to be lying over here?"

"'Twas from this side of the rail, sir, that he dropped. 'Twas the lantern that he saw and crawled to it. Like this, Master Modbury."

Graphically, Jeremy gave a lunging gait that resembled a long, crablike progress. It added emphasis to his story. Luval, eyeing Jeremy doubtfully, began to be convinced.

FRANCISCO LODERA had arrived from the castle. A few moments later, Gwendolyn appeared. The Spaniard saw the girl and motioned her back toward the door. He started to explain what had happened.

"Perhaps we should check this story, Mr. Modbury," stated Luval. "Mund is badly crushed. We ought to be sure about his fall. Was he on top of the rail in front of the windows, Jeremy?"

"Aye," the shrewd gatekeeper saw a chance for embellishment, "he was trying to clutch the vines ere he yielded his footing."

"It sounds true, Sir Rodney," remarked Modbury, turning to the man who was closest. "Would you consider that Jeremy had performed a duty?"

"Why not?" echoed Sir Rodney. "You are master here, Modbury. Jeremy is the man who patrols the grounds. Our task is to learn why this man Mund descended. Suppose we enter the castle."

Modbury followed Sir Rodney. Two servants came along and they went up to the front room. There, Sir Rodney tried the windows and found one that was loose. It was the window by which The Shadow had left.

"Halloo!" called Sir Rodney, to those below. "Look this way, gatekeeper! Was this the window by which the fellow left?"

"Aye, sir," called back Jeremy.

"That seems sufficient," decided Modbury.

When the men from above came out from the castle, Luval put a casual inquiry to Modbury.

"The window was unlocked, sir?" asked the secretary. "The one by which Jeremy said Mund had left?"

Modbury nodded.

"That makes it plain, sir," said Luval. "Mund has behaved suspiciously of late. Perhaps he was contemplating some theft; and wished to make sure of his exit."

"Some theft?"

"Yes, sir. He was about the second floor all evening, long after I had told him that there would be no more duty."

"Then look to the safe upstairs! Refer to the combination in the desk drawer. Mund may have found it. Open the safe, Luval; we shall follow to learn if everything is safe."

Luval hurried indoors. A few moments later, Modbury followed, accompanied by Sir Rodney and Lord Cedric. A cluster of servants still remained about Mund's body, while Jeremy stood by. Soon, Modbury himself returned.

"Nothing is gone," he told the servants. "The rascal had apparently postponed his theft until after he tested the ivy vines. What about your fowling piece, Jeremy? Have you reloaded it?"

"Nay, sir."

JEREMY handed the gun to Modbury. The

Shadow could see a slight smile on the gatekeeper's lips. Jeremy had been wise enough to unload. As for the barrel, it had not been cleaned for weeks. Inspection would indicate that the gun had recently been fired.

"Hasslett," ordered Modbury, "drive into Yarwick at once and inform the local authorities. Have them come here and make a prompt inspection. Tell them that we shall hold the body until their arrival.

"Jeremy, you must come into the castle. I shall have the constables talk with you. I shall testify that you were acting in discharge of your duty. This affair will bring us no trouble. Mund had no right to be leaving the castle."

Luval had come out again. The Shadow could see the secretary's face, for Luval had picked up Jeremy's lantern. Luval was wearing a satisfied smile. The Shadow knew why. Mund had been supposed to leave the castle quietly after certain work was finished. Luval thought the servant had been doing so; that Jeremy had actually spied him, then shot him down at the window.

Jeremy's own testimony; the unlocked window; finally, the emptied fowling piece all were points of proof. Luval's satisfaction was expressed because an unneeded tool had been eliminated. Mund had been useful for a while; but that period was ended.

Luval was an absolute wretch; a crook who played a part in deep-laid schemes. He was one who pretended to be a man of integrity—a man fit to hold a position of trust. Yet in this course of crime, Luval, himself, was a tool. The real crook who must be met was the master whose secret plans Luval served. The Shadow knew.

Francisco Lodera was still standing upon the porch, with Gwendolyn beside him. The servants followed Luval into the castle. Lodera and the girl were alone. Daylight was painting the upper floors of the castle; the last remnants of night clung to the ground alone. The Shadow still held a position of security. He waited. Gwendolyn spoke to Lodera.

"Could Mund have seen the ghost?" queried the girl, anxiously. "Could the poor chap have fled because he feared the same creature that startled me?"

LODERA considered. The Shadow could see his face tighten, for Lodera's profile was against the lights that came from the opened door of the castle.

"It might be so," decided Lodera. His tone, slow and deliberate, was one that gave an impression of either doubt or fear. "Yes, it could have been that, Gwendolyn. Either the ghost, or his belief in ghosts—"

"Such could have driven him to flight. Francisco, it is only right that I should speak and tell everyone of what I saw. If Geoffrey's ghost is the mischief maker—"

"Hush!" Lodera's command was a harsh hiss. "Would you spoil my plans, which you promised to aid?"

"But we must be honest—"

"Honest with ourselves." Lodera had changed his tone to a persuasive purr. "You know, Gwendolyn, that my ways are honest. I have explained to you why I have trusted Luval. You know that I intend no ill to anyone."

"Sometimes I doubt—"

"Not my honesty?"

"Your idea of honesty. Can't you understand, Francisco? This poor fellow—Mund—has been accused of crime. If he—"

"He has not been accused, Gwendolyn. He has been suspected."

"It is just as bad. If he is innocent; if he acted through fear, he must be cleared. His name—"

"His name is nothing. He was the last of the former servants. If no evidence is produced against him, Mund will simply be classed as a man who acted unwisely."

"Yet I am troubled."

"So am I for old Jeremy. There is a man who really deserves your pity. Think of him, with his poor family. He did his duty; yet you would want to make him a murderer."

"I, Francisco?"

"Yes. By worrying about Mund. Can't you see that Jeremy's best defense is the fact that Mund may have been up to mischief?"

THE girl nodded slowly. Lodera's clever twist of circumstances had begun to convince her. She was weighing the case of Jeremy versus Mund when a low roar came from beyond the castle. It increased; the whirr of an airplane motor. Lodera pointed upward to the lightened sky. The girl saw the monoplane.

"Dufour, off to London," exclaimed Lodera, with enthusiasm. "For us, Gwendolyn! For you, as much as for myself. Our cause is the same; a mutual one. You do as I tell you."

"I shall, Francisco."

"Say nothing about Mund, then. Do not mention ghosts. Remember, we shall be gone soon after dark tonight."

"You are right, Francisco."

Lodera and Gwendolyn went into the house; the last of all who had come out upon the porch. Hasslett had gone in the landaulet to Yarwick. The front of the castle was deserted. Now, it was illuminated by day, except for one angled sector that formed a blackened pathway toward the trees.

A shape stirred from the darkness of the wall and followed the streak of blackness. It was a cloaked figure, that of a being who had remained until the last fleeting moment in order to learn all. The tall, gliding form reached the trees just as the sun burst through the clouds to brighten the entire scene.

No darkness remained where the figure had been. The Shadow had vanished with the last vestige of night.

CHAPTER XVII
BELATED VISITORS

THAT afternoon, a new passenger stepped from the down train at Yarwick platform. The arrival was a well-dressed young man who surveyed his surroundings with interest. Chauncey, driving up in his victoria, was prompt to hail a possible fare. The young man shook his head, and Chauncey drove along.

When the squatty-carred local train had pulled from the platform, the young man went into the station. He saw the agent behind his counter; he also observed a package wrapped in a newspaper. When the agent looked up, the young man introduced himself as Mr. Ralph Jamison. He received the package.

Outside the station, the young man tore the newspaper and extracted an envelope which he found within. He discovered a message in the envelope and read its inked lines. The writing faded as he completed his reading of a simple code. Such was the way with all messages from The Shadow to his agents.

For it had been The Shadow, as Professor Roderick Danglar, who had left the package at the station. The young man who had received it, as Ralph Jamison, was none other than Harry Vincent.

Immediately after reading the instructions, Harry tucked the package under his arm and looked for a secluded lane. He found one, a narrow, hedge-flanked thoroughfare of the type styled a "smuggler's road." Stooping close to a hedge, Harry ripped the package fully open and extracted the garments which Nigel Chiswold had originally worn.

Harry donned the complete outfit, including the mask, which he managed in Nigel's fashion. With coat collar muffling his chin, he stalked from the smuggler's road and pulled his hat more firmly downward on his head. Harry had a hat of his own, an old soft one; and he kept it stowed beneath the bulky overcoat.

Following directions from The Shadow's note, Harry went to the Prince William Inn. He found Chauncey's carriage parked outside. The driver was evidently in the barroom. Harry, however, went directly through the main room of the inn. He saw Mullock behind the desk.

The proprietor looked up as Harry stalked by. He gaped at sight of the supposed Professor Danglar. A shaft of light struck Harry's face; Mullock spied the masklike visage, then gulped. He listened while the guest went upstairs and unlocked the door. Then Mullock wobbled into the barroom.

HARRY'S stay upstairs was a brief one. He came down immediately and walked through the lower room. With a sidelong glance, he spied the proprietor staring from the connecting door. As he passed, Harry grunted a statement:

"I am off to Highchurch; and afterward, the fenland."

Harry's face was turned. Mullock could not tell whether or not the fixed lips moved. Nor could Chauncey, who had regained his carriage, to gawk as the mysterious guest came from the inn. Harry turned on his heel and walked rapidly away. He started in the direction of Highchurch; then doubled through to the smuggler's road.

There, Harry discarded his disguise. He buried the garments and the mask beneath the thickness of a hedge. Cutting back, he strolled toward the inn, wearing his own hat and employing a leisurely gait.

The inn was buzzing when Harry reached it, but The Shadow's agent did not appear to notice the suppressed commotion. He entered the main room and inquired regarding Eric Delka. The proprietor told him that Delka was stopping at the inn, but was absent at present. Harry sat down to rest.

Half an hour drifted, during which time speculation subsided. All was quiet when a man came stamping in through the front door and growled a greeting to Mullock. Harry looked about. It was Delka, sour-faced and unshaven, his clothes crumpled, his shoes muddy.

"Inspector Delka!" exclaimed Harry, coming to his feet. "The very man I have come to see!"

"Hello, Vincent," returned Delka, in surprise. "What brings you here?"

"I called up Cranston," explained Harry, glibly. "He was gone from London, so I called Scotland Yard. I learned that you were up here."

"Humph. Sometimes they say too much at the Yard."

"I did not think that you would object to my coming here, Inspector."

"I don't. I am glad to see you, Vincent. Come on upstairs while I change my clothes. I want to talk to you."

Mullock had approached to hand Delka a telegram which had been delivered at the inn. The proprietor had heard Harry address Delka as "Inspector"; he had also caught the reference to Scotland Yard. As soon as Harry and Delka went upstairs, Mullock hurried from the inn.

DELKA became confidential as soon as he and Harry reached the room. The C.I.D. man opened his telegram, grunted, then began to change his clothes and prepare for a shave. He indicated that

Harry was to read the wire. As a friend of Cranston, Harry was a man in whom Delka might confide.

"'Professor Roderick Danglar'," read Harry, aloud, "'not connected with Cambridge University.'"

"That's the good word," nodded Delka, with a sour look. "The fellow led me a wild goose chase all through the fen district. I lost his trail at a hamlet beyond Highchurch."

"Who is the fellow?"

"Some mystery man who came to Yarwick. He had people talking, here at the inn, so I followed him. I thought I would find him at the Isle of Dean; but he never went there. I was stranded overnight."

A rap at the door. Delka, tugging on another pair of boots, gave an order to come in. Mullock entered, accompanied by a square-set, black-haired man.

"Mr. Delka," stated the innkeeper, "this is Mr. Hayman, our chief police inspector. He is quite anxious to talk to you."

Hayman nodded.

"I heard that you were here," he said. "I know you by reputation, Inspector Delka."

Delka smiled. He realized that Mullock had caught the conversation downstairs and had passed the word to Hayman.

"Yes," declared Delka, "I have been here investigating a rather unusual person—a man who calls himself Professor Roderick Danglar."

"He was back here, sir!" exclaimed Mullock. "Only half an hour ago. He has set out once more for Highchurch."

Delka leaned back and laughed.

"So that's it!" he guffawed. "Postponed his trip to the fens and returned here. Gone on his way again, has he?"

Mullock nodded.

"He stopped last night at Highchurch," stated the proprietor, "for Chauncey saw him there. He had a pair of long stilts, the professor did."

"A harmless idiot," decided Delka. "No more a Cambridge professor than I am. Nevertheless, I shall go to Highchurch to look into the matter."

"Would it be asking too much," queried Hayman, "if I requested a postponement of your journey, Inspector Delka?"

"Not if you have a good reason."

"There is one. A death at Chiswold Castle."

Delka came to his feet and stared. Harry Vincent could not restrain his own expression. He knew that The Shadow was at Chiswold Castle. Great though the confidence that Harry held in his chief, he knew that The Shadow's life was hazardous.

"Not an alarming happening," added Hayman, quickly. "Just a servant—a man named Mund. The fellow was trying to leave the castle just before dawn. He was challenged by Jeremy, the gatekeeper, who shot him."

"I see."

Delka was thinking as he spoke. He remembered Mund; also Jeremy.

"I must prepare a final report for the coroner," explained Hayman, in a troubled tone. "I am anxious that it should be in proper order. There is no blame upon old Jeremy, as I can see. But since I am riding out to the castle, 'twould be a favor if you would be kind enough to accompany me."

"Of course."

TEN minutes later, Delka and Harry were riding with Hayman in a tiny automobile that took the ruts like a jack rabbit. The cloudy sky was dusking, and gloom enwrapped them when they reached the trees before the landing field. Then they passed the clearing; and Hayman pointed toward the monoplane, which was moving along the ground.

"The plane flew in only an hour ago," stated the local inspector. "It had been in London for the day. I heard it roar overhead when I was at the coroner's home, a few miles east of Yarwick."

New darkness under the next trees; then the little car skirted to the gateway. Old Jeremy, anxious-faced, came out to open the barrier. The gatekeeper bowed as the little car rolled past.

"We sent Jeremy back to his post," stated Hayman. "Mr. Modbury accepted responsibility for him. 'Twas troubled, I was, about doing so; but the man will not flee. Did I act rightly, Inspector Delka?"

"I can tell later," replied Delka, "after I have learned the full facts about Mund's death."

"That will be quite soon."

Hayman drew the tiny car to a stop in front of the darkening castle front. Harry and Delka alighted with the local officer. Hayman pointed out the front windows above the door.

"'Twas yonder," he stated. "Mund, they say, was clambering from the balcony when Jeremy spied him from this spot. He fired his fowling piece, Jeremy did, after a command to halt. Mund fell, wounded. The fall, we believe, was what caused his death."

The castle door had opened. Luval stepped out and nodded to the visitors. One of the servants was behind the secretary. Luval gave an order and the man went back into the building.

Delka was looking upward, eyeing the lone turret high above. He turned to Hayman with a query:

"What about that turret? Could Mund have been up there, instead of on the balcony? It is straight above."

"We thought of that, sir," expressed Hayman, "but Mr. Modbury and others discovered the window open in the front room. Old Jeremy swore that Mund crawled forward after he fell."

Luval entered the conversation, just as the servant arrived from the castle, bearing Jeremy's fowling piece. The secretary handed the weapon to Delka; then spoke words that carried a tone of true conviction.

"THIS weapon," he told Delka, "could never have carried to so great a range as the turret top. Moreover"—he pointed upward—"how could anyone have aimed for a person there? See how the battlements project?"

"Right," agreed Delka. "The fellow would have had to be hanging over the side."

"Clutching the merlons," added Luval. "Besides, there is no way to reach the turret. It is merely an ornamental addition to the castle. You must remember that this building was erected when few archers remained."

"True," agreed Delka. "Otherwise it would have had many turrets." Then, to Hayman: "I believe that you have acted in due accordance with the law, Inspector. Jeremy was acting in discharge of his appointed duty. By the way, was Mund up to any definite mischief?"

"We believe that he intended to rob the castle," put in Luval. "He had been acting oddly. We think that he came out to test the ivy vines as a mode of escape."

Delka nodded. The theory was logical enough for acceptance. Others were arriving from the castle: Barton Modbury and Sir Rodney Ralthorn.

"Ah! Delka!" exclaimed Modbury, in a tone of surprise. "I am glad to see you back here. Has news of our trouble here reached Scotland Yard?"

"No," replied the C.I.D. man. "I was merely coming back through Yarwick when I met Inspector Hayman. He wanted my approval of his handling of this case."

"And have you approved it?"

"Yes. In every detail. The law has no case against old Jeremy. His story was certainly an honest one."

Another man had arrived to hear the words. It was Francisco Lodera; the Spaniard showed a pleased expression in the hazy dusk. Then his manner changed as Modbury gave an invitation. Delka was introducing Harry when Modbury spoke.

"Come, all three of you," suggested the diamond king. "Dine with us here at the castle. There are matters which I should like to discuss with you, Inspector Delka; and you also, Inspector Hayman. I have valuables here, you know."

Lodera glanced anxiously at Luval. The secretary's face showed nervousness. Then, tensely, Luval gave a signal to Lodera, to indicate that matters could be handled. The group started into the house, all except Hayman and Harry. The former wanted to move his automobile from the drive. Harry stood by to join Hayman when he came indoors.

Something had caused Harry to remain; it was an odd impression that he could not have explained. But the answer came, when Harry stood alone, there in the blackness that fronted Chiswold Castle. From the gloom of the walls came a whispered tone:

"Report."

The Shadow!

CAUTIOUSLY, Harry spoke in brief fashion. Then came The Shadow's new instructions, delivered in low tones from a place where he stood invisible. Harry was to watch happenings inside; to signal from a window should unexpected developments occur. Then he could report when The Shadow arrived to contact.

That was all. There was time for no more. Hayman had parked his tiny car and was returning. Eyes from the darkness watched Harry go into the castle with the local police inspector. Dusk had settled everywhere; for the cloud-fronted sun was now obscured completely behind the bulk of Chiswold Castle.

Silent and shrouded, The Shadow moved away. He skirted the castle at the stable side and reached the crags above Castle Cove. Through an opening, he peered toward the lost outline of Parrion Head, the distant promontory that jutted into the sea.

Parrion Head was beyond the far side of the cove; though a long way from the castle, it could be reached by a two-mile walk from the landing field on the other side of the gulch. As The Shadow watched the darkness, a bluish flame flickered upon Parrion Head. An interval; then the flare was repeated.

The Shadow laughed softly in the darkness. Then, as he spied a third and longer flame, he turned about and moved toward the front of Chiswold Castle. He was heading for the front trees, where both driveway and path afforded means of leaving the estate. Suddenly, The Shadow stopped.

A blink had come from the slitted turret. It was repeated, the flash of an electric torch. The Shadow waited. Again, the signal came. Once more, The Shadow delivered a whispered laugh. Then he changed his direction.

He had chosen a new destination: Jeremy's lodge.

CHAPTER XVIII
WITHIN AND WITHOUT

DINNER had been both prompt and informal within Chiswold Castle. Modbury and his guests had gone immediately to the table; they were half finished with their meal at the time when The Shadow had left the crags beside Castle Cove.

Then, during dessert, Barton Modbury had become loquacious. From the head of the table, he started talk of Mund's death; then, while his listeners were attentive, he had produced a small silver casket and had opened it.

Delka was on Modbury's right. The Scotland Yard man stared as Modbury poured forth a small pile of lustrous red gems that sparkled in the shimmering candlelight. Harry and Hayman both showed interest; and the regular castle guests delivered smiles.

"Fine rubies," explained Modbury, "which I purchased today from Lodera. That was why his plane flew to London. Dufour, the pilot, made the trip to bring back these jewels."

"How valuable are they?" queried Delka, examining the stones.

"I paid six thousand sovereigns for them," replied Modbury. That, to Harry, meant nearly thirty thousand dollars. "I consider them a bargain at the price."

"I had to sell them," remarked Lodera. "They represent about all of the fortune that remains to me. I lost a great deal of valuable property after the revolution in Spain. Next, I shall sell my airplane; then lead an economical life."

"Here in England?" queried Modbury.

"Perhaps." Lodera's eyes shifted momentarily toward Gwendolyn, who sat across the table. "Or maybe somewhere on the continent. I have not quite made up my mind. I think I shall first fly to London—say, in a day or so—and deposit my currency in the bank."

"You paid in cash?" asked Delka of Modbury.

"Yes," replied the diamond king, "but I am keeping the money in my safe until Lodera requires it. Come—we shall go up to the study and put the rubies away."

Delka and Harry went upstairs with Modbury. The South African diamond king opened the safe and showed the chamois bag, to give a brief display of its contents. He pushed aside the opened stacks of cash and tucked the rubies into a deep niche. Locking the safe, he led the way downstairs.

SIR RODNEY and Lord Cedric were in the great room, talking with Hayman. Delka caught their words; they were still wondering why Mund had avoided robbery until after making his test of the vines. Harry saw a sudden light gleam from Delka's eyes. The C.I.D. man spoke.

"I have it!" he exclaimed. "Tell me, Mr. Modbury, did Mund know that you intended to purchase those rubies?"

"He probably did," replied Modbury. "Why, Delka?"

"Because that would have meant a postponement of his burglary. It is quite plain. He wanted to wait until the rubies had joined the other wealth."

"Jove!" exclaimed Sir Rodney. "A clever stroke, Inspector Delka. That explains everything! The scoundrel knew that he would have six thousand pounds more for his bundle!"

"You are right," agreed Modbury, nodding. "Twenty thousand in diamonds; ten thousand in cash; six thousand in rubies. That sums the total. Last night, Mund was testing a means of escape. Tonight, he intended to rob my safe."

"Could he have cracked it, do you think?"

"I cannot say." Modbury spoke in troubled fashion, as he considered. Then, brightening: "But there is no need for further alarm. Mund was the only dishonest person who could possibly have been here in the castle. My other servants are all trustworthy."

Luval had entered from the hallway, in time to catch the conversation. Harry had noted the bespectacled secretary's face. Luval had kept a steady front. He sat down at the edge of the group.

Soon, Gwendolyn Ralthorn entered. Francisco Lodera was the only absentee. Five minutes later, he arrived, smoking a cigarette in the end of his long holder. Harry saw Gwendolyn gaze toward Lodera. The Spaniard gave a slight nod.

Conversation turned to the morrow's fox hunt. All joined, including both Gwendolyn and Lodera. At one interval, however, Gwendolyn left the great room and went upstairs. Soon afterward, Lodera strolled out through the hall. Both returned; but Harry had an idea that each might soon again go out.

Seated between Hayman and Delka, Harry could find no opportunity to leave. Nor did he wish to risk a signal to The Shadow; for as yet, he had observed nothing of alarming consequence.

Gwendolyn and Lodera appeared restless; but they were not the ones who Harry felt needed closest watching.

Harry had concentrated upon Luval; until the secretary made a move, Harry could see no need for action. Since Luval appeared quite content in an obscure chair near the flickering fireplace, Harry decided to wait.

At intervals, Harry's thoughts turned to The Shadow. He wondered exactly where his cloaked chief was located at this moment. He thought of various places, among them the gatekeeper's lodge. He rejected it as an unlikely place; nevertheless, that was where The Shadow stood at that very moment.

Despite the trees, there was one spot near the lodge from which the castle turret could be seen. Watching from that point, close by the fence, The Shadow had detected a repetition of the blinks. So had Jeremy; for the old gatekeeper had come out from the lodge. Coming through darkness almost to where The Shadow stood, Jeremy had spied Nigel's signal. But he had not detected the shrouded being who was present.

JEREMY had gone back into his little house; once again, he had come to the observation post, to mutter in troubled fashion because he saw no blinks. Then, as the gatekeeper turned to move away, The Shadow's ears caught the sound of a creeping approach. It was someone else, beside Jeremy; but the gatekeeper did not hear the newcomer until a low, accented voice whispered one audible word.

"Khyber."

Jeremy's gasp followed.

"'Tis thou," exclaimed the gatekeeper, in an undertone, "come from the gamekeeper's empty cot!"

"I have come."

The tone was that of Amakar, the Afghan. The dark-skinned giant was as blanketed as The Shadow, for the darkness here was thick. Jeremy's words explained a fact which The Shadow had supposed; but had not investigated by daylight. Amakar had occupied the one-room building that had been The Shadow's earlier headquarters.

"Look!" whispered Jeremy, to Amakar. "Master Nigel has sent the signal once more! Aye! 'Tis something he wishes; but I did not venture. 'Twould not be wise for myself to pass close by the castle."

"He signifies that all is ready," informed Amakar, soberly. "At times apart, my master will send his signal until I join him."

"Must that be soon?"

"I cannot tell. I, Amakar, shall approach and answer. Then will my master tell his need."

"How will you reach him?"

"He has long since told me the way."

Jeremy was blundering in the darkness. Amakar whispered soberly. Jeremy gave a grunt of understanding and went back to the lodge. The Shadow waited. He heard Amakar move softly forward through the trees.

With amazing precision, the big Afghan was picking a path through the woods, toward the castle. But his stealth was nothing compared with The Shadow's. Moving forward, the cloaked watcher kept silent pace with the Afghan. Amakar, because of his own tread, failed to catch the slight sounds behind him.

Amakar reached the outskirts of the trees. He paused; when Nigel blinked again, the Afghan delivered a strange, high-pitched wail. It was like the cry of a night bird, but one that differed from any heard in England. The wail, however, was restrained. The Shadow knew that Amakar had given it through cupped hands.

Moreover, the Afghan had turned his mouth upward. Through some uncanny ability, he had tuned the cry so that it scarcely reached the castle. His call had penetrated to Nigel; but it could not have been heard by those within the castle. Nor

would others, by the stable or in the woods, have heard it. Amakar had given his wail a straight direction, with an effect that matched the ability of a ventriloquist.

Blinks from the turret. They were signaling an answer. Nigel had heard. Amakar, understanding orders, began a new course along the front fringe of the trees. He saw an opened patch of protected ground and moved across it. Struggling moonlight threw a faint and unexpected glow that revealed the Afghan's bulk.

Amakar stopped as he heard a hiss behind him. Swinging, the Afghan saw a shrouded shape. The Shadow, too, had stepped from the trees. His hiss had been a challenge to the man. With a bound, Amakar leaped toward a tree and lowered his arms. The Shadow divined the purpose of his move. This was where Amakar had hidden his rifle.

SWEEPING grotesquely forward, The Shadow came driving into conflict. His arms were wide, in front of him. Amakar changed tactics. Lunging up from the ground, he shot his huge hands forward, to grapple with his eerie attacker.

The fighters met, as moonlight faded. Bare-handed, they struggled as they had in London. Amakar, huge of strength, again expected to crush his wiry foe. The Shadow, quick of action, sought means of countering the Afghan's power.

In this resumption of the duel, Amakar gained the first grip. As fierce as he had been in Whitechapel, the big man whirled The Shadow back and forth. With a furious lunge, he sought to fling his adversary against the nearest tree. The Shadow, however, clung. His choking hands caught Amakar's throat.

The Afghan doubled. The Shadow's feet struck ground. His body twisted; his arms worked like trip hammers. Amakar went sidewise; then The Shadow's footing failed. The black-cloaked fighter sprawled as Amakar rolled clear.

Regaining his feet, Amakar saw a slowly rising form that sank again in a shapeless fashion. A trickle of moonlight showed a waver; the shape rose again and faded sidewise. Amakar thought his foe was crippled. With a ferocious, half-hissed grunt, the mighty Afghan launched in a powerful plunge toward The Shadow.

His sweeping arms gripped nothingness. Plunging forward, Amakar sprawled rolling, his face and shoulders cluttered in the wrappings of a cloak. The Shadow had tricked him in the manner of a matador; for Amakar had come with the head-down attack of a bull.

The shape that Amakar had seen had been The Shadow's cloak, raised upward, forward, by a stooping figure beneath. The Shadow had given the cloak a sidewise shift, which had accounted for the wavering fade. Amakar had taken the bait. Releasing the cloak, The Shadow had twisted away, just as the Afghan charged.

Had this occurred upon a Whitechapel sidewalk, Amakar would have been stunned when he struck the paving, for the fury of his plunge was backed by all his weight.

Soft turf, however, was Amakar's final lodging. He was dazed by the force of his dive; but still ready for new fray. It was The Shadow's quickness that stopped Amakar's rise.

Bounding upon his fallen foe, The Shadow caught the big man's throat with one hand. With the other, he produced an automatic and jabbed the cold muzzle against Amakar's forehead. The Afghan felt the menace of the weapon. Groaning, he sagged backward to the ground.

A WHISPERED laugh sounded above him. The tone was weird; it stilled Amakar's hissed gasps. The overpowered Afghan expected death; instead, he listened to a voice that spoke in a sinister tone. Not in English; but in Amakar's own native tongue. The words that Amakar heard amazed him.

When The Shadow's speech was ended, Amakar replied. Unresisting, he blurted Afghan sentences that came in questioning tones. The Shadow replied. Amakar spoke solemnly. The statement that he gave was so important that when he had finished, he thought it best to repeat the words in English.

"You have spoken," stated Amakar slowly, looking upward with his head still prone. "I have heard. Your words bring those things which I did not understand. My mind has learned because your wisdom tells me much that was unknown.

"I, Amakar, shall serve you. You are the master; the one who knows. Whenever you speak, I shall obey. The little things that Amakar can tell, are to be yours. I, Amakar, obey."

Soon afterward, a shaft of moonlight showed the amazing sequel to the fray. The glow revealed the cloaked form of The Shadow moving along the fringe of trees. Behind him, an obedient slave, came the mammoth Amakar bearing his long-range rifle.

The Shadow had gained a double victory. He had overpowered the formidable Afghan; then, triumphant, had won the powerful victim to his cause!

CHAPTER XIX
THE NEW ALLY

SWIFTLY, steadily, The Shadow chose his course, in the manner of one who had studied the terrain. Passing the castle, he reached the cliffs above the cove; and all the while Amakar followed, silent and obedient.

Choosing a craggy path, The Shadow skirted the inner end of Castle Cove and turned toward the road that led between the castle and the aviation field. This course had saved much longer travel.

It was when they left the cove's end that Amakar made his first utterance since his pledge of loyalty. Tightening his grip upon his rifle, the big man spoke in his native tongue. His words were half a question, half a warning. The Shadow paused.

From faraway, carried through the funneled stretches of the cove came scraping, thumping sounds that were barely audible against the distant murmur of the sea. The cove was like a mammoth megaphone; The Shadow and Amakar were at the pointed tip of the great cone.

Listening, The Shadow knew that the sounds were faraway. Amakar, trained to the ways of the Afghanistan wilderness, had actually caught the noise before The Shadow. That and the formation of the cove were proofs of distance.

The Shadow spoke to Amakar. Obediently, the big man followed. He knew that there was preliminary work to be performed. He trusted in The Shadow.

AT a swift pace, The Shadow and his new ally came to the roadway and followed it to the landing field. Dim moonlight gave a fleeting view of Lodera's plane.

The Shadow chose it as his objective. He paced rapidly ahead, with just sufficient noise to guide Amakar, for clouds had thickened; and the ground obscured The Shadow's figure. When they neared the plane, The Shadow hissed cautiously for a halt. They heard a voice: Dufour's.

"Head for the castle road," the pilot was ordering. "Lay low and cover. Close in after Lodera and the girl go by. You know the rest."

"Wot about the other blokes?" came a query.

"They'll handle their job," returned Dufour. "You'll cover them when they come along. The bunch of you can scatter after we take off."

"Back to the boats?"

"Gonzales will decide that for you. He's with the other crew because it's more important. After you join, he will hold command. If you can't use the boats, he will guide you to the fens."

Buzzes of approval. The men who had congregated with Dufour seemed pleased at this suggestion of an alternative. The aviator gave final assurance.

"The boats should prove all right," he declared, "unless some coast patrollers caught my flares from Parrion Head. That is not likely, for I shielded them against view from the sea."

"But if blokes were staring from the castle—"

"Parrion Head cannot be seen from the castle. No one would have been on the cliff above the cove. Come! Along to the road. I'll point the way."

Soon afterward. a shaft of moonlight showed the amazing sequel to the fray. The glow revealed the cloaked form of The Shadow.

Dufour moved from the plane, with skulking men behind him. Then came a parting. The pilot was going to the cottage; his men were turning toward the road, to take their course toward the castle. The Shadow spoke to Amakar. Silently, they stalked after the men who had left Dufour.

There were six in that motley band; their low, gruff voices told their number. The Shadow gave them leeway until they were past the trees. He wanted to be far from Dufour's hearing. Then, when stilled blackness clustered overheard, The Shadow gave a soft whisper to Amakar. The giant drew up beside him.

The six men were moving slowly. One blinked a flashlight and pointed out the ground about. Bushes formed clusters beside the road. Here men could spread, yet keep within speaking distance. The ruffian crew was ready to form an ambush cordon between the castle and the landing field. The time had come for The Shadow's stroke.

The flashlight blinked off. Voices buzzed. Then came a sweeping avalanche in the shape of two forms that plunged into the clustered thugs. Side by side, The Shadow and Amakar swooped down upon their prey. Two against six, they struck with a tremendous fury.

RUFFIANS spun about at the first sound. The move added to their undoing. The Shadow, gripping the first foeman in his path, caught the fellow's body and swept it sidewise, like a human battering ram. Before the helpless man could struggle, The Shadow had piled him upon one of his pals. The two sprawled flat. The Shadow's fists then started flaying.

Amakar, his long arms wide, had clutched two ruffians at the same instant. With tremendous strength, he was whirling them about, handling each with a single arm. One man came from his feet; then sprawled as Amakar flung him face downward.

Wheeling, the big Afghan gained a double grip upon the other and hurled him bodily through the air. The whirling body plunged through bushes in its flight; then thudded against a tree in the darkness. A choked cry ended abruptly.

The Shadow had known what the other thugs would do. Had they seen their opponents, they might have sought flight; but in the darkness, with nowhere to turn, they chose the natural course of pitching in to the attack.

The Shadow had punched one thug into submission; he was holding the other prone, half stooped above him, when Amakar flung the man into the woods.

The Afghan stood between The Shadow and the new attack. Amakar's bulk came staggering backward as two attackers struck him before he could regain his balance. The Shadow drove his second adversary downward. The fellow's head cracked the hard dirt of the road. Then rising, The Shadow twisted inward and fell upon the pair who were pummeling Amakar.

One man lost his clutch, turned to battle with The Shadow. Shoulders dropped. The ruffian gave a gloating cry. Then The Shadow whipped upward and somersaulted his antagonist headlong to the bushy bank. The man rolled over, too jolted to rise.

Amakar disposed instantly of the final thug. Gripping the fellow with both arms, he raised him high above his head; then delivered a long, powerful heave. An interval seemed to follow; then came a violent thud in the road far ahead. The silence was disturbed only by outspread groans.

The Shadow's flashlight blinked. It picked out the sprawled thugs. Three were still capable of action; though their motions were slow. Amakar took care of them.

He rolled the trio close together; their bulging eyes showed horror when they saw the darkened face above the mammoth shoulders. Ripping away belts and tearing strips from flannel shirts, Amakar began to bind the subdued enemies.

With the task half completed, The Shadow moved about with the flashlight. He found the senseless man whom he had first encountered and pushed the fellow against Amakar's feet. From the furze, he dragged forth the thug who had ended up against a tree; then, from the road, he brought the man whom Amakar had tossed into oblivion. These two did not need binding.

An order to Amakar, hissed by The Shadow. The Afghan hoisted the first pair that he had bound and plunged off through the glade, a burden on each shoulder. He was taking a straight route to the old gamekeeper's cot, which was only a few hundred yards away. The Shadow finished tying up the next two thugs. He had them ready when Amakar returned. Again, the Afghan carried away a double burden.

THE SHADOW waited, listening. No sound came from the direction of the castle. Amakar, tireless, returned with amazing promptness. He lugged away the thugs whom he had finished with his tremendous tosses. This time, The Shadow, listening, caught faint sounds from the road. He edged into the bushes and hissed as Amakar came toward him.

"Dufour," ordered The Shadow. "Make haste."

Skirting the road, they came to the clearing. Amakar crossed, went toward the airplane. The Shadow heard approaching footsteps; then voices. Two persons had come along the road through the woods. One was Francisco Lodera; the other Gwendolyn Ralthorn.

"We are in the clearing," Lodera was saying. "Look, Gwendolyn; see the sky above us."

"The darkness was dreadful," protested the girl. "It was as fearful in the glade as in the castle."

"Look. The lights of the cottage."

"Are we going there?"

"No. Dufour is waiting for us by the plane."

The pair stumbled on through the blackness of the ground. The Shadow heard their footfalls fade. Then came another, more cautious tread. It was Amakar, returning. The Afghan was lugging Dufour.

He had plucked the sturdy pilot from beside his ship; and had conquered him without allowing a cry. Amakar never had difficulty with a lone adversary, except the one whom he now acknowledged as his master.

The Shadow ordered Amakar to stow Dufour with the other prisoners; then to meet him near the head of the cove. Moving toward the plane, The Shadow stopped and turned in the direction of the cottage. Lodera and Gwendolyn were going there, since they had not found Dufour at the plane. The Shadow could hear their voices.

The two appeared at the lighted doorway of the cottage. The Shadow saw them go in; gliding close, he caught their words. Lodera was speaking in a tone that showed mingled anger and perplexity.

"Dufour should be here!" was his exclamation. "Where can the fellow be? We cannot take off without him. Remain here, Gwendolyn, while I search for him."

"No, no!" protested the girl, excitedly. "I shall not remain alone, Francisco! You must wait with me until Dufour comes!"

"Very well," agreed Lodera, in a troubled tone. "I shall not leave you, Gwendolyn. But if Dufour does not learn that we are here—"

"He will see you, if you keep pacing about the doorway."

The Shadow saw Lodera nod in agreement. The plan was sensible; it was obvious that the Spaniard intended to adhere to it. The Shadow had no further need to remain. Since Lodera intended to wait for Dufour, it was plain that he would have to remain at the cottage. The Shadow moved away through the darkness, to rejoin Amakar.

Lodera, staring from the cottage door, was sharp of gaze. But no eyes could have discerned the cloaked figure that was gliding away in the darkness. Whatever his opinion of Dufour's absence, Lodera did not suspect the departing presence of The Shadow.

CHAPTER XX
CHANCE BRINGS ITS ISSUE

NIGHT had enwrapped strange doings about Chiswold Castle. The flares from Parrion Head; the blinks from the turret; The Shadow's fight with Amakar—like the succeeding captures of Dufour and his crew—all had taken place unwitnessed by those within the great stone walls.

Yet something had happened within the castle; and Harry Vincent had noticed it. Francisco Lodera and Gwendolyn Ralthorn had again departed from the great room downstairs. They had gone separately; and this time neither had returned.

Luval had also left; but the secretary's departure had not been voluntary. Barton Modbury had sent him upstairs to find a booklet that dealt with the subject of the Kimberley diamond mines. Luval was presumably in the study, hunting up the prospectus.

Chance had it that Hayman decided to go out to his car. The local inspector had remembered a report sheet which he wished to show to Delka. Harry, looking toward the hallway, saw Hayman go across. Then he saw the local officer stop short, to listen suspiciously. A moment later, Hayman returned.

"Come to the hall!" he whispered to Modbury. "I hear sounds from upstairs. I caught a glimpse of someone creeping upward. It could not have been Luval."

Modbury arose. Sir Rodney and Lord Cedric followed. Delka motioned to Harry. The entire group went out into the hallway and approached the stairs. Like a faint echo from above, they heard the sound of creaking floorboards.

"Let us go up," decided Modbury.

Though the group ascended softly, the sounds of their footsteps was audible. When they arrived on the second floor, they found the hallway empty. The only opened door was that of the front room. Hayman entered and glanced about suspiciously. He tried the windows. All were clamped.

"How about the study?" queried Delka. "Is Luval in there?"

"He should be," replied Modbury. "Perhaps it would be wise to see."

They went to the study door. Modbury opened it. Luval peered out from a closet, where he was deep in a stack of boxes, hunting for the Kimberley booklet. When he saw the group, Luval dumped pamphlets back into their place and came out to receive Modbury's question.

"Did you hear anyone up here?" demanded Modbury.

"No, sir," replied Luval. "I closed the door when I came into the study. Were the sounds from the hall?"

"Yes," cut in Hayman. "But someone was on the stairs to begin with."

Luval's lips tightened. Harry thought that he detected a worried look upon the secretary's face. But no one else noticed it. Sir Rodney Ralthorn had started another query.

"Where is Lodera?"

SUSPICION tinged Sir Rodney's tone. Lord Cedric Lorthing showed immediate support. He looked about the group; then demanded:

"And Gwendolyn? Where has she gone?"

Sir Rodney's face showed anger. He strode to the door and shouted. He called Gwendolyn's name; hearing no reply, he crossed to the girl's room and pounded the door. At last he opened the barrier and turned on the light. He came back to the study.

"Gwendolyn is gone!" stormed Sir Rodney. "She has eloped with that Spaniard, Lodera! I feared that something such was in her mind; but I did not believe that she would dare it—"

"Lodera may still be here," broke in Delka. "Hayman saw someone on the stairs. Suppose we search for him."

"Let us go to the landing field!" roared Sir Rodney. "We must seize Lodera's plane—"

"One moment." It was Modbury who interposed. He was staring sternly toward Luval; and the secretary was backing away. "Come, Luval. Your face betrays you. Tell us what you know."

Luval reached into his pocket. He drew forth an envelope. He approached Sir Rodney, handed him the object. Sir Rodney recognized Gwendolyn's handwriting. He ripped open the envelope and read the message.

"I am right," he bellowed. "The girl has fled! Come! To the plane's landing field!"

Servants had arrived in the hall, brought upstairs by the commotion. Modbury motioned everyone into the study. He closed the door behind him.

"One moment, Sir Rodney," insisted the diamond king. "Let us make sure of this. Luval—how much more do you know?"

"It is too late to stop them, sir," confessed the secretary. "They have been gone half an hour. I knew their intent as soon as Miss Gwendolyn told me to keep this letter for her father."

"Why did you not tell me?"

"I felt that it concerned Miss Gwendolyn only. She asked for my promise. I could not refuse."

"You are a fool, Luval. Nevertheless, we cannot hold you to great blame. The plane has gone by this time. Pursuit would be useless."

"They have probably flown to the continent," put in Delka. "They could land anywhere. You are right, Mr. Modbury, nothing can be done to overtake them."

"I advised against it," protested Luval. "I told Miss Gwendolyn that I did not trust Lodera—"

"You did not trust him?" demanded Modbury, suddenly. "On what account, Luval?"

"Only regarding promises," put in the secretary, hastily. "Do not misunderstand me. I thought Lodera honest. I merely believed that he might have made false claims about his social position, because he knew that Lord Cedric was his rival."

"I understand."

MODBURY expressed satisfaction with Luval's statement; but Sir Rodney came through with an objection.

"The fellow is a blackguard!" he cried. "Such a man would stop at nothing! He has behaved in an outrageous fashion! Only last night, he ventured into this room without permission. That was when you should have taken him to task, Modbury!"

"And where was he tonight?" demanded Lord Cedric, hotly. "Going in and out of the great room. I would wager that he was snooping hereabouts again!"

"Was Lodera in here tonight, Luval?" demanded Modbury.

"I could not say, sir," replied the secretary. "He may have come here, however. I saw him coming downstairs alone."

Modbury yanked open the desk drawer. He fumbled among papers there. His eyes showed excitement. He wheeled and went to the safe.

"What is the matter, sir?" queried Luval.

"The card is gone!" exclaimed Modbury. "I meant to have you destroy it; but I forgot. If Lodera took it, he carried away something more—"

Modbury stopped short as he pulled the safe door open. Then, with a rumbled cry, he raised up and pointed wildly. The front of the safe was empty. Diamonds, rubies, and cash were gone.

"Lodera's work!" bellowed the diamond king. "He was the one who waited for tonight! Not Mund; but Lodera!"

"He may have taken his cue from Mund," put in Delka, hurrying over to study the rifled safe. "That is the more likely answer. He did not need his rubies here."

"Except to get them out of London," stormed Modbury, "and to lull us by bringing them here!"

HAYMAN had grabbed Luval. The secretary was sinking into a chair, his hands raised pleadingly.

"I swear complete innocence, Mr. Modbury—"

Modbury heard Luval's appeal. His rage subsided; his face became stern but kindly. He motioned Hayman to one side.

"Luval is honest," assured Modbury. "I am sure that he would not betray me. He had access to the safe. I have trusted him with large sums in the past."

"I swear to it," repeated Luval. "I plotted, yes; but not toward crime. I knew that the elopement was due to come. I could not have prevented it. I was for Lodera, up until tonight; then suddenly I began to mistrust him.

"I believed that he was duping Miss Gwendolyn; but I knew also that her decision was made. I have been a fool—a terrible fool—"

"No more to blame than the rest of us," inserted Modbury. "We caught Lodera red-handed last night; yet we were too thick to realize it."

"Quite right," agreed Sir Rodney.

Lord Cedric nodded gloomily.

Modbury began to question the servants. None had seen Lodera and Gwendolyn leave the castle. After a brief quiz, Modbury turned to Delka and Hayman.

"We must drive to Yarwick," he decided. "From there you can call London, since there is no telephone here. This is a case for Scotland Yard. I shall go with you; we can stop at the landing field on the way."

"With a certainty," added Sir Rodney. "Yes, with a certainty that we shall find the plane gone. Well, Modbury, my sympathy is with you. After all, my daughter had a right to marry whom she chose. But you have suffered a financial loss."

"Your daughter has married a rogue," returned Modbury, sadly. "You are the one who deserves the sympathy, Sir Rodney."

Delka, with Hayman, had turned toward the door. Harry Vincent saw the C.I.D. man pause. The barrier was slightly ajar. Delka must have suspected that someone was on the other side. With a sweep, he yanked the door open and sprang straight toward the hall. He was in time to clutch a stooping man, before the fellow could spring away.

HAYMAN leaped to Delka's aid. Together, they dragged the intruder into the light. Startled cries came from Sir Rodney and Lord Cedric, while Barton Modbury stared, astonished.

Harry saw a wild look in Luval's eyes. One that he could understand, for Harry, too, was frozen in amazement. There were details which Harry had not yet gained from The Shadow.

Pale-faced, weary in the arms of his captors, the intruder at the door looked like a veritable ghost. That was what those in the room half believed him to be. Not one had ever expected to see that countenance again in life.

The prisoner was Nigel Chiswold, down from the turret room. Even in this light, he could easily be taken for another. Feature for feature, Nigel remained the image of his dead cousin Geoffrey, the former master of Chiswold Castle.

CHAPTER XXI

BENEATH THE CASTLE

DELKA and Hayman were the last to see the face of the man whom they had snared. Dragging Nigel into the study, they had thrust him forward; hence they were behind his shoulders. It was the consternation reigning on other faces that caused both captors to realize that they had gained a startling prize.

Hayman, twisting past Nigel, stared at the prisoner's face. A look of incredulity came over the local inspector. Hayman cried out the name:

"Geoffrey Chiswold!"

Delka spun Nigel toward him. The Scotland Yard man stared in amazement. He had seen Geoffrey's dead face in a London morgue. Here was the same countenance—a countenance representing the features of a living man!

Sir Rodney Ralthorn, stepping forward, was quick to clutch Nigel by the shoulders. Studying the prisoner's visage, Sir Roger nodded, as though he understood. Then, turning to the others, he stated:

"It is Geoffrey Chiswold, returned. Let us be thankful that the rumor was wrong. Geoffrey, we thought that you were dead!"

"Geoffrey is dead," declared Nigel, calmly.

Sir Rodney dropped back at the sound of the voice, so like Geoffrey's. Lord Cedric recognized the tone also; his eyes blinked, and his monocle dropped to his waistcoat. Barton Modbury sank back in his chair, half gaping. Luval huddled by the wall, while servants stared at one another.

Nigel shook himself from Delka's grasp. Hayman made a grab; but Delka motioned him back. There was no chance for the prisoner to escape. Nigel smiled wanly.

"Any cigarettes here?" he queried. "I've been out of smokes for ten hours."

Harry produced some cigarettes. Nigel lighted one and puffed serenely. The layman started to speak to Delka; Nigel caught the word "Inspector"; he looked at the C.I.D. man.

"Are you from Scotland Yard?"

Delka nodded!

"Good!" Nigel took another long drag from the cigarette. "You are the very man to hear my story. I am Nigel Chiswold, cousin to Geoffrey."

"I thought so." Delka's tone was firm as he nodded. "That idea just struck me. I saw Geoffrey's body in London. So you are Nigel Chiswold, back from India. You have been in England for some time, haven't you?"

"No," replied Nigel. "My paleness was due to the fever in Bombay. I came home on sick leave. I arrived just after a series of robberies had been committed in London. Those crimes impressed me; because I knew who could have had a finger in them."

TENSENESS had set upon all within the room. Delka stopped a buzz with a wave of his hand. He wanted to hear more.

"Clandermoor's—Kelgood's—Bond Street— Darriol's — the Smith-Righterstone's" — Nigel changed his enumeration—"gold plates—portraits— jewels—jade vases—tiaras and tapestries. I knew about them all from the past. But there was someone who knew more than I; someone who could have told exactly where they were at present."

"Your cousin Geoffrey?" queried Delka.

"Yes," answered Nigel, "I guessed that he was in back of the robberies. That is why I looked for Geoffrey in London. I found him in the fog."

"Near Whitechapel?"

"No, near St. James Square. I talked to him, intimated what I knew. Geoffrey was cagey. He had the cheek to accuse me in return."

Lord Cedric started to drawl a question. Delka called for silence. Nigel resumed.

"Geoffrey was leaving England," he said, tersely. "That fact troubled me. I realized that he had done his job; that a master crook was behind him. So, afterward, I sent my Afghan servant, Amakar, to find Geoffrey, with instructions to capture Jeff and bring him to me. Just as he captured Sannarak, the famous outlaw, at Khyber Pass, Amakar did that job single-handed."

"I have heard of Sannarak's capture!" exclaimed Sir Rodney. "He was the troublemaker who was brought to Calcutta; and afterward released, when he named Jahata Bey as the rogue behind the secret insurrections."

"Right," nodded Nigel, "and I intended to question Jeff as they did Sannarak. Unfortunately, Amakar failed to capture my wayward cousin. Geoffrey was murdered in Whitechapel, while Amakar was still on his trail."

HARRY VINCENT stared. Nigel's story was convincing. Harry remembered that surge of men who had come hurtling from the steps of the Whitechapel house. He realized that Geoffrey, already stabbed, could not have been the one who fought that group. It had been Amakar!

Harry had mistaken the big Afghan for an assassin. Then The Shadow had come to Harry's rescue. Amakar had fled; did The Shadow know that the Afghan was innocent of wrong? Had Harry been outside the castle tonight, he would have gained evidence of The Shadow's knowledge. The Shadow had divined the truth. That was why he had taken Amakar as an ally.

"Geoffrey was no longer useful to the master rogue who duped him," resumed Nigel. "That was why he was murdered. He was probably told to stop in Whitechapel on his way to the dock."

"Right!" exclaimed Delka. "It fits! I wondered what he was doing in that district. He must have gone there expecting to receive full payment for his part in crime. Instead, he was eliminated."

Again, Harry pondered. Delka had guessed this answer. Had The Shadow divined it previously? Harry felt sure that his chief must have seen through the game.

"Geoffrey had sold this castle," resumed Nigel.

"He warned me not to come here. He even continued his nervy bluff to the point of saying that I might be out to rob Modbury. I saw through it. I sensed that the master crook must be here, intending to do such a job himself. My task was to offset it.

"I intended to inform the law. First, however, I needed facts. I came here, wearing a mask, for my face—so like Geoffrey's—would have been recognized in Yarwick. I stopped, temporarily, at the Prince William Inn."

DELKA smiled sourly. He thought that this explained the mystery of Professor Roderick Danglar. However, he chose to let the subject pass, which was fortunate, to Harry's way of thinking. Both Nigel and Delka would have been puzzled had they gone into more details.

"How did you enter?" demanded Delka.

"Through a hidden opening in the rocks above Castle Cove," explained Nigel, "then through a vault below the castle; a place arranged to hide a company of soldiers in the days of the Pretender. I ascended a spiral staircase, straight up to the lone turret, where I occupied a secret chamber known as the spy room."

"Who else knew of this place?"

"Only Geoffrey. But he had informed the master crook. I gained evidence of that; and I learned that the man was here in the castle."

"Who is he?" demanded Barton Modbury.

"Francisco Lodera," returned Nigel. "Last night, I heard him talking to Luval—"

"He duped me!" protested Luval. "I swear it—"

"Silence!" ordered Modbury, in an indignant tone. "This refutes your story, Luval. You are in this deeply!"

"I do not think so," inserted Nigel, extinguishing his cigarette in an ash stand and reaching for another that Harry tendered. "Jeff was duped; and Luval could have been likewise. From the little that I heard, it looks as though Lodera left him here to take a false share of the blame."

Luval's bespectacled face showed a grateful expression.

"Gwendolyn saw me last night," added Nigel, "and thought that I was Geoffrey's ghost. Mund saw me also; and recognized me, for he was an old servant here. I fled back into the turret. Toward dawn, I signaled."

"To whom?" asked Delka.

"To Jeremy," replied Nigel, "because he had my confidence. Also I had expected Amakar. I was atop the turret; suddenly, Mund arrived. He tried to knife me. Amakar saw us against the sky; and finished the fellow with a rifle shot."

"So that was it," nodded Delka. "Jeremy took the blame."

"He did?" Nigel's eyes lighted. "Good, faithful

Jeremy. I had an idea that he had managed things somehow, to cover Amakar. However, I barricaded myself in the turret. Tonight, I flashed signals again."

"To Amakar?"

"Yes. I wanted him to come through the secret way and up into the turret. He has not arrived; if he is about, he is probably waiting. He does not know why I signaled for him, particularly because I did not urge haste."

"You had a special reason?"

Delka's sharp question showed that he had detected a significance in Nigel's tone. The young man smiled.

"Yes," he nodded, "a most important reason. I saw signal flares over upon Parrion Head. It was only by chance that I spied them from a slitted opening of the turret; but I knew their purpose."

He paused, then stated:

"Flares were used there, in the days of the Pretender, to bring men hidden in the inlet past Parrion Head. Another of Geoffrey's confidences in Lodera, I decided. That pilot at the landing field must have sent up the flares. Men are coming here to Chiswold Castle, to enter the secret vault from the passage by the cove.

"Wait. Hear me out." Nigel smiled serenely. "Geoffrey did not know the difficulties of boating through the cove. I did, for I navigated it often. It will take much longer than Lodera supposed. Men could have landed already on the far shore of the cove; but not on this side. They are not yet here from Parrion Head."

"But Lodera is gone!" stormed Modbury. "His plane has had time to take to the air. He is the man we must overtake—"

"And we are too late," inserted Sir Rodney, angrily. "Too late to save Gwendolyn. Why did you not come here sooner?"

"Lodera is not yet gone," replied Nigel, with a shrewd, wise smile. "He has to wait until his men complete their work; until they carry their burdens from the castle, then place the cargo aboard the plane."

"What cargo?" queried Modbury.

NIGEL leaned forward and advanced his right hand in a dramatic fashion. Harry Vincent could feel the spell which this keen informant placed upon his listeners.

"The swag from London," declared Nigel, emphatically. "The wealth that I expected to find here, once I knew of Geoffrey's complicity. The treasures that I knew would be more important to Lodera than the jewels and the money that I heard you speak about, not long ago.

"Gold plates—portraits—jewels—vases—tiaras—tapestries—all are stored below, in the place where I shall lead you. Three hundred thou-

sand sovereigns' worth of swag, almost ten times the amount of wealth that Lodera has stolen from you, Modbury.

"Not too heavy—not too bulky. It's an easy load for Lodera's powerful plane. Lodera has duped your daughter, Sir Rodney. She has gone, to become the thieving Spaniard's bride. But Lodera, at this minute, is fuming because of the delay.

"He is waiting at the landing field, wondering why his men are so belated, not knowing how long it takes to land at Chiswold Castle after a trip from Parrion Head. Lodera will not go until he has his stolen wealth."

Pausing, Nigel turned deliberately, swung open the door to the hall. He pointed in the direction of the front room; then looked across his shoulder to the others.

"The path is open to the vault below," announced Nigel. "Follow me, and find the proof of all that I have told!"

CHAPTER XXII
CRIME STANDS REVEALED

SUDDEN exclamations burst from many lips. This time Delka raised no hand for silence. The dramatic finish of Nigel Chiswold's story had left the Scotland Yard man utterly dumbfounded. Then, to Delka's ears came excited words.

"To the landing field!" Sir Rodney was shouting. "We must capture Lodera! At once!"

"Hold on!" Hayman had entered the argument. "We must not forget that men are coming here below!"

"A double attack!" put in Lord Cedric, coming from out of his shell. "Jove! We should do both!"

"Hear me!" boomed Modbury, in a commanding tone. Then, as excitement stopped, he turned to Luval. "Here is your chance to show your colors, Luval. Go and unlock the door of the gun room. Take the servants with you so that they may arm themselves. Have them bring other weapons here."

He passed a key to Luval. The secretary dashed out willingly, followed by a flood of servants.

"Our first task lies below!" exclaimed Modbury. "Once we have trapped this boat crew of Lodera's, the rest will be swift. We can capture Lodera." He turned to Sir Rodney: "And with no harm to your daughter Gwendolyn."

Sir Rodney stared puzzled, along with Lord Cedric. Harry Vincent caught the thought, however, and so did Eric Delka. The Scotland Yard man gave his prompt approval.

"Excellent!" affirmed Delka. "We can capture the crew by ambush. Then we, ourselves, can go to the landing field. Lodera will think his own men are arriving. We shall trap him with Dufour. The girl will be unharmed."

"Right, Delka!" approved Hayman. "As representative of the local authorities, we must use our full strength for that ambush. 'Twould be folly to break forces and send some to the landing field too early."

The servants were returning with the weapons. Revolvers, rifles, a varied assortment from which all could choose. Each man picked his weapon; Nigel then gestured impatiently toward the front room. Accepting him as the temporary leader, all followed.

The paneled wall was open. Nigel stepped through to the staircase. Modbury gave a hoarse whisper.

"Two of my servants should remain here," he suggested. "They can cover us in case Lodera or some others should return to the castle."

"Good," approved Hayman. Then, turning to Delka, said, "You shall be our leader, Inspector."

Delka nodded to Modbury, to place two men on guard. Nigel was wagging a flashlight from the spiral stairs. Delka reached him and beckoned for the others to follow.

THE corkscrew steps led to musty depths. The journey resembled a visit to an ancient tomb. Nigel's blinking torch stirred flapping bats from nesting places. These creatures flapped blindly upward while descending men beat at them with their hands.

Nigel extinguished his torch for the final stage of the descent. Then his carefully treading feet struck stone instead of iron. He whispered for silence. The others heard him creep forward. Finally, his flashlight came on to stay. The followers clustered in to join him.

Harry Vincent, next to Delka, was astounded by the size of this lower room. The vault was hollowed from the very rock upon which the castle stood. Its ceiling was high; its length and breadth were great. Nigel's flashlight threw but a weakened glow until other torches joined it.

At the far end of the chamber was a blocking barrier of wood, with a metal sheathing. It served only as protection against the elements, for its hinges were weak; its lock was useless. Nigel whispered an echoed explanation.

"Rocks hide the entrance," he said. "Only those who know of the door can find it. Geoffrey knew; so did I. He told Lodera, while I explained the way to Amakar. If my servant comes, you will recognize him. He is huge and dark-faced."

NIGEL'S light blinked on a stack of boxes at the side of the vault. He led the way and ripped back canvas sides to reveal the slats of crates. He tore at paper wrappings. Gold plates glittered under his light.

Delka, stooping, spied painted canvas in another crate. Square boxes, wedged in place, were containers for jewels and tiaras. Nigel raised one lid to show a sparkle of gems. Hayman ripped heavy

paper from a tightpacked bundle to poke the cloth of gold-threaded tapestries.

Delka clapped Nigel on the shoulder. The Scotland Yard man was pleased. Wheeling about, he began to post his men. He took one side, with Sir Rodney and Lord Cedric. He sent Hayman to the other, accompanied by Harry and Nigel.

Modbury and Luval had four servants with them. Delka indicated that they were to guard the inner depths, at the foot of the spiral stairs.

"Keep contact with the two upstairs," ordered the C.I.D. man. "One man will do as messenger between."

Modbury spoke to Hasslett. The chauffeur had happened to be in the castle when the robbery of the safe had been discovered. Hasslett became the messenger. Delka gave word for the lights to be extinguished. In the darkness, he whispered final orders that toned through the vault.

"Let them enter. Once they are well inside, give them lights and cover them. If they throw a torch-light toward anyone, act in response. I shall watch and be ready with a prompt order."

Echoes died. Solemn silence persisted through the vault. Nigel, close to Harry, buzzed that the wait would not be a long one. Tenseness continued; only the trifling sound of Hasslett's footsteps could be heard from the spiral stairs.

Then, without warning, came the surprise.

A click. Light flooded the vault, from incandescents set deep in the high ceiling. Powerful bulbs had flashed from everywhere, exposing all within the underground room. A harsh snarl echoed; not from the outer door, but from the innermost spot, at the spiral stairs. Delka and Hayman wheeled, their companions with them. They stopped short.

Modbury's servants had crept forward, joined by the men from above. With leveled revolvers, they were covering both groups at the sides. Centered between were two gloating men, each with a raised rifle. Modbury and Luval!

NO words were needed to explain the changed situation. Barton Modbury's large face had taken on an evil glare which he had managed to suppress in the past. He stood revealed as a murderous master of crime, while Luval, his teeth gleaming in a leering grin, proclaimed himself as the master rogue's lieutenant.

"Stand where you are!"

Modbury's rasp was menacing. Hayman and Delka dropped their revolvers; those beside them did the same. Resistance was useless; for they were under the very muzzles of looming guns.

"Fools!" sneered Modbury. "Not one of you would have guessed my game had Nigel Chiswold not blundered into it. Even he was tricked. But he learned enough to spoil my plans.

"I came to England bent on robbery. I wanted a tool. Geoffrey Chiswold served. He knew the places to rifle. He worked with my gang in London. But not until after I had bought Chiswold Castle; then had learned its secrets from Geoffrey.

"The swag came here, shipped with my new furnishings. Luval and these servants stored it here below. Mund was also in my employ, for we kept him after the old servants were gone. We knew Mund for one of our own kind.

"I invited guests to serve me as new dupes. You, Sir Rodney and you, Lord Cedric. The pair of you would do to vouch for my integrity. But that was not all. I wanted another; I chose Francisco Lodera, because I knew that he and Gwendolyn were in love.

"Geoffrey gave me all these details. He planned with me. I needed a way to get the swag from England. Lodera had a plane; I saw to it that Dufour was recommended as a pilot. Dufour is another of my men."

Chuckling, Modbury approached closer to the silent men whom he had tricked.

"Luval talked to Lodera," he added, "and offered to help him sell me the rubies and elope with Gwendolyn. Lodera fell into the snare. He needed money; he wanted the girl. All the while, we were framing him.

"I wanted him to be branded as a thief who had robbed me—not too much, however, for I did not want him to be classed as a crook with a great capacity. The jewels and the money were just right; for they would have appealed to a shrewd opportunist.

"What was to happen to Lodera? It has already begun. His fate—and the girl's—are settled. They were seized on their way to the landing field. Bound and gagged, they are aboard the plane. The swag will go there also.

"Dufour will fly to the continent and there unload the massed wealth for disposal. He will fly back to the coast, take to the chute, then let the plane crash with Lodera and Gwendolyn aboard. They will be found later, dead, the jewels and the money gone.

"No one will ever know that the spoils of London robberies went from England aboard that ship. I shall return to South Africa. There I shall receive the bulk of the money that the swag will bring."

Modbury paused. His face took on a look of disappointment.

"I SPOKE of matters as they were to be," he growled. "I had Geoffrey murdered after he was no longer useful. He went to Whitechapel, expecting payment, then received death instead. His former crew killed him—the men who had aided him in robbery and murder—and they came here, to lie in wait above Parrion Head.

"I had not reckoned with Nigel. When he bobbed up, Mund saw him and explained matters to Luval in the study. Later, I talked with Mund. He was kindling my study fire. I deputed Mund to murder Nigel; then to flee the castle. The body was to stay in the turret chamber.

"Old Jeremy fooled us. Neither Luval nor I knew that Mund had gone to the roof of the turret. We thought that he had finished Nigel in the spy room, for he had no knife upon him. We actually believed Jeremy's story, thinking Mund had been leaving by the front window.

"All was well tonight. We planted the blame on Lodera; but chance brought the issue too soon. I was delaying, pretending that there would be no hope of catching Lodera. I wanted to give my boat crew time to remove the swag and take it to the plane.

"When Nigel reappeared, the game was finished; at the very time when I had removed blame from Luval. The moment Nigel told that the London swag was in this vault, my plan was ruined. Why? Because the great point to conceal was the fact that the stolen goods were ever in this castle, or had ever been here.

"I had but one remaining course. To speed all of you into following Nigel. To make this vault a trap, where all of you will die and remain forgotten. As soon as the spoils have been removed, I and my servants shall quit this castle, leaving your dead bodies buried in this secret vault."

One last pause. Then Modbury sneered:

"Fools! Had anyone examined facts, he might have found the clues. Geoffrey, to begin with; then his death in Whitechapel. My furnishings in the great room. Luval plotting with Lodera, duping him all the while. How could Lodera have been the master crook, while I owned this castle and held full control?

"Luval talked to Mund; but Lodera did not. Luval talked with me; so did Mund. You fled too quickly to your turret, Nigel. Had you remained, you would not have made the mistake that you did. Had anyone of keenness examined all angles of my scheme, he would have guessed that I was the brain behind it.

"But no one was close enough; nor shrewd enough. You knew a little, Delka; but it was too little. You were less informed than Nigel. You knew nothing, Hayman. Why do you think I covered Jeremy? I shall tell you. Because the fellow had unwittingly rendered me a service—at least so I thought—in finishing Mund, who—like Geoffrey—was no longer useful.

"Jeremy will be handled later"—Modbury clucked in an evil fashion—"and he will lead us to the hiding place of Nigel's Afghan servant. We will deal with him as well.

"We have new plans, and they are completed; all

successfully arranged, because no one was capable of noting the points that I have mentioned. Those points and many others—all so perfectly covered that I held success within my grasp.

"Until Nigel blundered. Nigel, the only one who might have guessed the truth. A proof that no one in the world could have divined my schemes. None of you need look for rescue. It is hopeless—"

Modbury stopped, staring. His hard eyes bulged.

A LAUGH had quivered through the vault, a mighty taunt that awoke horrendous echoes. A burst of challenging mirth that swept from the darkness by the forgotten outer door, the spot where Modbury had believed that his boat crew would soon arrive.

Swinging into the light of the vault's brilliant center was a figure cloaked in black. Harry Vincent gasped his recognition. It was The Shadow. He had come to rescue.

No one, Modbury had said, could have known the depth of crime. Modbury was wrong. The Shadow had long since guessed the game, through the very clues that the master villain had claimed no one could gain!

CHAPTER XXIII
THE DOUBLE STROKE

THE SHADOW, like Modbury, had planned with thorough purpose. A hidden being in the darkness, he had matched every move that the master crook had made. He had tabulated every fact that Modbury had mentioned; and more.

Upon that first night in the vicinity of Chiswold Castle, The Shadow had observed the meeting between Nigel and old Jeremy. He had heard Nigel's story, had recognized it as the truth. Nigel's mention of the vault below the castle, with the spy room in the turret above, had been sufficient to inform The Shadow that swag must be located here.

Listening to Lodera's talk with Luval; watching the moves by Nigel, The Shadow had recognized at once that Lodera was a dupe. He had known that Luval, like Geoffrey, was too small to be the master crook; that some stronger, hidden hand must have shaped this entire setting.

Crime in London—the purchase of the castle—the choice of guests who fitted perfectly into the scheme. Only one plotter could have framed the game. That one was Barton Modbury. No deep-dyed villainy could have been hatched and carried through without an inkling reaching the self-styled diamond king.

Modbury's close adherence to Sir Rodney and Lord Cedric had shown The Shadow that the super-crook was using those guests to have them support his alibi.

The Shadow, sole witness to the fray between Nigel and Mund, had been ready to protect Nigel. Amakar had saved him that necessity, by the long-range rifle shot. Listening later, The Shadow had heard Jeremy's bluff. It had passed with both Modbury and Luval. The Shadow had known that Nigel would be safe; for rogues believed him dead.

To counter Modbury's evil schemes, The Shadow had chosen Amakar as an aide, knowing the strength and loyalty of the big Afghan. The Shadow had recognized Amakar's true worth that night in Whitechapel. He had fought Amakar then, only because of Harry's blunder. Both Harry and Amakar had been mistaken; each thinking the other to be one of Geoffrey's assassins.

The Shadow's words to Amakar, tonight, outside the castle, had been given in support of Nigel Chiswold. That was why Amakar had accepted The Shadow as his master. Together, they had set out upon a triple mission.

First, to deal with rogues at the landing field, Dufour included. Then, to intercept and overpower the crew that was coming for the swag. Finally, to enter the castle, bring Nigel from the turret, and unmask Modbury in the presence of the law.

ONE man had unwittingly ruined The Shadow's threefold plan. He was the very one who had also thrown chaos into Modbury's scheme; namely, Nigel Chiswold. Neither The Shadow nor Amakar had learned that Nigel had seen the flares from Parrion Head. There had been no call for haste when Nigel had signaled Amakar. The Shadow had supposed that Nigel would stay placed until Amakar came.

Coming back from the end of Castle Cove, The Shadow had chosen a spot outside the secret entrance to the vault, which Amakar—informed by Nigel—had shown to him. There he was in wait for the belated landing crew. As Nigel had guessed, Modbury's mob had struck trouble with the rocks. They were still picking their way up from the cove.

Posted some distance from the hidden entrance to the vault, The Shadow had not detected the first glimmer of flashlights from within, nor had he heard the sound of whispered talk. But when Modbury had clicked the light switch from beneath the spiral stairs, The Shadow had spotted the lines of glow from the edges of the buried, battered door.

The Shadow had known the answer. Modbury. Servants of the master crook had installed those lights; and only Modbury would have risked their use. His outside men were coming; glimmering edges of light would hasten them, when they observed the glow. But Modbury had drawn a foe whose presence he had not suspected: The Shadow.

Approaching, The Shadow had dropped to the level of the secret door. He had edged past the broken barrier. Creeping inward, he had chosen the right moment for action. In uncanny fashion, he had revealed his presence. Through sinister mirth, he had drawn all eyes to himself.

Modbury and Luval, their rifles half lowered, were caught flat-footed. The servants—evil thugs in disguise—were more ready than the crooked chief and his bespectacled lieutenant. Those minions whirled when they heard Modbury's snarled gasp. Following their master's glaring gaze, they saw The Shadow.

This was the move that The Shadow wanted; the one that he had forced. His automatics were ready in his fists, pointing outward at an angle. His fingers pressed their triggers just as Modbury's henchmen aimed to fire.

ROARS boomed through the vault as big automatics stabbed their message. With The Shadow's shots came the answering barks of revolvers. Thugs were surging forward, shooting wildly as they came. The Shadow was thrusting carnage into their ranks.

Slugs found living marks with every jab, while hurried bullets from thug-gripped guns were sizzling close past The Shadow's fading form.

It was The Shadow's battle; and he would have cleared the field, but for the action of the men whom he had come to rescue. Of those huddled prisoners, only two used their heads: Eric Delka and Harry Vincent.

The Scotland Yard man and The Shadow's agent were at opposite stations. Both dropped to the floor and snatched up their lost pistols, to deliver a flanking fire that would break the surge of Modbury's eight servitors. Others, however, acted with less wisdom.

Sir Rodney and Lord Cedric from one side; Hayman and Nigel from the other—all four leaped forward weaponless to grapple with the driving mob. Before The Shadow could wither more than half of his opponents; before either Delka or Harry could aid him, future chance was ended.

Instead of four thugs charging hopelessly against a cannonade, there was a cluster of fierce, fighting men. Four against four, and half of them, men who must be saved.

Harry and Delka gained a simultaneous thought. From opposite sides, they pitched into the milling throng. Four unarmed men were wrestling valiantly to drag guns away from crooks. The odds were against success; but Harry and Delka changed the tide. Snatching at thugs, they used their guns as bludgeons, to smash down opposition.

Men sprawled everywhere, rolling, scrambling; while muffled gunshots told that tumbled crooks were trying to use their guns against the fighters who had downed them. Delka slugged one thug who wrested free from Nigel. Harry grappled with another who had managed to wound Lord Cedric.

As he rolled, slashing at his antagonist, Harry saw both sides of another duel. Modbury and Luval had sprung forward with their rifles, under cover of the sprawling forms in the center of the floor. Then, as the path cleared, both were aiming. Their rifles had gained a single target: The Shadow.

Two against one. The Shadow's guns were leveled. But Modbury, shrewd in strategy, had chosen a position of security. He had dropped behind Luval; half crouched, the master crook had thrust his rifle barrel beneath the aiming secretary's upraised right arm.

Luval had become a living bulwark!

Two rifles were about to spurt as one. Should The Shadow beat them to the shots, it would be of no avail. His bullets could not reach Modbury until Luval had toppled.

As he had sacrificed Geoffrey and Mund, so would Modbury let Luval die in this emergency. Luval, intent upon beading The Shadow, was ignorant of Modbury's move.

In that tense instant, The Shadow fired. With split-second swiftness, he ripped bullets toward his foemen, while their fingers were still on the move. Luval was the only target; yet Modbury never fired in return.

Timed to the instant with The Shadow's gun bursts came a sharp crackle from the outer door. Amakar had followed The Shadow. The huge Afghan had thrust the broken barrier aside, to arrive just before the climax of the mad, swift fray.

Amakar, like Harry, had seen the final duel in the making. He had raised his rifle; like The Shadow, he had fired straight at Luval.

AMAKAR'S high-powered gun possessed a quality that The Shadow's automatics lacked. Luval's body could stop the bullets from The Shadow's pistols; but a human form was tissue against a close-range fire from Amakar's rifle.

Amakar had aimed for Modbury, through Luval. The Afghan, like The Shadow, had beaten the foemen to the shot. His timely bullet, winging through Luval's breast, found its lodging in the man beyond.

Luval was sprawling crazily, after a backward stagger. His rifle had clattered to the stone floor. Modbury had straightened; but his gun was lowered. Nerveless fingers clutched it, while bulging eyes stared glassy from a distorted visage.

Lips, curling uglily, sought to deliver a defiant snarl. They failed. Amakar's steel-jacketed missile had done its work. With a sickening gasp, Modbury collapsed upon Luval's body.

The master criminal, like his lieutenant, was dead. The Shadow and Amakar had gained a simultaneous triumph!

CHAPTER XXIV
THE LAST TRIBUTE

A SINISTER laugh wakened the echoes of the vault. A knell from hidden lips, that told of valiant victory. That mirth was solemn as a knell; for it betokened the delivery of doom that was deserved.

The Shadow had spotted the source of deep-laid crime. He had interposed to rescue trapped men from certain death. Backed by Amakar, he had completed a swift victory. All that remained was to end the efforts of underlings, who did not know that their evil chief had died

Not those who were still here in the vault; for their struggles had ceased. The battle on the floor was ended. The last of Modbury's servants had succumbed. The Shadow turned and spoke to Amakar. The mammoth Afghan bowed and followed toward the outer door.

Thanks to the intervention of Harry and Delka, the stubborn crooks had been unable to dispatch any of the men who had surged upon them.

Lord Cedric Lorthing had received a bullet in his left shoulder; but he was managing to come to his feet, aided by Sir Rodney Ralthorn, who had come through the fray unscathed.

Nigel Chiswold was uninjured; and he was also giving aid to a companion who was weakly rising. This was Hayman, wounded less seriously than Lord Cedric, but dazed from the furious fray. Hayman was clutching his right forearm; the local inspector had suffered a flesh wound.

Harry Vincent, rising from above a crook whom he had subdued, was quick with a call to Eric Delka. Looking toward the outer door, Harry had seen The Shadow wheel. With Amakar beside him, the cloaked victor had left the vault. Harry pointed; Delka understood.

Leaving Nigel Chiswold and Sir Rodney in charge of the vault, Harry and Delka dashed for the secret door. Past the broken barrier, they clambered upon the ledge that partially hid the opening. Lights were blinking on the rocks, just below. Guns had begun to crackle.

Harry and Delka saw the issue. The Shadow and Amakar had separated. One from each side, they were flanking the delayed crew from the boat. Savagely, thugs returned the fire of booming automatics and sharp-cracking rifle fire.

Crooks sprawled wounded. As the flankers cut in behind them, those who were still unscathed came clambering up toward the entrance to the vault.

Flashlights spotted them when they reached the ledge. Delka's growled order stopped them. A quartet of vanquished ruffians threw up their hands. Delka and Harry marched them into the vault.

While they were lining up the prisoners, Amakar arrived, carrying two wounded prisoners from the cliff. The Afghan deposited his burdens on the floor; then solemnly went out to bring in more.

He made no comment while he performed this action. Amakar was acting under final orders. When he had brought in four other groaning captives, Amakar stood before Nigel Chiswold and delivered a salaam.

The bow meant that three trips were all that Amakar needed. It meant also—Harry Vincent understood—that Amakar's service with The Shadow was ended. The master of darkness had told Amakar to join those within the castle. From now on, Amakar's orders would come from Nigel Chiswold.

LATER, rescued men thronged the great room of Chiswold Castle. They had left the dead below; they had made the prisoners carry the wounded up the spiral stairway. Hard upon their assembly into the great room came the chug of motors from the front driveway; then pounding fists at the great door. Backed by Amakar, Delka opened the barrier.

Men had come from Yarwick. Local police and physicians, as well as the coroner. With them were the two who had summoned this aid: Francisco Lodera and Gwendolyn Ralthorn. Then came old Jeremy, with news of prisoners in the gamekeeper's lodge. With a smile, Lodera informed that men had already dropped off to bring in those captives.

"Dufour is among them," explained the Spaniard. "He had a small automobile in back of the cottage. We started for Yarwick, Gwendolyn and I, after we were told to go."

"Told?" queried Delka. "By whom?"

"By a ghost," smiled Lodera. "At least by someone whom Gwendolyn thought was a ghost."

"The weird person whom I saw upon the lawn!" exclaimed the girl. "He spoke to us at Dufour's cottage. He told us about Nigel Chiswold being here at the castle. He said that Barton Modbury was a plotter who had sought our deaths."

Pausing, Gwendolyn looked about for her father. At that moment, Sir Rodney appeared from upstairs. Happily, he embraced his daughter with one arm; then, from beneath the other, he produced a package that he was carrying.

"I found these stowed deep in the filing cabinet," said Sir Rodney to Delka. "The diamonds, the rubies, and the money. Luval must have buried them there after he took them from the safe."

"At Modbury's order," added Lodera. "We were told that also. We were to look for the gems and the money. As for the other treasure—"

He paused. Already, heavy footsteps were descending the stairs. Amakar had directed men to the vault. They were bringing the first crates from below, up by the spiral stairway, which was wide

The master criminal, like his lieutenant, was dead. The Shadow and Amakar had gained a simultaneous triumph!

enough for the long boxes; then down by the front staircase to the hall outside the great room.

"This settles everything," chuckled Delka from the doorway, while he watched men from Yarwick pry open the first box and draw out stacks of gold plates. "All the stolen goods are intact. Modbury was smart enough to preserve everything. He wanted to dispose of his spoils at full value, on the continent. Yes, everything is settled."

"Not quite."

IT was Lord Cedric Lorthing who drawled the

statement. A physician had just finished binding his shoulder; though pale, Lord Cedric smiled as he adjusted his monocle. He approached Lodera and thrust forward his right hand.

"Congratulations," remarked Lord Cedric. "We did you an injustice, Francisco. Since Gwendolyn chose to elope with you, there is no question regarding whom she loves. Accept my wishes for a happy marriage."

Gwendolyn looked toward her father. Sir

Rodney nodded his approval. Smiling happily, the girl nestled against Lodera's embracing arm.

"You are right, Inspector," nodded Lord Cedric, to Delka. "All is settled to everyone's satisfaction."

Hardly had he spoken, before a rhythmic buzz sounded from above the castle. Delka started for the front door; and others followed. Lodera and Gwendolyn joined the group, with an explanation.

"It is my plane," stated Lodera, "our friend has taken it to London. He told me that the ship will be left at Croydon Airdrome."

Twinkling lights against the darkened sky; at last, a broad-winged shape that swept beneath a faint trail of momentary moonlight. A blackened token high against the clouds, the departing plane seemed symbolic of the mysterious flier who manned it: The Shadow.

Eric Delka watched from Harry Vincent's side, as they stood upon the porch. Light from the doorway showed the set smile upon the Scotland Yard man's lips. Delka, like Harry, had long since recognized The Shadow's prowess.

Two others watched; their silence betokened different thoughts. One was Nigel Chiswold; his face was one that registered deep gratitude. Nigel had seen the avenging of Geoffrey's death; the finish of Barton Modbury, master schemer who had lured the other Chiswold into wrong.

Deep had been Nigel's regard for Geoffrey, despite the latter's weakness. Nigel had come with hope of making amends for Geoffrey's misdeeds. His wish had been realized, thanks to The Shadow. Moreover, the settlement with Barton Modbury had paved the way for Nigel to gain an unexpected reward.

Instead of being a man who needed protection; Modbury had proven to be the hidden plotter, whose transactions would be repudiated by the law. Nigel Chiswold would soon receive a heritage. He would be recognized as the owner of Chiswold Castle.

THE other who watched was Amakar. Whatever the Afghan's memories of the past; whatever his desire for the future, no one could have told; for Amakar's face was steady and expressionless.

One gesture alone betokened Amakar's respect for the cloaked master whom the Afghan had served; and the huge fighter reserved it until the others had turned to enter the castle.

Then Amakar raised his huge right hand to his forehead. Slowly, in native fashion, he delivered a last salute. Harry Vincent, turning at the door, was the only person who observed the action.

Harry Vincent understood. The giant Afghan would not forget the mighty prowess of that cloaked leader whom he had followed and served amid successful frays. Nor would The Shadow forget the aid that his ally had given in return.

That was something that Amakar knew. That last salute had become the Afghan's privilege. In that gesture was embodied the respect of all who had profited by The Shadow's deed. This was the final tribute.

Amakar's farewell to The Shadow.

THE END